Highest Praise for
THE CRUELEST CUT

"As authentic and scary as crime thrillers get, written as only a cop can write . . . A verygood and fast read."

—Nelson DeMille

"A tornado of drama—you won't stop spinning till you've been spit out the other end. Rick Reed's writing crackles with authenticity."

—Shane Gericke

"Put this one on your must-read list. *The Cruelest Cut* is a can't-put-down adventure. Readers will definitely want to see more of Jack Murphy."

—John Lutz

"A jaw-dropping thriller that dares you to turn the page."

—Gregg Olsen

THE
CRUELEST
CUT

RICK
REED

PINNACLE BOOKS
Kensington Publishing Corp.
www.kensingtonbooks.com

PINNACLE BOOKS are published by

Kensington Publishing Corp.
119 West 40th Street
New York, NY 10018

All Kensington titles, imprints, and distributed lines are available at
special quantity discounts for bulk purchases for sales promotions,
premiums, fund-raising, educational, or institutional use.
Special book excerpts or customized printings can also be created
to fit specific needs. For details, write or phone the office of the
Kensington special sales manager: Kensington Publishing Corp.,
119 West 40th Street, New York, NY 10018, attn: Special Sales Department; phone 1-800-221-2647.

This book is a work of fiction. Names, characters, businesses, orga-
nizations, places, events, and incidents either are the product of the
author's imagination or are used fictitiously. Any resemblance to
actual persons, living or dead, events, or locales is entirely coinci-
dental.

PINNACLE BOOKS and the Pinnacle logo are Reg. U.S. Pat. &
TM Off.

ISBN-13: 978-0-7860-2483-4
ISBN-10: 0-7860-2483-6

First printing: November 2010

10 9 8 7 6 5 4 3 2 1

Printed in the United States of America

PROLOGUE

The late-May rain came down hard as the Evansville PD detectives, uniformed officers, and SWAT team staked out the downtown alley behind Turley's Jewelers. Thanks to a tip from a reliable informant, today they would take down the Solazzo gang, armed robbers who had done a Godzilla on the downtown small businesses recently.

Bobby Solazzo had recruited the team carefully, finding only the most vicious and psychotic bastards and leaving the ones with an ounce of compassion in them to join Kiwanis or Civitan. Solazzo's crew were the kind of guys that said, "Give me the money *and* I'll kill you."

Solazzo and company had already eluded authorities in a high-speed chase and a shoot-out at a liquor store that left two employees dead in a pool of blood, and had been lying low for the past ten days, but now they were ready for their next heist.

Detective Jack Murphy was in charge of the stakeout. He was crouched uncomfortably behind a Dumpster, wiping rain from his eyes, while the deputy chief of detectives was on the store's rooftop, along with one of the SWAT snipers and a reporter from the local rag who was pressing for the perfect shot for their headline: SOLAZZO GANG GOES DOWN. Other sharpshooters were strategically located in vantage points overlooking the alley, already designated the "kill zone." They didn't have to wait long.

An older black Suburban with darkened windows slid into the mouth of the narrow alley and eased along, coming to a stop directly behind Turley's Jewelers. The next two minutes seemed to run in slow motion, beginning with the doors of the Suburban flying open and four large and well-armed men emerging.

One man approached the back door of Turley's and pointed a sawed-off shotgun at the door's lock. The shotgun blast that shattered the lock on the door spooked one of the cops, who had his pistol pointed into the alleyway, and some reflex caused him to yank the trigger. Jack half-stood and looked around, thinking, *Must be the deputy chief. Leave it to him to screw things up.*

The shot went wild, but the reaction of the four men below was that of a well-trained military squad, as two men rushed into the back entrance of Turley's, and the remaining two returned fire at the rooftop snipers' position and back down the alleyway. Although the original orders to all of the ground team were that no one fired except the SWAT snipers, the air was suddenly filled with deadly projectiles. A bullet zinged into a nearby quad of electrical transformers high up on a telephone pole just above the west half of the stakeout team, sending a shower of fiery debris down on them. The uniformed cops positioned above the kill zone continued their barrage of gunfire, effectively immobilizing their team members on the ground.

Murphy had been waiting for the Suburban to come to a stop before giving the order to the SWAT commander to move in when he'd heard the single gunshot and then all hell breaking loose. Now he was in the middle of a goddamned war, and he was fucked no matter which way he ran. He could flee into the raging fire at the west end of the alley where there were some backup officers at least. Or he could chase the asshole he saw take off east down the alley when the shooting started. Staying put was not an option.

He bolted from his hole and chased the lone runner. The good news was that he'd gotten a pretty good look at this character and was pretty sure it was the leader of the pack, Bobby Solazzo. The bad news was that it *was* Bobby Solazzo, and Bobby had a sawed-off shotgun and liked to use it.

What kind of moron chases a guy who's got a shotgun? Murphy thought. But he plowed ahead through cascading rain, the smooth soles of his dress loafers slipping on the wet brick-worked street surface, the smell of sewage from the overflowing storm sewers barely registering.

He gripped the polymer handle of his Glock .45 standard police issue semiautomatic and slowed his pace—listening, watching for any movement or lack of movement. The alley was so narrow that a shotgun blast down the middle would take out anyone standing there. Not Jack's idea of a fun time. With the damn rain coming down in waves he could only see a few feet in any direction. For all Jack knew, Bobby was ten feet away, just waiting for him to come into view.

Murphy's Law says, "Never take a pistol to a shotgun fight." But, then, he wasn't supposed to be taking on Bobby's gang alone, was he? He was a detective. He was supposed to be directing the stakeout at a safe distance, watching the action as the uniformed officers and SWAT team took these assholes down. And that reminded him that Murphy's Law also says, "Anything that can go wrong, will always fuck you sideways."

He took a deep breath, let it out, and then moved forward again. *Bobby's got to be close now,* he thought, as he neared the end of the alley where it turned to the right. He stopped and, blading his body against the concrete-block wall, he glanced around the corner and spotted a shotgun lying on a pile of trash.

He's unarmed! Jack thought, as lightning flashed overhead. The resultant thunderclap was immediate and deafening in the tight alleyway, and it couldn't have come at a worse time. He had just moved out from cover when another flash caught his eye. This one close. Too close. Moving at him with the speed of lightning. But not lightning. *A blade,* he thought, then, *too late,* and tried to turn away, but he felt the point of the blade cut into his face and scrape downward, gouging a path through flesh and bone.

He lifted his .45 toward the direction of the attack . . .

CHAPTER ONE

Dr. Anne Lewis stood in the doorway of her garage and looked toward the back door of her house. The television weatherman had it wrong again. "Partly cloudy with a ten percent chance of rain" had turned into a raging thunderstorm. *If I wait it will stop soon. It can't rain this hard for long, can it?* she wondered.

Then she heard the phone ringing inside the house.

She muttered an expletive and ran. She was thoroughly soaked when she got inside and, of course, the phone had stopped ringing.

"Probably just a telemarketer," she said out loud, a little put out that her husband, Don, had not answered the phone. Since his retirement last year, all he had done was lie around the house, read the newspapers, watch sports, and make a mess.

She sighed and straightened a picture frame near the back door on her way into the bathroom for a towel. At the sink she dried herself and looked in the mirror. Her hair had turned prematurely gray in college—many years ago—but still had a shine to it that made it remarkable. Not that Don noticed anymore.

But she wasn't really being fair to him. After all, they had been married forty-three years. Both of them had been driven by careers, so they had never found time for children. Also not his fault, but still she wondered sometimes what her life would have been like if they'd had kids.

With Don's retirement last year, and her planned retirement at the end of this year, maybe she was just going through growing pains. Thirty-plus years of working in the psychiatric field had made her too introspective. She leaned close to the mirror and looked into her sky blue eyes.

What do psychiatrists do when they retire? she wondered. *Teach? Travel? Slowly go insane?*

She pushed the thought away and glanced once more at herself, smoothed her damp hair, and then dabbed a tissue at the eyeliner that streaked her face.

"Not bad for an old dame," she said and smiled. But as she started to leave the bathroom she noticed an odor. "My God, something smells like a wet dog!" she said and sniffed the hand towel. That wasn't it. "Please don't let it be the septic." The last time it had cost them a small fortune to repair the septic system, and then there was the smell and the mess with the whole backyard dug up.

How could he put up with this smell all day? Where is he?

She left the downstairs bathroom and walked through the house.

Surely he isn't still in bed!

She started up the stairs but stopped at the top step; a cold chill ran the length of her spine.

"Hi, Doc. Remember us?" A fist slammed into her sternum, crushing the breath from her and causing an explosion behind her eyes.

*   *   *

She woke to the most extreme pain she had ever experienced. Wherever she was, it was pitch black and her eyes hurt.

How long have I been unconscious? What happened?

She couldn't see, but she could tell she was propped into a sitting position against something hard. She tried to move but could only turn her head from side to side. She managed to wiggle her fingers and toes but could barely feel them. Something was crammed into her mouth, causing her jaws to ache.

Then she remembered the man. Although she couldn't place him, he had looked familiar. The professional, analytical part of her mind kicked in. Had she seen him in the newspaper or on television recently? No, that wasn't it. Was he a patient?

Whoever he was, it was clear that he was angry and quite capable of hurting her. And where was her husband? She wondered if Don, too, had been tied up somewhere.

Sudden pain. A blindingly bright light shone in her eyes. She tried to close them but couldn't.

"Wakey, wakey," a voice said.

She tried again to shut her eyes.

"Your eyelids are taped open. We don't want you to miss anything, Dr. Lewis."

He knows my name!

She tried to talk, to ask him what he wanted, why he was doing this to her, but was unable to speak because of the gag.

"Yeah—taped your mouth shut, too."

Oh my God, where is Don? What has happened to my husband, you bastard?

As if he had read her mind, the intruder trained the flashlight beam next to her and, with a gloved hand, turned her head in that direction.

Anne Lewis looked into the bloody and empty eye sockets of her husband's face. His body was bound and propped on the bed beside her. Where his mouth should have been was a bloody, cavernous hole. His lips had been crudely cut off, most of his teeth smashed out or broken, tongue cut out. She tried to look away but couldn't. Hot bile rose from her stomach and, finding no other avenue, it erupted from her nose.

"Now look what you've done, Anne," the voice chastised softly, as if correcting an errant child. "And you're supposed to be a professional woman."

The blow to her face came unexpectedly, and she almost choked on the gag. Her vision blurred, and she felt herself blacking out.

"Don't you pass out on us, bitch!"

The intruder yanked her head up by her hair, slamming the back of her skull into the headboard hard enough to make stars swim behind her eyes. Another blow to her chest took her breath, and she felt an explosion inside her skull as the world danced around her.

She heard something ripping and then felt her head being secured to the upright rails of the headboard with something sticky. Tape.

His voice took on a childlike tone. "Punch and Judy fought for a pie. Punch gave Judy a knock in the eye. Says Punch to Judy, will you have any more? Says Judy to Punch, my eyes are too sore." He laughed heartily.

Fear racked her body as she, too late, recognized her assailant. She was quite certain she was going to die.

"Well, Anne, Bobby's waiting, and I promised that I'd make this quick." He grabbed her by the throat, and said, "But I lied. I'm gonna make it as painful as I can. Practice makes perfect, you know."

CHAPTER TWO

Jack wiped the shaving cream from his face and looked in the mirror.

"Why, Detective Jack Murphy, you are one good-looking hunk of manliness," Susan Summers said from behind him.

Murphy looked in the mirror again and then gave her a questioning look. "Are you seeing the same thing I am?"

His face was cleanly shaven, but that only made the thick, white scar—running from below his right ear, across his chest, and ending above the left nipple—stand out from his skin like a thick, white snake. It was hard to believe that he had been put in the hospital twice in as many months

He smiled at Susan. "You're right. I'm a stud muffin," he said in a sarcastic tone.

She laughed and snuggled against him, nuzzling his neck. "Don't be so vain, Jack. The scars make you look dangerous. Women can't resist a dangerous man."

She backed away, and he watched in the mirror as she slipped into one of his long-sleeved shirts. He admired her body and wondered for the umpteenth time how he had ever attracted a beautiful woman almost ten years his junior.

Susan was a runner and had already completed three miles along the river roads before he had gotten out of bed. Her body was tan, her muscles firm, and the curves were all in the right places. Her strawberry-blond hair, which she usually wore down, was pulled back to show the smooth curve of her neck; her eyes were a bluish-green that reminded him of the sea.

She gave him a peck on the cheek and headed toward the kitchen, and as she did he checked out the part of her that never failed to make his heart race.

She said over her shoulder, "If you don't stop checking out my butt and get dressed, you'll be late for your first day back, Romeo."

"Whoops," he said, and looked one more time in the mirror at the scar on his neck. The doctor said the itching was a good thing; it meant his cut was healing. It had finally stopped keeping him awake with its insistent, burning itch, but it looked like hell. The doctor had also said the scar would eventually blend in. He wondered what it would blend in with, and then thought that if his face were a pizza, it would probably blend in. Meanwhile, he looked like shit.

With Susan in the kitchen, the sounds of pots and pans rattling and banging could never be mistaken for cooking, but her skills with a microwave were superb and she had a thorough knowledge of pizza delivery routes.

The thought of Susan naked made him smile. She was an excellent lover and a kind and caring woman. When he was released from the hospital, Susan had taken over as his personal nurse. That was a real step up from the physical therapist who had kept him screaming profanities in the hospital. The nurse's name tag identified her as an R.N. Jack had asked her if that stood for "Retired Nazi," and she had stretched his painful wound even tighter. *So much for the "angel of mercy" label*, he had thought.

Susan, however, had babied and pampered him, and spent

more time at his cabin than at her own home. She had fed and dressed him, treating him like a sick child.

At first he'd enjoyed the attention from Susan, especially the sex. But there was a problem. His ex-wife Katie. She seemed to pop into his mind daily. Everything they did, places they went, and somehow he couldn't help but compare everything in his present life to his past life with Katie.

He and Katie had been married for five years, divorced for almost a year now. He'd hoped they could fix the problems between them, and maybe get on with their life together, but the things that had driven them apart were still there. He was still married to his job. He was still someone who would stupidly run into danger instead of away from it. And when he got on to a case, he couldn't let go. He would work day and night until it was finished.

Katie had wanted a stable, safe relationship. One where her man came home from work at five, ate a meal and chatted about how their days had been, made love, and then didn't have to leave at the drop of a hat. That would never be his life.

"Are you ever coming out of there?" Susan's voice came from the direction of the kitchen.

Jack closed his eyes, willing the thoughts of Katie from his mind, and feeling guilty about having them. He rallied and stepped into the kitchen, naked. "No. I'm not coming back to bed. And you can't make me, woman. By God, you're an animal."

She unbuttoned the shirt she was wearing and walked slowly toward him, and then let it slide to the floor.

"I told you that you couldn't handle me," she whispered in his ear.

Later, he took a quick shower and dressed in the clothes Susan had laid out. He normally wore a suit and tie to work, but today he was going to wear slacks with a soft knit golf shirt. There was no way he could stand a tie around his neck.

"Susan, have I told you how much I appreciate everything you've done?"

"Yeah. Only about ten thousand times," she said and rolled her eyes. "I've never met anyone so reluctant to be taken care of. Before I met you, I thought men only wanted a maid that would sleep with them."

"Well, now that you mention it, I still have about thirty minutes before I have to report in."

"You're a bad man, Jack Murphy."

He wrapped his arms around her small waist and said, "I mean it. I can never repay you for what you've done. All of it." He bent and kissed her on the forehead.

"Oh. I think you can do better than that," she said and gave him a long, deep kiss.

When their lips parted, he looked at her and felt himself becoming aroused again. She must have felt it too because she pulled away, saying, "I've made coffee."

"Be right there," he said as she left the room. He took his department-issued pistol out of the dresser drawer, released the clip, dropped it onto the bed, and worked the action several times. He deftly disassembled the pistol, blew lint from anyplace it had accumulated during the month he had been home, reassembled it, then slammed the loaded clip into the butt and jacked a round into the chamber.

The Model 36 Glock .45 is a work of art. Weighing seven ounces less than its big brother, the Model 21, it is more compact and carries an awesome ten rounds of .45-caliber firepower. Unloaded, the pistol weighs about the same as the ammunition. Each round of .45-caliber, brass-jacketed, hollow-point ammunition is capable of striking the human body with the force of a sledgehammer.

Jack slipped the gun into its holster and slipped it onto his belt. He'd forgotten how heavy the gun was and was surprised to see that he'd lost a bit of weight. He tightened his belt to the last notch.

Going into the kitchen he poured a cup of coffee and saw that Susan had gone out to the front porch.

Eddie's normally close-cropped dark hair had gotten long in prison. He liked it that way. And his almost waiflike physique had turned into a sculpted mass of muscle. Lifting weights several hours a day, eating regularly, and the desire to stay alive tended to do that to a convict. The only thing he'd changed after he got out of the pen six weeks ago was his tan. The constant fluorescent lighting had a way of making a man's skin look like roadkill, but there was no way he was going in the outside exercise yard without a shirt and denim jacket. Denim didn't stop a shiv—a homemade knife—but it was better protection than nothing.

Eddie picked up the binoculars when he saw a light come on inside the cabin. Someone was moving around, but his angle of view didn't allow him to see inside. He had first spotted some movement over an hour ago. *Murphy must be putting on his makeup,* Eddie thought and smiled at his own humor. But then he thought maybe Murphy had gone back to bed because it had been so damn quiet for the last hour. His ass was hurting, and his legs were getting stiff from sitting on the wet ground along the river bank.

He twisted the focus knob and grumbled at his brother, "Dammit! I told you we shoulda got the good ones!"

"We ain't got no money, Eddie," Bobby said.

Eddie couldn't help but notice how bad Bobby was looking. His skin was sallow, and his muscle tone was that of a man thirty years older. Bobby had always been the leader. The strong one. The one that all the girls wanted. But being on the run for the better part of a month was taking its toll on them both.

Bobby stretched out on the ground, hands tucked behind his head, and stared up into the empty October sky. Eddie didn't understand how Bobby could be so calm. It was all Eddie could do to keep from kicking in the cabin door and finishing this business.

"We could find a cabin like Murphy's to stay in. I'm sick of livin' in roach-infested motels, Bobby. Worse yet, I'm fucking tired of sleeping on the ground out here. That damn river stinks worse than you do." He hoped that would get a rise out of Bobby, but Bobby just looked at him and shook his head.

"And if we take over one a these cabins out here, what do we do with whoever's living in the cabin, Eddie?"

Eddie thought about it. "We kill 'em. Sink their bodies in the river."

Bobby sat up and looked at his brother.

"Well," Eddie demanded. "Why not?"

"Because someone might come around looking for them, ya think? And then what? Kill everyone that comes to the door?"

"Well, shit!" Eddie spat on the rocks. "That's bullshit." But he knew his brother was right. Bobby was always right.

Motion from the cabin caught Eddie's eye. He raised the binoculars again just in time to see the cabin door open and a very shapely strawberry-blond woman walk onto the porch. She was carrying a coffee mug and wearing only a long-sleeved shirt, unbuttoned most of the way down. When she lifted the cup to drink he could see her panties. He'd never seen her almost naked before.

"Well, I'll be damned," he said to his brother, and as much as he hated Jack Murphy, he had to give him credit for his taste in women. Of course, that meant that he was disappointed in Susan Summers for exactly the same reason. What would she see in a piece of shit like Murphy?

"Looks like Murphy's shacked up regular-like with our lady parole officer," Eddie said.

The look on Bobby's face said it all. He couldn't believe

Murphy's luck either. Murphy didn't deserve any luck. He was a bastard.

Eddie sat down next to his brother and said, "This is what kills me, bro. Here we are, almost homeless, and that murdering asshole is living it up." He jabbed a finger at the cabin. "Look at that place. He's got a nice boat and even got a goddamn private dock!"

Bobby just shrugged.

"Fuck him, man!" he said and spit in the water. "Why him? Why not us?"

"Let it go, Eddie," Bobby warned. "Murphy's only got one thing we want. We don't need his cabin, or his boat, or even that slut of a parole officer. When we're through with him, he won't have nothin'—not even his life."

Eddie focused the binoculars across the river again. Susan was a nice piece of ass, but she'd always acted like she was better than them. Treated them like dirt.

He wondered what it would be like to slide into that, do the nasty, hurt her a little. Women liked that—being hurt.

His thoughts were interrupted when Murphy came out onto the porch of the cabin. Eddie zoomed in on the face.

"Son of a bitch!" he said as he watched Murphy move behind Susan and put an arm around her waist. Murphy was tall, at least five-ten, maybe six-foot even, and it was obvious he was built lean and hard like a fighter. From what Bobby told him about that night, Murphy was lucky to be alive. But to watch him move you'd never know he'd been hurt. Eddie smiled, thinking he'd have to do something about that.

Susan leaned into Murphy and nuzzled his neck.

"You shoulda cut his dick off, Bobby!" Eddie said and spat into the rocks. "I can't do this, Bobby. We gotta do it now. I ain't hiding like some goddamn Peeping Tom."

"Just watch him, bro," Bobby said patiently.

"I'm watching, dammit!"

Eddie's hands sweated against the metal body of the binoculars as he twisted the focus knob. He concentrated on Murphy's face. "You gave him one hell of a scar, bro."

"Time to go." Bobby was on his feet, making toward the area where they had hidden the van. "We need to get over there and follow her. She may come in handy later."

"Just a minute," Eddie said, and watched as Murphy turned Susan around to face him. She leaned forward on her tiptoes and gave Murphy an unbelievably unchaste kiss.

"Houston, we have tongue," Eddie said with a snicker. "Maybe we'll send him that pretty little tongue as a gift, but not before I get a chance to check out the rest of her." Watching Susan respond to Murphy's caresses excited him. He could feel the pressure building in the front of his pants.

"We stick with the plan, Eddie."

"First we punish him, then we finish him. Right?" Eddie said.

Bobby grinned. "Ab-so-fucking-lutely."

CHAPTER THREE

The fish aren't biting. Damn the luck!

Timmy Ryan expertly cast his weighted line into the river, dropping the cornmeal-encrusted hook in between some overhanging branches like he'd been shown. The guy that owned the cabin down the way was a cop, a detective, and he fished here all the time. Timmy had watched him from a distance until his curiosity finally won out. He'd approached the man and found out his name was Jack.

His new friend, Jack, had shown him how to make cornmeal bait, and although Jack would never talk about his work, Timmy had heard stories about him, had found out his name was Jack Murphy, and that he was sort of famous around Evansville.

What would it be like to get shot? Or kill someone? Timmy wondered.

He'd seen the scar on Murphy's neck and had asked him once if it hurt. Murphy just said, "What do you think, tough guy?"

Murphy called me "tough guy." Wow!

"You won't catch nothing here, Tommy," the voice stole into his thoughts, and came from close behind him.

Timmy turned and saw a man sitting in the rocks. The guy was dressed like a soldier—beige pants tucked into desert boots, mud-colored T-shirt, and deeply tanned skin—but Timmy knew this creep wasn't a soldier. His dark hair was long and greasy, and his eyes were the color of the sky, except cloudier, like he was looking off somewhere.

"Did I get your spot, mister?" Timmy asked out of politeness. He knew it wasn't the stranger's spot. He knew it was his and Murphy's spot. And the guy had called him Tommy, so he sure as hell didn't know him. *What a dweeb!* But since Timmy was playing hooky from school, he didn't need any trouble. The guy might be a creep, but he was a grownup creep, and grownups were grownups.

The man chuckled and tossed a rock into the river. The rock came close to Timmy's head.

"Hey! You don't have to do that. I'll just move on, mister."

"Tommy, Tommy, Tommy," the man said almost caressingly. "You don't need to worry, little man. Everything will be okay."

Of course everything will be okay. Why wouldn't it? And quit callin' me Tommy, shit-for-brains, Timmy thought.

Timmy started to reel in his bait. He wanted to be quit of this place and this guy as soon as possible. Then a thought struck him: this was "his" fishing spot, his and Murphy's. Why should he let some dirt bag run him off? Murphy sure as hell wouldn't run. Murphy'd do some fancy moves and this ass-wipe would be swimming in the river.

Showing more courage than he felt, he said, "I fish here a lot, mister. And my friend fishes with me. He's a famous police detective." He hoped that would shut this guy up.

The man stood slowly and said, "I know."

He came down the rocks and stood beside Timmy Ryan, placing a dirty hand on his shoulder. "Tommy, me and my brother seen you down here with Murphy. You think he likes you, don't you?"

Timmy was more surprised than he was scared, and he didn't care for the way this guy was talking. "Me and Murphy are friends, ass-wipe," Tommy said, pulling away from the hand on his shoulder. "And how come you keep calling me Tommy if you know so much? You don't even know my name."

The man laughed and said, "You ever heard of Tommy Tittlemouse, little man?"

The heavy blade appeared magically in the man's hand. Timmy put his hands out defensively, but the heavy steel sliced through fishing rod and flesh until it found its mark, deep in the tendons and bone of Timmy Ryan's neck. He was dead before he hit the ground.

When Maddy Brooks found the envelope, her first instinct was to throw it in the trash with her junk mail. But the envelope was addressed in red crayon, her name written in a childlike, scrawling hand. She opened her middle drawer and pulled out the letter she'd found on her desk last week. That one had contained a poem or something about Punch and Judy, or some such nonsense. She looked at the crayon-scribbled handwriting on the two envelopes, and they appeared to be the same.

As one of the top news anchors for Channel Six, she had made more enemies than friends. Making it to the top wasn't easy for a woman in the news business, but she'd found that most men could be led around by their lower extremities. She knew she was beautiful, and she felt no shame for using her God-given looks to attain her goals. But she could be as treacherous as she was beautiful, and when she found out who was playing these practical jokes on her . . .

"Not funny, guys," she said loudly enough for everyone

in the newsroom to hear and tossed the envelopes back onto her desk. She would need them when she filed her "hostile work environment lawsuit" against the station. At the very least, the letters would give her some leverage for another promotion.

Her phone rang. She picked it up and said, "Maddy Brooks, Channel Six News." She listened a moment before hanging up and yelling for her cameraman. Then she was out the back door and heading for the Jeep Liberty the station let her use.

CHAPTER FOUR

Jack was bored. Two hours of riding a desk, and he was beginning to think he'd made a mistake coming back to work early. His first day, after four weeks of sick leave, and his mind had turned into mush. He couldn't concentrate for shit.

Since he had walked in the back door of headquarters this morning and parked his ass, all he'd done was read reports, drink coffee, field questions about how it felt to be back at work, and feel his blood pressure rise with the insistent stress of the job. Everyone was congratulating him on not getting killed and reminding him how close he'd come. On television the detective-hero gets shot, beaten, run over, blown up, attacked by dogs, and stuff like that, and even does it all with a snappy line like "Hasta la vista, baby," or "Is that the best you got?" But, in the real world, all those things hurt like hell, and the only thing the detective says is "Get me an ambulance."

He'd forgotten how it felt to be in the same room with twenty detectives—listening to their constant bickering, insults, bad jokes, inappropriate laughter, and petty jealousy, not to mention the general depressed atmosphere that would smother a sane man. Luckily, he wasn't quite sane.

Old memos, wanted posters, bulletins, and even active case reports were stuck haphazardly here and there, littering the top of his desk. He'd spent an hour sorting through the mess, tossing most of it, and piling up things that looked important. He was just going through it a second time when he felt a nudge.

He looked up to see his partner, Liddell Blanchard. Jack was tall, but Liddell's six-foot-five hulking figure made him look like a midget. "Saddle up, pod'na," Liddell said. "We've got one down at the river. Out by your place."

In her haste, Maddy Brooks tripped in the big rocks lining the steep bank along the Ohio River and tumbled to the bottom of the embankment.

"Maddy, are you okay?" her cameraman asked, trying to fight down a chuckle. He carefully made his way down the rocks to where she was sprawled out.

She rolled into a sitting position, blew strands of hair out of her face and looked up at him. "Yeah. Just wonderful." She looked around, hoping no one had seen her fall. It wouldn't do for her embarrassing moment to show up on some home video footage.

Dex, her cameraman, said with a grin plastered to his face, "Maddy Brooks always gets to the bottom of things. One way or another." He chuckled and reached down to give her a hand.

She pushed his hand away. "I will do it myself, thank you," she said icily. She knew he secretly had the hots for her, and she didn't want him touching her.

She made it to her feet and brushed herself off, surveying the damage to her clothes. She had lost the heel of one shoe and knew she was going to have bruises all over her body, but somehow she had not broken anything and thankfully hadn't damaged her face.

"Maybe we better get you to the hospital . . . you know . . . to get checked out," Dex offered.

She fixed him with a stare and said, "This never happened. You understand?"

He held his hands up in surrender. He knew what an icy bitch she could be, and he definitely didn't need her gunning for him. But he couldn't help but smile inwardly at the memory of the Ice Queen tumbling head over heels down the rocky embankment. *Too bad the camera wasn't on. That footage would make for some pretty fun halftime entertainment with the guys.*

Maddy kicked at one of the large rocks until she dislodged the heel from the good shoe, and then scampered down the river in the direction of the crime scene. If she was lucky, she would find an opening in the police line and get some good shots of the body before the detectives ran them off. That was why she had opted to come down the sharp rocks instead of driving straight to the crime scene. She would find a way in. No way was she going to be shut out of the scene after losing an expensive pair of shoes.

"The old guy with the dog pulled the kid out of the water," Corporal Timmons said to Liddell, and nodded in the direction of an elderly gentleman wearing a red, shawl-neck sweater and tweed, snap-brim cap. The dog—a mostly white Jack Russell terrier mix—pulled anxiously at his lead, casting nervous looks at the throngs of policemen.

Liddell said to Jack, "I'll go talk to him," and headed in the direction of the man and dog. They both knew Jack was better with the dead than the living, so Jack went to check out the victim.

The first rule of a crime scene is to not touch anything. This scene had been fucked sideways before the police arrived. First by the old man, and then by the Fire Department Rescue Squad. It was understandable that the old man would pull the kid's body from the water, because he wouldn't know any better. But a fire department rescue crew had arrived before the police did, and had thrown a tarp over the body. He knew they did it out of some misplaced respect for the dead, or to protect the kid's body from prying eyes. But he'd been through this with them before and could not seem to get them to understand that they should leave the body exactly as it was found. Now he would have to learn where the tarp had come from and what it had last covered because of the possible contamination and/or transference of evidence.

Jack donned a pair of latex gloves and carefully lifted the tarp slightly to peer underneath. The body was that of a small boy, maybe ten to twelve years old. The body had apparently been head down on the muddy bank, maybe partly in the water, but he now lay on his side, his jeans, T-shirt, face, and hair smeared with dark river mud. "Can we get some shots, Jack?" one of the crime scene techs asked. "Then we'll uncover the body and get a better look."

Jack stood back and let the tech shoot several digital photos of the area and then helped the techs carefully lift and fold the tarp so that any possible evidence that had come in contact with the body would remain on the inside of the tarp.

"He's been moved," the tech said.

"Corporal Timmons said the old man pulled the body from the water," Jack explained to the tech.

"Well, he probably wasn't in the water," the crime scene tech replied, pointing out the partly dried mud on the face and in the ears and mouth.

Jack whistled at Liddell, got his attention, and held up his cell phone. When Liddell came on the line Jack said, "Ask him if the boy was actually in the water." Liddell asked. The old man replied, "He was lyin' in the water just like I said. I pulled him out. Me 'n' Belle pulled him out."

Jack had punched the speakerphone button and held the phone out so the tech could hear.

The tech shook his head. "Belle must be the dog?"

Jack shrugged.

"The boy's body was moved, Jack, but not from the water. If he had been in the water he wouldn't have that amount of mud still on him. He was probably faced down in the mud, maybe near the water's edge, and then was turned over."

Liddell heard what the crime scene tech said, and Jack heard him using a stern voice on the old gentleman. A moment later he came back on the line and said, "He admitted that he turned the body over. Said he was checking to see if the kid was breathing. Then when he saw he was dead, he made up the story about pulling him from the water because that gave him more of a reason to have touched the body. He wants to know if he's going to jail." Liddell chuckled.

"Tell him he's been watching too much *CSI*," Jack said and hung up. To the tech, he asked, "Any idea yet how he died?"

The tech looked at the back of the victim's upper torso and whistled softly. "Well, I don't know if it is the exact cause of death, but someone tried to cut his head off."

Jack looked at the boy's body again, more closely now that the tarp was removed. He could see the victim's head was twisted in an odd position, but until the coroner arrived they wouldn't be able to do a more thorough examination.

"Something else, Jack," the tech said, and pointed to something lying partially under the victim's side. Jack looked but couldn't see what the tech was talking about. The tech pointed again, and said, "I might be wrong, but that looks like intestines."

The tech was right. But there was nothing else they could do until the coroner arrived and they took tons of photos.

"I'll get some more photos before I move him. And we need to clear an area around the body until we can check everything," the tech said.

Jack thought about shoe prints. He would have to get one of the techs to look at the old man's shoes, maybe take a picture of the bottoms, for later elimination. He looked up and saw the mobile crime scene van parking at the top of the road. He also saw Maddy Brooks hobbling down the shoreline with a cameraman in tow.

Jack keyed his radio and advised the uniformed sergeant in charge of the scene that they had company. In less than a minute two uniformed officers were headed down the bank to cut off Maddy Brooks and get her out of the crime scene.

He watched the two uniforms corral the news crew, and although he couldn't make out any words, he could hear her exasperated voice rising above the others as she was ushered out of the area. He could imagine the threats she was hurling down on their heads. He knew she had a job to do, but he couldn't care less about her damn television station or her bastardized idea of the U.S. Constitution. The public's right to know didn't outweigh the rights of the victim. At least on that count, the fire rescue crew and Jack were in complete agreement.

CHAPTER FIVE

"He'll see you now," the mayor's administrative secretary said.

Chief Marlin Pope put down the *Evansville Living* magazine and nodded at the woman. He guessed her age as in her early forties, but the perpetual scowl she wore made her mouth into a straight-line gash with concentric wrinkles emanating from it, creating the effect of a broken pane of glass. Her hair was tightly permed and short like the geriatric set seemed to prefer. Her pinstriped black pants, coarse black blazer, and thick-soled, ugly shoes gave her the look of a stern jail matron. She was quite a contrast to the last secretary, who had looked to be all of seventeen years old, was a knockout, and was rumored to be extremely loyal to "his honor, the mayor," but not too bright.

Maybe he's finally realized that youth and beauty do not necessarily equate to brains and ability, Pope thought. *But, more likely, his wife hired this one.*

"Good morning, Mayor," Pope said as he entered the spacious office. He didn't bother to attempt to shake hands. It was no secret that Mayor Thatcher Hensley hated the very air that Pope breathed and would do everything in his power to replace him as soon as it was possible. The only thing stopping Hensley from replacing him *now* was a serious lack of backbone.

Pope knew that he had the distinction of being the first black man in the history of Evansville to attain the promoted rank of deputy chief and the appointed rank of chief of police. The person the mayor was considering as a replacement for him was Deputy Chief Richard Dick—blond-haired, blue-eyed, tall, and lean, every bit the Aryan poster child.

Mayor Hensley believed that replacing the popular Marlin Pope with the decidedly unpopular Richard Dick would be tantamount to political suicide. But in truth, it was an accepted political practice for an incoming mayor to replace the chief of police with his own selection.

To his regret, when Hensley took office he delayed in naming a new chief of police. Now, almost a year later, the rumor that Hensley was considering doing so was viewed by the black community as a racial slight, by the public as a weakness, and by his own party as outright stupidity.

But like any politician worth his salt, he had a backup plan. All he had to do was find good cause to dismiss Pope, maybe some type of malfeasance of office, or a corruption charge, and Hensley would be home free. The trouble was, Pope was good at what he did, and as far as Hensley had been able to ascertain, the man was as honest as, well, the Pope.

"Have a seat, Marlin," Hensley said, not bothering to address him by his title or even his proper name. Pope pretended not to notice the intended slight and sat directly across from the mayor. Thatcher Hensley leaned back in his chair and crossed his legs, a smile playing at the corners of his lips. "Where are you on the murder of Dr. Lewis? And don't bullshit me."

* * *

James Kuhlenschmidt hated his nickname. "Kooky" wasn't exactly a confidence-inspiring moniker. *Why couldn't I have gotten a cool nickname, like "Gunner" or "Robo" or something? Why do I always get the shit jobs?*

He made his way through the large riprap and head-high brush along the shoreline, where his training officer had sent him on a fool's errand. He was supposed to be looking for evidence. *The body is way back there. It's obvious there's nothing down here.*

But he had seen one interesting thing when that newswoman had gone down on her keister in the rocks. *Man, that will give me some stories to tell at the FOP Club later.* And then he'd watched from behind the bushes as she and her cameraman scurried down the shore with her yelling orders at the poor guy like he was some kind of pissant. He wondered briefly if he should stop them from sneaking into the crime scene, but then he remembered that he, Officer James Kuhlenschmidt, was also being treated like a pissant. *Let one of the hotshot cops down there do something about that pair.*

His mind was still occupied with these thoughts when his feet tangled up in something and he went sprawling onto the hard rocks and sharp brush. As he struggled to his feet, he noticed that his pants leg was torn and there was blood all over his hands. "What the fuck?" he said out loud and wiped at his hands. The blood wasn't his. Then he noticed the clear, plastic line twisted around his boots. And there was something else.

Maddy Brooks had just about made up her mind to call Deputy Chief Richard Dick and insist that she be allowed to do her job, when she saw a young, uniformed officer running toward the crime scene. He was screaming something over and over, but she couldn't quite make the words out. It sounded like "Buckets of blood!" She turned to order Dex to film the scene unfolding below them, but he had already shouldered the camera and was getting it all.

CHAPTER SIX

Eddie watched from a distance as the skinny cop ran up to Murphy and tossed his cookies.

"Must've found the stuff we left behind," Eddie said to Bobby. "Took 'em long enough."

He watched Murphy pull something out of his back pocket and hand it to the skinny cop. It was a handkerchief.

"Oh, ain't that special? He's helping that young cop clean hisself," Eddie said.

"Better get some rest," Bobby said. "We got a lot to do tonight."

Eddie turned toward the parking lot where he'd left the van. *Murphy's one cold son of a bitch.* He had expected a stronger reaction when Murphy saw the kid's body, but instead of getting angry, or crying or getting excited in any way, Murphy had just squatted down and checked the kid out. Like he was looking at a dead dog. It was very disappointing. Bobby'd said that killing the kid would get to Murphy. And this particular kid should have been special.

"I know what you're thinking, Eddie," Bobby said. "But before we're done, we'll get that bastard's attention."

"Yeah, whatever."

CHAPTER SEVEN

The room smelled of bleach and formaldehyde and something more unpleasant. Death could not be scrubbed away or covered up, and Jack had learned over the years that the smell of a violent death was as much in the mind as in the air. He knew he'd smell the corpse of this poor kid every time he closed his eyes for the next week. Or at least until the next corpse came along.

"Need this?" Carmodi asked, holding out a small glass container of mentholated cream. Carmodi had dabbed some under his own nostrils.

Jack shook his head. "Let's just get to it. The longer you try to fight the smell off, the longer it takes to get used to it."

"Your partner's a little testy today," Carmodi said to Liddell.

Ignoring Carmodi's remark, Jack said to Liddell, "Call dispatch again and see if anyone's reported a missing kid."

"I just got off the phone with them, pod'na," Liddell answered.

"Well, then try the shift commander," Jack said angrily. "Are those guys checking the schools?"

Liddell nodded his head. "I talked to him right before I called dispatch. No one has a missing kid."

"Well, someone's missing a kid!"

Liddell put a big hand on Jack's shoulder. "You okay?"

Jack looked at the body on the table. The boy was about ten or twelve years old. No one knew he was dead except the cops. No, he wasn't okay, but he lied through his teeth, "Yeah. I'm just great." To Carmodi, Jack said, "Sorry, Doc. I've been off work a while."

Carmodi shrugged and pulled on latex gloves. He was used to cops. Some of them joked, some cried, and some got angry. It was a way to deal with the stress of the job. It was like a pressure release valve, and a good thing to have. If you couldn't let it out, the things these guys saw in their careers would make most people blow their brains out. Actually, he'd done autopsies on a couple of those.

Two crime scene techs were busy snapping digital photos while Carmodi and his assistant turned the body onto its side to remove the body bag from underneath. Having done that, he began removing the muddy clothing.

Jack had been to several hundred autopsies, but this was the part he hated most. Stripping the clothing from a dead body was dehumanizing in a way that nothing else could be. As a policeman, he was supposed to protect people, and in death, a person was at their most helpless. Although, in his rational mind, he knew he couldn't save everyone, he always experienced a personal sense of failure that he had not kept the person safe.

He forced himself to look, to pay attention, to discover any clues, as Carmodi and the assistant prepared the body to be dissected. He wanted to scream at them to stop and just bury the poor kid. Instead, feeling like a pure bastard, he pulled on some gloves and searched the mud-stiffened clothing as it was removed.

Carmodi and his assistant turned the body onto its back.

The autopsy table is almost seven feet in length, and slightly tilted toward a huge stainless-steel sink with a filter on the sink trap. A microphone is suspended over each of the three stainless-steel autopsy tables, and the forensic pathologist can start recording by simply stepping on a foot pedal. Carmodi stepped on the pedal and spoke into the mike, saying the date, time, and location of the autopsy, as well as his own name and those of everyone present during the procedure.

"The body appears to be that of a young white male, age approximately eleven years old . . ."

And so the autopsy began. After giving the overall description of the body, Carmodi instructed the assistant to help him wash the body clean. A length of hose was coiled under the sink, and the assistant used this to start washing the mud and other detritus from the body to enable closer examination. The mud was washed away from the face and neck, revealing a considerable cut running down the neck and chest, continuing into the abdomen.

A crime scene tech snapped high-resolution digitals of the wound while Carmodi spoke into the microphone again. After the dictation was finished, he spoke to Jack and Liddell. "Almost took the boy's head off."

"Can you put that in layman's terms, Doc?" Liddell said and chuckled.

Carmodi was about to respond when he noticed Jack fingering the scar on his own neck. "It's no contest, Jack. His is bigger than yours."

Jack shot him an angry look and was about to respond to his callous remark, but Liddell put a hand on his shoulder.

"Jack, I got this. Go back to the scene if you want—you know—coordinate things," Liddell offered.

"Yeah. Leave the Cajun behind and scoot," Carmodi said to Jack. "You're ruining my normally pleasant demeanor."

Jack ignored the men and walked around the table, getting a good look at the boy's face for the first time. His own face went white.

"What's the matter, Jack?" Liddell asked.

Carmodi was staring at him also.

"I know this kid," Jack said.

CHAPTER EIGHT

Mayor Thatcher Beauregard Hensley's office wasn't as spacious as he would have liked, but to move to a larger office he would have had to give up his private bathroom, and that would never do. His middle name, Beauregard, had come from a French great uncle on his mother's side of the family. It meant "beautiful outlook." Unlike his namesake, he had not seen any beauty in life, except what he could buy or control. So he had opted for commandeering the office next to his and had the wall replaced with thick soundproof glass and a heavy glass door. The stolen office was now his private conference room and made his domain look twice its original size.

Mayor Hensley informed his secretary that he would not be taking calls and had her usher his waiting visitor into the conference room via a private and seldom-used entrance.

Deputy Chief Richard Dick took a seat across from the mayor. Hensley forced a smile, and said, "What have you got for me, Richard?"

"I think we may have an opportunity here, Mayor."

Dick outlined what he knew of the murders for the mayor,

explaining how he felt the current chief had handled the investigations poorly. He omitted the fact that he, Richard Dick, was the commander of the investigations unit and had done nothing to solve the murders himself.

Hensley smiled. "Malfeasance," he said, as if tasting the word. "That might work, Richard. But what if this detective . . ."

"Murphy. Jack Murphy," Dick said.

"So what if this Detective . . . Murphy . . . catches the killers?"

Dick made a dismissive gesture with his hand. "Murphy's not as good as he thinks he is."

"But what if . . . ?" the mayor persisted.

"Well," Dick said, "if he does, then you and I take the credit. But if he doesn't . . ." He paused deliberately. "And God forbid there is another murder . . . well . . . I am the commander of the detective unit, and Chief Pope is breaking policy by not allowing me to run the investigation. If it blows up in his face, we can point that fact out in his dismissal hearing when you appoint me as the new chief of police."

"Has the chief ordered you not to work on these murders, Dick?" the Mayor questioned.

Instead of answering, Dick shrugged and gave Hensley a sardonic smile.

Hensley's sources within the police department had told him that Dick wasn't respected and that behind his back the men called him "Double Dick." Obviously some play on his name, Richard Dick, but in any case it wasn't good that he had no support within his own ranks. Dick was a bumbling, arrogant asshole, but he was a cunning asshole, too, and could be a useful ally. Hensley made a mental note to keep an eye on him and wondered if his choice of a new chief of police wasn't made a little hastily.

"Keep me informed, Deputy Chief," the mayor said.

* * *

"You know this child?" Carmodi asked.

Jack stared at the face of the little boy. He'd first seen the kid about a month ago. It was one of those early mornings. The sun was not quite up, and Susan had gone for her run. He'd taken advantage of the quiet to make coffee and go out to his back porch to watch the threads of brilliant red and crimson colors spread across the horizon to the east. That's when he heard someone down near the riverbank, cursing a blue streak. The voice sounded young. He'd looked over the porch railing and seen a kid yanking the end of a long, thin stick for all he was worth.

He remembered how amused he was, watching as the kid wrestled a large catfish from the river and then had to chase its flopping body around the bank.

"Timmy," Jack said. "His name was Timmy."

"Last name?" Carmodi asked.

Jack thought about it, but didn't think he had ever asked. "Just Timmy," he said. "That's all he told me."

Then Jack told them everything he knew about Timmy. How he had found him fishing on the riverbank below his cabin, and how the kid never seemed to run out of questions once he found out Jack was a cop.

"He was always asking things like, 'Have you got a gun?' 'Have you ever shot anyone?' 'Have you ever killed any bad guys?' You know stuff like that," Jack said. "I lied to him and told him it was mostly boring paperwork, but he saw my scar and started asking questions about that."

While he spoke, Jack absent-mindedly began going through the pockets of the muddy jeans. In the right pocket he felt something mushy, but grittier than mud. He pulled out his gloved hand and saw something yellowish on the fingers.

"What's that?" Liddell asked.

"Fish bait," Jack said and looked at what was left of what

had once been several cornmeal balls. He had taught the kid how to mix cornmeal with a little egg white and roll it into balls. Overnight it would harden and make bait that catfish couldn't resist.

"Ah shit," Jack said, and left the room.

Jack stood in the hallway near the coroner's office. He pulled the latex gloves off and pitched them in a biohazard container. He had never walked out during an autopsy before, but this one was getting to him. There were other things he could do.

Jack almost laughed at that thought. "What to do next?" he said in the empty hallway. There was a long list of what needed to be done. None of it would bring back the curious little boy who would rather hang around a broken-down cop and ask questions, or fish in the river with a long stick and fishing line he'd found along the riverbank. *Why couldn't he just go to school like other kids his age?*

He needed to make a bathroom stop. Then he would call the motor patrol lieutenant at the crime scene and juvenile detectives to tell them who he suspected the deceased child might be. They could get busy shaking the bushes again. He had only a first name for the kid, but he knew Timmy lived somewhere in the area of the museum. There were a lot of large, older homes that had been divided into apartments around there. Juvenile detectives would canvass the schools. Maybe they'd get lucky and find the kid's folks.

I need a quiet place to make a call, he thought, and re-membered that the closest phone was in the office of the chief deputy coroner—a diminutive woman named Lilly Caskins whom everyone called "Little Casket." It was a nickname that suited her well, for she was evil looking, with large dark eyes staring out of extra thick lenses, and horn-rimmed frames that had gone out of style during the days of

Al Capone. But the thing that bothered Jack was her blunt-
ness at death scenes. For a woman, she had absolutely no
compassion for the dead, or the living.

He decided he didn't want to run into Lilly. At the other
end of the building there was a bathroom, and after going
there, he could take his cell phone out into the garage.

He headed in that direction, and as he passed the conference room he spotted the pale face of the rookie cop that had
thrown up at the crime scene. He was little more than a kid,
and Jack guessed his age at barely twenty-one, just old
enough to be hired by the police department. He was shirt-
less and sipping ginger ale from a can. His uniform shirt lay
stretched across a couple of chairs, drying.

Scratch the bathroom stop, Jack thought, not wanting to
smell vomit on top of everything else today.

"You feeling better, Officer, uh . . . ?" Jack asked. He'd
forgotten the rookie's name.

The young man looked up with red-rimmed eyes and
said, "Kuhlenschmidt," then returned to staring at the floor.

Kuhlenschmidt was a wreck. He had just seen his first
murder victim, his first mutilated body, and had the bad luck
of humiliating himself in front of the news media and his
peers by soiling himself and screaming and crying hysterically. Eventually he would have to be interviewed and file a
complete report as he was the one that had found the actual
scene of the murder. But Jack could see that questioning him
right this minute would be fruitless.

Not everyone is cut out to be a cop. He wanted to tell
Kuhlenschmidt he should look at other career options, but
instead he said, "Look, Officer Kuhlenschmidt, don't be so
hard on yourself."

The young cop looked up hopefully. "This ever happen to
you, Detective?"

"No," Jack said, and watched as the darkness crept back

into that face. "But I can tell you some whopper stories on your training officer when you get off probation."

Kooky looked up and said, "I'm sorry I screwed up out there, Detective Murphy."

Jack had to turn away from the tears welling up in the young man's eyes. It had been a long time since Jack had seen his first ugly murder, and had become the hardened bastard he was today. It was a cop's lot in life to lose faith in humanity to the reality of evil.

"You married?" Jack asked, changing the subject.

"No. Got a girlfriend though."

"Go home," Jack said. "Take a shower. Have sex. Drink a beer or two. Have some more sex."

Kuhlenschmidt looked up and grinned.

"Did I mention that you should have sex?" Jack said in a very serious tone, and Kuhlenschmidt chuckled.

"Yeah, I get it, Detective Murphy. Thanks."

"Do not get drunk," Jack said sternly. "That's not the way to deal with this."

"I understand," he said, "but what about Corporal Timmons? I'm on shift until three."

"I've already taken care of it," Jack lied.

Kuhlenschmidt picked up his shirt and started to get up.

"Wait here," Jack said. "I'll have someone take you home. You can come back to get your personal car later."

Jack was about to leave when Kuhlenschmidt said, "The deputy chief will never let me be a detective because of this, will he?"

Jack pulled out a chair and sat down beside the man. "Let me tell you a story about Double Dick."

Kooky glanced up, and a grin spread across his face. "Double Dick? Are you talking about the deputy chief, sir?"

"Yeah," Jack said, and told the young officer how Deputy Chief of Police Richard Dick had earned the nickname Double Dick. It wasn't because Dick was short for Richard, which would make his name Dick Dick. The name had come about because Dick had a reputation for screwing everyone over and fouling up every case he was involved with. He also briefly told the story of how Dick had screwed up the last robbery stakeout that Jack was on and the lawsuits that were still being settled because of it.

"So you're saying that when he shows up at a scene, everyone gets Dick'd, sir?" Kuhlenschmidt said with a crooked smile.

"You got it, partner."

Kuhlenschmidt smiled brighter at the word *partner*. *Maybe Kooky isn't such a bad nickname, after all,* he thought.

"Gotta go pee, Kooky."

Jack left the rookie in the conference room. He hoped the poor guy was in better shape, mentally at least, than he looked.

Jack walked into the garage and punched the numbers for the motor patrol shift lieutenant into his cell phone. He passed on the first name and information they now had for the victim, and the lieutenant promised to get some guys out re-canvassing the area around the museum. Before he hung up, Jack told the lieutenant that Officer Kuhlenschmidt would need the rest of the day off and a ride home. Probably needed some time with the department shrink, too.

Having done his good deed for the year, he called the Juvenile Division and got some good news. And a lot of bad news. The good news was that juvenile detectives already knew the kid's last name and where he lived. The bad news was there was no missing persons report on Timothy Ryan, and the kid's mother had taken off years ago and left him with one of her boyfriends. There was no mention of a father. The juvenile detective working this was trying to find the boyfriend to come and identify the body, but so far had been unable to locate him.

Jack hung up thinking that couples should have to apply for permits and prove they have a collective IQ over twenty to have children. Unfortunately, they don't even have to have a full set of teeth between them to breed.

His cell phone rang. "Murphy," he said. It was Liddell.

CHAPTER NINE

Jack entered the autopsy room again to find Carmodi, Liddell, and two crime scene techs leaning over the table near Timmy Ryan's head.

"Check this out," Liddell said and moved aside.

At the bottom of the table, one of the crime scene techs was unfolding a wadded-up piece of paper.

Liddell said, "Carmodi found it stuffed in the kid's throat."

The tech finished unfolding the paper, and they could see there was something written on it.

"Shit!" Carmodi exclaimed softly. The crime scene techs began snapping digital photos excitedly.

"What is it, Doc?" Jack asked. It seemed everyone in the room knew something that he didn't.

Liddell leaned toward Jack and said in a whisper, "We found one of these notes last week, Jack."

Liddell had been back to work for several weeks, and had kept Jack up to date on some of what was happening, but he didn't remember being told anything about a murder where a note was left at the scene. He hadn't been much interested in what was going on while he was recuperating at home, but now he wished he'd kept up.

"Crayon," one of the crime scene techs said. "Just like the last one."

The note was scrawled in red crayon in what looked like a child's handwriting. Jack read the note:

> he caught fishes
> in other mens ditches
>
> they pay for your sins

"What the hell does that mean?" Jack asked. No one seemed to have a clue.

Maddy Brooks threw her ruined shoes at the trash can in her office. She was furious. Not only did she ruin a pair of expensive shoes, but that incompetent, damned detective had shut her out of the story.

Who the hell does Murphy think he is? She was imagining ways to make his life miserable when she noticed the two envelopes that still lay on her desk. In her haste to get to the murder scene at the river, she had not thought them important. She tore open the newest one and pulled out the note inside.

Once again, in a childlike scrawl, in red crayon, was written:

> he caught fishes
> in other mens ditches
>
> they pay for your sins

Really! she thought angrily. *Enough is enough. If these yokels think they can scare me into quitting, they don't know who they're messing with.*

She debated the merit of going to the station manager, but realized that she didn't have any evidence as to who was leaving the notes. And if she started asking who had left them on her desk, it would just make her look panicky, and that would never do.

She decided to wait and watch. But right now she needed a smoke.

Eddie awakened with a start. His pillow was damp, and his long hair clung to his face. His eyes hurt, and his throat felt strained, like he'd been screaming. He sat up on the edge of the couch where he had fallen asleep and shielded his eyes from the sunlight that bled through the mostly missing window blinds of his motel room.

From the room next to his someone was banging loudly on the wall. A raspy voice accompanied the banging. "Shut the fuck up over there! I'm trying to sleep!"

"I oughta kill that bastard," Eddie said through clenched teeth, then yelled at the wall, "Shut up, ya rat fuck!" He slammed his hand against the wall hard enough to rattle the windows.

Sitting across from him, his brother shook his head sadly. "How many times I gotta tell you, bro? Complaining don't get the job done."

Eddie jumped up from the couch and grabbing the huge corn knife, headed for the door.

"I'll get the fuckin' job done, all right," he said as he swung the thirty-inch blade of the corn knife around in the air. "I'll cut him a new asshole."

Bobby didn't move from the bed where he was reclined, head cradled in his hands, with a huge smile playing across his face.

"What?" Eddie asked. Then he looked in the cracked mirror behind the couch, and saw what Bobby was grinning about. Eddie's damp hair stood out in all directions, he was naked, and in his hand was the antique harvesting knife he'd stolen from behind a junk store.

Bobby started to chuckle, and Eddie had to admit he was quite a sight.

"Guess I'll just cut the shit heel's tires later," Eddie said and sat back down on the couch. He held the knife at arm's length, checking it out. He'd always liked knives, maybe not as much as Bobby, but even Bobby would have to admit this was the "mother of all knives."

The thirty-inch hammered-iron blade was a quarter of an inch thick at the back and razor sharp along the wickedly curved blade. The long wood handle was at a forty-five-degree angle to the blade and, like a scythe, was designed to swing with one or both hands to harvest corn.

"Save it for Murphy," Bobby said.

Eddie put the knife down and slumped back on the couch. He was tired. The one thing he'd never had trouble with in his life was sleeping, at least until now. Booze, even drugs, didn't help anymore. He pulled his knees up under his chin, wrapped his arms around his legs, and began rocking. Pieces of memories flashed in his mind, sparking raw emotions. The waking nightmares were all too familiar now. *An old church building, stairs, a locked door, a boy shoved over an altar, a splash of blood dripping onto a wooden floor, screaming, screaming, screaming . . .*

"Hey, snap out of it, bro." Bobby's voice brought Eddie back. Bobby was sitting at the foot of the bed, a sad look on his face. "You were thinking about the preacher, weren't you?" Bobby was referring to their deceased father. He had been a self-professed preacher of sorts.

Eddie nodded, not trusting his voice. He was too big to cry, and too proud to let his brother see how close he was to doing just that.

"I told you how to make the dreams go away, Eddie," Bobby said. "Complaining don't get the job done."

Eddie hated it when his brother said that. "Complaining don't get the job done, Eddie. Sorry don't get the job done, Eddie." Those were the preacher's words. Nothing ever seemed to get the job done where his father was concerned.

"What do you want me to do?" Eddie asked.

Bobby looked at the corn knife, and Eddie felt a shiver of excitement.

"Who?"

"Get the book and I'll show you," Bobby answered.

Maddy Brooks looked around before sneaking out the back door of the television station. She wedged a Popsicle stick between the door latch and the strike plate so the door wouldn't lock, made sure the coast was clear, and then took out a pack of smokes. The last thing she needed was for the station manager to catch her smoking near the building. Actually, she didn't want anyone to see. Evansville had passed a nonsmoking ordinance that forbade smoking in or within one hundred feet of an occupied structure. Of course, the two-faced assholes at city hall had made an exception for the Blue Star Casino and for most taverns. When it came to politicians, money always spoke louder than words.

And the thought of someone being allowed to smoke in the confined spaces of the riverboat, while she had to sneak off to light up, made her angry. You'd think her job as news anchor for Channel Six would give her a few privileges. Like being able to smoke in her office. *Like Bob Sampson. I can smell smoke in his office all the time.*

But Bob Sampson was a man, and as such, was immune from the same rules as women at the station. She wondered briefly if Sampson was the one leaving the notes on her desk, but quickly dismissed the idea. Sampson was a dickless little shit. He wouldn't have the nerve to do something like that.

Maddy sucked the smoke deep into her lungs and held it. What she wouldn't give for a joint right now. But smoking cigarettes outside the back door, and smoking dope outside the back door, were two different things. She smiled at the thought of getting caught smoking a doobie, and just then the back door crashed open.

"Maddy?"

The party crasher was Lois, the television station's secretary. Lois Hensley was short, paunchy, wrinkled, and an annoying little twit that Maddy knew was trying to get her fired. Lois had been with the station almost twenty years before Maddy had been hired.

"Yes, Lois." There was no hint of annoyance in her voice. She hated Lois, but she respected the power that Lois had with the station manager. Maybe Lois had never been a reporter, but she was not someone you wanted to piss off. She knew more about the operation of the station than God, *and* she was the mayor's mother.

"I found this taped to the front door." Lois handed Maddy an envelope with Maddy's name scrawled on the outside in red crayon.

"Is this a joke, Lois?" Maddy asked before remembering that Lois was dispossessed of a sense of humor. "Sorry, Lois. Who left it?"

Lois looked haughtily at Maddy. "I did say I found it taped to the front door, didn't I?" She turned to leave, and then, as if she had just remembered, Lois said, "Oh yeah, there was another of those silly notes, and I put it in your mail slot."

"When was that, Lois?" Maddy asked. She could barely contain her agitation, and Lois seemed to be enjoying herself.

"Well, it didn't look important. I really don't remember. Yesterday, today, I really don't remember."

Maddy tried to control her temper. She'd love to slap silly Lois—well, silly. *So, it wasn't someone playing a joke on me,* she thought. Lois would never take any part in an attempt at humor or playing a joke on anyone. And there was no one in the building who would dare involve Lois in something for fear it would come back on them.

She took the note and said, "Thanks, Lois." Lois gave her a smug grin and turned to go back inside, then turned back again, long enough to say, "You know there is no smoking near the building, Maddy."

Maddy dropped the cigarette on the concrete. "Bitch," she snarled as the door shut behind the older woman. Then she had a thought and pulled the door open.

"Lois, did you leave some other notes on my desk? Notes like this one?" Maddy asked, hoping that Lois had noticed something that might help her learn who was doing this.

"If you got notes, I'm probably the one that left them," Lois answered nastily. "That's my job."

Maddy barely heard the response. Her mind was trying to wrap itself around something just out of her reach. She opened the note Lois had just given her. *Oh my God!* she thought.

In her bare feet, she rushed down the hallway, stopping just long enough at her own office to collect the other two notes, then straight to the station manager's office. They would need the station's legal counsel.

The recaps of the day's events were as disappointing as they were time consuming. Marlin Pope, as chief of police, had made them go through every detail of the case from beginning to end at least a dozen times. Captain Franklin had asked both the forensic pathologist and the coroner to be present at the meeting, but Carmodi was unable to attend. Lilly Caskins was there representing the coroner.

Liddell leaned in to whisper in Jack's ear. "I wonder where Double Dick is."

Jack shrugged. "In hell, I hope," he said, causing Liddell to chuckle a little too loudly.

"Do you have something to add, Detective?" Chief Pope asked.

Liddell turned red. "I was just noticing that Deputy Chief Dick was not present, sir."

Lilly Caskins guffawed. She had overheard Jack's response and couldn't agree more. She hated the deputy chief for reasons unrelated to anything to do with the police department. Her job as chief deputy coroner gave her an inside ear to the current political arena, and she had heard some things regarding Dick that she was not happy about. The very idea of him becoming chief of police sickened her. She respected Marlin Pope, but more than that, she respected the position of chief of police. A man like Richard Dick would fuck up everything he touched.

Pope waited until Caskins got herself under control, then cleared his throat and said, "Now, if we can continue. I need to know what our plan of action is. Captain?"

Franklin looked at Jack and Liddell before beginning. "Summarizing all this, we have two sets of murders that may, or may not, be connected by notes left at the scenes— more particularly, left on the bodies of the victims. No progress was made on the Lewis case, and now we have a killing on the riverfront, where a note, similar to the one left on the body of Anne Lewis, was discovered shoved down the throat of this boy, Timmy Ryan. Crime Scene can tell us that the wounds in both cases were caused by a large, heavy, sharp instrument, like a machete, and that in both cases the bodies were moved after death. No witnesses in either case. No suspects. Nothing so far on the neighborhood canvass-

ing, and in the case of Timmy Ryan, we have been unable to
locate a next of kin. Is that about right?" Franklin asked Jack
and Liddell.

Jack answered. "We also have no connection between the
victims—outside of cryptic notes written in red crayon, that is."

Chief Pope looked around the room until his gaze rested
on Captain Franklin. "What I want to know is how in the hell
did I not know about the first note? The one left on Anne
Lewis's body."

"It was lying on the floor when crime scene and detectives arrived, Chief," Franklin explained. "Apparently the
cleaning woman that found the bodies called for an ambulance, and by the time dispatch figured out what was going
on, the ambulance crew had moved the note and covered the
victims with sheets."

Chief Pope ran a hand down his face. He knew all that,
but he also knew after reading part of the files, that the first
detective on the scene was Detective Jansen, and that Jansen
probably screwed the pooch, so to speak.

And so the meeting went into the late hours of the evening, until finally, everyone was told to go home and get some
rest. Fresh minds see fresh details. They would start again
before the sun was up. Then they would meticulously go over
every report, recanvass every neighborhood, reexamine every
speck of physical evidence, re-interview everyone, and with
any luck, find a next of kin for Timmy Ryan.

As Jack was getting into his personal vehicle to go home,
Liddell stopped him.

"How in the world can a kid be murdered and there is no
one to claim him? No one to mourn him." Liddell shook his
head sadly.

Jack could see the sadness in his partner's eyes. "He's got
us," Jack said.

CHAPTER TEN

The neighborhood had seen better days, but the residents were rallying, trying their best to create a quaint atmosphere that would attract family buyers and keep the slumlords at bay. What they didn't want were more rental properties. They weren't being snobbish. It was logical that renters would have less money to put into landscaping and/or other eye-pleasing decor.

Even though Elaine Lamar was an outsider—not really a homeowner—she had been asked to join the Homeowners Association. She had gone to one meeting, and that was enough for her. Between finger sandwiches and tiny cups of punch, she had been told by at least ten different people that they would "be happy to help her come up with some ideas for giving her house a face-lift." What they didn't offer was the money to do this with.

Elaine leaned against her ten-year-old Toyota Camry and looked up at the peeling paint and warped wood of the two-bedroom home she was renting from a friend. The grass needed cutting, and weeds grew in the gravel driveway. She couldn't remember the last time she'd given the inside of the house a decent cleaning. She inwardly groaned and thought, *There's just not enough time in the day.*

She looked at her watch. It was only noon, but she was dead on her feet and two hours late getting home on a Saturday that she wasn't supposed to be working. Not to mention that her children had been left home with orders to stay inside on an absolutely beautiful day, when they should have been outside playing or riding their bicycles, or doing something with their mother.

Working a full-time job and taking care of three kids with no help or financial support was killing her, but it wasn't like she had any choice. When her husband left her and their three children behind for a younger woman, she had been angry at first, and then the shock set in. She had almost had a nervous breakdown from worrying how she could support them or put them in a good school. Then a friend had found her the rental house, and another friend got her on at a realty firm as office manager.

The job had been an answer to her prayers, and though she loved her work with the realty company, sometimes the hours she had to put in did not seem worth the money when she considered how much of her children's lives she was missing.

The thought of how Carl had treated his children would normally infuriate her, but tonight she was just too tired to care. She was so tired, in fact, that she didn't notice that the front door was standing wide open until she reached to put the key in the door.

Jenny left the front door unlocked. What was that girl thinking? Jenny was her oldest. Ten years old going on twenty, and the only girl. Elaine knew it had been hard on her daughter to be strapped with caring for two younger brothers when Jenny was a mere child herself. But, if it hadn't been for Jenny's maturity, Elaine would have given up long ago and lived on the welfare system. The little girl's positive and uncomplaining attitude had been the one thing that had given Elaine the courage to keep working a full-time job and taking night classes until she got her Realtor's license.

Elaine walked into the living room and called out, "Jenny? Jeremy? Ricky?" No answer. She smiled when she thought about how the two younger boys, ages three and four, still called each other "Icky" and "Germy" instead of Ricky and Jeremy. And how Jenny would patiently correct them, telling them both that they were special and shouldn't make fun of their names.

Are they hiding from me? she wondered. *Is that why the door was left unlocked?*

"Okay, you guys, game's over. Come on out." She walked into the kitchen expecting them to leap out at her and try to scare her, but the house was quiet. A short hallway led to the two bedrooms. The bedroom on the left was Elaine's. The bedroom on the right had been the master bedroom, but because it was bigger, her three children were sharing it. If she could just keep up these hours a little longer, she would have the money to move them into a real house where they could all have their own rooms.

She stopped at the door to her bedroom and found it closed, as it should have been. When you share a small space with three children, you value all the privacy you can get. But the door to the kids' room was also closed, and that was never the case. One or the other of them was continually running in and out of that room.

So this is where they're hiding, she thought. She grabbed the door handle, intending to rush into the room growling to play into their little game. But when she tried the handle, it wouldn't turn—the door was locked. When she'd first moved in she had thought it strange that all of the bedrooms had doorknobs that allowed the door to be locked from the inside. But it had been explained to her that because the house had been a rental property, that some of the renters had in-

stalled locking knobs on their rooms for privacy. She'd
meant to put regular bedroom doorknobs on at least the children's room, but when was there time for things like that?
And, she'd never imagined a scenario where the children
would lock her out.

"Come on. It's not nice to lock the door on Mommy," she
said, teasingly at first, and then she began to get a bad feeling.

"Jenny. Open the door, honey. You're scaring Mommy."

There was no response, and she started to panic, but then
remembered that the door lock could be defeated by insert-
ing a slender pushpin in a hole on the outside of the knob.
She rummaged in her purse and found a paper clip. She
straightened one end and plunged it into the hole in the center knob and heard the inside button pop open.

Anxious, and a little scared, she pushed the door open.

Susan Summers was a vision of beauty with her tanned
and fit body and long, strawberry-blond hair as she walked
from her car to the side door of the Indiana State Parole
building.

"I could eat her up," Eddie said, and grinned at his
brother. But Bobby was looking pale and nervous. "What's
the matter, bro?" Eddie asked. "No one's going to see us
here." Bobby didn't answer. He didn't seem himself lately.
He hardly spoke, and when he did it was negative.

"You worried they got warrants out on us?" Eddie asked.
They had violated parole many times before, and Eddie had
missed the last four or five appointments with them. But
Bobby was acting funny, and if Eddie didn't know that
Bobby was incapable of fear he would swear his brother was
scared.

"What the fuck, Bobby? So we get busted sittin' out here.
They don't have nothing, so we go in front of a judge for vi-

olatin' parole, get a slap on the wrist, and back out the fuckin' door."

Instead of speaking, Bobby pointed to the Mother Goose book. Eddie reached in the glove box and pulled out the only thing left from his childhood, a tattered copy of *Mother Goose Rhymes*. This was the same book Bobby had read to him when they were kids. He opened it to the page his brother had marked and read the passage out loud:

> *"Little Nancy Etticoat,*
> *In a white petticoat,*
> *And a red nose;*
> *The longer she stands,*
> *The shorter she grows."*

This was one of his favorite riddles. It had been a game he and Bobby had played when he was little, and Eddie was always good at guessing the answers. The answer to this one was "a candle." Nancy Etticoat was a tall white candle, and the red nose was the flame. The longer the candle burns, the shorter the candle gets. This would be the next riddle, because the candle was burning for Murphy, and time was running out. *Too bad Murphy's too stupid to figure it out,* he thought.

Murphy was supposed to have caught on when they killed the kid along the river by Murphy's cabin, but Murphy hadn't reacted like they thought he would. Eddie had watched from a distance as Murphy and that big partner of his walked around the body, giving orders and looking all smug, with not one tear or look of anger or anything. Murphy hadn't even seemed to notice that the kid was cut up just like Bobby had done to him a while back. *Damn near cut Murphy's head off,* Eddie thought. *Too bad Murphy didn't die when Bobby cut him.*

So it was Murphy's fault that three more kids had died,

Murphy's fault he had to up the ante. If Murphy had paid attention to the notes, maybe they wouldn't have killed the kids. But he had to admit, "The Old Woman Who Lived in a Shoe" was the perfect rhyme for the three brats he'd killed that late afternoon. *She had so many kids she didn't know what to do,* Eddie thought. *Well, I knew what to do. Now she won't have to worry no more.*

In a way, Eddie was sorry the mother wasn't home when they'd done the kids. His own mother had run off and left him and Bobby when he was too little to know what was going on. Everything the preacher had done to him and Bobby was her fault. Yeah, he would have done the mom with the kids if she'd been home. But, what the hell, maybe they'd be back for her later. Right now he had things to do. Someone else was about to have a very bad day. Too bad it wouldn't be Susan Summers. She would have to wait.

CHAPTER ELEVEN

So many children
There will be more

The words were scrawled on the wall over one of the twin beds; the blood, still wet, was an obscene mockery of the innocent lives it had been taken from.

"What does it mean?" Jack asked in a whisper, not really expecting an answer.

The two detectives stood just inside the doorway of what would have been a typical kid's bedroom, with brightly colored clothing, tattered jeans, and scuffed tennis shoes scattered around the floor along with a mishmash of comic books, schoolbooks, and toys. But this room had been transformed by sprays of dark blood clinging to the walls, the curtains, the well-worn carpet, and what they saw was right out of a horror movie.

There were two twin beds in the little room. Jack guessed that one bed belonged to the little girl and the other was shared by the boys. The three little bodies lay side by side on one bed, posed in death by the killer, as if they were laid out for a wake. Little arms were crossed over unmoving chests, skinny legs straightened with toes pointed skyward, and each head brutally removed. The heads had been carefully arranged on one pillow at the foot of the bed, the faces wiped clean of blood so that the expression of fear and pain was clearly visible in their features. A blanket had been pulled up over the bodies when the mother had found them, and according to the crime scene guys, she had pulled this off in her panic. It lay on the floor beside the bed now, waiting to be methodically documented, photographed, and collected.

"Christ almighty," Liddell muttered, and covering his mouth, he fled from the room.

Jack surveyed the room. It was a bloody mess. Curtains, carpeting, mattress, pillows, ceiling, and walls all stained with sprays of blood. It was as if these children had been put through a shredder. He didn't have the stomach to look closely at all of their wounds, but the on-scene deputy coroner said they all were killed by repeated cuts and stab wounds from something sharp and heavy and long, like a sword or a machete. Jack could see the little girl—Jenny was her name—had cuts on the soles of her feet. Her brothers had been luckier or had died first, leaving the killer to vent his rage on the remaining victim.

He imagined how they had been rounded up in the living room by the intruder and carried or dragged to the bedroom. *They tried to run,* he thought, looking at the different locations of blood spatters in the room. Their young ages would have precluded them from putting up much of a defense. *They were killed in this room.* There was almost no sign of a struggle in the other rooms. Apart from an overturned end table and a general disarray of couch pillows and rugs, there was almost no sign of a struggle in the rest of the house. And the absence of blood in the other rooms meant they were most likely killed in this room.

Jack looked one more time at the words on the wall. *So many children. There will be more.* There was no mistaking that the killer intended to kill again, and maybe the words meant he would kill more children. But why? Why kids? What did these children have to do with Timmy Ryan? And what did any of this have to do with Anne and Don Lewis? Did Anne Lewis or her husband have anything to do with the killer? Maybe he, or she, lost their children because of the Lewises? He didn't know. All he had were questions, no answers. And even the questions didn't make sense yet. He had never felt this helpless in his life. Children were dying, and he couldn't do a damn thing to stop it.

The mother was such a wreck at the scene that the responding emergency medical crew had sedated her and had taken her to the hospital before the detectives had arrived. The first officers on the scene said she had been "ranting" and didn't seem to understand anything. Jack and Liddell would stop at the hospital later, and Jack hoped she would be able to answer a couple of questions.

He left the bedroom and found Liddell in the kitchen. No surprise there.

"Crime scene's done in here." Liddell was sitting at the kitchen table with a bottle of water. He offered one to Jack, and then took out his notebook and rattled off the report given to him by the officers that had canvassed the neighborhood.

"Mother—Elaine Lamar—age twenty-nine. Divorced from Carl Lamar. Works for Need-a-Home Realty and puts in a long week according to the neighbors." Liddell gave Jack a glance, and said, "Carl's an asshole, but I don't figure him for this." He continued. "The neighbors say she leaves the kids by themselves at times, but never for a long period of time, and it doesn't happen often. The kids are Ricky, Jeremy, and Jenny, ages three, four, and ten. The neighbors also say she is a great mother and that the children are so well behaved that it never occurred to anyone to report them being left alone."

"The little bungalow over there"—Liddell pointed over Jack's shoulder—"is occupied by Missus Geraldine Truitt, age eighty-three and a widow. She heard the children screaming a few hours earlier, but she thought they were playing. In fact, she said the kids are so quiet normally, that she had been pleased at hearing them being loud for once. She couldn't be sure of the time, but she takes her heart meds around noon, and it was somewhere around then."

Jack had sat quietly through Liddell's report, but he now got up and checked the refrigerator.

"Already looked," Liddell said. "There's plenty of food. One beer. Part of a bottle of wine, nothing stronger. She's clean, Jack."

Jack knew his partner was right. When he checked with the Department of Public Welfare, they would tell him they had no record of Elaine Lamar or the children, meaning there had never been complaints of child neglect or abuse.

"Any boyfriends? Visitors?" Jack asked.

"Mother Teresa, I'm telling you, pod'na." But Jack wasn't listening. "Jack, you okay?"

Jack started, and realized that he had been fingering the scar along his neck. The burning pain that had finally disappeared weeks ago was back with a vengeance. But the discomfort was nothing compared to the rage that gripped him. The pure hatred for the killer felt so natural, so welcoming, that it freed him for a moment from the worry of the investigation. He let the rage wash over him, giving him the confidence that he'd catch the person responsible for this. And when he did, he'd wallow in their bloody carcass like a dog rolling in a pile of manure.

"I'm going to find him," Jack said. "Then I'm going to shit in his skull."

Liddell's features hardened. "I'm with you, pod'na."

*   *   *

Chief Marlin Pope's secretary was a mousy young woman with sharp, bookish features and oversized clothes that hung on her thin frame, making her look anorexic. Her face seldom showed any expression other than boredom, but as she entered the chief's inner sanctum she was almost out of breath with excitement.

"Chief!" she said.

"What is it, Jennifer?" Pope said without looking up.

"Maddy Brooks and an attorney for Channel Six are in the waiting room."

"I'm busy, Jennifer," Chief Pope said, motioning to the pile of paperwork on top of his desk. "If they want information, they have to go through our public information officer like everyone else." He was surprised at her barging in like she had. She never cared much for the media before.

"I think you had better talk to them, Chief," Jennifer Mangold said in a conspiratorial whisper. "She says they've been in touch with the killer."

"Get Murphy and Blanchard in here," Pope said. "And call Captain Franklin."

"Do you want me to call the deputy chief, too?" she asked.

"Let's not bother the deputy chief yet," Pope answered. "Tell Maddy Brooks to wait a few minutes." She nodded and left the office.

Pope looked at the stack of paperwork that had to be sorted. "The city attorney will just have to wait," he said to himself and cleared the top of his desk.

Tisha Carter crossed the parking lot, glad to be through with her morning shift as a physical therapist for St. Mary's Hospital. It was a late September afternoon, and the heat index was in the triple digits, but inside the hospital it was as cold as the inside of an igloo. She shrugged out of the sweater she had been wearing and wondered why the hospital was always so cold. But she wasn't going to let anything spoil her mood today. She was off work, it was Friday, and she had a date tonight with that nurse she'd been admiring.

Thinking about Janet made her smile. Tisha had discovered in high school that she preferred women and was very comfortable with her life choice. But Janet was an emotional wreck about her sexuality, and so their first date was comically laid out. Tisha had to drive to a neighboring city, get a place to stay under an assumed name, and then call Janet at a telephone booth to tell her that it was okay to come over. She had opted for renting a cabin near Patoka Lake. It was over an hour drive from Evansville, secluded, and they would be totally alone.

In a way, Janet's suggestion was very romantic. But women were much better at romance than men. To men, sex and romance were the same. She could feel her heart beating faster as she got behind the wheel of her car and drove out of the parking garage. She was so engrossed in her thoughts that she didn't notice the older, white van pull out of a parking space and follow her.

CHAPTER TWELVE

"So what are you after?" the police chief asked the man he knew to be legal counsel for Channel Six, David Wires. He was afraid he knew the answer to his question, but so far they had only hinted at what their information was. He wanted them to put it in their own words so there would be no misunderstanding. He'd found over the years that the best way to deal with the media was to be honest, even if it meant telling them nothing more than "Sorry, we're not releasing information yet." He knew that if you tried to cut them out of the loop, they would report whatever they had no matter how wrong or harmful it was.

Maddy looked pleased. She was sure the police chief wouldn't have interrupted his day if she wasn't on to something big.

"We want in," Maddy answered for Wires, and smiled. David Wires, the attorney, was smiling, too. He had said little, but he was the hammer poised to drive the point home if they didn't get what they wanted. Maddy knew it, the attorney knew it, and she was sure that Chief Pope knew it as well.

Before the chief could answer, his secretary peeked in to announce that Captain Franklin and the detectives were there. Pope let out an audible sigh and motioned for them to be shown in.

Eddie sat in the van watching the silly bitch flitting from one aisle to another in the roadside store. She had deviated from her normal route home, and it was pissing him off. They had driven all the way out of Evansville on Highway 57, where she then stopped in the little town of Daylight. He'd taken advantage of the stop to fill his gas tank, but now he cursed under his breath as he waited for her to head home.

It didn't help that Bobby was in one of his silent moods and hadn't said a word since they'd left the parking garage at the hospital.

Finally Eddie could stand the silence no longer. "Okay. So what's the fuckin' deal, Bobby?"

Bobby looked at him without answering, which only added to Eddie's anger. "We followed this nurse twice last week, and both times she went straight home. What the hell is she doin'?" Eddie demanded.

Bobby shook his head and smiled. "Eddie, you gotta relax, man. It don't matter where you do her. You just do her and leave the note," he said with a smirk.

"Well, what if she's driving to fuckin' New York or somethin'? We gonna follow her to New York, Bobby?"

"Hell, if we whack her out of town, so much the better," Bobby said calmly and leaned back and closed his eyes.

Eddie was starting to smile now. Bobby was right. If they whacked her somewhere out of town, it would show Murphy how far they would go to get at him.

"Like a long-distance wake-up call," Eddie said happily, and Bobby winked at him.

"Now you're getting the picture, bro," Bobby said.

* * *

Introductions were made and then Wires stood and shook hands with Captain Franklin, but didn't offer to shake hands with Jack or Liddell.

"Guess they don't teach etiquette in law school," Liddell whispered loud enough for the attorney to hear.

Chief Pope gave him a cautioning look and continued, "And of course, you all know Maddy Brooks."

Liddell grabbed Maddy's diminutive hand in his huge ones, shaking it so hard it rattled her. "Big fan! Very big fan, Miss Brooks," he said. Jack could tell she wasn't sure of his sincerity, but had no doubt that she could take care of herself.

"Well, you *are* big," she said, looking Liddell up and down, to which everyone laughed. "Can I have my arm back now?" she asked, and they all laughed some more.

We're having such a wonderful time, Jack thought. He wondered when he and Liddell would have to bend over and take one up the rear for the team. He already had an idea what was going on here because the chief's secretary had filled them in on what she had "accidentally" overheard. Apparently Channel Six had some source inside their murder investigation and was strong-arming the chief to go public. But out of respect for the chief and captain, Jack kept his thoughts to himself.

Chief Pope offered beverages, which were declined by everyone except Liddell. After Jennifer had brought his coffee, they all looked at each other.

Jack broke the silence. "Well, this was nice, but I have a murder or two to investigate, so if you'll excuse me." He stood to leave, and Chief Pope said, "Sit down, Murphy!"

Liddell rolled his eyes at Jack like he was an incorrigible child, but Jack was out of patience. He said, "Oh, come on, Chief. We all know what this is about. These two are black-mailing you."

Captain Franklin put a hand on Jack's arm and said, "Shut up, Jack, and sit down." Jack took a deep breath and sat back down. A line from a sci-fi movie ran through his mind: *Resistance is futile, earthling.*

Chief Pope addressed Maddy, saying, "Okay, Miss Brooks. If you have what you say, and you continue closely cooperating with my men, I will give you limited access to our investigation."

Dave Wires spoke for the first time. "We will have full and continual access, or we will air the notes on the five o'clock news." Wires didn't have to say that Maddy would also report on air that the police would not comment on the notes, which was as good as saying, "and the police, in an attempt to cover up, et cetera, et cetera."

Captain Franklin looked at the chief, trying to read his expression. "I don't know what's going on here, Chief," Franklin said. "But maybe we should see what Maddy actually has before we compromise our position."

Maddy looked at David Wires, Esq., and he nodded. She opened her purse and pulled out several clear, plastic document protectors, each containing an envelope. Franklin took them from her and handed them to the chief. Pope's face took on an ashen tinge. He passed the papers to Franklin. Jack and Liddell looked over his shoulder.

All the papers and envelopes appeared to be handwritten in red crayon. The envelopes were all made out to Maddy Brooks at Channel Six. Jack recognized the first note as similar, if not identical, to the one he had recently seen in the Lewis murder file. The note read:

> Will you have any more
> My eyes are too sore.
> they pay for your sins

The second note was identical to the one that Dr. Carmodi had found stuffed in Timmy Ryan's throat. It read:

> he caught fishes
> in other mens ditches
> they pay for your sins

But what caught Jack's attention was the last note:

> so many children
> there will be more
> Jack

No note had been left at the murder scene of the Lamar children. But, except for the addition of his name, the killer had written these same words in blood on the wall of that room.

Franklin looked at Jack but addressed his question to Maddy, saying, "When did you get these, Miss Brooks?" Jack could feel his pulse rising, and then Maddy asked the question he had feared.

"We're talking about a serial killer who has something against Detective Murphy, aren't we?"

Liddell picked up the notes and was looking at them when he murmured, "Guy's leaving messages, but they don't mean anything."

Chief Pope cast an angry look at Liddell and put his hands up. "Okay. Let's not get carried away here, folks. We don't know if these notes are involved. We've never said anything about notes being left at murder scenes. These notes are written in crayon. Anyone could be sending these notes to you, Maddy. Maybe someone at your job is playing a practical joke?" he suggested. "So, what makes you so sure of this?"

Jack thought the chief had a point. Nothing had been released to the public about notes being left behind at any of the murder scenes.

Maddy looked like the Cheshire Cat as she leaned forward in her chair. "I knew you would ask that, Chief. And the truth is that I didn't know the notes were definitely involved until I got this one."

She reached in her handbag, and brought out another plastic bag with a note inside. But before she would show it to the men she said, "When I got the third note, the one about the children, I started thinking these must be about the murders. So I confirmed with a source that you found notes at two of the three murder scenes." She held up three fingers and counted off, "Dr. Lewis and her husband were murder number one. Timmy Ryan, murder number two. And last, the Lamar kids, where, as you can see, he clearly refers to Detective Murphy. But you didn't get a note at that scene, Jack. The killer left another kind of message there, didn't he?"

Jack ignored her probing question and said, "Let's see the new note."

Maddy tried to stare him down, but she could see he wasn't going to answer her question before he saw the latest note. "I received this at the station about an hour ago." She handed the bag to Jack, who glanced at it and handed it to the chief.

As Chief Pope read it, his normally dark complexion turned to the waxy color of yellow coal. He handed the note to Franklin, who read it out loud:

> Jack be nimble
> Jack be quick
> Jack jump over
> the candlestick

Franklin traded a look with the chief, and then to Maddy he said, "Okay. Who's your source?"

"Oh, no you don't. You know I don't have to name my

sources," she said smugly. "Let's just say it's a reliable source that's close to the investigation."

Chief Pope looked around the room. He knew that none of the men in this room would ever talk to the news media about an active murder investigation. But he also knew that policemen loved to brag about their importance, so it could have been any one of the dozens of officers that were at any of the three crime scenes. Or a crime scene tech. Or another detective. Then he remembered that the investigation of the death of Dr. Lewis and her husband had been the responsibility of Deputy Chief Dick. Any investigation Dick was involved in was sure to spring leaks big enough to sink the *Titanic*.

Jack, also, had an idea who had leaked to the news media, but it didn't really matter, because from the look of resignation on the chief's face, he was sure they had bigger problems.

Pope stood up and said, "I think I should call the city attorney."

"We'll wait," Maddy said, and Chief Pope left his own office to make the call in private.

Maddy looked around the walls of the chief's office. She noticed the diploma from the University of Louisville, awarded to Marlin L. Pope, master of science in criminology. In another frame next to it, was a master's degree in business administration, an MBA, from Indiana State University.

Liddell saw her checking out the diplomas and said, "He's a smart man. We all respect him."

Maddy feigned a hurt look. "I respect him," she said.

"I'm just sayin'," Liddell said in a cautioning tone. Wires looked as if he wanted to defend Maddy, but then, seeing the size of his opponent, he opted to keep quiet.

Chief Pope came back in the office and sat behind his desk. "Okay, this is what we are willing to do," he said.

CHAPTER THIRTEEN

The Indiana State Parole Office was in a yellow-brick building with a full glass front that had been built around 3000 BC, so it was pretty new as far as government buildings go. The heavy glass door in front sported the Great Seal of the State of Indiana, which looked like some guy with an axe chasing a buffalo through the woods. Jack had never seen a buffalo until he took a trip to Montana a couple of years ago, but in the great way-back there must have been buffalo in Indiana. Guys with axes probably chased them all out of the state.

Jack entered and walked down a narrow hallway to the receptionist window, making note of the fist-sized holes in the drywall on both sides where misunderstood criminals had vented their frustration at the attempts of the state to keep them from reoffending.

The receptionist, Ms. Johnson-Heddings, sat in her usual spot behind the thick glass window, with her lined and leathery hatchet face, and her hair pulled back in a severe bun so tight it seemed to give her a face-lift.

"You're looking especially lovely today," Jack remarked with what he hoped was a disarming smile.

Her face cracked into a smile that could melt the heat shields off the space shuttle, but Jack had learned not to look directly into it.

"Do you have an appointment, sir?" she asked icily.

Thinking that her hair was pulled back so tight that it might have caused some brain damage, Jack said, "It's me. Jack!" He smiled and pinched his own cheek in a grand-motherly way. "You know—your favorite son. Little Jacky."

"You're not my son," she said severely.

"Can you tell Susan I'm here?" he asked.

"Jack. Come on back." Susan's voice came from around a corner.

He did a short drumbeat on the counter. "It's been great seeing you again," he said and walked down the hall, feeling the heat of her stare.

Susan's office always looked like an earthquake had hit. She sat behind a pile of books and folders that Jack knew had a desk under them somewhere. He'd been to her house a couple of times and always wondered how the clean freak that lived there could have an office like this.

"I'd give you a pure and chaste peck on the cheek, but Ms. You-Know-Who might forcefully evict me," he said and was rewarded with a chuckle.

"She takes her work very seriously, Jack. Be nice," Susan chastised him.

"Okay. I'll try." Jack looked for a chair, and then remembered that there were three in the office the last time he was there. Now he couldn't see any lump that looked like it might have a chair under it, so he gave up and stood.

"I need you to do something for me, Susan," he said.

"That's it?" Susan said, getting up and coming around her

pile of papers. "No foreplay? No 'My, you look stunning' or even a 'Hello'?"

She wrapped her arms around his neck and gave him a full-body kiss that made his knees sag. He was still standing there as she sat back in her chair, smiling. "Okay, now what else can I do for you?"

Jack cleared his throat and to his shame actually did look around to see if Ms. Heddings was lurking nearby with a Bible and a leather belt. "Wow! Okay," he said, and then told her about the developments of the day—the murders, the notes, the imbedding of the news media, and his reason for being there, the personal nature of the notes.

Susan was a pro, but she seemed shocked by the revelation of the notes. "I heard about the children, Jack," she said. "I started to call and see how you were doing, but I know how you hate to be fussed over."

Jack looked at her with renewed respect. It was great to have a relationship with someone who could understand what you were doing and give you the support you really needed without reminding you how much you needed mental help. He would never have been able to talk to Katie, his ex-wife, about any of this. She was a sixth-grade teacher, and her worst day was a kid throwing up in the classroom. He envied Katie that innocence and had always believed that keeping his dark view of the world from her was a noble thing. But it was different with Susan. His world was almost the same as hers. He didn't have to sugarcoat.

"I need you to go through your records and see if anyone is out on parole that might be doing these things, sending these notes—someone who would have a personal grudge against me," he said.

"Already on it," she said and indicated a stack of files on the floor beside the doorway. "Ms. Heddings made copies for you." Jack raised an eyebrow.

"She's been listening to the news, too, Jack. I think she

has a soft spot for you. We didn't know about the notes, of course, so those are all the files we came up with as possible for the killer. On top is a list of all of our parolees, but there are hundreds of those."

"Well, I had better get back," Jack said and collected the folders from the floor.

"If you need anything . . ." Susan said.

"This will get me started. Thanks," he said.

Ms. Johnson-Heddings was scowling as he stopped at her counter.

"Thanks, Mom," Jack said, indicating the stack of folders.

"I'm sure I don't know what you're talking about," she said.

After Jack left, her face softened. *That man can really be a smart-ass,* she thought, and allowed herself a smirk.

CHAPTER FOURTEEN

When Jack entered the back door of headquarters he became aware of the curious looks he was getting from other detectives and uniformed officers. They were milling about in the hallways, seeming to work, but no one was really doing anything. It reminded Jack of a school of fish swimming aimlessly and only reacting to things that threatened the group.

"Detective Murphy," a loud voice said from the detective lieutenant's open doorway, "so nice you could join us."

Jack recognized the voice and immediately realized that there was a shark among them, and Jack was the target. His fear was confirmed as the roomful of detectives and uniformed officers seemed to shimmer and disappear.

"You're working late," Jack said to Deputy Chief Dick, who was sitting in the lieutenant's chair as stiff and straight as a mannequin, and like a mannequin, had no real spine.

"Come in and have a seat," Dick commanded, although the only other chair in the tiny office was occupied by a harried-looking detective lieutenant named Lou Gilbert.

Gilbert looked around as if he was wondering if another

chair was in his office that he had never noticed before. Then, realizing that he was being dismissed, he cleared his throat and excused himself to go and do something administrative. When he left the room, Jack pushed the door shut and sat down. The wooden seat was still warm. He wondered how much warmer it would be when he left.

Deputy Chief Dick tried to stare him down, lost, and turned his head. "Anything new in the case, Detective?" he asked at last.

Jack noticed that Dick had failed to call him by name. Dick's way of reminding him that he was just an underling. "Which case?" Jack paused and then added, "Deputy Chief." Department protocol demanded that a deputy chief be called "Chief" unless the actual chief was present, in which case you would call both men by their actual rank. It was all very confusing. But calling Double Dick "Chief" was like passing a kidney stone. It was hard not to disrespect the man.

Dick pretended to ignore the slight and handed Jack a business card. Jack looked at the card. Dick had written two numbers on the back of it.

"Those are my mobile and home numbers," Dick explained. "I want you to keep me apprised of any developments."

"Yes, sir," Jack said and pocketed the card. He had every intention of throwing it away as soon as he left.

"And," Dick said, pausing for effect, "Maddy Brooks will be in touch with you this evening. You will extend every courtesy to her and her cameraman."

"Why isn't she here now?" Jack asked.

"She has some business to clear up, and the station has some legal matters to discuss with her," Dick began to explain, and then realized that Jack was being facetious. "Listen to me carefully, Detective Murphy. You seem to be an intelligent man—" he began.

Jack smiled, tried to look bashful, and said, "Thank you, sir."

"Dammit, Murphy," Dick said, and then composed himself. "Listen, Jack. I know we've had our personal disagreements. But this killer . . ." He seemed to be genuinely concerned even if he couldn't decide how to address Jack. "This is no time for personality clashes. I know you want to catch this killer. And I know you will do your best."

Jack wondered what the punchline was. It wasn't normal for Double Dick to be complimentary. He had to be up to something.

"So, what do you want, Deputy Chief?" Jack asked point-blank.

"Believe it or not, I want to help you," he said and smiled. "I'm even going to assign another detective to help you."

Jack's shoulders slumped. Now he knew what Dick was up to. He was going to put one of his cronies on Jack's team to do his evil master's bidding. The question was, which of the worst detectives in the department would he saddle Jack with? He didn't have to wait long for the answer.

"Detective Jansen has been told to report to you," Dick said, and before Jack could protest he added, "and I want you to bring him up to speed on everything. After all, he has some knowledge of the Lewis case."

Jack almost said, "Yeah, Jansen was the one that screwed up the case," but he caught himself in time.

Seeing the look on Jack's face, the deputy chief stood, straightened his clothing, and said, "This is not a request, Detective. You will do this or find yourself on administrative leave. Do you understand?"

Jack stared at the power-hungry, ladder-climbing asshole of a career politician and nodded. He didn't trust himself to respond verbally.

* * *

Jack left the meeting with the deputy chief with his head swimming. Jansen was the worst of the worst—a black cloud. He was officially assigned to the Missing Persons Unit, but in reality was a missing person himself. Jack had seen the man only a few times in the past year, and then it was as he was skulking down a hallway like a shadow. This was just getting better and better.

He was so angry when he left the lieutenant's office that he'd forgotten the files he'd gotten from Susan. He went back down the hallway and knocked on the lieutenant's door, which was closed now.

"Come in," came a timid voice, and Jack opened the door.

Lieutenant Gilbert sat behind his desk in the seat Deputy Chief Dick had so recently occupied. The difference between the two men was more than mere difference in rank. Where Dick was pompously officious, tall, and gangly, Gilbert was short, grossly overweight, and so pleasant that he made you want to sit and visit a spell. Gilbert was flipping through the folders, and Jack felt a twinge of compassion.

"I used to love this work," Gilbert said.

It didn't sound like a question, and Jack didn't have a satisfactory response, so he collected his files and left. He could hear the lieutenant whistling a happy tune and wondered how the man had managed to keep his sanity all these years. *But then, maybe he isn't sane,* Jack thought glumly.

As he walked down the hall toward the detective squad room, he saw Liddell coming from Records with a stack of files at least as thick as his own.

"Hey, Jack," Liddell said, puffing from the heavy load. "If a man can be measured by the number of people that want him dead, you're top dog."

"Very funny, Bigfoot," Jack said.

"These are the files of people you arrested that might want you dead," Liddell said, as if to prove his point.

Jack looked at the stack. "I've arrested that many people?"

Liddell laughed. "No. These are just the ones I thought might want to kill you. I couldn't carry the rest."

"You missed your calling as a stand-up comedian," Jack said, and added, "He's not going to be in there."

"How do you know, O Great One?" Liddell asked.

"Because if it was that easy, you'd be able to figure it out by yourself."

"Bite me," Liddell said.

"You first," Jack answered, and they entered the detectives' office with their files.

Maddy Brooks was sitting at Jack's desk, looking through the murder case files and sipping from a Starbucks cup, as the detectives entered.

"How are you doing, Maddy?"

Liddell dropped his weight into a chair, and said, "Wassup?" while slouching like a gangbanger. Maddy ignored him and came around Jack's desk.

"What's all this?" She motioned at the stack of records the men had set on the desks.

"That stuff. Oh, Jack's a popular guy," Liddell said and grinned. Maddy leaned over to read a file label and deliberately gave the men a view of her cleavage.

Her eyes widened, and she asked, "Are these all cases you are involved in, Jack?"

"Past tense," Jack responded blankly.

"You must have some fascinating stories," she said.

Jack sat down and stared at her. "I've been ordered to cooperate with you. You don't have to suck up to me. Both Liddell and I know that you couldn't give a shit about us or anything we've done, or are doing, except how it will affect a story for you."

Maddy looked as if she had been slapped in the face, but Jack had to give her credit—she recovered fast. She sat back, crossing one long leg over another, shamelessly allowing her skirt to ride up her thigh. "Okay. Let's start over, guys," she said neutrally. "What are we doing with these files?"

Jack handed her a short stack. "We're going to look through them and see if there's anything that would make someone want to kill people and leave messages for me."

Maddy gave him a smug look, and said, "I thought you said the messages weren't about you?"

"Look for any psychiatric reports, past violent behavior, childhood problems, things like that," Liddell suggested.

Maddy shot him a contemptuous look. "I am an *investigative* reporter, not your secretary," she said, stressing the word *investigative*. She hesitated as if she had something else to say.

"Spit it out," Jack said.

Maddy gathered herself up and looked at Jack. "Well, I was curious about the notes and went to see our corporate shrink. Just to see if he could give me a psychological profile on the type of person that would write those notes." She looked from Liddell to Jack, seeking approval but finding only closed expressions. "And he said that he didn't have any experience in this sort of thing," she continued.

"Well, duh," Jack said.

"You didn't let me finish," she protested. "He said that all the notes seemed to refer to nursery rhymes or riddles, and he gave me this book from his office." She reached into her handbag and pulled out a thin, hardback book whose cover had the picture of a grandmotherly looking woman, riding on a large, white goose.

Liddell chuckled and said, "Imagine that, Jack. A psychiatrist who just happens to have a Mother Goose book in his

office? I wonder which one of his clients that one is for."
They both looked at Maddy, but she didn't seem to notice.

"He said that most people think Mother Goose rhymes
are for kids—you know, entertainment—but in reality
Mother Goose rhymes are all about violence and death," she
said.

Neither man spoke. "I'm just telling you what he told
me," Maddy said. "Don't stare at me like that."

Liddell looked at the stack of files and shook his head.
"Well, thanks for that, but we've got some files to go
through, and I'm getting hungry."

"But I think he may be on to something," Maddy protested, and flipped through the pages of the book, stopped at
a page, and began reading out loud, "There was an old
woman who lived in a shoe, she had so many children she
didn't know what to do. She gave them some broth without
any bread, she whipped them all soundly and put them to
bed."

Liddell looked up from the folder he had seemed ab-
sorbed in.

"That was the last note. The three kids," Jack said and remembered the writing in blood on the wall of the tiny room,
and the little bodies beaten and put to bed. "So many children," he said. "The killer was quoting part of the rhyme. Let
me see that." Maddy pushed the book across the desk. He
flipped to a page and read out loud, "Little Tommy Tittlemouse lived in a little house, he caught fishes in other men's
ditches."

He stressed the last three words, "other men's ditches."
Just like the note, he thought, and near the back of the thin
book he found what he was looking for:

Punch and Judy
Fought for a pie;

Punch gave Judy
A knock in the eye.
Says Punch to Judy,
"Will you have any more?"
Says Judy to Punch,
"My eyes are too sore."

CHAPTER FIFTEEN

Well. Didn't expect this, Eddie thought, and watched the nurse pull the curtains over the windows of the tiny cabin. He'd followed her from the gas station, where she'd bought a bag full of goodies and a case of beer, to somewhere called Patoka Lake Cabins, almost a two-hour drive northeast.

It hadn't been hard following her on Interstate 64. Hell, he was right behind her a couple of times, but he allowed a car or two to get between them from time to time. She'd turned off on Indiana 231 North, taking the back roads through small towns that were sometimes nothing more than a truck stop with a few mobile homes. Eventually, when she'd stopped at an office that looked like a log cabin, he pulled off the road like he was checking a map.

The hard part was the last couple of miles as she wound her way into the woodlands, back through gravel and then hard-packed dirt roads, climbing steeply at first and then dropping down into the valley that made up Patoka Lake.

When Eddie saw her slow, he pulled off in a turnaround and waited. She turned down a short gravel drive and stopped in front of a cabin surrounded by trees.

He and Bobby had given her a few minutes and then walked the last couple hundred yards, circling around the cabin to the west, and then coming back around to a densely grown area where they could watch the front of the cabin without being seen.

Until a few moments ago she had been scurrying around. Then he heard music coming from inside. Romantic type stuff. Apparently she was expecting someone. To Bobby, he said quietly, "If a dude shows up, I'll just do him, too."

"I wonder if her nose is itchin'?" Eddie asked, and then answered his own question. "'Cause she's about to get company."

That was when she shut the curtains and the front door. Eddie hoped it wasn't locked. It was such a nice-looking little place, he'd feel bad about huffing and puffing and blowing her house down.

Inside the cabin, a disappointed Tisha Carter was just closing her cell phone. Janet had changed her mind again. After all the planning, not to mention the expense, Janet was not coming. *Well, there's nothing I can do now,* she thought. *I can't get my money back. Might as well enjoy the cabin.*

"Dammit!" she said, and just as she got the word out she heard the cabin door. Her heart leapt with anticipation. *It's Janet. She was just teasing me,* she thought. It was the last happy thought she would ever have.

Captain Franklin leaned back in his chair and listened to Jack and Liddell's theory. Maddy Brooks remained quiet, letting the detectives take credit for what she considered her own idea.

"So, let me get this straight," Franklin was saying. "You're telling me this nut is sending these notes to us as messages about whom he's going to kill next?"

"Well, more precisely he's sending the messages to Maddy.

We are finding notes at the scenes of the murders, but, the best we can figure it, she has gotten a note in advance every time," Jack said. "And the note about the Lamar kids had my name on it. We didn't find that at the scene."

"And you can't tell us anything about how the notes are getting there, Miss Brooks?" Franklin asked.

She blushed slightly before answering. "Our receptionist was the one that found the notes." She seemed to weigh her words before going on. "Lois is her name. Lois Hensley." She waited to see if anyone recognized the name. Franklin did.

"Hensley? As in Mayor Thatcher Hensley?"

"That's her," Maddy said and made an ugly face as if to say, *See what I have to put up with?*

Franklin asked, "Has anyone questioned her yet?"

"We wanted to bring you up to date first," Jack responded.

"Well, what are you waiting for?" Franklin said.

Maddy cleared her throat. "There's something else you need to be concerned about, gentlemen."

Franklin noticed Maddy looking at Jack, as if waiting for him to explain.

Jack looked at the floor while Liddell spoke. "We think the killer might be targeting Jack."

"What!" Franklin exclaimed, although he privately had believed the same thing.

Maddy jumped in. "The last note to me wasn't a rhyme—it was a riddle."

"So," Franklin said, "this guy is nuts."

"Maybe nuts, but very shrewd," she said. "I think—we think—that the last note is a riddle for Jack to figure out."

"Are you saying he's doing this to get Jack's attention?"

"Not only for that reason," Jack said. He felt a knot forming in his stomach. "It's more like I'm having my nose rubbed in it."

Maddy said softly, "He may have already killed again."

"Deputy Chief Dick said I was supposed to report to you, Captain," a voice said from the doorway.

They all looked up to see the haggard-looking figure of Detective Jansen leaning in the doorway, wheezing like he'd just finished a marathon race.

"What's he doing here?" Liddell asked.

"Detective Jansen is on the case with us now," Jack said. "I'll fill you in later."

"So who's gonna fill me in?" Jansen asked and lecherously eyeballed Maddy Brooks.

Franklin spoke up. "Detective Blanchard is going to take you to the squad room and get you started," he said to Jansen, and then to Jack, "Jack, I need a moment of your time."

Liddell looked at Jack, then turned and led the missing persons detective out while Maddy watched their retreating figures. "Detective Blanchard doesn't look too happy," she remarked.

Jack, who was barely holding it together, shot her an angry look.

"Maddy," Captain Franklin said quickly, "would you give us a moment, please?"

Before she left the office, Franklin called out to her, "Maddy."

She turned and smiled, expecting to be let back into the meeting, but Franklin said severely, "Not a word about any of this on the air."

She assumed the look of a deer caught in headlights and wondered if he had been reading her mind. "Not a word, Captain. I promised, didn't I?" And she left the office.

When Jack came back into the detective squad room, Liddell was explaining to a half-interested Jansen that they were going through the files to see if they could find a connection between the victims and the killer, or between the killer and Jack.

Liddell looked relieved when Jack came in. "Maddy said she was going back to the station to see if she could narrow down when the notes actually arrived," he said.

Jansen looked up, saw Jack, and said, "How we gonna find anything in these damn files, Murphy?"

Jack responded calmly, "The captain wants you to go to Channel Six and try to nail down the exact times those notes were delivered. See if they have security cameras. You know the routine." But he only half believed that Jansen really knew what he was doing. And even if he did, he didn't think Jansen would give half an effort. Jack added, "We'll deal with these files."

Jansen paused, weighing the possibility of losing track of Murphy against the idea of being at the television station around gorgeous babes like Maddy Brooks. The deputy chief would be pissed if he found out Jansen had left Murphy alone. But he could always say that he was ordered to by the captain. "Captain Franklin, huh?" he said, and put the file down that he hadn't opened yet.

"Yeah, the captain," Jack lied. "I guess he figured since the mayor's mother is going to have to be interviewed, it should be someone with more seniority and tact than me doing it."

"The mayor's mother?" Jansen said to Liddell. "You didn't tell me nothing about the mayor's mother being involved in this shit." His face took on a pained look, as if he'd just swallowed an ice cube and gotten brain freeze.

"Well? You didn't tell me you were blowing Double Dick," Liddell responded. "So we're even."

Jansen ignored the insult, grabbed his hat, and waddled out of the squad room. As soon as he was out of earshot, Liddell asked, "What's really going on, pod'na?"

Jack told him about the conversation with Captain Franklin. How Franklin said the mayor was putting pressure on the chief, and that he believed that there was going to be a coup attempt by Deputy Chief Dick to replace Pope.

"Chief Double Dick." Crossing his arms across his big chest, Liddell said, "Ugh, me Chief Double Dick. Me fuck-'em up'em wet dream."

Jack didn't laugh. The thought of Dick becoming chief wasn't funny.

"Is that really possible?" Liddell said, getting serious. "Is there no God?"

"God's got nothing to do with it," Jack said. "If he did, Jansen would be a wart on Double Dick's ass."

Liddell laughed until he almost choked.

"Okay, that's enough. We've got work," Jack said, looking at the two large stacks of folders.

"Do warts wear hats?" Liddell asked.

CHAPTER SIXTEEN

Jack tried to concentrate on the stack of files on his desk, but the last riddle kept nagging at him until a sense of urgency swept over him. This case was like nothing he had ever come across, and the normal methods of investigation didn't apply. Murphy's Law said that if something could go wrong it most likely would at the most inopportune moment. Not only had Maddy Brooks broken her promise to the captain, by going on the six o'clock news and hinting that the police suspected the recent killings were the work of a serial killer, but she had also claimed the police had dubbed the killer "Mother Goose." That would bring every nut job out of hiding to get their faces on camera.

These cases had been screwed from the beginning, which only confirmed the rule. There were no witnesses to interview, the bodies were hacked into sushi, and the victims seemed to have nothing in common.

That last thought brought him out of his reverie. "Liddell," he said.

"Huh," Liddell said, his nose still buried in a file.

"What if these victims *are* all connected somehow?"

Liddell stopped reading and looked at him. "Connected how?"

"Well, why did the killer pick these particular people? What did they have in common?"

"We've been through this, buddy. They didn't have anything in common except dying a horrible death."

"I knew Timmy Ryan," Jack said. "And Anne Lewis's name sounds familiar. She was a psychiatrist or psychologist, right?"

Liddell leaned back, and his chair creaked loudly with his weight. "But she wasn't your psychiatrist, was she?"

"No," Jack said, and wondered if his partner could ever be serious. "Wait a minute. Where's that file?" He rummaged around on his desk and found the case file on Anne Lewis and her husband. Flipping through some of the reports, he finally stopped and pulled a page out.

"Here it is," he said, holding up the paper. "Jansen worked on this case," he said, and Liddell moaned and covered his face with both hands. "Let me finish. Jansen said in the one and only supplement he wrote that besides her private practice, Anne Lewis worked as a court-appointed psychiatrist."

Liddell caught his meaning. "And what if she knew the killer?" he finished Jack's thought. Then he looked at the pile of paper on his desk. "That means more files, Jack. We'll need someone to put all this stuff into a database so we can search for connections."

"I'll see the captain," Jack said. "See if he can spare some *real* help."

"Better get that corporate shrink of Maddy's in here, too," Liddell said, causing Jack to turn and look questioningly at him. Liddell explained, "Well, he seems to be an expert on Mother Goose."

"Don't you start it, too, Bigfoot," Jack said and left. He'd had all of the Mother Goose crap he could stand for one night. Even the mayor had come in to ream the chief and demand to know what was being done about "Mother Goose." When the chief couldn't produce a solid suspect, the mayor suggested that the police should "bring in a psychologist, like on *CSI*."

Jack wondered if the mayor really didn't know that *CSI* was just a television show, and not real life. Also, that the police department didn't use psychologists to solve cases. But then he would have to explain that *Ghost Hunters* was also just entertainment for the weak-minded or bored, and that they probably wouldn't be able to speak to the spirits of the deceased to get information. Sometimes it's better to just keep it zipped and let them think they're helping. But if the mayor kept this up, the investigation would turn into a circus and Jack would be just another clown.

"The bitch clawed me, Bobby!" Eddie screamed. He sat on the floor of the cabin with his hand clamped to his right ear. Blood seeped between the fingers of his hand, and his ear burned like hell.

Eddie picked up the corn knife and started to get up. "I'm gonna take her fuckin' head clean off."

Bobby just shook his head sadly. "She's dead, bro. Besides, that would mess up the message."

Eddie dropped his arm. Of course, Bobby was right. When she was found, she had to look just like this. If he did any more cutting it would screw things up.

"Okay, I guess we can get out of here, Bobby." Eddie started toward the door, but then remembered the note. He took it out of his pocket, grabbed the woman's face roughly, and forcing the jaws open, shoved the note into her mouth and as deep as he could into her throat.

Eddie stood back and looked at his handiwork. *Something's missing,* he thought. He dipped his finger in her blood, and then dabbed it on her nose.

"That's better," he said and smiled.

Captain Franklin had promised Jack someone to help sort through the mounting files and, thankfully, had rejected the idea of bringing in a psychologist. But before Jack went back to his office, he had to see someone. He left headquarters and drove the short distance to the neighborhood he had grown up in, and parked a little way down from the familiar house so he would have more time to think up a good reason for being there. But the truth of the matter was that he wasn't sure himself why he was there.

The sky was dark, threatening rain, and the air had turned cool. Winter was months away, but, according to the old-timers, it would be an especially harsh one.

He walked down the brick walkway that he and his father had laid when he was a kid, and up onto the porch of the house he had grown up in. His ex-wife, Katie, opened the door before he could knock. When they had divorced, they'd agreed that she would keep the house, and he moved into the river cabin that his grandfather had built.

"I saw you coming up the walk," she said, and smiled at him.

Even with everything that was happening, Katie's smile warmed him, and he wondered, not for the first time, how he could have managed to screw up their marriage so completely.

"Hi, Katie," he said, and waited to be shown into the house they used to share. He knew every nook and cranny of the house, from which floorboards creaked to how the wind would sometimes whistle in the bathroom window if it wasn't shut tight. She led him into the living room and sat on the recliner, leaving him to the couch, and the thought struck him that Katie had remembered that he couldn't sit in the chair when he was wearing his gun. He'd always sat on the couch, where he had more room. But even with the fact that she had remembered such a trivial point, he still felt uneasy here. It didn't feel like his house anymore.

"How've you been?" he asked, inwardly groaning at his stupid question.

She averted her eyes and said, "Oh, you know . . . fine, I guess. How's Susan?" she asked.

The remark had surprised him. Embarrassed him. *Why should I feel guilty? It's not like Susan and Katie aren't on friendly terms. Sometimes a little too friendly.* In fact, Katie and Susan had become such good friends that he sometimes felt like the outsider. He would have understood it better if Katie and Susan had felt threatened by each other, but instead they had formed a bond around a common cause. And that cause was Jack Murphy.

He also knew that Katie was dating an attorney. How could she possibly be attracted to an attorney? He had often wondered if she was doing that just to spite him, but Katie wasn't like that. After he had been released from the hospital, both she and Susan had taken turns caring for him, feeding him, changing his bandages.

But recently it had all become very uncomfortable for him. And when he was alone with Katie, which didn't happen often, she seemed uncomfortable as well.

He realized she was talking to him, and said, "What?"

"Why are you here, Jack?" Katie asked. Her features clouded with a familiar look of worry. He wanted to apologize for coming over without calling and then run for his car. But he needed someone to talk to that had nothing to do with the case, or the police. When they were married, no matter how serious a case he was investigating, he would sit with her and talk about nothing. Just being near her helped him clear his head, helped him realize that there were still good people in the world, and that he was putting up with this job in the sewer of society for the protection of people like Katie. He had never shared his concerns or the ugly part of his life with her because he was protecting her. He had to keep her clean of all of that. He had to have something unblemished, untouched by evil, to come home to.

But he knew, in his own way, he had ruined the very thing that he needed the most. She had been right to divorce him. He thought he should leave before he made her worry, or made more of a fool of himself. But then he had an idea.

"Look, Katie, do you still have those—" He paused, almost saying Mother Goose books, and said instead, "nursery rhyme books you use for class?" Katie taught sixth grade at a school for troubled children, and he knew she had a score of children's books lying around. He had the book Maddy had acquired from her company shrink, and he was sure he could find hundreds of articles on the Internet, but he had needed to see Katie, to see that she was okay, and to tell her . . . to tell her what?

"What's going on, Jack?" she asked.

Now it was his turn to look away. *Shouldn't have come,* he thought. "Oh, it's nothing important. I just need to look up some stuff. Research, you know?"

"You're doing research with a Mother Goose book?" she asked incredulously, and he shrugged in response. She left the room and came back with a stack of books of various sizes with colorful covers.

"And this has nothing at all to do with that 'Mother Goose killer' they were talking about on the news tonight?"

Jack didn't answer.

"If you don't want to tell me what you're doing, it's okay," she said.

"There's nothing to tell, Katie," he said defensively. "Why do we always have to do this?"

"*We're* not doing anything, Jack," she said.

Why do women have to be so complicated? he wondered. *Everything they say has two or three meanings.*

"I didn't come to argue," Jack said, and picked up the books. "Thanks. I'll get them back to you."

"There's no hurry." The iciness was gone from her voice.

Jack stopped in the doorway and turned around. "Maybe you should go and visit your sister in Maine," he said. "Just for a few days."

"Why?"

"Dammit, Katie! Why can't you just go and visit your sister for a while?"

She pushed him out of the door. "We're not married anymore, Jack. I don't do things just because you tell me to." She looked worried again. "What's really going on, Jack?"

The last thing he'd wanted was to worry her, but that was what he had done. He really had no evidence that this killer was sending these messages because of him. The only victim he even had a passing acquaintance with was Timmy Ryan, and he had barely spoken to the boy. Fished with him a couple of times.

"I'm sorry," he said, not wanting to leave on an angry note. "You're right—I shouldn't tell you what to do. Just promise me you'll keep your doors and windows locked for a while."

She looked at him and then asked, "Does this have something to do with the murders I saw in the news?"

"Just promise me you'll be extra careful for a while. Okay?"

"Okay, Detective," she said, and smiled. "I'll lock up. But

I'm not leaving town. Not unless you can give me a good reason."

That was something, at least.

Liddell was still at his desk poring over arrest records when Jack came in. There were no second-shift detectives still in the office.

"Where'd you get the Mother Goose books?" Liddell asked with a smirk on his face.

"You're a detective," Jack said. "Figure it out."

Before Liddell could start ragging on him, Jack said, "How's Jansen doing with the mayor's mother?"

Liddell's smirk widened into a full-blown shit-eating grin. "Get this," he said. "Jansen starts going ape-shit on the station manager for not having security cameras outside the building, and the old lady, the mayor's mother, comes to the manager's defense."

Jack was surprised that Jansen would be interested in the case enough to go to that trouble, but then he remembered that Jansen was probably trying to impress Maddy Brooks or some other young lady. He had a reputation for fancying himself a ladies' man. "So what happened?"

"Jansen called her an old biddy," Liddell said, barely able to contain himself.

"That's it?"

"Guess where Jansen's at right this minute," Liddell said. "Go on. Guess."

"I give up," Jack said. "Where is Jansen this very minute?"

Liddell looked around out of habit. "In the mayor's office with the mayor, the chief, Double Dick, and Captain Franklin."

"You think that means we're rid of him?" Jack asked.

"Probably not," he conceded. "But I'd love to hear what's going on."

"That's why I love you so much, partner. It doesn't take much to entertain you." Jack started rummaging through his desk drawer.

"What're you looking for?" Liddell asked.

"I've got a ball of yarn here somewhere. Thought I'd throw it for you."

"Asshole," Liddell said.

"Let's get something to eat. I can't think anymore."

"Two-Jakes?" Liddell asked.

"Where else?"

Two-Jakes was the adopted name for Two-Jakes Marina and Restaurant, a combination restaurant, bar, and water-craft storage facility. It was the largest of its kind along the stretch of Ohio River from St. Louis to Louisville. In the winter, the rich folks stored their large summer crafts there with confidence that the boats would be serviced and pampered until they were ready to play ship captain the next spring. In the summer, visitors would travel up the Mississippi River from as far away as Tomato, Mississippi, or come down the Missouri River to just north of St. Louis where it joined with the Ohio River.

Because Two-Jakes was set out over the Ohio River, travelers along the waterway could tie off at the restaurant's floating dock and enjoy fine dining and an assortment of imported and local beers that would make an Irishman weep with joy.

One reason Jack wanted to go to Two-Jakes was because his father had been one of the original Jakes. Jack had inherited half ownership upon his father's death a few years ago. The other reason was the food.

Jack and Liddell drove separately with the idea of eating a late supper and then calling it a night. Jack had called the charge nurse at St. Mary's Hospital and was informed Elaine Lamar was still heavily sedated. Maybe they could talk to her in the morning. So far, police records had yielded zip information on a next of kin for Timothy Ryan. Juvenile Division thought they might have a lead on the mother's last boyfriend who was supposed to be caring for Timmy, but so far that had gone nowhere. Tomorrow Jack would have the additional help the captain had promised. Sleep was what was needed now.

Correction. Food first, and then sleep.

On his way to the restaurant Jack called Susan Summers.

"I was just heading home," she said.

"Your home or mine?" Jack asked.

When he had first come home from the hospital, Susan had stayed at his cabin for several nights, only going back to her own home to do laundry and pay bills. But as he got back on his feet, she spent more nights at her own home than with him.

"Mine," she answered. "I thought you would be tied up on this case."

He was surprised to feel disappointed that she wouldn't be at the cabin tonight, not that he would be any kind of company. He looked at his watch. It was almost nine o'clock.

"Kind of at a dead end until the morning," he admitted. "How about dinner? On me."

"That sounds lovely," Susan said. "Two-Jakes?"

"Ah, you know me well," Jack said. "We're going to meet Liddell there, too, if that's okay?"

"Of course it's okay," she said. "You know I like big, strong men."

"You don't have to kiss up to me. I already said I was buying," he said, and she chuckled.

"You don't have a jealous bone in your body, do you?" Susan asked in a feigned hurt tone.

"I think I broke that one, too," Jack responded. "See you in a few minutes."

"I can hardly wait," she said and hung up.

The parking lot was almost full when he arrived, which was a good thing, and Jack spotted Liddell standing at the side door. As he walked up Liddell hooked a thumb toward the business and said, "You got to be making a fortune."

"Yeah, that's me. Daddy Warbucks," Jack said. "Susan's coming."

"You old dog." Liddell playfully punched Jack on the shoulder. It hurt.

"It's the least I could do," Jack said, rubbing his shoulder. "I mean, she is helping with these cases."

"And she's beautiful and sexy, too. Right?"

"I hadn't noticed," Jack lied. "Have you called Marcie today?"

"Yeah. She said to tell you to be careful."

"You're the one Marcie should be worried about, Bigfoot. I have a pure heart, and therefore, am impervious to evil, whereas, you have very big feet and seem to step in it up to your fat head."

"So, that begs the question, why is this asshole trying to get at you and not me?" Liddell said. It was a fair question.

CHAPTER SEVENTEEN

After the hullabaloo at the station late last night, Maddy had given up and gone home exhausted. It had been nearly impossible to drag out of bed at five o'clock in the morning, but the first thing she did was check her answering machine and her e-mail. *Nothing.*

She turned on the radio in the bathroom and stripped off her nightgown, stepping into the shower and turning it as hot as she could stand it. In her mind, she went over a list of things to do today.

She had managed to sneak in to the Lamar woman's room last night, but the nurse had given the woman something so strong that all she could do was grunt. Then when she got back to the station, Detective Jansen was being led out by an angry Captain Franklin. She wasn't present during all the excitement, but several employees told her that Jansen and Lois Hensley had gotten into a verbal knock-down, drag-out fight. In a way, she felt a little sorry for Detective Jansen. Although he could be very crude, he had been a good source of info for her at times. But calling Lois a nosy old biddy was just plain stupid.

She looked in her closet and laid out clothes appropriate for the morning's tasks. She planned on going directly to the police department first, to see what progress they had made. She knew they were upset with her for last night's story, but they surely didn't expect her to keep it quiet that there was a serial killer loose in Evansville. Well, maybe she had stretched things a little calling the killer "Mother Goose," but that was her job. She was doing a public service.

She selected a black skirt, short enough to complement her long legs, and a silk blouse. Now, all she had to do was slip on a jacket, and she was ready to go on air.

She looked for the high heels she'd worn yesterday and remembered she'd thrown them away. She made a mental note to have the station reimburse her.

She quickly dressed, touched up her makeup, and wondered, not for the first time, what life would have been like if she had stayed in Atlanta. The news station she worked for there was much larger, the pay had been better, and she had been closer to her family. Of course, in Atlanta, she had been just another pretty face among even more beautiful and aspiring news women. After two years of hard work and asskissing she had only gotten as far as writing for the talking heads. At that rate she would be sixty before she landed an anchor position.

Here in Evansville she was better looking than most, and had needed to kiss fewer butts to get ahead. In less than a year she had moved into a co-anchor position. She hoped this story would send her over the top. Then she could think about going back to Atlanta on her own terms.

She walked out of her back door, still immersed in thoughts of Atlanta, when she sensed his presence. Before she could turn, a hand covered her mouth, and a strong arm wrapped around her throat, choking off any possibility of screaming.

"Don't scream, pretty lady," the voice whispered in her

ear. "I got a present for you." As he said this she was slammed against the vehicle's trunk and thrown to the ground, where she was pinned by her attacker's weight.

Her mind raced, and she thought of the little can of pepper spray she kept on her key chain. But her keys had been knocked from her hand and she couldn't see them. She tried to struggle, but he was too strong, and he was slowly squeezing the air out of her. She began to feel light-headed.

"Don't scream and I'll let you breathe," he said.

She could feel the spittle from his lips and could sense his excitement, but she knew she had no options. She nodded her head slightly and felt the arm loosen from her throat.

She sucked in grateful gulps of air.

"There. All better now," he said, and she did feel better. Angry now, she said, "Get off of me! What do you want?"

"Told you, Maddy. I got you a present," he said, and reached down behind her, his hand slowly moving across her back and buttocks, until she thought she would scream. But then the hand stopped and came back up to her face. He held something in his hand.

"Open your mouth," he ordered.

She could feel his breath in her ear, and the hardness in the front of his pants. "How do you know my name?" she asked, hoping to stall him, hoping he wouldn't kill her. The other murders ran through her mind. The attacks, the notes.

As if he had read her mind, he said, "I'm not goin' to hurt you, girl. If I was goin' to kill ya I'd of already done it, know what I mean?" He shoved his crotch down against her buttocks, and his voice became threatening. "I got something for you, dammit. Now open your mouth."

She did as told, and he stuffed something into her mouth. He whispered in her ear, and then he told her to nod if she understood. She did. And then he was gone.

She didn't know how long she lay on the ground beside her car, but eventually she realized he was gone. *I'm alive!*

She tried to get on her feet, but her muscles wouldn't cooperate. The best she could do was to drag herself into a sitting position with the note still in her mouth. She suddenly gagged and spat it out, feeling bile rising in her throat. She rolled over just in time.

CHAPTER EIGHTEEN

"Nine-one-one," the Dubois County Sheriff's Department dispatcher said. "Do you have an emergency?"

There were sounds of crying, then, "I want to report a murder."

"Did you say a *murder*?" the dispatcher asked.

"She's dead. Someone killed her. In the cabin."

Gladys had been a dispatcher for the Dubois County Sheriff's Department for twenty-three years. She looked at her display screen, and then did a double take. She wrote the incoming telephone number on a piece of scrap paper, and then waved it at the young deputy who had been injured and was working in a "light duty" capacity in dispatch. He looked up from his *Field & Stream* magazine and lazily took the note. Gladys put the caller on speakerphone.

"Didn't you hear me?" the panicked voice of a young-sounding woman cried. "She's dead! She's been murdered!"

The deputy looked at the note, where Gladys had written: *Get the Sheriff. This call is from Evansville.*

"Just calm down, hon. Tell me where you are," Gladys said soothingly.

CHAPTER NINETEEN

When Liddell arrived on Chestnut Street, Maddy Brooks was sitting on the bumper of an ambulance arguing with the medical crew. An older gentleman in a gray suit with gray hair was trying to calm her down. Maddy saw Liddell approaching.

"The bastard!"

"Are you okay, Maddy?" Liddell asked. She turned on him like a wounded animal.

"Do I look like I'm O-KAY?"

He ignored her tone of voice. "Yeah," he said, looking her over. "Your makeup's a little messy, but you look nice."

Jack pulled up in his personal car and got out next to the ambulance. "What happened? Who did this, Maddy?"

Maddy's eyes looked frightened, but her voice remained angry. She was running on pure adrenaline right now. But Jack knew that when the adrenaline rush was over she was going to crash.

The man in the gray suit and gray hair stepped up to introduce himself. "I'm Bill Goldberg, the station manager at Channel Six," he said.

"I was coming out to my car, and he grabbed me," Maddy said, ignoring Goldberg. She pulled her thin suit jacket closer around her. "I thought someone was behind me. When I started to turn around, he grabbed me and threw me down." She was too humiliated to tell the men that he had felt her up and humped her like a horny teenager.

Jack looked around, but there was just the usual throng of curious onlookers. No one he recognized, anyway. "Tell me the rest," he said.

"Don't you think you should wait for our lawyers, Maddy?" Goldberg said. Maddy gave him an angry look, and then remembered something. "Excuse us, Bill," she said, and motioned for Jack and Liddell to follow her.

The detectives followed her down the side of her rental house toward where her car was still parked.

"When he stuck the note in my mouth, I was so afraid that I just froze. I couldn't move."

"What note?" Liddell asked, but she started trembling and didn't answer.

"Why didn't he kill me, Jack?"

"You think it was our guy?" Jack asked, and then noticed that she was barely able to stand. He put an arm around her and led her to the back steps, where he helped her sit. She was shivering as if freezing. *May be going into shock.*

"I'll get the ambulance guys," Liddell said, and took off around the house.

Jack put his jacket around her shoulders and sat by her, rubbing her arms and gently holding her. He could feel her breathing deeply, as her muscles trembled and she cried so softly that it was barely audible, and he wondered why she thought she had to be so tough. She couldn't just let go and bawl her eyes out like a normal woman.

When her shaking lessened, he gently asked, "You said there was a note, Maddy?"

She looked up at him and said, "I'm not normally this emotional."

"Aw, Maddy. You did just fine."

"Don't say you would have done the same thing, Jack Murphy, or I'll brain you," she said, as she regained her icy self-control. Liddell came back with the paramedics, but she waved them away, saying, "I'm okay now."

She stood up and walked to her car, opened the front door, and took something from the front seat. "Sorry. I've handled it," she said, and handed Jack a crumpled piece of paper.

"It's all right," he said and slipped a pair of powder-free, nitrile gloves from his pocket before he took it. Smoothing it out with the gloves, he saw that it was written in red crayon.

> Jack
> the right answer is
> Little Nancy Etticoat
>
> Mother Goose

"Have you looked at this?" Jack asked, thinking that the killer was now calling himself "Mother Goose," thinking that the killer must be following the news, but more particularly, following Maddy Brooks.

"Yes. It must have something to do with the other rhymes, or maybe with the last one, the riddle. Maybe it's the answer to the riddle," she suggested.

"Maybe," Jack said, but it didn't seem to fit. For if he remembered his nursery rhymes correctly, "Jack Be Nimble" referred to a candlestick, but more particularly was about time. He'd never heard the Little Nancy Etticoat thing.

"It looks like the other notes," Liddell said. "I'll call Crime Scene."

After he got off his phone he said, "Franklin is on his way out here. He said he would notify the chief and Double Dick."

Maddy gave him a curious look, and he corrected himself, "I meant Deputy Chief Dick."

"Don't worry, Detective," Maddy said with a sardonic smile. "I know you all call him Double Dick."

Liddell looked away. "I don't know what you're talking about, Miss Brooks."

Maddy looked at Jack, and he held his hands up. "Leave me out of this."

Eddie had spotted the big detective arriving and decided it was time to hit the road. He had a knife with him, but it wouldn't do to take the one called Blanchard out this early in the game. Besides, he looked like he would be a handful in a fight. He'd have to take him from behind. That was something he'd learned in prison. *Maybe later*, he thought.

He drove slowly away from the area, turning into the parking lot of the Evansville Museum. A bicycle path and several footpaths ran down the levee behind the museum. It was barely light out, but the parking lot was already full of cars and SUVs that sported bicycle carriers. His old van blended in well here. He climbed in the back of the van to think, leaving Bobby asleep in the passenger seat.

How can he sleep through all this? Eddie wondered. *Man, I got a woody that won't quit,* he thought, and lay on the floor with his hands shoved down the front of his jeans, touching it. When he finished, he drifted off to sleep with the smell of Maddy Brooks's hair still in his mind.

Franklin was talking to the station manager, Bill Goldberg, when the two detectives brought Maddy Brooks back to the ambulance. She had finally agreed to let the paramedics check her over.

Franklin and Bill Goldberg were talking and laughing comfortably like old friends.

"If we were caught on camera at a serious crime scene laughing, the news media would castrate us," Liddell observed.

"Yeah," Jack said. "But how would that affect you, Bigfoot?"

"Hey!" Liddell exclaimed. "There's no need to get nasty. Besides, I bet I get laid more than you do."

Jack ignored the challenge, because he knew Liddell was probably right.

Maddy was finally released by the medical crew and came over to them with the station manager in tow.

"This is Bill Goldberg," she said, seeming to forget that they had already been introduced. They all shook hands.

Jack whistled at one of the crime scene techs. "Can you bring a Tyvek blanket over here?" he asked the tech, then to Maddy and her boss said, "Maddy, we'll need to take your clothes for evidence."

She looked at the station manager, and Jack realized how much her life was controlled by station policy, just as his own was controlled by department policy.

"It's okay, Maddy," Goldberg said. "What's important is to catch the guy that did this to you."

She leaned in and whispered something to Goldberg, who nodded, and then he whispered something back to her. Just then the crime scene tech arrived with a white Tyvek blanket, wrapped it around Maddy's shoulders, and shuffled her toward her door.

"Try to remember what you can and we'll talk in a little while," Jack said, and she turned slightly and smiled. He knew that victims of trauma sometimes had a temporary loss of memory just after the incident, and that it wasn't unusual for them to remember things hours or even days later. He believed it must have something to do with the mind protecting itself. But it was just as likely that she would try to hold out some information from them because that was what newspeople did.

Maddy came out of her house wearing a faded pair of blue jeans, a baggy purple sweatshirt with the Channel Six logo, and fluorescent yellow flip-flops. Liddell looked her over and gave him a thumbs-up. She gave him her middle finger, but was smiling while she did so.

"She wants me," Liddell said to Jack.

"Do you really need my clothes?" Maddy said to no one in particular. "And my shoes? Or are you merely trying to humiliate me?"

"Oh, we're trying to humiliate you. Big-time!" Liddell said with a grin.

"Well, it's working," she said to Jack. "Where'd you get this guy anyway?" she asked and hooked a thumb at Liddell.

"Believe it or not, when he was little someone stuffed him in my mail slot and I didn't have the heart to get rid of him," Jack said.

Maddy giggled and sat down on her back steps.

"I don't believe he's ever been little," she said.

"Thank you," Liddell said, and Maddy turned red.

"Are you feeling like answering some more questions?" Jack asked.

"If you don't mind talking to someone in a purple top with yellow flip-flops."

Jack gave her a serious look. "I want you to close your eyes."

Maddy stared at him.

"Just humor me," he said.

She let out a breath and closed her eyes. "Okay, now what?"

"This might be unpleasant, Maddy, but in your mind I want you to picture leaving your house. Like a movie, but seen through your eyes."

"You're kidding, right?" she asked, opening her eyes again.

"I told you she wouldn't do it," Liddell remarked.

Maddy shot him an angry look and closed her eyes again. "I'm leaving the kitchen," she said.

Liddell and Jack exchanged a smile.

"What is the first thing you remember seeing?" Jack asked.

"What kind of question—" Maddy started.

Jack interrupted her, and said, "For God's sake, just answer the question, Maddy."

She took a few breaths, slowly letting them out, eyes closed. "Okay. I'm facing toward the backyard." She opened her eyes and said, "It might be easier if I just go back and walk through this again."

"Are you sure you're up to it?" Liddell asked.

"No," she admitted. "But I need to do this. Will you guys go with me?"

"I could never turn down a woman in yellow flip-flops," Liddell said.

True to her word, Maddy reenacted leaving her house and hesitated at the part where she was grabbed from behind, but then continued like a real trouper. Jack knew this must be draining her emotionally, but she did remember a surprising amount of details this way.

Although she hadn't really seen her assailant's face, she could tell the men that he was a white male, maybe twenty-five to thirty years old, taller than Jack but not as tall as Liddell, thin but not skinny, and his breath smelled peppery, like Dentyne gum or licorice or something. Being alone with the two men, she confided that he had rubbed his hands over her breasts and other places she didn't want to talk about.

Jack could sense that she was holding something back, but he knew that asking her now was a waste of time. She had told them everything she was going to.

"What about hair length?" Liddell asked.

"Have you not been listening? I was attacked from behind. I didn't see his hair."

Jack said, "What did his face feel like? Facial hair? Anything else you can remember, Maddy."

She closed her eyes again for a minute or so, and then opened them. "His hair was long!" she said excitedly. "And he needed a shave and a bath, but he didn't have a beard or mustache. At least I don't think so. But I do remember his hair falling across the side of my face when he was whispering in my ear."

She looked at Jack with admiration, and said, "How do you do that?"

Liddell snickered, and said, "Because his heart is pure and chaste."

Maddy looked curiously at Jack. "Don't ask," he said.

"What did he whisper?" Jack asked, and a look came into Maddy's expression like someone pulling down blinds.

Just then, a Jeep Liberty with Channel Six News markings pulled up, and Bill Goldberg spoke to the driver. In moments, the Jeep sped off, and Jack noticed that Maddy carefully looked the other way.

What was that about? he wondered.

CHAPTER TWENTY

Maddy absolutely refused to have a police officer stay with her. Bill Goldberg had halfheartedly attempted to get her to change her mind, but in the end she was like any other reporter Jack had ever met—hardheaded and secretive. She had finally said that, as she wasn't under arrest, she was going back inside to change, and then go to work, and would they all please leave her alone.

Jack and Liddell met Captain Franklin on the street and stood around their cars discussing their next move.

"What do you think?" Franklin said, and looked around to be sure no one else was listening.

"I think they would sacrifice their own mothers for a personal interview with the killer," Liddell said.

"You talked to the station manager, Goldberg. Do you think they will keep their word and cooperate with us?" Jack asked the captain.

"He was lying through his teeth," Franklin said conspiratorially, "but there's not much we can do about it."

"I wonder what Maddy was whispering to him about?" Liddell said.

Jack thought again about the Channel Six vehicle speeding off after meeting with Goldberg. Could have been on a hot call. Maybe the mayor had gotten caught skinny-dipping in the Civic Center fountain. Probably not.

Franklin's phone rang. "Excuse me a minute," he said and walked a few feet away. He came back and handed the phone to Jack. "You need to take this," he said.

"Detective Murphy," Jack said, and then, "Wait a minute. Let me get something to write on." He fished through his jacket and found a coffee shop receipt and a pen. "Okay, go ahead, Sheriff." He wrote a couple of things on the paper and then flipped the phone shut and handed it to Franklin.

"That was Sheriff Tanner Crowley. Dubois County," Jack said. "They're working a murder scene at a cabin near Patoka Lake."

"So?" Liddell asked.

"The killer left a message in blood for me."

"How do they know it was for you?" Liddell asked.

Jack looked at Franklin. "He wouldn't say. Captain?"

Franklin looked at his watch. "It'll take you about an hour to get there the way you drive." It was about an eighty-mile trip to Patoka Lake from Evansville. "Keep the wheels on the road, Jack," he said. "And call when you know something. Liddell can take over here."

Franklin walked away, and Liddell turned to Jack, saying, "Give me the keys to your Cherokee, and you can take my unmarked car. I'll leave your Jeep at the station and drive your unmarked until you get back."

"Good idea," Jack said and traded keys.

"You always get to go on the trips. How come I never get to go?" Liddell complained.

"Keep an eye on Maddy, will you, partner?" Jack asked.

"If you don't hurry, she may beat you there," Liddell answered.

                              * * *

Interstate 64 runs east–west at the northern edge of the
county. Jack went up U.S. Highway 57 and then turned east
toward Louisville. He opened his phone and dialed the number for Sheriff Crowley. When he came on the line, Jack asked
some questions he hadn't previously thought of. Crowley
said he'd get back to him.

Jack was just passing the Interstate 164 bypass near the
Vanderburgh County limits when his phone rang.

"Murphy," he said, listened, and then said, "Damn!"

He told the sheriff where he was, hung up, and stepped it
up. Eighty. Ninety. At one hundred-ten miles an hour he set
the cruise, turned on the wig-wag lights, and gripped the
wheel. Traffic was light but would be getting thick with
morning work traffic soon.

Crowley had told him that they found a note, stuffed in
the victim's throat, just like Jack had told them. But they
were hesitant to remove it until their coroner arrived.

Crowley hadn't told him much except to get his ass over
there and answer some questions, and Jack could understand
where the sheriff was coming from. It was an election year.
Dubois County had a small sheriff's department, and Crowley was hoping to have a handle on this before the state police got involved. Once the state police got there they'd start
ordering the sheriff and his men around, and Crowley would
probably like to get the credit himself.

About twenty minutes out he began looking for Exit 57
that would take him north on 231 through the little town of
Huntingburg. That route would take him off the interstate,
but if traffic was light he would pass through Birdseye, English, and St. Anthony, and come out at the spot the sheriff
had chosen for the meet.

He spotted Exit 57 too late and had to stomp on the
brakes. He took the right ramp to the top, then turned north
onto State Road 231. Less than a mile down the road he

spotted a cow standing in the road; then a couple of deer darted across his path. Up ahead was a black buggy being pulled by a pair of horses. *Should have stayed on the damn interstate.* He reluctantly reduced his speed to sixty-five, then to forty-five, and then he was in Huntingburg. Rush-hour traffic was an oxymoron.

CHAPTER TWENTY-ONE

Liddell and Franklin had set up a loose surveillance team on Maddy Brooks, but it wouldn't be easy. She was within her rights to refuse protection from the police, as crazy as that sounded, and could even file a complaint or federal charges for violating her civil rights. And that posed a problem. Franklin needed experienced detectives because of the nature of the assignment, but Deputy Chief Dick had interceded and selected the two newest detectives for the job. Franklin hoped he had made it crystal clear to the two men that they were to observe and report and not talk to her.

Then Liddell got down to the tedious work of going through the records once more. He had not even made a dent in them, and wasn't really sure what he was supposed to find. He'd been at it about ten minutes and was hoping that Jack would call soon to let them know what was going on in Dubois County, when Captain Franklin came in with an embarrassed-looking Detective Jansen following close on his heels.

"You won't need to finish that, Liddell," Franklin said.

Liddell looked from Franklin to Jansen. "I think I should do this myself, Captain," he said, casting a furtive glance at

Jansen. Not that he wanted to do Jansen any favors by keeping him from a grunt job—he just didn't trust him.

Franklin said, "I want you to meet your new help," and a smallish young woman stepped from behind him. Liddell hadn't noticed her come into the room.

She smiled and extended a hand. It was very soft, but her grip was strong. Her skin was the color of yellow coal, with dark hair and even darker eyes that bordered on black. Without waiting for Franklin to introduce her, she confidently said, "My name is Angelina Garcia. I'm a civilian intel analyst for the Vice squad."

Franklin added, "And the best damn computer operator you will ever meet." He then turned to Garcia and Jansen. "I want you two to take all of those files"—he indicated the folders covering Jack and Liddell's desktops—"and come with us."

Jansen let Garcia pick up the majority of the files, and he reluctantly picked up the rest and followed the trio down the hallway.

"Where we going, Captain?"

"Chief's conference room," Franklin answered. "He's given us his rooms until this is over."

Liddell grabbed the stack of files from Garcia and, piling them on top of Jansen's, said, "You heard the captain. Let's go."

A desk had been brought inside the chief's conference room, and several computer and telephone lines had been set up in preparation. Power cords snaked along the walls and under the thirty-foot-long conference table.

"I'm moving into the chief's office temporarily," Franklin said.

"Where's the chief going?" Liddell asked.

Franklin allowed himself a tiny smirk. "He's going to take the deputy chief's office temporarily, and the deputy chief is going to be working out of the Vice unit for a while." Liddell raised his eyebrows, and Franklin continued, "To gather intelligence for us."

"I see," Liddell said. The chief had effectively neutered Double Dick while making it look like he had given him an important job. *That's why he's the chief,* Liddell thought.

"Show me what you've got. And call me Garcia," Angelina said to Liddell.

Liddell explained what the stacks of files were and briefed her about the notes that were found at the scenes of the murders. He also told her about the corresponding notes sent to Maddy Brooks at Channel Six and about the ties to Mother Goose nursery rhymes.

"Mother Goose, huh?" Garcia said. "Where's the book?"

Liddell promised to bring her the stack of books that Jack had gotten from Katie. "Are the books important?" he asked.

"Don't know that yet," Garcia said and looked thoughtful. Then she asked, "And your partner is going to yet another murder scene?"

"Yeah," Liddell answered. "Patoka Lake area."

"Be sure you tell me what he finds there as soon as possible," she said and picked up the nearest stack of files and set them on top of a desk. To Jansen, she said, "I'll work here, if that's okay, and you can have that end of the table."

He grumbled and excused himself to go to the restroom.

Liddell started to pick up the other pile, but she put a restraining hand on his arm. "I'm quite capable of doing this work, Detective. You catch this bastard and leave the paperwork to me."

"If Jansen gives you any problems, call me," he said.

Garcia threw her hair back and laughed. "I can take care of that pip-squeak, Detective Blanchard," she said confidently.

He could get to like this little dynamo. "Okay, Garcia. You can call me Liddell."

She smiled and then ignored him totally as she lit up her monitor and got to work.

CHAPTER TWENTY-TWO

Jack had entered the lake region, but it took him almost five minutes to locate the sign that pointed left to Panther Creek. He took this road for about a hundred yards, and when he turned into the lot he got a clear view of part of the lake. The water was deep blue and green, and the sun sparkled off its surface. He pulled up behind a brown and tan Jeep Cherokee marked DUBOIS COUNTY SHERIFF and came to a stop.

The man inside pulled himself from the Jeep, and it rose several inches. Sheriff Tanner Crowley was a big man. He wasn't fat. He might have been in his fifties, but he looked strong and fit.

Jack rolled his window down as the big man came up to his car.

"Murphy?"

"You got me," Jack said. "You Sheriff Crowley?"

The sheriff nodded his head and grinned a little. "Your captain said you were a smart-ass. Is that right?"

"Guilty as charged, your honor," Jack said.

"You 'n' me'll get along just fine," Crowley said. "Call me Tanner." He put out a large hand, and Jack shook it.

"You will want to ride with me. Some of these roads are not fit for travel except in a four-wheel drive, and we got a little piece to go to get to the cabin."

Jack got in the passenger side of the Jeep and was surprised at how roomy it was even with all the radio equipment and a computer mounted between the seats. A 12-gauge Winchester pump shotgun was mounted above their heads in an electronically locked quick-release carrier above the windshield. A half-dozen pairs of handcuffs and ankle cuffs stood up in a wooden box between the seats.

The sheriff saw Jack eyeing the box of handcuffs and said, "It's a quiet little county most of time. At least until a bunch of drunked-up fishermen start tearing the place apart." Jack could understand that. He was an avid fisherman himself and was known to have a drink or two—or twenty—when he was out on the water.

Tanner drove expertly down a path that led into the woods and back out onto a gravel road. "Shortcut," he said as they bounced over some small downed trees. He consulted a GPS mounted to his dash and said, "We should just about be there," and cut the wheels sharply off the gravel road and into the woods. They traveled uphill a hundred yards or so and made a sharp right turn, traveling along a shallow stream and coming out below a gravel parking area. Jack could see two other sheriff department SUVs and a huge, white Ford pickup with monster tires parked in the lot.

As Tanner parked, a deputy ran up to the car. This one was as big as Tanner but younger. They talked for a minute, and Tanner introduced them.

"This is detective Murphy from Evansville," he said to the deputy, then to Jack, "This is my chief deputy, Mark Crowley." Tanner saw Jack's expression and said, "Yeah, he's my son. You gonna say something smart-ass about it?"

"I just want to get back to the road before the banjos start playing," Jack said with a grin.

"Hear that, Mark?" Tanner said.

"Yeah, Sheriff, he's a hoot," the younger Crowley said.

"Why don't you fill him in on the way, Bubba?" Crowley said to his son.

He actually called him Bubba, Jack thought, but didn't interrupt.

They walked up a gravel path. The sheriff had said it was about fifty yards to the cabin, and Jack wondered why they had parked so distant from the crime scene. As they walked farther down the path and into the woods, it became clear to him. He'd seen an SUV with K-9 markings parked in the outer perimeter. They must have brought the dog out to see if they could get a direction of travel on the killer.

"Dog do any good?" Jack asked.

Mark Crowley answered, his voice sounding hollow. "Dad'll fill you in on that. You probably should look at the scene first."

They arrived at the front, wraparound deck of the cabin. An older deputy stood just outside the front door with a notebook in his hand. The deputy's uniform was faded to the point it was almost colorless, but Jack was impressed to see he was wearing a Glock .45 in a Class III retention holster.

The older deputy's name tag read VODKA WILSON, and although Jack thought that was quite a remarkable name, he was glad the older man wasn't Grandpa Crowley. Even nepotism had to have limits.

They walked onto the deck, and Vodka was already writing in his notebook. "This the guy, Sheriff?" Vodka asked without looking up.

"It wasn't me. I got witnesses," Jack said, holding his hands in the air, to which the older deputy chuckled, then coughed into his cupped hands like he would spit out a lung.

"Gotta quit smoking," Vodka said when he recovered enough to speak; then to the Crowleys he said, "His captain was right, Sheriff. He's a real smart-ass." He then wiped his right hand on his pant leg and held it out to greet the new-comer.

Jack would have liked to glove up first, but he reluctantly took the offered hand. He was a guest here, so it wouldn't do to be rude. As he shook hands, Jack wondered how many people the captain had talked to. Probably everyone on the lake knew he was a smart-ass by now. *I'm going to have to talk to Captain Franklin about this slander when I get back,* Jack thought.

Every light in the cabin was on in addition to several work lights on tripods set up to illuminate the body. The lights were so glaringly bright, the body so badly abused, that Jack winced at the grisly scene. During the ride to the cabin the sheriff had informed him that the victim was a white female about twenty-five years old and that she had been employed by St. Mary's Hospital in Evansville. She was found by a female friend who had come to visit her at the cabin at about three o'clock that morning.

"This is exactly how her friend found her," Mark Crowley said.

"Is she still here? The friend?" Jack asked. He hoped she was available to answer a few questions. Like, why was she going to the cabin at three o'clock in the morning?

"Well, that's part of the weirdness we got here," Mark answered. "Our office got the call from a pay phone in Evansville at four thirty-five this morning. A female caller. Said she wanted to report a murder. She wouldn't give her name at first, but the deputy finally convinced her we needed to talk to her, and she agreed to talk to you."

"Me?" Jack said, surprised. "Why me?"

"Her name is Janet Parson. She's a nurse, a physical therapist of some type. Works at the same hospital as the victim. She says she knows you," Mark answered.

The name sounded familiar to Jack, and then he remembered that when he had been in the hospital, his physical therapist was named Janet. Her name tag had read JANET: R.N., and he had kidded Liddell that the R.N. stood for "Retired Nazi." Liddell thought she had a cute butt, but Jack was so busy screaming profanities during the treatments that he hadn't noticed.

"So why did she leave the scene and drive all the way back to Evansville?" Jack wondered out loud. Both Crowleys just shrugged.

"She's on her way back here," the sheriff said. Just then they heard tires crunching in the gravel, and Deputy Vodka Wilson stuck his head in the doorway.

"Sheriff," he said in his gravelly tone, "I think that 'friend' a' hers is here." He made little quotation marks in the air with his fingers when he said "friend."

Sheriff Crowley told him to have someone hold her at the outer perimeter until they were done inside and they would talk to her. The deputy relayed the sheriff's orders to someone, and the door closed again.

The men went back to examining the body.

"We got a name on the victim yet?" Jack asked. It occurred to him that he hadn't asked yet.

"Yeah," Mark Crowley said. "Her name is Tisha Carter. She's a nurse. Unmarried, no kids. A deputy is trying to run down family and history, but you know how it is when you have to go through another agency to get info." Jack nodded. He knew how bureaucracy slowed things down to a death rattle.

The body was in the center of the one-room cabin, hanged by the neck from a wood ceiling beam in a kneeling position. She was facing away from the door. Her hands were tied behind her back with a cord that looked similar to the one around her neck, and she was partially clothed in a bloodstained white garment that might have been the top of her nursing uniform. Long bloodstained gashes in the clothing suggested she had been slashed with some type of long-bladed instrument. The skull showed through several gashes in the top of her scalp. She was naked from the waist down. Her feet were bare, and the soles of her feet had gashes in them.

Just like the Lamar child, Jack thought. He pointed to the blood pooled around the body. "It looks like she was overpowered right here. Maybe strung up before she was killed, because all the blood is beneath her."

"Yeah, that's what we figured, too," Mark Crowley said. "The killer hacked her to death while she was hanging. Some kinda sword or something. Then he gutted her."

Sheriff Crowley looked pallid. "She was probably dead before most of this was done, don't you think?"

"Yeah," Jack said, but he didn't believe it. For one thing, her pants were gone, suggesting a sexual assault before the murder. But he didn't want to suggest that yet without more evidence.

Mark Crowley squatted down and pointed to some marks in the pool of blood that encircled the body. "There are some spots here that look like bare footprints." Jack looked at where Mark was pointing and thought he could make out some depressions that would be consistent with a set of toes and maybe a heel.

"The size of that print is bigger than this little gal's foot," Sheriff Crowley said. Mark nodded in agreement.

"I found several more, I think," Mark said. "It looked like someone was walking around the body barefoot."

"Admiring his work," Sheriff Crowley offered.

Jack inched his way around to the front of the body and had to get on his knees to look up into the victim's face. It was remarkably free of blood except for the tip of her nose.

The sheriff nodded and said, "Remember I told you that there were a couple of things really strange about this?"

Jack nodded, wondering how much stranger the sheriff imagined things could get.

"There are a couple more things." He pointed at the wall behind them.

Jack stood up and saw a forty-two-inch, flat-screen television mounted on the wall. It was turned on, and something was smeared on the screen. Jack walked over to it and saw that there were words written in something red and sticky. He could make out the words:

You killed her
Jack

Without taking his eyes from the screen, Jack asked the two men, "How'd you know I was the right Jack? It wasn't just because the victim was from Evansville. Or because the witness wanted to talk to me. Was it?"

The younger Crowley pulled a small, plastic envelope from his pocket. Inside was a business card and the back of it was smeared with blood. The front of the card read *Detective Jack Murphy*. It was his business card.

"Where?" Jack asked.

"Stuck to the television screen."

"So, I'm a suspect?" Jack said, only half-jokingly.

Sheriff Crowley leaned in and said in a low voice, "I've heard stories about you, Murphy, and I know you're a hard man. But you better be careful." He and his son looked at each other, and then Tanner said, "This kind of shit don't happen in my county. It's a quiet place."

"Except for drunken fishermen," Jack corrected.

"Yeah. Except for them," Tanner Crowley said, shaking his head. "But the state police will take this scene over pretty soon, and if they found this," he said, nodding toward the business card, "they'd tie you up in so much red tape you wouldn't be able to do what you do best."

"I haven't been doing too hot, so far," Jack said.

Mark Crowley looked at the television screen. "Whatever you're doing—or whatever you've done—is pissing this guy off. I'd say he wants to kill you or get you to kill him, you know?" He opened the front door, and they walked onto the porch.

Sheriff Crowley let out a long sigh and looked at the sky. "Cheese 'n' crackers," he muttered, and put a big hand on Jack's shoulder. "This guy has probably hightailed it back to your neck of the woods. I got no problem with however you plan on handling him in your own county. Hell, I wish you'd kill the son of a bitch if you want the truth."

"What are you going to tell the state police?" Jack asked.

"Hell, boy, they think we're a bunch of dumb rednecks down he'ah," he said with an exaggerated hillbilly accent. "I ain't telling 'em shit. It'll be their case soon, so fuck a bunch of state cops."

Jack looked down at the sheriff's SUVs on the perimeter and a familiar face peered out of one of the windows. *Janet. Retired Nazi,* he thought, and walked down the steps.

CHAPTER TWENTY-THREE

"Hi, honey." Marcie said into the phone. She knew that if he was calling her at this hour in the day that he was either going to be late, or may not be home at all that evening. Being a policeman's wife, she was used to it. But it was neither.

"I just wanted to hear your voice," Liddell said.

She could tell there was something bothering him, but she would wait for him to tell it in his own way.

Finally he said, "This isn't going too good, babe."

"Tell me," she said gently, and he did. He told her about the whole frustrating mess, and how Jack was in Dubois County checking out another murder that might be, probably was, related to the recent ones. He told her how the killer was sending these messages to Jack, seemingly taunting him. He was worried about his partner and knew that Jack would likely go after this guy alone.

And Marcie, good wife that she was, listened. She didn't offer advice because she knew he wasn't asking for any. He was using her as a sounding board to work this out in his own mind. And it was okay with her. It was okay because

Liddell was calling *her*, and not anyone else. That meant a lot. When he was through he told her, "Sorry for bending your ear, hon."

"Liddell," she said, "you can bend anything I've got," and heard him chuckling on the other end.

"Love you, hon," she said.

"Back at cha," he said, and slowly hung up.

Marcie held the line open until she heard his end go dead; then she hung up and dialed another number.

The phone was answered on the second ring. "Hello," Katie Murphy said.

Eddie finished writing the notes and laid them on the console. The map of Mother Goose Land lay open on the dash, and a new character had been marked.

"When are we gonna do the cop, Bobby?"

Bobby shook his head. "When you gonna learn, Eddie?"

"I know. I know. First we gotta make him pay. But I'm getting tired of this shit, Bobby, and you ain't done much since we started except give me orders."

Bobby said nothing, and so Eddie looked at the map again. He had to admit that Bobby had a pretty cool plan. So far, all of the murders, except the nurse, had followed the map. The nurse would have fit perfectly, too, if she hadn't taken it in her head to drive way the hell out to that lake. *What was the bitch doing out there anyway?* Eddie thought. *She had someone coming out there, I just know it.*

Eddie had wanted to stay and see who it was. Maybe have a little fun. But Bobby wanted to leave right after they did her. *"Stick to the plan, Eddie. Stick to the plan." That's all he ever says.*

Well, Eddie was getting sick of being bossed around and doing all the work to boot. He'd do this next one, but then he was going to have some fun.

"Bobby, I don't understand all this shit. I just want to get even."

"We are getting even, Eddie. First, we destroy the man's reputation, and then we destroy everything he cares about. When we're done with him, he'll be begging us to kill him. Trust me, Eddie."

"I do trust you, Bobby. I trust you with my life, man." Eddie smiled, but Bobby didn't smile back.

Maddy Brooks was putting the finishing touches on the script that would be sent to her TelePrompTer in the newsroom when they televised her "Breaking News Special" this morning. The police department would have a fit, but she couldn't keep this under wraps any longer. The killer had made that very clear.

She shuddered when she remembered his lips pressed against her neck, whispering the most awful things to her, giving her instructions that had dire consequences if she disobeyed, but promising to keep in touch if she did what he said. She didn't shudder because of fear, but from disgust. The man exuded rot and decay, and even taking a scalding hot shower hadn't erased the feeling he left behind.

But, in truth, this was just too good of an opportunity to pass up. She was in the driver's seat, and even the police didn't have the right to stop her from telling—no, warning—the public about this freak.

She smiled. The station's ratings would go through the roof, and with the higher ratings would come a promotion for the woman that made it possible.

The station manager, Bill Goldberg, stuck his head in her office where she was touching up her makeup. "You ready, tiger?"

"You got it covered with the lawyers?" she asked, but didn't really care. She just wanted to sound concerned for the station. Show that she was a team player.

"The attorneys say we have a green light, kiddo. Let's do it," Goldberg said with enthusiasm.

Maddy stood, looked in the mirror one more time, and followed Goldberg down the hall to the news desk. She was about to become a star.

CHAPTER TWENTY-FOUR

In the conference room and on Garcia's desk were files that had already been entered into the database that Garcia herself had developed. With it, she could search for any name, date, location, time, weapon, charge, conviction, or any of a dozen other items. The program she had written could also streamline the data into comparisons between cases. It was all beyond Liddell, who was grumpily flipping through pages of old cases and wondering what Jack was doing.

"Detective Blanchard," Garcia said.

Liddell looked up to see her offering him a cup of coffee. He took the coffee and thanked her, then stared again at the pile of papers in front of him.

"Why don't you call Detective Murphy? Maybe he's found something out by now," she suggested.

Liddell closed the file and picked up the stack that was in front of him. "He would have called if he had anything," he said. "But I can't just sit here waiting for something to happen. No offense meant," he added hastily.

Garcia smiled. "None was taken, Detective Blanchard. I

can call you if I get anywhere. I should have all of this entered in the next couple of hours, and then we can start the real research."

"That'd be great, but you have to do one thing for me."

She raised her eyebrows. "You mean besides bringing you coffee and kicking you out so you don't feel guilty about leaving me with this mess?"

Liddell chuckled. It would never do to underestimate Vice Technician Angelina Garcia.

"Stop calling me Detective Blanchard," he said. "Makes me feel like an old man. Just call me Liddell, or hey you, or something else, but not Detective Blanchard."

"Hey you," she said, "scoot before the captain comes back. Just leave your cell number, and please don't let that nasty little grouch back in here."

Liddell didn't know who she was talking about for a moment and then remembered that Jansen had excused himself to make a call. He was probably outside smoking and updating Double Dick on their progress.

"I'll find something for him to do so he'll stay out of your way."

"Thanks," Garcia said and made a face. "He gives me the creeps."

"You should be safe," Liddell said with a serious look on his face. "I hear he likes little boys."

"Liar," she said, grinned, and then shoved him toward the door.

"So you say this killer is focusing on Detective Murphy?" Mayor Hensley asked the two men. Chief Pope and Deputy Chief Dick had been called to discuss the mayor's possible comments to the media about the string of recent murders. The fact that the mayor had called this meeting, Pope knew, meant he was planning on going public with the murders even if the media, by some miracle, kept cooperating.

It's just too good for him to pass up, Chief Marlin Pope thought. He looked over at Richard Dick. The man was openly gloating. Dick could smell the blood in the water. *And that blood is mine,* Pope thought. If this case wasn't closed soon, Pope knew he would be out of a job.

"That's not how I would put it, Mayor," Pope responded.

"But you said the killer is leaving notes for Murphy. Taunting him," Hensley said, waving his arms to emphasize his point.

"Yes, that's true, Mayor, but . . ." Pope started to say, but was rudely cut off by Deputy Chief Dick.

"Look, let's not fool each other about this maniac's intentions," Dick said and leaned back in his chair. "The fact is that he has left a message in each case. He has used Murphy's name on one or two notes sent to, uhm, what's her name . . . that Channel Six woman, Brooks."

Pope almost let out a laugh. "You know her name very well, Richard. Now who is trying to fool whom?"

Dick drew himself up, perfectly portraying a wounded innocent, but Pope moved in for the kill. "You've had Maddy Brooks in your office more than the cleaning people, Richard. I'll bet you have her on speed dial."

Mayor Hensley let himself chuckle at the last remark. It was a known fact, and not just among the police officers, that Richard Dick was a news whore.

"Gentlemen, let's not lose sight of why we are here," Hensley said, and Dick eased back in his chair, once again calm and in control. "Maddy Brooks already leaked the possibility of a serial killer to the public." He stood up and walked to the bank of windows that made up the wall of the office. "Hell, she even dubbed him 'Mother Goose.' And she hinted that he was after Jack Murphy." As he said this, he turned on Chief Pope. "Need I remind you that I wasn't informed when all this was done? I didn't even know about the Mother Goose angle. The public should have confidence in their mayor. If I'm not informed in a timely manner it makes me look weak and ineffectual."

Pope thought that description fit him perfectly.

"If I have to respond to the news media," Hensley continued, "I need to know what to say. The citizens of this city are going to be extremely upset that we kept quiet about this killer. They do have a right to know. To protect themselves. The question before us, gentlemen, is this: Is it appropriate to allude to the connection between Murphy and the killer?"

Pope saw the mayor and Dick exchange a look. *They're going to take me down and take Murphy down with me,* Pope realized. This had nothing to do with protecting the public or the public's right to know there was a killer among them. It was all politics.

Pope could understand the mayor taking advantage of this type of sensationalistic journalism; after all, that's a politician's bread and butter. But Richard Dick was a police officer, sworn to protect the public. Pope knew that Dick hated the very air Murphy breathed, but he didn't think, until now, that the man would allow people to be killed to get his revenge on Murphy. He suddenly wished he had retired before all this had started.

The meeting had ended just like Deputy Chief Dick thought it would. Pope had blustered and tried to cover for that damn Murphy, but the mayor was having none of it. Now all that remained was for someone to leak the story to one of the television stations in competition with Channel Six—preferably Channel Eleven as they had always been a supporter of the mayor—and then all he had to do was sit back and watch the media frenzy do the rest.

Maddy would be furious with him that they had not given

her the exclusive story. But he was confident that people would be calling for results in the investigation, and of course, Dick would be their man. He would take Pope's position as chief of police and then suspend Murphy for mishandling the case. Even if they never solved it, he could always blame the results on Pope and Murphy. It was the perfect plan. It was a shame that he couldn't just give the story to Maddy Brooks, but then all the other stations would complain, and, well, he had to start thinking like a chief. This plan was better. And, as they say, all is fair in love and politics.

He sat across from the mayor and looked through the notes he'd gotten from Detective Jansen. Jansen was a scumbag and a pitiful excuse for a police detective, but he was very detailed and loyal. Of course, he'd expect some reward when this was over, so he'd have to throw the man a bone. Maybe promote him to sergeant and make Murphy work for him. *If Murphy's still on the job by then.* That thought made him smile.

"What's funny?" Hensley asked.

"Nothing really, Thatcher," Dick said. "I was just remembering an old joke."

"Tell me," Hensley said. "I could use a laugh right now."

"Okay," he said, and quickly thought of a joke so as not to let on what he was really thinking. "Why do people get upset when a Chrysler with four attorneys goes over a cliff?"

Hensley just looked at him, dumbfounded. *Doesn't this moron even remember that I'm an attorney?* he thought.

Misunderstanding the mayor's silence, Dick continued, "Because a Chrysler seats six." He laughed out loud. "Get it?"

CHAPTER TWENTY-FIVE

The Channel Six newsroom was buzzing with excitement. The cameras were wheeled into place and cued on the news desk where Maddy Brooks sat beside the senior news anchor, Clark Jameson.

"Check her makeup," the director yelled from behind the cameras, and a cute, young guy rushed to Maddy and dabbed at imaginary blemishes in her immaculate complexion. "On the air in one minute," the director announced.

The TelePrompTer was rolled into place, but Maddy didn't need it. She'd been writing this story her whole life. She looked over at Clark, and he was looking straight ahead at the camera. *Mr. Professional,* she thought. She could feel his tension, knew he was deliberately ignoring her, could almost hear him thinking, *Just who does this bitch think she is?* But Maddy didn't care about any of that.

"Thirty seconds," the director said.

I'm going to be a star after this story breaks, she thought.

"Twenty seconds."

This will make my career. Maybe give me a chance at Chicago. Or New York.

"Ten seconds," the director announced, and everything became quiet. The small light on top of camera one lit, indicating that camera one was operative. Camera one's operator took over the cue at this point, holding up both hands, palms pointed toward Clark, while he mouthed the countdown. *Five, four, three, two, one*, and Clark expertly began, "Hello, I'm Clark Jameson, and bringing you a breaking news story is our own investigative reporter, Maddy Brooks, who has been working side by side with Evansville Police to investigate a string of murders that have now spread to Dubois County. Maddy?" he said, and the light atop camera two lit.

Maddy took a breath, looked into camera two, and began. "Thanks, Clark. On September fifteenth, a prominent local psychiatrist and her husband were brutally murdered in their north-side home. Doctor Anne Lewis and her husband of forty years, Don Lewis, lived and worked in this community for most of their lives until those lives were brought to an end by a sadistic killer the police have dubbed Mother Goose."

"Is it important?" Tanner Crowley asked.

Jack leaned over and examined the chewing gum wrapper again. It was from a stick of Black Jack gum. He hadn't seen that brand of gum since he was a child. He stood up and looked southward. The front of the cabin could be seen clearly about forty yards away. One of the deputies had done a perimeter search and found the spot in the woods where someone had recently trampled a young pine sapling, left a dozen or more boot prints, and apparently had chewed a stick of Black Jack gum.

"A television reporter was attacked a couple hours ago in the parking lot," Jack said.

"Gee, I'm real sorry to hear that," Mark Crowley said with a satisfied grin.

"If you knew the whole story, you'd have to go home and change into something more comfortable and have a cigarette," Jack said, and Mark chuckled with delight. "Anyway," he continued, "she said the guy's breath smelled like Dentyne gum."

"Coulda been Black Jack gum," Tanner Crowley mused. "I'll check with all my guys to be sure no one is chewing gum."

"I'll do it," Mark said and ambled back toward the parking area.

They had interviewed Janet Parson, who was reluctant to answer questions, and at one point asked if she should have an attorney present. The sheriff had assured her that she wasn't a suspect, but she had finally insisted on talking alone with Jack.

Sheriff Crowley scratched his head and looked down in the parking lot where their star witness leaned against her car, smoking cigarette after cigarette. "So you say she's gay?" he said to Jack.

"Yup," he answered.

"And she was up here to spend the night with the victim, for whom she had romantic inclinations?" Tanner continued.

"You do have a way with words," Jack answered. "But, yeah, that's about the size of it."

"And that's why she wanted an attorney?" he said as if he didn't believe her story.

"I think she's conflicted," Jack said.

Sheriff Crowley shook his head. "I'm too old for this shit. In my day . . ." he began, then seemed to think better of it and said, "Well, never mind that. So she told you she got cold feet about coming, and then decided to get here about three o'clock this morning and surprise her friend. When she got here she found the cabin door open and her friend was dead?"

"Sheriff, if she's accurate on the time, I'd say you're lucky you don't have two murders to investigate."

"I hear you," the big man said.

CHAPTER TWENTY-SIX

Sheriff Crowley pulled his Jeep into the parking lot at the Panther Creek boat ramp, where Jack had left his car, and cut the engine. Jack stepped out into the cool breeze coming off the lake. The serenity of the blue water made it difficult to believe that such an atrocity had been committed less than a mile away.

Janet Parson had been of little help to them, and her confusion over the extent of her relationship with the victim didn't help things. She had been inside the scene of the murder and left. She then waited four hours to make an anonymous call to report it. And then she was hesitant to answer any questions about why she was there at the lake in the first place and about her relationship to the victim. Jack didn't really give a damn why she was there, except for how it related to the death of Tisha Carter. But he knew that after the state police investigators were through with her, she would wish she had been more forthcoming with him and the sheriff. The staties would not be sympathetic.

Of course, she had to be considered a suspect in the death for all of the aforementioned reasons. Could she have done it? Hell, yes. Jack had seen firsthand the results of the revenge of a jilted lover. But if Janet was telling the truth, they weren't lovers. Not yet, at least. So she would have no reason to kill her friend.

At the end of the interview, Jack was pretty sure that Janet was merely an innocent who had been caught up in something horrible. Both he and the sheriff had left business cards with her, promising to keep in touch about the case, and she was taken to the Dubois County Sheriff's Office to wait for the state police to be involved.

He waved good-bye to Sheriff Crowley and was about to get into his car when his cell phone rang. He answered.

"Jack. Why didn't you tell me the truth? It's all over Channel Six," Katie said angrily.

Coin was hunkered down in a downstairs doorway of the Old Courthouse building when Liddell found him. It was around nine o'clock. Most of the street people would be up and moving about, spurred by the noise and foot traffic of the more fortunate. Liddell was surprised to find any of his older snitches except the prostitutes and some of the regular drug users. But Coin was homeless, had been since Liddell had first run across him, and would sleep in trash bins, public restrooms, or any place that was abandoned or had an unlocked window. He smelled like dried urine, feces, and smoke. The last place Coin had stayed was in the basement of an old theater, The Alhambra, in the Haynie's Corner district downtown. There'd been a fire there a few days ago. Most of the building was gone now. He was surprised Coin hadn't been caught in the fire.

"Liddell, my man!" Coin greeted him with a huge grin that showed what was left of his summer teeth. They call them summer teeth because sum'r there 'n' sum ain't.

Liddell didn't know Coin's real name was. He wasn't sure

Coin knew his real name. But he had earned the nickname "Coin" because he would sell out his own mother for a few coins. He was snitching useless information to half the police force before everyone figured out his game. Now, no one would give him the time of day, except Liddell.

"Hey, I got some good stuff for you, Liddell," Coin said, trying to stand but not quite able to get his feet under him. Two Mad Dog 20/20 wine bottles lay empty near him, and he had made a bed of wadded newspapers.

Glad someone appreciates the local newspaper, Liddell thought and reached in his back pocket, pulling out the small brown paper bag. "I got something for you, pal," Liddell said, handing the bag to Coin.

Coin peeled the bag down and twisted the top from a half pint of MacGregor scotch like a kid with a Christmas present. He turned the bottle up and downed half of it before grimacing and coughing, and then he rubbed his watery eyes with the back of one grimy hand and got quiet.

"You okay?" Liddell asked. He'd tried to get Coin into every homeless shelter in Vanderburgh County, but the man stunk, thieved, and fought his way out of so many that no one would take him. He'd finally given up trying to rehabilitate Coin and had decided to let him live his life the way he wanted.

Coin sniffled and rubbed at his nose with his sleeve before looking up with moist, rheumy eyes. "You're the only friend I got," he said and hacked up a wad of phlegm into his hand, then started crying.

Liddell stuck a twenty in the old man's shirt pocket and left. He'd just walked back to his car when his cell phone rang. When he looked at the screen he saw it was Murphy.

"Wha'sup, pod'na?"

"It was him," Jack said. "This time he wrote 'You killed her Jack' in blood on the television screen."

"Find a note on her?" Liddell asked.

"Yep," Jack answered. "The sheriff has to wait for the state police. They're a small department and don't have the forensics for something like this. Where are you?"

"I was going crazy back at headquarters," Liddell said truthfully. "I had to get out and do something. Oh yeah, the chief gave us his conference room and outer offices to work from. We got a sharp gal from Vice working with us now. She's some kind of computer genius. All the files we were trying to go through should be entered into a search program before you get back. If you are coming back, that is?"

Jack had to chuckle, even though it became obvious to him that Liddell hadn't yet heard about Maddy Brooks giving everything away.

"You haven't been in touch with the office, have you?" Jack asked.

"Nah. I just found Coin and was getting ready to run down some of the others. You know, Tennessee and BoJack and some of those guys. See if anything's shaking."

"Well, shake it back to headquarters," Jack said. "Maddy Brooks released the story."

"Fuck me!" Liddell said.

"Yeah," Jack agreed, and while Liddell drove back to the station Jack filled him in on Patoka Lake. By the time they hung up, Jack was back on Interstate 64 and pushing.

He flew by the Lynnville exit and pushed harder, running with his grille-mounted lights only, not expecting to see any state police between Patoka and Evansville because they would all be going to Patoka. His cell rang again. It was Franklin.

"Yeah, Captain," he answered.

"Fill me in," Franklin said calmly. "But make it brief—we have some, uh, issues that have developed here."

Calling what Maddy had just done "issues" was classic Franklin. He would call an alien invasion a little problem.

"I'm aware," Jack said. "Katie called me, after Marcie called her. Liddell's on his way back to the office. I'll be there as quick as I can."

"Katie called?" Franklin asked, and the way he said her name made Jack grind his teeth. Franklin had always had his eye on Katie, even when she and Jack were married. But it wasn't proper to cut the testicles from your boss, so he ground his teeth instead.

"She said Maddy spilled the whole deal this morning and released some things that even we hadn't released yet. Like this Patoka connection. The sheriff's guys turned a Channel Six news crew away before I got here this morning. That was the one we saw leaving from Maddy's place."

"I kind of assumed that's what she was telling Goldberg this morning. We knew they were lying about something. But, Mother Goose?" Franklin said. "She says that we came up with the name."

"What a surprise," Jack said. He filled the captain in on the Patoka crime scene, leaving out the part about his business card being left behind by the killer. It wouldn't help the case right now, and he didn't want to be pulled off. After he hung up with the captain, an idea struck him. He hit the speed dial.

Sheriff Crowley answered on the first ring. "Murphy? I was just getting ready to call you," he said.

Jack didn't wait for him to finish. "Listen, Sheriff, you have to get the note out of her mouth. Do it right now!"

"Calm down, boy," Crowley said. "We already got the note. That's what I was calling you about."

Well, then what the fuck does it say? Jack wanted to scream into the phone, but he took a deep breath.

"It's some kind of damn poem or something," Crowley said.

"Read it to me," Jack said impatiently.

Crowley looked at the note and read:

> little nancy etticoat
> in a white petticoat
> and a red nose
> the longer she stands
> the shorter she grows

"That mean anything to you?" Crowley asked.

Jack thought for a moment. "Yeah. I think it's another rhyme or a riddle or something. This bastard has been using Mother Goose rhymes for his messages."

"Mother Goose?" Crowley said.

"Yeah. Listen, Sheriff, the white petticoat could refer to the nurse's clothes. I got a look at her face, and there was blood on the very end of her nose. Like it had been dabbed on. A red nose."

"Damn!" Crowley said. "The longer she stands, the shorter she grows, might refer to how he hanged her in a kneeling position like that."

Jack thought that sounded about right. "But taken together, what the hell does it all mean? What's he trying to tell us?"

"Damned if I know," the sheriff admitted. "Well, the state police just showed up, so I guess I'll have some explaining to do about why I dug this note out of her mouth."

"Just scratch your head and spit on the ground. Works for me," Jack said.

"Shucks," Crowley said, "why didn't I think of that? You take care, Jack. Oh yeah, when you catch up to this guy, don't worry about us, if you get my drift."

Jack closed his phone and wondered, *What the fuck does*

it all mean? Then he thought about Maddy Brooks and wondered if she had received a new message yet. That was the
pattern, after all. But since she had fucked her deal with the
chief of police, he wasn't sure she would play nice anymore.
He fumbled his phone open again. *Only one way to find out,*
he thought.

CHAPTER TWENTY-SEVEN

"Maddy, someone on the phone for you!" Lois yelled from down the hallway.

Maddy shook her head and wondered what it would take for the old witch to lose her job. She was totally worthless as a receptionist and, except for getting rid of that even-more-worthless Detective Jansen, she had been nothing but a pain in the ass since day one.

"Lois, honey, can you transfer it to my phone?" Maddy purred. *No need to cut my own throat now,* she thought.

"I'm not your personal secretary," Lois yelled back at her. "He says he is Mother Goose," she said with contempt. "Shall I give him your desk phone number?"

"No! Don't hang up!" Maddy said in a panic and rushed to the front. *Don't hang up, don't hang up,* she desperately thought. *If you hang up, I'll kill you myself, you old bitch.*

Maddy leaned across the counter and grabbed the phone from the older woman's hand. "Hello. Hello!" she said into the silence at the other end. *Jesus H. Christ, the woman's hung up on the killer,* she thought frantically, and was about to hang up when a familiar voice came on the line.

"Mother Goose?" the voice asked.

Maddy was almost breathless. "Listen, don't be offended. I did what you wanted."

"And what was it I asked you to do?" Jack asked.

Mayor Hensley was furious. "Weren't you supposed to take care of this, Richard?" he yelled at Deputy Chief Dick.

Dick didn't answer because he knew it wasn't really a question. How could he have known that Maddy Brooks would break her deal with them? How could he know that?

Hensley paced the glass wall of his office that looked down Main Street toward the river. In a few weeks the Christmas parade would be filling Main Street. Thousands of voters with their children would be standing and sitting on both sides from Martin Luther King Boulevard to Second Street. He was supposed to officiate and judge the band playing the best music, the most colorful float. Now he would be a target of derision for the media, maybe the whole city.

It was already beginning. His secretary had already lied to three reporters, claiming that the mayor was in an emergency meeting. It wouldn't be long now before the media representatives that were scooped by Maddy Brooks would be clamoring at his office door demanding a story. He could hardly blame it all on the chief now, could he? And he would look totally incompetent trying to blame it on the deputy chief. *What to do?* he thought.

"If your damn detective hadn't pissed off Channel Six, we wouldn't be in this mess," he said, knowing it wasn't true. It didn't matter. He just wanted to punish Richard Dick. Why shouldn't Dick sweat a little more?

"I've taken care of Detective Jansen," Dick said.

*   *   *

While the mayor and the deputy chief were in their meeting, Detective Jansen was parked in the front drive of the Civic Center Complex, pointing a directional mike at the mayor's window. What he was doing was illegal, but it didn't matter. No one would ever know he had taped all of their conversation. No one would know the juicy things they had committed to his device. No one except the deputy chief and the mayor, that is. And it would certainly come in handy if they tried to get rid of him.

He smiled and drank his Irish coffee.

CHAPTER TWENTY-EIGHT

The phone went silent, and then Maddy Brooks went on the offensive. "Don't start with me, Detective Murphy," she said. "I'm exercising my Constitutional rights to inform the public of a menace. I don't know why I let you all talk me into sitting on the story in the first place."

Jack couldn't believe what he was hearing. "Listen. You approached us. You're not going to change the subject by getting me angry, so tell me the truth. Are you expecting a call from the killer? What haven't you told me, Maddy?"

She was silent. Thinking. Then she said, "Let me interview you for the next segment, and I'll tell you everything I know."

"How about I put your skinny ass in jail and let the lawyers fight it out?"

"You're not a very pleasant man, Detective Murphy."

"Honey, you haven't seen unpleasant yet, but I promise you it's coming," Jack said and broke the connection. He thought about it and then hit redial.

Maddy answered on the first ring. "Is that a yes?" she asked.

* * *

The chief's conference room was still being used to grind down information into usable bits, and so it was not available for the hastily arranged meeting.

Jack looked around Deputy Chief Dick's office and couldn't help but notice the spaciousness and expensive decor. *You could fit the entire detectives' office in here,* he thought. All that was missing were the marble Roman columns outside the doorway, draped with grape leaves. The chief, deputy chief, Captain Franklin, and a smallish woman he assumed was Angelina Garcia were in attendance along with Liddell and himself.

Liddell said, "Jack, this is Detective Angelina Garcia," nodding toward the woman as they were finding their seats.

"I'm not a detective actually," she said, somewhat embarrassed. "I'm a computer technician. Kind of an intelligence gatherer."

"You ought to see her work, Jack," Liddell said enthusiastically, and this time she did blush.

"Well, I think I may have found some things for you," she said.

Before she could tell them what she had, the chief called for quiet.

"You all know of the recent issue with the news media," he began, and everyone became silent with their own thoughts. "Deputy Chief Dick is working with the mayor's office on what to release to the rest of the media at this point, so any further information for the press is to go through him. Is that understood?" Everyone nodded assent.

Liddell leaned toward Jack and whispered, "I bet Double Dick has a woody right now," which earned him a stinging look from Captain Franklin.

"Do you have something to say, Detective Blanchard?" the chief inquired.

"Yes, sir," Liddell said. "I was wondering if Detective Jansen was supposed to attend this meeting, sir."

Jack had to admire his partner. For a big guy, he was fast on his feet.

The chief shook his head. Not a yes. But not a no. "Any other questions?"

"Yes," Jack said, and told them about his conversation with Maddy Brooks ten minutes earlier.

"You should have called me before you committed to that interview," Deputy Chief Dick said, and the red began creeping up his neck.

"This was before I knew you were the PIO . . . sir," Jack replied. PIO stands for public information officer, and Dick was offended immediately that he would be considered to hold such a lowly position.

"Let me remind you, Detective Murphy"—Dick began angrily, then seemed to think better of it and lowered his voice. "I am your superior officer, and if you are to remain on this case you will work through me in the future. Do you have a problem with that?" He sat back haughtily.

"No problem at all, sir," Jack said. This wasn't a battle he needed to be fighting.

Chief Pope interceded and said, "What's done is done. After this meeting, Murphy will get with you, Richard, to go over the details of what he can release to Maddy. Let's get back to the other issues here. This is Technician Garcia." He introduced her around the room. "I've asked her to crunch some information for us, and she may have some answers. Angelina."

She pushed some stapled handouts to the men seated around the conference table. "I didn't have much success with the police files that I started with," she said, "but if you look at the top page of your handouts, you will see that I created some lists of suspect possibilities based on arrests and incidents involving Detective Murphy over the last several years."

Jack noticed how easily she had captured everyone's attention. He also noticed that she wasn't half bad to look at. His handout contained about twenty pages, and he wondered if he had really pissed that many people off over the last several years.

Garcia continued. "If you go down about five pages, you will see that I have copied several news articles from recent years." The men flipped through their handouts, and she continued. "The first article is about the Lamar family. I noticed when I was going through the police records that Jack had worked a domestic violence case against Mrs. Lamar's ex-husband. I found the case file and read it."

"The first victim, Mrs. Anne Lewis, was the court-ordered psychiatrist that was involved in that case. She interviewed Mrs. Lamar, her ex-husband, and the three children. It was because of Anne Lewis's testimony that the ex-husband was convicted and sent away for five years. It was because Jack had gotten Anne involved with the case that this story made the newspaper."

They all looked at the story. The article itself looked like a filler column that was probably buried near the classified ads, but the importance of the story was that there was a photo of Jack inset next to a photo of the ex-husband, and below those a photo of Mrs. Lamar and her three children, one of them an infant.

The story was at least three years old, because the youngest Lamar kid was still a baby. Jack vaguely remembered the case, but even looking at the story and photos it didn't really register.

"You remember this one, Jack?" Pope asked.

"No, sir, not really. Well, maybe. I've worked a lot of cases, sir."

Garcia plowed on. "And the next page is the story about Jack recuperating in the hospital after the shootout at the casino a few months ago."

The men flipped to the next news article that Garcia had photocopied. The caption under the photo read: *Detective Murphy receives care at St. Mary's Hospital after knife attack.* The photo was one of Jack in a wheelchair being pushed by a nurse.

"Shit!" Jack said. "That's Tisha Carter."

CHAPTER TWENTY-NINE

Deputy Chief Dick had stormed from the meeting after ordering Jack not to talk to the news media without consulting him first, and then hurried down the hallway toward the main Civic Center building. Liddell chuckled at the retreating gangly figure.

"What's so funny?" Jack asked.

"Double Dick getting mad and running out of his office," Liddell said and laughed even harder.

"Don't laugh too hard, gentlemen," Captain Franklin said, coming up behind them. "It's not over yet." Franklin told the men to meet him in the chief's complex in five minutes, then stepped back into the meeting room with the chief and closed the door.

"How does the captain do that?" Liddell whispered. "One minute he's not there, and the next minute he's right on top of you. Spooky, that's what it is."

Jack wasn't concerned about Franklin. He was worried about what Franklin had said. Chief Pope had looked worried, and Franklin had been complacent during their meeting. That wasn't in the nature of either of them. The only thing Jack could deduce from their behavior and the aggressive behavior of Double Dick was something that he couldn't bear thinking about. *Chief Double Dick,* Jack thought, then pushed the thought away. His dad had taught him that you don't worry about things you have no control over. But if he had a chance, he would deep-six any plans Double Dick had of becoming chief of police.

He and Liddell headed for the next meeting. More and more, that was what police work was becoming. A bunch of meetings with people who had nothing more to worry about than what the news media was going to say. It was no wonder the older cops were retiring in droves.

"How bad is it?" Franklin asked Chief Pope.

Pope was seated at Deputy Chief Dick's desk, and Franklin sat on the edge of the big desk. Pope looked at his detective captain and wondered what would happen when they had both been replaced by the mayor's men. Well, at least Captain Franklin was safe as far as rank and pay were concerned, since captain was a merit system rank. His own position as chief was less tenable, however, and he would go back to his former rank of lieutenant when he was no longer the chief.

The irony of it was he had never been interested in making rank, so he had stopped testing at the rank of lieutenant. Then he had been appointed by the previous mayor to the position of chief of police. In the ten years he had held the position, he had never been inclined to test for rank. Now he would pay for that.

But his thirty-plus years on the department had been good for the most part, and he had no big regrets. He could step down while he was still the chief and pull the pin on his badge—retire. *But what about these poor guys?* he thought.

"Charles," he said, always opting to use first names when

they were alone, "this is what's going to happen." And he told Captain Franklin what he knew of the mayor's plan. When he was finished, he took a deep breath and asked, "Would you like to be reassigned anywhere while I still have the authority to do it?"

Franklin shook his head. "Believe it or not, I still have faith in these guys," he said more confidently than he felt.

"I've got faith, too," Pope said. "But the cold facts are that Hensley is going to replace me regardless of the outcome of this case."

Franklin was silent. He knew Pope was right.

Garcia had given them their first solid connection in these cases, but it wasn't one that Jack would have preferred. It was bad enough when he suspected the killings were aimed at him, but now it appeared that these particular victims had been targeted because of their connection to him in the news media.

They were back in the chief's conference room, and Garcia had put a city map up on one wall. Over this she had pinned a clear sheet of plastic. All the locations of the murders were marked with red grease pencil. Jack started to correct her, to tell her that the actual scene of Timmy Ryan's death was where the fishing rod was found and that Timmy Ryan's body had been carried to the place it was found, but he didn't want to interrupt her thought process.

"And down the side here I've put pictures of the victims along with a few photos of the scenes," she said. "I thought this would help you visualize the cases as a whole instead of individually."

Liddell put his arm around her thin shoulders. "I love this little gal," he said with a grin.

"Don't break her, Liddell," Jack said.

"Sorry," he said, and sat down.

Garcia pointed to another display. This one was complete with photocopies of the notes that had been received by Maddy Brooks at Channel Six and those found with the bodies.

"These are the notes. As you can see, the notes sent to Maddy Brooks are slightly more complete than the ones found with the bodies."

"He likes her," Liddell suggested.

"Well, I think it might be deeper than that," Garcia said, and then stopped as if she had overstepped her duties. "I mean, I had some, uh, thoughts on something else."

"Go ahead, Angelina," Jack said.

"Call me Garcia," she said, then, "Well, this is going to sound crazy."

"This whole thing is crazy," Jack reminded her. "Go ahead."

She picked up one of the Mother Goose books that Jack had gotten from Katie and flipped to the back where there was a foldout map of Mother Goose Land. "I found this in the back of this book and, well, it struck me as kind of, I don't know, kind of important."

Jack and Liddell looked at the colorful map complete with characters, houses, Humpty Dumpty's great fall, haystacks, and all the other rhymes in Mother Goose's world come to life. Jack saw what she meant in a heartbeat.

"Can we blow that up to a bigger size?" he asked her.

She reached behind her and unrolled a poster-sized transparency copy of the map. She then put the transparency over the city map marked with all the scenes, and it all came together.

There at the top of the map was Punch and Judy, not quite directly over the house of Anne and Don Lewis, but close enough. Near Jack's cabin was the setting where Tommy Tittlemouse was fishing in a large ditch. The Old Woman in a Shoe was to the west.

"Where's Little Nancy Etticoat?" Liddell asked. He had caught on easily.

"Yeah," Garcia said sadly, "that's where I kind of lost my idea."

Jack had been studying the map. He said to Liddell, "Do you have the address for Tisha Carter? Her home address?"

Garcia pointed to the lists of victims and witnesses she had pinned to the board. "Her address is in those apartments near Green River Road and Bellemeade Avenue," she said.

Jack lifted the Mother Goose map, found Tisha's apartment on the city map, and marked it with the grease pencil. When he overlaid the Mother Goose map on the city map, Tisha's apartment location showed through, but there was nothing on the Mother Goose map associated with it.

"Wow!" Liddell remarked. "Why didn't I think of that?"

"Bite me," Jack said, then, "Sorry, Garcia."

"If you hadn't said it, I would have," she said, surprising both men.

CHAPTER THIRTY

"He says you are to go right in," the mayor's secretary said to the angry deputy chief.

Dick ignored her and pushed through the mayor's inner office door. "You've got to appoint me now, Thatcher," he said.

Mayor Thatcher Hensley sat behind his desk and leaned back in his comfortable leather chair, a smile playing on his lips. He was used to the deputy chief's tirades. He also knew that Chief Pope was currently occupying the deputy chief's office space after lending his own several offices to the investigative team working on the recent slayings. He had to hand it to Pope. It was a gutsy move to kick Dick out of his own office. But he knew what Richard Dick had overlooked. He knew that it was the move of a desperate man. Pope knew he was out on the plank, and all it would take is one small shove.

"Calm yourself, Richard," he said. "Have a seat."

Dick hated it when the mayor was condescending like this, and that was exactly how he took the mayor's cool and calm demeanor when everything they had planned was going to hell. He wondered again how he could have ever tied his career to this priggish, spoiled, rich kid.

"Well, you won't be calm when you hear the chief's new plan, Thatcher. I can tell you that," Dick said hotly.

Mayor Hensley leaned forward, elbows on his desktop, fingers steepled. "Tell me."

"What the hell do you mean, she won't interview me?" Thatcher Hensley yelled.

Deputy Chief of Police Richard Dick smirked at his boss. He was glad to see the man humbled, even if it was just a little. *Now who needs to remain calm?* But it was not a time to gloat. It was important that they regain control of the situation.

"Thatcher, she's just one station. We still have good contacts with the other television, print, and radio media," Dick said.

"Just one station!" Thatcher yelled. "She's got the goddamn exclusive on this," he blustered, "and it's your fault, Dick! It's all your fault!"

"Now wait a minute. I'm not the only one that decided to let her tag along with Murphy," Dick protested. He could see where this was going, and he didn't need the mayor looking for plausible deniability by making a "scorched earth" scenario out of a plan that was still salvageable.

He looked at Mayor Thatcher Hensley. He had known Thatcher's father, Thatcher Hensley Senior. Senior was almost as tall as Dick was, with a muscular frame and dark Hollywood looks. He'd been successful in everything he had tried and had made a fortune in the steel industry before getting involved in politics. He'd served four consecutive terms as mayor by popular vote.

Thatcher Junior must have been a true disappointment to his dad. He had none of the old man's looks and seemed to be the antithesis of his father, this most recent outburst only proving what a loser young Thatcher was.

Thatcher's lower lip was trembling, and he nervously rubbed at a spot over his right eye that had developed a nervous tic.

"We can still come out of this all right," Dick said, and the mayor's face eagerly turned toward him. "I've got control of any media releases now, *and,*" he stressed, "I've got control of the investigation as well."

The mayor's face turned dark, and he said, "How the hell does that help us?"

Dick spoke in a conspiratorial tone. "We let Murphy do his damn interview."

The mayor looked dumbfounded. "I thought that was something we wanted to avoid, Richard."

"Trust me," Dick said and smiled. "By the time this is over, you will be able to fire both Murphy and Pope."

The television stage lights were hot. Jack felt a trickle of sweat running down his neck as he sat alone, onstage, while a dozen or so people rushed about the newsroom like their asses were on fire. Jack noticed that Maddy Brooks seemed to be the only person in the room unaffected by the frantic atmosphere. He watched her going over last-minute directions with the two cameramen, marking a correction, giving instructions, nodding. While she was in her element here, he was nervous.

He'd given dozens of interviews to the news media in his career, but they were mostly impromptu, on the spot, and he was usually more confident. He had never been in the television station until recently and wasn't prepared for the "hurry up and wait" attitude.

He'd arrived exactly on time and had been instructed to sit in one of the chairs behind the news counter. The chairs looked comfortable, but in reality they were so worn with use that the seats were lumpy and hard, and he didn't want to think of the sorts of "funk" he was sitting in.

A station flunky had rushed over to him "to get him ready," and Jack had refused both makeup and a bottle of water. Ten minutes later, under the hot lights, he now wished he had taken the water. If they didn't get this interview over soon, he would melt into a little puddle.

Maddy came over exuding phony gratitude and sat in the chair next to him. The stage set was divided into two areas by the long, curved, desktop. To Jack's right was the main stage where the news anchor team would start the session, and then the cameras would commit to Jack and Maddy. Or, at least, this is what Jack imagined.

"You look great, Jack," Maddy said, smoothing his jacket lapels and repositioning his clip-on microphone.

He wanted to say "bite me" and get up and leave, but it was too late. The lights came up to full intensity and then dimmed, and one of the cameras cued to the main stage. Clark Jameson and Tonya Simpson, the Channel Six news team, were smiling their postcoital smiles at no one.

"Showtime," Maddy whispered to Jack and patted his hand.

CHAPTER THIRTY-ONE

Thatcher Hensley sat in his conference room with Deputy Chief Dick and Chief Pope, all of the men watching the wall-mounted plasma screen intently.

The news announcer said, *"You're watching Channel Six television. All the news, all the time."*

"You know this is crazy, don't you?" Chief Pope said to Dick.

"What? You don't have confidence in your own man?" Dick responded. The mayor stared at the screen, ignoring the talk.

"Did you even get an outline of the questions they're going to ask Murphy?" the chief asked.

Dick grinned. "You can't really think Murphy will stick to the questions," he said and looked back at the television as the faces of the Channel Six news team filled the screen.

Pope wished he could put a stop to this, but the mayor seemed in total support of Dick. *Still.*

"Mayor Hensley, I really don't think this is the way to do this, sir," Pope said.

Hensley ignored him, and then it was too late.

The news announcer said, *"And now for the news."*

A strikingly handsome and smiling face filled the screen. *"Hello, I'm Clark Jameson."* Then Jameson's face was replaced by an equally striking woman's face. The smile on her face was practiced, but no less pleasing for it. *"And I'm Tonya Simpson. Tonight, our own Maddy Brooks is bringing you more on the Mother Goose killings. With her, to tell the story in his own words, is Detective Jack Murphy, the chief investigator assigned to these horrendous murders. Maddy?"*

The camera angle changed and zoomed in on Maddy Brooks. She jumped right into the story.

"With me tonight is one of the Evansville Police Department's most decorated officers, Detective Jack Murphy."

The camera panned out, now showing both Maddy and Jack Murphy. His expression was deadpan, his message to the viewers an obvious "I was forced to come here." Maddy smiled and continued.

"Detective Murphy has been kind enough to come into the station to answer questions about the string of recent murders committed by the sadistic killer the investigators have dubbed 'Mother Goose.'"

The camera panned in for a full-face shot of Jack. He looked barely restrained but said nothing.

The camera panned back to Maddy Brooks.

"Well, uh, Detective Murphy. Can you tell us how many murders you have attributed to the Mother Goose killer?"

The screen filled with Jack's face, and he leaned forward slightly, looking stern.

"First of all, Maddy, your television station came up with the name 'Mother Goose.'"

Off-camera, Maddy's smile slipped, her face flushed with embarrassment and anger.

"Maddy, the Evansville Police Department is currently

investigating numerous homicides of which we believe some share a commonality. But we haven't said that any of these were committed by one individual or set of persons. This information was something that you came up with in your last broadcast and, quite frankly, I don't know where you got it."

The camera panned back to Maddy, who was struggling to overcome her anger.

Maddy looked toward the director, then back into the camera.

"Detective Murphy, don't you feel that our viewers deserve to know all there is to know about a psychotic killer that is loose among them?"

Jack looked away from his camera and directly at Maddy Brooks.

"Maddy, I believe the public has a right to protection by their law enforcement officials. And that includes protection from an unscrupulous news media that wants to raise their ratings by causing panic and chaos." Maddy tried to talk over him, but Jack had turned back to his camera and continued.

"Ladies and gentlemen, please don't be used by these people. I assure you that when we, your police, have something to release to you, or if we feel that there is something we can tell you to better protect yourselves, then Marlin Pope, our chief of police, will release the information to *all* of the media"—he stressed the word *all*—"and not just to one station that is trying to scoop everyone else."

While Jack was speaking, Bill Goldberg was standing and looking dumbfounded, and Maddy Brooks was looking angry. But Clark Jameson and Tonya Simpson seemed to be enjoying the show, since it was not at their expense.

"As far as the name Mother Goose is concerned, you may have something, Maddy. Who knows? Maybe his mommy or daddy didn't love him. Maybe he was sexually abused by the family dog. Maybe he didn't get a Game Boy when he was little. Sick people do sick things. But we will catch the killer. We always do."

The director was frantically waving his arms for the cameraman's attention, then making slashing motions across his throat. "Go to commercial. Go to commercial!" the director yelled, and an advertisement for some new piece of personal workout equipment guaranteed to give you tighter butt muscles in one week came on the television screen.

Back in the mayor's conference room, a shocked Marlin Pope looked down at his hands. His career was over. So was Jack's.

The cheap television set exploded against the floor of Eddie's room. He stomped back and forth through the rubble, crushing the pieces under his heavy camo boots.

"Sadistic?" he screamed. "Psychotic?" He picked up the broken television tube and threw it through the window. "Did you hear that bastard, Bobby?" But Bobby just sat on the edge of the bed, unconcerned.

"I shoulda killed that bitch!" Eddie spat the words out and looked angrily at Bobby. "Why didn't you let me, Bobby? What's wrong with you, man? All you ever do is tell me to do shit. You don't do anything, bro. Know what I mean? When are you gonna step up, man?"

His anger had boiled over and was starting to cool. He knew it wasn't Bobby's fault. It was Murphy's fault. Hell, Murphy hadn't been angry. Or scared. "I'll make him scared, Bobby," he said through clenched teeth. "I'll make them all scared."

Someone started banging on the door to his room. He could see through the shattered window that it was one of the Indians that owned the place. They had probably already called the police. He grabbed his duffel bag and looked around the shitty room. Nothing he could do about finger-prints now.

He kicked the door open in the startled woman's face and knocked her to the ground. He delivered another kick to her face, then stomped her head repeatedly until she stopped moving. He hoped he had killed her, but there wasn't time to hang around. They had to move.

Jack walked into the detectives' squad room to the deafening sound of applause and cheering. Several uniformed officers and civilian employees had come to greet him as well. He couldn't have felt worse.

He had ended the interview at Channel Six by getting up, yanking his microphone from his jacket, and walking off camera. It had been a soul-cleansing experience, having the last word with the likes of Maddy Brooks, but it had been career suicide, and he was afraid that it would cost more than just his career by the time the dust settled.

Double Dick had set him up, and he'd played right into the devil's hands. At first he had been glad that Dick hadn't shown up at the station, and then he became a little angry that he was being left there to field questions that should have been answered by the administrative types. But it had all been a trap. Dick had expected Jack's temper and arro-gance would get him in trouble. Hell, he'd been counting on it.

Jack looked around the room at the brightly smiling faces, but instead of supporters and friends, he saw a pack of hounds baying and gnashing teeth. In a way, what he'd done, and the way these professionals had reacted to his behavior, was no different than the animalistic behavior he'd just ac-cused the news media of displaying. Like a crowd cheering on a fight, except the crowd wouldn't be bloodied or bruised by the encounter. And in Jack's book, that made them all cowards. They wanted to see the bloodshed, but at a distance. He shut the door on their surprised looks and their calls for him to join them and walked to the chief's complex.

In the chief's conference room, he found Liddell and Angelina Garcia huddled around her computer screen.

"Jack, you've got to see this!" Liddell said and moved back to let Jack stand behind Garcia.

Jack was relieved that no one was asking questions or talking about what he'd just done at Channel Six.

Garcia had created a map on the computer. She punched a key, and the Mother Goose Land map was layered over the city map. Jack didn't see the significance at first. This is the same stuff they had already done on the wall maps. Then she highlighted only the nursery rhyme locations. She struck another key, and the computer generated a dotted line, traveling from the first rhyme to the second and so on, and when the line was complete the computer had drawn the shape of a five-point star, a pentagram.

"I programmed parameters into a search engine that would instruct the computer to ignore any correlates outside the city limits, with a secondary set of instructions that if a correlate was outside the city it would search for any secondary correlates for that particular piece of data. The program was searching for recognizable patterns including geometrical patterns and . . ." Jack put a hand on her shoulder.

"I didn't understand anything you just said, Garcia. But I can see the star. Good work," he said and smiled at her when she looked up.

Liddell smiled at him, leaned in to Jack's ear, and whispered, "She's single, Jack."

"Would you grow up?" Jack said, pushing him back.

"Besides, I might be gay," Garcia said from across the room.

Both men looked at her. "She's got good hearing, too, pod'na," Jack said.

"But I'm not gay," Garcia said hurriedly. "So don't repeat that."

Captain Franklin stuck his head in the doorway and said, "Jack. A minute," and disappeared again.

"Try not to stick your other foot in your mouth while I'm gone," Jack said to Liddell and went to see the captain.

Liddell yelled after him, "You don't have to talk without an attorney present!" Then to Garcia, he said, "If they fire him, I'm quitting."

She looked sympathetic, then curious. "Is he always so brash? Jack, I mean. You know, telling that reporter off like that." Liddell didn't answer, and she continued. "Not that he wasn't right. But I would never have the nerve to do something like that."

Liddell looked at her and smiled. "Nerve is one thing Jack has plenty of, darlin'."

CHAPTER THIRTY-TWO

Eddie drove the van to the North Park Shopping Center and left it in the busiest part of the parking lot. The van was stolen and so were the plates, but not from Evansville, where someone might accidentally find it. The cops in this town were so stupid they would never get him anyway. The only thing he'd done to attract attention so far was beating up that dumb shit at the motel. He'd told Bobby that the cops weren't going to give a shit if some Indian broad got clobbered, what with 9/11 and all that. But Bobby looked pale, and had not said a word since they left the motel except to criticize Eddie for losing his temper.

He had never parked the van at the motel, opting instead to park on a nearby residential street and walk. And he had never used his real name anywhere he stayed. But just to be safe, Eddie decided to leave the van somewhere for a while until he heard the news. See if the cops were looking for him or the van.

He hit on the idea of riding the city bus for a while until he could come up with a plan. No one would pay attention to him on the bus, and he wouldn't have to worry about moving the van until later in the evening, when the lots started clearing off. It wouldn't do to have some nosy cop poking around and running the license plates. He still needed the wheels for a while.

It was a good idea, even if Bobby didn't like it. The only drawback being that a lot of creeps rode the bus. He wondered where the hell they all came from.

CHAPTER THIRTY-THREE

Jack had come back agitated and sulking after his meeting with Captain Franklin. Then, in true Jack Murphy style, he immersed himself in work until, after several hours of bitching and moaning, Liddell finally threatened to handcuff Jack unless he went with him to eat. Bigfoot was getting hungry, and it was getting late.

Liddell drove the unmarked Crown Vic east on the Lloyd Expressway while Jack rode in silence. "Guess I'd better speed up a little," Liddell said, getting no response. "We're supposed to meet the girls at seven, right?" Jack silently stared out the passenger window.

Traffic was light, so Liddell crept up to sixty-five in the fifty-five zone, hoping the troops would recognize his unmarked sedan and not give him any grief. It was almost seven o'clock, and he had promised Marcie they would be there at seven o'clock sharp.

"So Double Dick is really the chief now?" Liddell said in disbelief.

Jack grunted in reply, not wanting to think about it anymore. When Franklin had asked to see him that afternoon, he would never have guessed that it was to tell him that Dick was assuming the reins as police chief. Marlin Pope had taken vacation and was waiting to be reassigned, or if the rumors were to be believed, possibly retire.

The news of the chief being replaced shoved Mother Goose out of the limelight, and the "hastily arranged" press conference was so elaborate that it must have been planned for years. The press conference was held in front of the Civic Center that evening, and the incoming chief, Richard Dick, had assured the public that his primary focus would be on catching the killer. When asked if the police had any leads on the murders, Dick responded by blaming Marlin Pope for "dropping the ball."

Jack had always known it was a possibility that Chief Pope would be replaced by the incoming mayor's appointee. But it was also just as easy to believe that a plane would drop from out of the sky on top of him. And the longer the new mayor hesitated in removing Pope and replacing him with Double Dick, the more relaxed Jack had become. It had been two years, halfway through the mayor's term, and it just didn't make sense to change horses in midstream, so to speak.

But what really bothered Jack was the thought that his interview at Channel Six might have been the straw that broke the camel's back. He would never forgive himself if he was the reason Hensley had replaced Pope with a media whore like Double Dick.

Although his own mood was somber, Liddell seemed to be in good spirits, as he thumped out a beat on the steering wheel.

"What are you so happy about?" Jack said.

Liddell looked at him and grinned. "I'm not happy. I'm just not unhappy."

Jack was unhappy. Liddell continued to thump on the wheel, and it was getting annoying. "You want to stop that?" Jack said, grumpily.

"Don't you like Bon Jovi?" Liddell said, and then started singing loudly while Jack stared out the window.

When they pulled up outside the Olive Garden restaurant, Liddell spotted Marcie's car with Marcie and Susan standing beside it.

"Hello, girls," Liddell said, and then put his arm around his wife.

"You look beat," Susan said to Jack as they all entered the restaurant.

"That good, huh?"

Susan knew what was bothering him, but she also knew that Jack wouldn't talk until he was ready.

Sunset Park covered a sprawling ten acres of riverfront along the east side of the Evansville Museum. Before Eddie went to prison, it was nothing more than woods, trails, and a couple of outhouses. Now the wooded areas had been thinned out, eliminating the need for trails, and the outhouses had been replaced with restroom facilities like you saw along the interstates. There was also a playground for the kiddies called Kids' Kingdom.

While Eddie was still inside, he had talked to a couple of junkies from Evansville that told him two cops had been responsible for raising the money and supplies to build it.

Wouldn't they just love to see what I'm going to do with it? he thought, and had to smile as he spotted the perfect place to leave the next body.

The stray cat's neck snapped like a twig in Eddie's strong hands. He liked cats, but he needed the blood, and Kids' Kingdom seemed to attract the scarred-up tomcats like catnip, so there was no shortage of targets.

He'd brought a knapsack with him and had three other

dead cats stowed away in it near the monkey bars. Taking a folding Buck knife from his pocket, he slashed the throat of the cat he was holding upside down by the tail and let the blood drip, creating a trail down the narrow sidewalk between the teeter-totter and the swing set, past the jungle gym made to look like a castle with turrets and murder holes, leading to the monkey bars. He smeared the last of the drained cat's blood on the note he pulled from a pocket and dropped the cat.

He stuck the note to the upright wooden post of the monkey bars with the Buck knife. He then hung all the cats by their necks from the monkey bars and was about to leave when he heard the voice behind him say, "Mister, you shouldn't do that to them kitties."

Eddie was startled. He had been so caught up in his work that he hadn't noticed anyone approaching. From what he could see, the boy looked no older than fifteen.

"I'm playing a joke on a friend," Eddie said to the boy.

The boy was very fair of hair and skin. Even in the darkness he seemed to glow with the vitality of youth, and Eddie knew at that moment he would kill him.

"What you doing out here at night?" Eddie asked the boy.

The kid didn't even blush. He looked Eddie in the eye and said, "I need money. I come here to make money for me and my mom."

Eddie had spent a lot of his youth in prison. He'd seen these punks before, just not this young. It infuriated him that this kid was coming on to him. But the way the kid talked and looked made him think of a rhyme from the Mother Goose book.

"Monday's child," Eddie said, and the boy looked querulous. "That's what I'm naming you," Eddie explained.

"Whatever, mister," the boy said.

"Monday's child is fair of face," Eddie said sweetly, "but

the child born on the Sabbath day is bonny and blithe and good and . . . *gay*."

It was getting nasty out, drizzling rain and threatening to storm. The boy just wanted to make a few bucks for some smokes and then head home.

"Mister, it's starting to rain. You want something from me or not?"

"Yes," Eddie answered. "I certainly do."

The corn knife slashed down.

CHAPTER THIRTY-FOUR

Jack had left the Olive Garden and drove straight to his cabin. Alone. He didn't have the energy or desire for love-making with Susan, and admitting that to himself was just another failure. He'd been unable to keep any meaningful relationship for long, and had justified this by feeling that his work was important and meaningful. But what had he really done? The Lewises were dead. Timmy Ryan and Elaine Lamar's children were all dead. He'd been impotent to stop the killer, and there was no miracle drug, like Viagra or Cialis, to aid him with that.

Jack slept fitfully for less than four hours when the call came in from dispatch. Another body had been found. Jack dressed and picked Liddell up at home, making his apologies to a yawning Marcie, and they drove in silence toward the scene. Liddell was subdued for a change, and that was demoralizing as well.

The crime scene mobile unit was already on scene, and a uniformed officer strung yellow caution tape across the parking lot entrance to the park behind their car. Halogen lamps were set up on tripods and plugged in to the power generator on the mobile unit. When the lights came on, Jack looked in horror at the scene in front of him.

Almost every surface of the playground equipment was smeared with dark stains that could only be blood, and still looked wet in the harsh lights. Crime scene techs snapped photos from every angle as they worked their way toward the center of the scene where the body of what appeared to be a young boy was hanging by the neck from the center bar of the monkey bars. He was cadaverously thin, face twisted into a surprised look, and his bare feet were not touching the ground. What appeared to be a pile of clothing lay under his naked body, and on top of that his insides had spilled out. On both sides of him, hanging from the other bars, were the carcasses of cats, all strangled, like the boy. All gutted, like the boy, with their entrails hanging down.

Jack turned his back on the scene and took some deep breaths. As he looked toward Waterworks Road, he could see the lights of Two-Jakes restaurant in the distance. His cabin was only another mile or so downriver from there. This was the second murder that had been committed almost in his backyard.

Kids' Kingdom had been opened to the public less than a year ago. It was the brainchild of two Evansville policemen, both with children, who had taken it upon themselves to raise the money, material, and support to build a playground safe for children and parents alike. This particular patch of ground had been home to "night people" for years and was known as "Blow-job Alley" for as long as Jack could remember. It had been a hangout for dopers, sexual deviants, and the insane.

But Kids' Kingdom had changed that. The trees had been cleared to make room for swing sets, jungle gyms, seesaws, and other playground equipment. Although the city of Evansville had donated the property for the project, it had been slow with assistance in the form of utilities. Port-a-

johns were finally replaced with a nice restroom facility, but
there was still no lighting except in the parking area. The
current mayor, Thatcher Hensley, had cited budget concerns
as the holdup in getting adequate lights in the area. This
coming from a man who had run for election on a platform
of crime prevention.

Liddell walked up beside Jack and stood stiffly, rubbing
at the back of his neck. "He's not human," Liddell muttered.

"I demand to be let in," said a voice from the parking
area, and when Jack turned he saw Maddy Brooks and a
cameraman attempting to get through the caution tape.

Jack wasn't sure how she had managed to get that close to
the crime scene, but something in him snapped and he acted
without thinking.

"Don't do it, Jack!" Liddell yelled, grabbing at Jack's
coat sleeve but missing.

Jack reached the yellow tape, grabbed Maddy's arm, and
dragged her underneath. "You want to see this up close?
Okay! You got it, lady!"

Maddy came willingly the first few yards, but then, upon
seeing the grisly scene at the monkey bars, turned her head
away and tried to stop. But Jack still had her arm and dragged
her to within feet of the dangling body whose intestines
hung to the ground. She pulled her eyes away and looked
around at the gutted cats. Her shoe kicked something soft,
and when she looked down, she was standing on the man-
gled remains of yet another cat. This one had been partially
skinned with flaps of fur stuck to the meat.

"Oh my God!" she moaned. She tried to yank her arm away,
but Jack held on tightly, and shoved her toward the boy's body.

"Go on," he yelled, "take a good look! You need all the
facts. Go on. I said look, damn you!"

He let go, and Maddy fled toward the yellow tape with
one hand over her mouth, the other clutching her stomach,

and made retching sounds. Jack didn't care. *In for a penny, in for a pound.* He was almost certainly going to be taken off the case or suspended, or both, anyway, so he may as well go out with style.

Liddell caught up with Jack and moved in front of him, trying to block the cameraman's view. "Jesus, Jack," he said. "What's got into you, pod'na?"

Jack was embarrassed, but he was still angry. "I've got to leave before I go over there and shove that camera up her ass."

"Come on, Jack, don't let them get to you," Liddell was saying, just as one of the crime scene technicians came up.

"Jack, you'd better come take a look at this," said the tech.

Jack was still examining the body when Captain Franklin arrived at the scene. Franklin walked up to the detectives and said, "What happened with her?" He jerked a thumb over his shoulder indicating Maddy Brooks, who was being comforted by her cameraman. He seemed to ignore the grisly scene in front of him, as if a boy and some cats mutilated and hanging from monkey bars were an everyday sight.

"You don't want to know, Captain," Jack assured him, knowing that Maddy would get her pound of flesh from him later. "But take a look at this."

Captain Franklin moved around to the back of the body, where Jack and Liddell were standing, and the crime scene tech shined a bright flashlight on the boy's back. Carved into the boy's flesh were the letters:

    Jack

"Ahh, shit!" Franklin said and looked away.

* * *

Eddie slept. In his dream he was in his old room, in his old bed. A part of his mind knew that was impossible because the house had burnt up with the preacher still in it. But here he was, in his room, in his bed, listening. Listening closely. He knew the noise would come, and his heart thundered in his chest.

Where is Bobby? his dreaming mind wondered. Why isn't he in the room? But then he remembered that the preacher had locked them both in the basement and had let only Eddie out to confess his sins. And Bobby had been left in the dark, dirt-floored basement with the spiders and other creepy stuff, but Eddie had been told to go to his room, where the preacher said he would be along shortly to administer his punishment.

Eddie waited for his punishment to come. He'd been a bad boy because the preacher had caught him and Eddie reading from a Mother Goose book instead of the Good Book during one of the preacher's daily services. The preacher hadn't punished them right on the spot, in front of his tiny congregation. He'd waited until the service was over, and then he'd shaken hands with everyone and smiled and told them how much he appreciated them coming to listen to the Lord's message, and how he would pray for all of them. And then when the congregation members were all out of the little one-room church attached to the preacher's two-bedroom house, he and Bobby had been led painfully by their ears to the basement's trapdoor hidden behind the pulpit. The preacher had made Eddie yank the door open, and both boys had been shoved brutally into the darkness below.

Eddie waited and remembered how he hated the preacher, how he wanted to kill him, how Bobby promised they'd get even one day, and he was about to remember something else when he heard the sound he'd been dreading.

The creak of the stairs was sharp in the darkness of his room, and he wondered why it was so dark. Is it always this dark? he wondered, but he couldn't remember.

There came the sound of metal on metal, something turn-ing, the doorknob, the latch to his door. His heart pounded so hard his chest hurt, and he wanted to scream but he couldn't.

"Wake up, bro. Wake up, man," Bobby said, and Eddie snapped out of the dream. His hands shook. He was embar-rassed to find he had an erection, and he wondered what the fuck was wrong with him. He hoped Bobby wouldn't notice he had a hard-on, and he shoved his hands into his lap.

"You were dreaming about the preacher again, weren't you?" Bobby said. "You were dreaming about what he did to you. What *he* made *us* do to him."

Eddie pounded his fists on his thighs and began to cry.

The old man and his dog were in the back of a police cruiser. He was petting the dog's head and muttering sooth-ing things to the little Jack Russell terrier. The dog seemed calmer than the man.

Jack was surprised to see it was the same old gentleman who'd found the body of Timothy Ryan.

"This guy should play the lottery," Liddell said.

"This would not be an example of good luck," Jack re-sponded. "If it was the lottery, he'd probably get a ticket that said he owed them money."

"Yeah. Guess you're right. By the way, his name is Duke Gibson," Liddell said.

"The dog or the man?" Jack said, and then added, "Never mind. Bad joke."

Jack opened the back passenger door of the police car and leaned down to scrub the dog's head. "Mr. Gibson, I'm Detec-tive Murphy. You remember my partner, Liddell Blanchard?"

The man nodded his head straight up and down and tried to swallow. "What's going to happen to me?" he asked ner-vously.

Liddell straightened up so the old man wouldn't see him

smiling. Jack looked at the man and said, "Mr. Gibson, this is a very serious police matter, and I expect you to tell us everything you know."

"What'll happen to me then?" he asked.

"Then the police officer here"—Jack pointed to the uniformed officer whose car they were using—"will take you and your dog home. I don't want you coming back down here until we catch whoever did this. Do you understand, Mr. Gibson?"

"Yes, sir. Yes, sir, I understand, and I thank you for not taking me in, Detective Murphy. You're a good man. Thank you, sir."

Jack straightened up and grinned at Liddell. "You want to do the honors again?" he asked.

Liddell theatrically rubbed his hands together and said in a high-pitched voice, "Oh, I'll get him, my pretty—and his little dog, too."

Jack shook his head and walked off to interview the uniformed officers and anyone else that had information about this, which included two fire paramedic units, an ambulance crew, neighbors living around the area, dispatchers, and the original call taker. It would be a long morning.

His cell phone rang, and it was Liddell.

"The old man said his dog was acting funny, then took off running ahead of him. By the time he caught up with the dog on the playground, he said the dog was carrying something around in its mouth."

"Let me guess," Jack said. "A dead cat."

"Yeah."

"Better tell the crime scene guys that there may be dog hair contaminating the scene," Jack said.

"I'll do it," Liddell said and hung up.

What a cluster fuck, Jack thought.

CHAPTER THIRTY-FIVE

Captain Dewey Duncan was sixty-three years old and had been a policeman for forty-two of those years. He'd never been a detective, or even a good street cop, but he'd been good where it mattered. And that was at taking tests. He could memorize almost anything set in front of him, so testing for promotion had been simple. But by the time he reached the rank of captain, he realized that if he tried to go any further he would have too much responsibility, and that was something he avoided like death itself.

When he'd come to the attention of Deputy Chief Richard Dick, he was working as the "accreditation commander" for the police department. No one really knew what an accreditation commander did, so he had been able to slip into that netherworld of invisible employees that he had longed for. He drew a captain's pay and did whatever pleased him. It didn't get any better than that. Or at least that's what he thought until he was approached by Richard Dick.

Dick had offered him a position as "administrative assistant," not if, but when, Dick became the chief of police. He'd been assured that his job would be simple and that he would act as personal driver for the chief. Dewey Duncan knew how treacherous Double Dick could be, but he believed an old saying of Winston Churchill's that went "*Keep your friends close, but keep your enemies closer.*" He'd made a habit of placating everyone inside his sphere of influence and especially those who had influence over him. With Dick's offer he knew he'd hit the mother lode.

Now he was wearing his dress blues with all his meritorious decorations and driving the new chief, Richard Dick, to the scene of a homicide. The only thought that troubled him was that he'd never actually seen a homicide, or a dead person for that matter, if you didn't count his Aunt Lucy, whom he'd accidentally found after she died in her sleep. He'd been living in her attic for his first few years on the force and had gone down for breakfast and couldn't wake her. From that point on, he knew he wanted nothing to do with real police work. He'd come a long way.

He stopped the unmarked sedan outside the yellow caution tape and hurried out to open the door for the chief. He fervently hoped he would not be required to go any farther.

"Uh oh," Liddell said, causing Jack and the captain to look up from the body.

"Let me take care of this, gentlemen," Franklin said and walked toward the approaching figure of the newly appointed chief of police, Richard Dick.

Jack watched as Double Dick strutted toward them and was once again reminded of how much Dick resembled a flamingo, or perhaps Don Quixote, with his tall and gangly body, protruding Adam's apple, beak nose, and skinny legs. As Double Dick stooped to go under the yellow caution tape, Jack decided he looked more like a flamingo dipping for a tasty fish.

"We just got Dick'd," Liddell said with not quite a smirk.

"This isn't going to be pretty," Jack said, seeing Chief

Dick walk right past the captain, making a beeline for the two detectives.

"Just what part of 'orders' do you not understand, Detective Murphy?" Dick said, drawing himself up to his full height. He didn't let Jack answer. "I specifically told you that you were not to have any more contact with the media without my presence, did I not?"

Jack wondered which contact with the media he was referring to. The botched interview at Channel Six, or the abuse of Maddy Brooks here? He said nothing because he knew that Dick didn't really want an answer. Dick wanted his head.

"I was told by my driver that Maddy Brooks called, almost hysterical, complaining about your behavior here," Dick said.

"I can explain that, Chief," Liddell said, but Dick gave him a cautioning look.

Captain Franklin caught up with them, but Dick directed his question at Murphy. "Were you not aware that I was in charge of this case, Detective Murphy?"

"Yes sir, I am aware of that," Jack said, looking him directly in the eye.

"Then why did you go to this crime scene without contacting me first? Or without contacting me at all, for that matter?" Dick asked, and when Jack didn't respond immediately, he added, "Well, Detective Murphy, I'm waiting for an answer."

"Chief, it's partly my fault," Franklin said, trying to intercede.

"Captain, if that is true, then you will suffer the same fate as your stooge here," Dick said, almost spitting the words out.

Franklin started to interrupt, but Jack spoke up. "It's not anyone's fault, Captain. I was just doing my job. It's what we do."

Chief Dick's eyes seemed to bulge in their sockets. His

mouth drew into a tight line. "It may be what you 'did,' but it is not what you will do as long as I'm chief."

Jack clenched his jaw, trying to keep his mouth shut, and Dick saw it. Couldn't let it go. "Do you have something else to say, Detective Murphy?"

Oh well, Jack thought. *In for a penny, in for a pound.*

"Well, Chief," Jack said, and Franklin rubbed a hand down his face, knowing he couldn't stop him, "I came here because I was dispatched to the scene of a murder. You asked why I came here without calling you. The truth is that if I called you, we would all be standing around with our dicks in our hands waiting for you to arrive with the news media, and then we'd waste more valuable time while you got your fucking Kodak moment and tramped through the evidence. So what am I doing, you ask? I'm standing here talking to an asshole while my murder case gets cold. Sir."

"Captain," Dick said, still looking directly at Jack, "take possession of Detective Murphy's weapon and credentials. He won't need them for a very long while."

Franklin hesitated, but Chief Dick spoke again. "I've given you an order, Captain. You will carry it out, or you will surrender your weapon and identification to me."

Franklin still hesitated, and Jack stepped up and handed the captain his police ID, then pulled his Glock .45 out of the holster, dropped the ammunition clip, ejected the live round out of the receiver into his hand, and surrendered these to the captain.

"Jack," Franklin called out to Murphy's retreating figure.

"Let him go, Captain Franklin. The man's a disgrace," Dick said, and Liddell felt his face get hot.

Captain Franklin must have read his mind, because he put a hand on Liddell's arm and squeezed. "What are your orders, Chief?" Franklin asked.

"That's more like it," Dick said smugly.

CHAPTER THIRTY-SIX

When Eddie had gone to Kids' Kingdom he hadn't planned on leaving a human body, just the cats. The note he'd made out was another clue for Jack, and he didn't need a body for that. But the kid had changed those plans, and so, he'd had to improvise. He cut a message into the boy's hide for Jack. After what Murphy said about him on television, that was as good a message as anything. But Maddy Brooks had proven she couldn't be trusted. He'd deal with that.

He'd played with the idea of running by Channel Six and leaving Maddy Brooks a note so she could find the body, but she had seriously pissed him off. And so, there had been nothing all night about Kids' Kingdom on Channel Six or any of the other channels. Just went to show that Maddy wasn't shit without him giving her the notes. She was as stupid as the police.

He was sure he hadn't missed any of the news. The Mt. Vernon Inn, where Eddie had stayed overnight, was just thirty minutes from Evansville and got all the Evansville television stations. The rooms were cleaner than the strip motels in Evansville, but they were still used mostly by

long-haul truckers looking for a little slap and tickle with the
ladies of the night. Or, as Bobby put it, "a little Pokey and
Gumby."

The motel had been Bobby's idea. It was outside the ju-
risdiction of the Evansville cops, and one thing Eddie and
Bobby had learned through their many contacts with the law
was that law dogs didn't cooperate with each other very
good. It was a weakness the cops were probably aware of,
but never seemed to correct.

The sun was just cracking the horizon when Eddie
walked a mile down the road to the Whistle Stop restaurant.
He had reclaimed the van from the North Park Shopping
Center in Evansville and had it safely tucked away behind
the motel, where a lot of the clientele seemed to prefer to
park.

They would have to move again tonight, keep moving
until this was over. It would make them harder to track that
way, but it was a pain in the ass. *That fucking Murphy,* Eddie
thought.

Bobby had disappeared sometime during the night, and
when Eddie woke up hungry, he had hoped to at least eat
with his brother before he delivered the next message. But
he found the van, parked behind the motel still, and no sign
of Bobby.

Fuck him, Eddie thought as he entered the restaurant. The
Whistle Stop sat at a crossroads on Highway 69 next to railroad tracks. When Eddie was a kid, the preacher had taken
him and Bobby to a tent revival in a cornfield near there, and
on their way home he had treated them to a caboose burger
at the Whistle Stop. That was when his mom was still around
and the preacher was different. Everything was different.

Back then there had been nothing around but farm fields
and a rundown gas station. Now there was a Huck's Conve-
nience Store, an Ace Hardware Store, and dozens of other
businesses lining both sides of the highway.

Inside he looked around and was glad to see that nothing in there had changed. One entire wall was a chipped and faded mural of an old steam engine. The model train tracks still crisscrossed overhead and along the walls. The only things missing were the little toy trains that used to run around the tracks, and every now and then, one of them would let out a whistle and smoke would come from the train smokestack. It was the most interesting thing Eddie had ever seen, but they had never gone there again.

Eddie sat at the counter and a rabbit-faced woman with stiff graying hair banged a chipped porcelain mug down in front of him. "Coffee's over there," she said. "Help yourself." Then she turned away and began yelling at the cook in the back. "Ernie, put some more bacon down."

Eddie looked at her piteous figure. Her frame was so frail that her faded tan waitress outfit hung on her like a skeleton. Her name tag read BERNICE. For some reason, maybe because he hadn't been here since he was very little, she reminded him of his mother. She had been a waitress, too. But the preacher had killed anything good he remembered about his mother. All that was left was pity, and he didn't even know why he felt that.

"Hey, Bernice, how 'bout some of that apple pie," Eddie said, nodding toward a pastry case that had two pieces of pie and something else he didn't recognize.

Bernice was at least sixty years old, but she strutted to the counter where Eddie was sitting like she had a million-dollar figure.

"You sure that's all you want, sugar?" she asked.

"Bernice, I like my women like I like my coffee," Eddie said with a grin. "Hot and black."

Bernice chortled and slapped a piece down in front of him.

A trucker came in and sat two seats down, while the efficient Bernice banged an empty mug down on the counter and said, "You know where it's at, Herb." The driver chuckled and blew a kiss at her and made grinding motions at her with his hips like a dog humping a leg.

"Herb, someday I'm gonna spray you with pesticide," Bernice said, her face drawn into a serious expression. To Eddie she said, "Let me warm that pie up for you, hon." She grabbed Eddie's plate before he could protest and headed to the kitchen, saying over her shoulder, "Some people get treated better cause they got manners, Herb."

Eddie shuddered at the thought of Bernice and the driver doing the nasty. But then, truck drivers weren't known for having the best taste in women. His mind slowly returned to the problem at hand. Jack Murphy. And he was just getting an idea when the truck driver began making loud slurping noises with his coffee. Eddie looked at him and shook his head and thought, *Fuckin' asshole truckers. Cowboy boots, the fuckin' hat, and no fuckin' manners.*

Bernice returned with the warmed apple pie and set it in front of Eddie. She scooped up the newspaper that someone had left behind and was about to put it behind the counter when Eddie spied the headlines.

"Gimme that!" he said, and grabbed the paper from her.

"Well, hon, you just had to ask," Bernice said in a hurt tone.

Eddie stared at her for just a second and said, "Shut the fuck up, you wrinkled old bitch," and before she could react he shoved the pie and coffee over the counter onto her feet.

The dishes smashed, and hot coffee and apple pie exploded onto her legs and dirty sneakers. When she looked up, Eddie was gone. The trucker who sat two seats down just shook his head and continued slurping his coffee.

*   *   *

Sleep hadn't come easily to Jack, and he didn't so much "wake up" as just "get up" the morning after his suspension from duty. He didn't mind being suspended, but it killed him to be taken off the case and he regretted going so quietly. But what good would making a big scene do? *Nothing*, he decided. *But it sure would have felt good.*

The Evansville morning paper lay on his kitchen table. The headline read: DECORATED COP DUMPED FROM INVESTIGATION.

The article didn't really say much, but Double Dick was quoted at least twice in the first paragraph stating that Murphy was suspended indefinitely pending an internal investigation. The rest of the story recounted some of his past cases and talked about how many bad guys he had killed during his career and posed the old question of whether he was maybe a little gun happy. Then, way down in the last paragraph, they mentioned that Richard Dick had replaced Marlin Pope, suggesting that Marlin Pope was incompetent and that Double Dick was now "cleaning house," so to speak. Jack wondered who the mayor owned at the newspaper to be able to get away with saying that shit.

He was about to make coffee when he heard tires crunching on the gravel parking area behind his cabin. Before he could put the coffee in the filter, Susan was on the porch, tapping lightly on his front door.

"It's unlocked," he called, and she came in with a sack that said DONUT BANK BAKERY on it.

"I come bearing gifts," she said and placed the sack on his kitchen table and sat down. She saw the newspaper and looked at him.

"Don't want to talk about it," he said, and he noticed she was wearing warm-ups and running shoes. "You run this morning?" he asked and peeked in the top of the donut sack. Susan pushed his hands away.

"Not yet," she answered. "I was going to see if you were up to a little exercise."

"You bring donuts to a cop and then expect them to go out and run first?"

"Yeah," she said. "Otherwise your ass will get flabby, and I'm not dating a guy with a fat tushy."

"So you didn't really come bearing gifts," Jack said. "You really came bearing a bribe, didn't you?"

"Well. Yeah," she said and smiled.

Jack gave up. "Okay, I'll run with you." He headed to the bedroom to put on running gear. From the bedroom he yelled, "I'm going to expect more than donuts when we get back. You can check out my tushy to see if it qualifies."

"I'm not promising anything, pervert." She stood in the bedroom doorway.

"Then how about prepayment," Jack said, and stood naked in front of her.

She giggled and pushed him down on the bed. "You really should run, you know. It would be good for you."

He rolled over on top of her. "Maybe later."

He kissed her and felt her arms go around him, pulling him closer.

"If I'm still breathing, that is."

The knock at the door made him jump. He looked over at the nightstand and saw that it was seven o'clock. Susan had left only ten minutes ago after making him promise to run with her after she got off work. *Couldn't be Susan.* He reached in the nightstand drawer and pulled out his Glock model 36. It fired the same .45-caliber ammunition as his duty weapon but fewer rounds. It was smaller and lighter, but not less dangerous.

Pulling a sheet around his waist, he made his way to the front door to find it standing open and Katie outside the storm door with something in her hand. He must have forgotten to shut the front door when Susan left. Not very smart for someone who lived his kind of life.

"Katie," he said and opened the storm door. "Come in."

She went to the kitchen and noticed a bag on the kitchen counter identical to the one she was carrying. "Well, I see someone beat me to the punch," she said, and Jack noticed she was holding another bag of donuts.

"You're not going to ask me to run, are you?" he asked.

"What?" she asked confused.

"Nothing," he answered.

"So what have you been doing this morning?" she asked.

"I was just taking a nap," he lied.

"Jack, I just got off the phone with Susan. You don't have to lie to me," Katie said with an uncomfortable smile. "She didn't say anything about donuts, though." Katie stared at the sheet Jack was holding around his lower torso.

Jack's face turned red, and he stammered, "Be right back," and headed to his bedroom. *Shit!* he thought. *Like getting caught by your mom, only worse.*

He dressed quickly in some Rural King–brand painter's jeans, a loose button-up shirt, and deck shoes. This was the good part about being suspended. Wearing anything you wanted.

He walked back into the front where Katie was trying to make coffee. *Trying* was the operative word.

"Let me do that," he said. She gave in too easily. Cooking had never been her forte.

"I never could figure that thing out," she said about the coffeemaker, as if it were some type of alien technology that only someone with a degree from MIT could operate.

"Susan told me you were suspended?" Katie said. It was not quite a question.

"Yeah. It's okay though," he said, but he didn't feel okay at all.

Jack finished the coffee and pulled out a kitchen chair for her.

"No, I can't stay long," she said, and Jack wondered why she was making coffee if she wasn't going to stay, but then that was Katie.

Not knowing another way to approach the issue of her being there, he decided to just ask. "Why are you here, Katie?"

She started to speak and then stopped and turned away from him.

He waited, but she seemed to be staring outside as if deep in thought. "What's wrong, Katie?" he asked.

She faced him again, and he could see there were fresh tears in her eyes. She plopped down in the chair he had offered and began to cry in earnest.

"Aw, Katie, it's all right. It'll be all right," Jack said soothingly with a hand on her shoulder, although he had no idea what she was crying about.

Katie patted his hand and looked for a tissue.

Jack pulled a paper towel off the dispenser and handed it to her. "Sorry, Katie, I'm out of tissues and stuff," he said. She tried to smile, but the tears came again, harder this time.

"What's wrong, Katie?" he asked, but she stood and walked to the door.

"It's nothing, Jack. I'm just . . . never mind. I shouldn't have come," she said, and left.

An hour later there was another knock at Jack's door. He had just finished the last of the coffee and had eaten half a dozen donuts and was going out of his mind. Maybe it was the sugar, maybe it was Katie's unexpected visit, maybe it was everything that had happened, but he knew he didn't want any more company. He ignored the knock and took another bite of donut.

The knock became more insistent, and then he heard his partner yelling, "Open up! Vice squad. We know you're watching kiddie porn in there!"

Jack padded barefoot to the door and unlatched it. "Come on in, it's just getting to the good part of the flick where the cop puts a bullet in the hairy monster that's attacking the cheerleader."

Liddell ducked his head to get in the door and looked around, sniffed, and then found his way to the kitchen and the uneaten donuts. "No. This is the part where the hairy monster discovers the joy of a good donut instead of eating human cheerleader flesh and goes his merry way with a sack of glazed goodies."

Jack grinned at him. "Knock yourself out," he said, and Liddell inhaled a chocolate-covered long john.

"Thanks," Liddell said and dug deeper into the sack. "What's up?"

"Well, let's see," Jack said. "Susan came in early this morning with the first bag of donuts and wanted me to go running with her."

Liddell raised his eyebrows and said, "First bag?"

Jack ignored him and continued. "Then Katie came by a few minutes after Susan left and broke down in tears."

"What's the matter with Katie?" Liddell said, the donuts forgotten for the moment. "Did something happen to her?"

"Nothing happened to her," Jack said angrily, though he didn't know why he was angry. "At least, that's what she said." He sat on the loveseat that served as his couch and picked up his pistol from the table and dropped the clip out of the grip.

"Nothing?"

"That's what she said. I asked, 'What's the matter?' and she said, 'Nothing.' "

"That's it?" Liddell said.

"Yeah. Why do women do that?"

Liddell shrugged. "Marcie's not like that," he said. "When something's on her mind she spills it."

"Maybe you could have Marcie talk to her."

"No problemo, Jack," Liddell said; then, nodding at Jack's pistol, "Glad to see you have your backup piece handy."

Jack stuck the Glock in his back pocket. "That's what Boy Scouts say. 'Always be prepared.'"

"You know what else Boy Scouts say?" Liddell asked.

Jack didn't want to play the game. He knew it was going to be some lame joke, but what could he do? "I'll bite. What else do Boy Scouts say?"

"Don't touch me there," Liddell said with a straight face, then started to crack up. "Get it? Don't touch me there."

"Real funny, Bigfoot. So why are you here? I know you didn't bring donuts, too, and you sure as hell don't want to run. I hope you're not going to start crying, because I don't think I have any more paper towels. Of course, as big as you are, I would probably have to get a beach towel anyway."

"If we don't get a break in this case soon, we'll all be crying," Liddell said, and both men became somber.

Liddell had called Jack several times to update him on developments in the Kids' Kingdom case. Unfortunately, there were no updates. No missing child report. Nothing. The boy's picture would go on television at five o'clock if they didn't have someone come forward before then. But right now, they didn't have shit, except another dead body, and this one with Jack's name carved in it.

CHAPTER THIRTY-SEVEN

In the dining room of Two-Jakes, one of the servers, Vinnie, polished the tabletop to a high shine, and then put paper coasters down for the men. Jack, Liddell, and Captain Franklin sat in a back booth away from the long glass wall overlooking the river. Jake Brady brought coffee and shook hands with Franklin, assured them the doors were all locked and they wouldn't be disturbed, and then headed off to the kitchen to let the men talk.

"Any news on the last body?" Jack asked Franklin.

"Chief Dick is doing a news conference at five with all the media. So far we haven't had anything but crank calls," Franklin answered, then changed the subject. "Liddell said you wanted to talk, Jack, but I have to tell you, this isn't off the record," Franklin said.

"That's okay," Jack said, knowing the risk that Franklin was taking even being near him without Double Dick's knowledge and approval. Liddell had told him that Double Dick had created a whole new meaning for the word *micromanage*.

Liddell stood and said, "Plausible deniability." The other

men looked at him, and he explained, "I learned that from Bill Clinton." He chuckled and went to mooch breakfast from Vinnie.

When he was gone, Jack said, "I appreciate your coming, Captain. I wouldn't ask if it wasn't important."

Franklin remained quiet.

"First of all, the Black Jack gum wrapper that was found in Dubois County," Jack said.

"What about it?"

"Mark Crowley is the chief deputy, and he's the one that found that particular piece of evidence. It hadn't been on the ground long, Captain. It could've been dropped by someone watching the cabin."

"Jack, that's a state police case now. Dubois isn't in it anymore. And neither are we."

"I know, but Mark Crowley is a very, uh, industrious investigator. He probably would get us a copy of any prints they lifted."

"What would that do?" Franklin asked. "If the state police came up with a suspect, they would share."

Jack gave the captain a sardonic look.

"Okay. Maybe they wouldn't share," Franklin conceded. "But eventually, we would find out."

"Yeah. You're probably right," Jack said sarcastically.

"It's not a contest, Jack," Franklin said.

"The hell it isn't! The bastard is killing kids," Jack said.

Franklin leaned closer to Jack. "What can we do about it?" Jack knew he was really asking what they could do about Chief Dick, but the captain was a professional and would never bad-mouth the chief. Even Double Dick.

Jack looked away from the captain and said, "What if someone was to deliver copies of the state police fingerprint evidence to you?"

"I probably don't want to know who that would be, but I guess if someone were to have evidence that related to our killings I would be negligent in my duty if I didn't look into it," Franklin said.

Jack sat back and sipped his coffee.

"You're just like your dad, Jack," Franklin said.

"I forgot you and my dad knew each other," Jack said. "Actually, I thought he retired before you were hired."

"He was my training officer," Franklin said to Jack's surprise.

"No kidding? I'll bet that was an experience," Jack said. Jack's father had retired as a motor patrol officer. He'd never had any aspirations of doing anything but working the street. When Jack had been sworn in as an officer, his father had set him straight about who did the heavy lifting on the police department. "It sure isn't those sissy pen-pushers," his dad had said, meaning the detectives. But to his credit, when Jack had transferred into the investigations side, his father had been as proud as a man could be.

"Yeah," Franklin admitted. "We had some different ideas about how to do the job, but he was a good cop. Would have made a good detective. But he didn't know when to shut up. Just like you."

Jack grinned. "Yeah, I guess I can see that. But you have to admit, Captain, I went out with style."

Franklin tried to hide a smile and got up to leave.

"See you, Jack," he said, and Vinnie unlocked the door to let him leave.

Liddell came over and sat down. "Well?"

CHAPTER THIRTY-EIGHT

Two days later...

The identification of Kyle Bannock as the victim at Kids' Kingdom was front-page news for all of one day. But the murders had stopped as quickly as they had started. Maddy had received no further notes from the killer and had resorted to rehashing the story of Jack's humiliating suspension. The newspapers had also picked up on this, but because they were courting the mayor's favor, they were giving the mayor credit for replacing the chief of police and thereby putting pressure on the killer. Chief Dick had taken to wearing SWAT attire, minus the helmet and ballistic vest, but keeping the spit-shined combat boots. He believed this gave him a forceful look. A man of action. A man that gets things done.

What a joke, Jack thought as he drank coffee and browsed the newspaper, looking at a picture of Double Dick in SWAT tactical attire. The front-page stories didn't report that absolutely nothing had been done on the case since Jack's suspension. Or that they hadn't had any cooperation with the state police with the Dubois investigation. So, they didn't have a clue what was being done. In reality, except for the discreet inquiries being made without Double Dick's knowledge, no one was really assigned to the case anymore.

Double Dick had reassigned Angelina Garcia to her previous duties so that he could have the chief's conference room back. Detective Jansen had somehow become Dick's PIO, or public information officer, and so no one was actually compiling information on the case except Liddell.

In other words, no one—the news media, the cops, nor the politicians—knew anything. All they knew was that the murders had stopped, and like all good sheep, they could go back to their mindless grazing until the wolf reappeared at their door and took another of their children.

Because of the lull, Maddy's big dreams were falling apart, and with the drop in viewers, it wouldn't be long before she would be out covering church bake sale stories.

Jack had contacted Chief Deputy Mark Crowley, and his proposition of working together was met with enthusiasm. Sheriff Tanner Crowley gave his son some much-deserved time off, with the usual warning that he was not to be working on the murder case—*wink, wink*.

Jack and Liddell had their first member for the team they would put together in spite of Double Dick. Within a matter of hours they had assembled what Liddell jokingly referred to as "the Holy Jihad team": Jack Murphy, Liddell Blanchard, Susan Summers, Mark Crowley, Detective Walker from Crime Scene, and sometimes Captain Franklin. Their "war room" was a back room of Two-Jakes that was used for small gatherings and birthday parties.

Jake Brady and Vinnie kept them in coffee and they never lacked for food, but what they didn't have was the freedom they needed to use the vast resources of the police department. Liddell had been effectively gelded by Double Dick and couldn't have a thought about the cases without clearing it with Dick first.

That was where Susan Summers and Tony Walker came in. Tony was their mole in Crime Scene and had access to police data, reports, and some crime scene equipment, while Susan was their communications. She was able to use her position as a state parole officer to make inquiries of other law enforcement agencies, jails, and prisons. It wasn't the ideal way to conduct an investigation, but by working together they had found a way around Jack's suspension.

Susan and Franklin were absent from this meeting— Susan, because she still had parolees to supervise, and Franklin, because he had to keep up appearances at work.

It was already getting dark by the time Mark Crowley had obtained a good copy of the partial latent fingerprint taken from the Black Jack gum wrapper. He faxed this copy to a nervous Tony Walker, and then drove to Evansville. By the time he arrived at the Two-Jakes, Walker had examined the copy of the latent print and entered his results into the state database of latent prints, Indiana Automated Fingerprint Information System, or IAFIS, and was now giving the assemblage a report. "I couldn't get into the FBI's fingerprint system," Walker explained, "because that computer is in the Central Record room. If I go in there and get caught, Chief Dick will be on me like stink on shit. He's got spies everywhere."

"We'll ask Franklin to check on doing that," Jack said.

Tony continued. "The IAFIS system spat out about two hundred possible matches. The print wasn't very good to begin with, so that is all we're going to get. I don't think even the FBI will do any better."

"Get this," Crowley said, looking over the autopsy report findings, "The state cops have a DNA sample." He was referring to the Indiana State Police investigation into the murder at Patoka Lake. "Apparently our girl took some skin out of her attacker's hide."

"But it'll take weeks to get the results back," Liddell reminded him.

"Yeah. There's that," Crowley conceded. "But if we ever catch the bastards, it could make the court case a lot easier."

Jack looked at Crowley. "You just said 'bastards'—plural."

"Yeah," Crowley said, rubbing the back of his neck. "Guess I did."

"Up to now we've been thinking we only had one killer," Jack said. "Maybe we should widen our thinking a little— while the pressure is off?"

"But that takes us back to square one," Liddell said.

"Maybe that's what we need. Some new perspective on this," Jack said looking around the table. Then to Liddell, he said, "You still got the phone number for Garcia?"

While Liddell called Angelina's cell phone, Jack filled in the other members about her involvement. They agreed that Garcia would be an immense help. If she agreed.

Liddell got off the phone and smiled. "Fuck Double Dick and the mayor he rode in on," he said. "Her exact words."

"Let's start again early tomorrow," Jack said. Then, remembering that Crowley had driven for an hour, he added, "If that's all right with you, Mark?"

Crowley grinned. "Well, I was thinking of heading down to the riverboat and trying my luck anyway."

Liddell took out his cell phone. "I can get you a free room at the casino hotel," he said.

"Can you get me some playing money, too?" Crowley asked, unashamedly.

Liddell just rolled his eyes.

He'd been surprised that there was nothing in the newspaper about him beating that Indian woman at the motel.

Eddie could tell he'd hurt that woman badly. He'd beaten and stomped her unconscious, and there was a lot of blood. So much, in fact, that he'd had to stop at a nearby car wash and spray the blood off his boots. Surely the cops were combing all the cheap motels trying to identify him. But it had been three days since the killing at Kids' Kingdom and there was plenty in the newspaper about that, but not a thing about the motel.

In a way it pissed him off that he'd rushed out of his room and spent his dwindling cash supply to lay low. If he'd have known the police didn't give a shit about some Indian broad, he'd have just woke her up, dusted her off, and given her a few bucks for her trouble.

He had laughed the incident off, but Bobby had gone apeshit at the time. *There you go thinking with your dick again,* Bobby had said. *Are you trying to get us caught?*

Eddie wasn't trying to get them caught. But he wasn't going to take any shit off some fucking motel maid either. He was beginning to think that Bobby had lost his nerve, and that wasn't good. It bothered him that Bobby was so quiet. Quiet unless he had something bad to say about the way Eddie was doing things.

If Bobby wasn't the only family he had left, he'd tell him to go to hell. But it had always been him and Bobby against everyone else—when they were kids, when they grew up, while they were in prison, and back on the street. Bobby was the only one he could count on. He wanted to tell Bobby how he felt, but he knew Bobby'd just tell him he was acting gay or something.

Eddie looked at the newspaper on the table in front of him. DETECTIVE MURPHY STILL ON SUSPENSION, the headline read.

"Do you think they figured it out?" Eddie asked his brother. "Do you think they pulled Murphy off the case? Or did he get scared and quit?"

"Eddie, get your head outta your ass," Bobby said. "They think we won't finish this if they pull his ass off the case. They think we're weak, or stupid, or both."

"What are we gonna do, Bobby?" Eddie pushed the newspaper off the table and onto the floor with the fast-food containers and empty beer cans.

Bobby looked at him and shook his head sadly. "Whining don't get the job done, bro."

Eddie winced at the reprimand. There Bobby went again saying shit that the preacher used to say. "I ain't whining, Bobby. This was your idea in the first place." Eddie was getting mad, building up some steam as he spoke. "So why don't YOU quit complaining and calling me dumb and come up with a fuckin' idea?"

Bobby didn't seem to notice Eddie was mad. Or if he did notice he didn't seem to care. He just sat on the couch and rubbed at his right eye with a knuckle, like he had something in it or had an itch. Eddie had noticed him doing that a lot lately.

Finally, Bobby stopped rubbing his head, and said, "Okay, here's the plan."

CHAPTER THIRTY-NINE

Jack sat in his Jeep, behind his cabin, the engine running. He wanted to check on Katie, but the last time he'd spoken to her she had broken down crying and then wouldn't tell him what was wrong.

He made up his mind to go inside and put his feet up, have a beer, try to relax enough to think this stuff through. He'd call Katie. See which way the wind was blowing.

He stepped out of the Jeep and hit the lock button on the Jeep's key. Some part of his mind connected hitting the button with the sound the Jeep's horn made, with the sudden blackness and pain that crawled behind his eyes. Then he was down.

Jack opened his eyes and a tide of pain washed over him like a debilitating hangover. He was nauseous and could feel himself spinning and floating. He could see a shadow moving across the moon, but he couldn't tell if he was sitting, standing, lying down, or even alive. He wondered for a moment if he'd had a stroke, but the pain behind his ear told him different.

And then it started raining, and something was buzzing inside his head, over and over, like a stuck record, finally settling into separate noises, muffled words, then nothing at all.

When he opened his eyes again, the pain was still there. The moon had come out from the shadow, and the spinning had stopped. It was no longer raining. He tried to lift himself up and felt something click off inside his head.

"If you killed him, Eddie, the game's over bro," Bobby said.

"He ain't dead, Bobby. I seen him being put in the ambulance," Eddie said. He pronounced ambulance *am-boo-lants*. "Besides, I only hit him the once."

Bobby sat on the rocks at the edge of the river. The same place where they had watched Jack's cabin the first time. Bobby was shaking his head, but Eddie didn't want to hear any more of his shit, so he said, "You were the one that said we needed to shake things up. Get him mad so's he wouldn't quit."

"Ain't this just fucking dandy," Bobby said.

"Jack. Jack," the voice said softly.

He squinted his eyes open just a slit. The light was dim. He was vaguely aware of noise, talking in the background, something rattling, a muted laugh, a cough.

"Oh, Jack," came the voice again. It sounded familiar. His eyes closed again, and he eased back into the friendly darkness.

*   *   *

"Welcome back, pod'na," Liddell said, seeing Murphy open his eyes.

Jack looked around and realized he was in a room, in a hospital, in daylight. It was hard to mistake the mint-green paint and the hospital smells.

"What happened?" he asked, cutting his eyes instead of turning his head. The back of his neck felt like a piece of wood.

"Somebody whacked you in the head," Liddell said. "You've been out of it for a while."

Jack motioned for Liddell to come closer. Liddell scooted his chair closer, and Jack said in a low voice, "Get me out of here. No more hospitals."

"I don't think that would a good idea, sir." The nurse had appeared from out of nowhere and stood at the bottom of Jack's bed. "You've had a serious concussion." She moved around to the side of the bed and offered him a sip of water from a Styrofoam cup with a straw sticking out.

Jack took a sip, and the coldness caused a spear of pain to shoot up the back of his throat and into his skull.

"Can you tell me your name?" she asked.

"Mud," Jack replied.

"What day is it?" she persisted.

Jack just looked at her. She made a note on his chart.

"One last question, Mr. Mud," the nurse said, and Jack tried not to smile, but did, and it hurt. "Do you know who the President of the United States is?" she asked.

"Does it matter?" Jack answered. "They're all a bunch of assholes."

"Yeah, he's back to his normal self," Liddell said with a chuckle.

The nurse took the chart and left the room. Jack knew the doctor would probably be in soon to tell him all the things he couldn't do for a while.

"Get me out of here," he repeated to Liddell.

"Let's talk to the doc first, Jack." Liddell handed him the morning newspaper.

Jack looked at the date, then up at Liddell's concerned face. He'd been out for two days.

"I told you that you got whacked," Liddell said.

"What with? A truck?"

"Doc said it might've been an axe handle or something. I'll let him explain."

"Katie?" Jack said, and then thought how strange it was that his first concern was about Katie and not Susan. Katie wasn't even talking to him.

"She's fine. She's been up here a lot. Marcie and Susan, too."

Jack closed his eyes again and felt the room tip slightly.

"Don't go into the light," Liddell said.

"Fuck you," Jack said and looked at his grinning partner. "Where are my clothes?"

Liddell ignored him and explained the condition he'd found Jack in.

"Clothes," Jack said again and tried to sit up. He didn't make it. The room was spinning.

"Susan and Katie went to the cabin yesterday and brought a clean set of clothes for you," Liddell said.

"So who found me?" Jack asked. "Wasn't that old guy with the dog was it?"

Liddell laughed out loud this time. "No. His luck has gone away. I found you, buddy. Again. It's getting to be a habit with us."

Liddell was referring to the incident a few months back when Jack had nearly bled to death. Jack's fingers unconsciously traced the scar that ran down his neck and chest, and he thought about how he had cheated death not once, but twice before. And how he would have died back then if Liddell hadn't somehow tracked him down and stanched the flow of blood until medical help got there.

He closed his eyes, but it made the dizziness even worse. Thoughts flashed through his mind about how he had chased the robber down an alley, lost sight of him, and then saw the discarded shotgun on the ground. It had been raining, coming down so hard he couldn't see ten feet in front of him, couldn't hear anything but the heavy droplets pinging on the metal roofs of buildings on either side of the alley. Then an arm, a face, something slashing down. Jack opened his eyes, not wanting to see the blade coming at him again. He had to get his mind around something else and said, "Was it raining again?"

"What?" Liddell said.

"When you found me, was it raining?"

Liddell's mouth pinched into a tight line, and he said, "Get some rest. I'll fill you in later."

Jack closed his eyes and slept until the doctor came in.

The doctor was a small man with dark hair and a short growth of beard on his chin. He asked the same questions the nurse had asked. The doctor didn't have a sense of humor either.

CHAPTER FORTY

Jack was in the hospital for another full day while they ran tests, MRIs, X-rays, and probed and prodded his nether regions before the doctors finally gave in and released him. He was still having dizzy spells, but that was the least of his worries. It had been almost a week now since the killing at Kids' Kingdom, and there had been no other incidents, but also, no new leads.

Liddell had picked him up at his cabin this morning and driven him to Two-Jakes, where the others were scheduled to gather in the war room. As Liddell's unmarked Crown Vic pulled up in front, Jack felt a wave of nausea wash over him. The familiar glass façade of the main restaurant wasn't comforting anymore. It felt too open, too exposed.

"You okay, pod'na?" Liddell asked.

"Does the Pope shit in the woods?" Jack answered.

"How many fingers am I holding up?" Liddell asked, and displayed his middle finger to Jack.

"You're a fucking riot, Bigfoot."

Vinnie was waiting at the front door to let them in. He

locked the door behind them and then rushed away toward the kitchen without saying anything. He knew when Jack was in a mood, and he knew when to disappear.

As Liddell and Jack entered the war room, Jack looked around. The only new face was that of Angelina Garcia.

She gave him a sympathetic smile and said, "You don't look too good."

He had news for her. He felt even worse than he looked. This morning when he'd dressed he noticed that he had dark rings around both eyes and the roof of his mouth was tender.

A round of greetings and sympathies was given before they settled down to business. Mark Crowley asked the question they had all been thinking.

"Do you have any idea who it was, Jack?"

Jack knew that Crowley was, of course, referring to the remote possibility that it could be the killer they were hunting. Jack didn't know how to answer. He felt that he knew who the killer was. It was as if the name was just out of reach of his conscious mind. But whoever clobbered him was a shadow.

"I really can't say," Jack answered and could see the collective disappointment in their faces. "One minute I'm getting out of my Jeep, and the next I'm in the hospital."

"We do have something, though," Liddell said, looking at Jack.

Jack gave a nod, and Liddell continued.

"I already told you all that I had been calling Jack, and when he didn't answer I went to his cabin to talk to him, and that's when I found him on the ground." Liddell took a breath and looked at Jack again. Jack looked embarrassed and got up and left the room.

When he was gone Liddell cleared his throat and continued.

"Well, there's some things I didn't tell you folks."

So he told them. And when Liddell finished the story

everyone remained silent until Mark Crowley stood up, anger in his face. "The bastard urinated on him?"

Liddell felt like shit. Some sick fuck had almost killed his partner and then had pissed on him while he was down. He hadn't been there when Jack needed him, and it didn't set well.

"Yeah, that's what I said, ain't it?"

Crowley saw the red creeping into Liddell's face and said, "Hey, I didn't mean anything bad. Sorry if I sounded insensitive, but I just can't get my mind around someone doing that. You know?"

"Forget it, Mark. I'm just a little touchy. But . . ." He paused and looked at everyone. "I don't want none of you talking about it around Jack. He's not even supposed to be on his feet, but the guy's too stubborn to lie down."

Tony Walker asked the obvious question. "Did you keep any of that stuff for me?"

Liddell looked chagrined.

"Tony, we can't use it. I didn't even make a report, so it would never be usable as evidence."

What he said was true, but Liddell still had Jack's soiled clothes. He had bagged them at the hospital and put them in the refrigerator in his own garage. He wanted Jack to file a battery report, but Jack wouldn't budge.

"But if we can match the DNA to the evidence from my case, at least we can be sure it's the same person," Mark Crowley said.

Liddell looked at him directly. "Your partner wasn't almost killed. The reason I waited to do anything until now was to be sure it was what Jack wanted. After all, it was his head that was caved in. If he don't want to make a report, he don't have to make a fucking report."

Crowley stood his ground.

"I just want to be sure what we're doing here, Liddell. It feels like we've crossed some kind of line. I don't want to

see this guy get away with what he's done while we all lose
our jobs—or worse—for doing things outside the system."

Liddell understood exactly what Crowley was saying.
They *had* crossed the line. If Double Dick got wind of this
informal alliance and what they were doing, they'd all be
charged with obstruction of justice. But he also knew he
couldn't stop, wouldn't stop, and that what they were doing
was the right thing. The system wasn't working. Double
Dick had assumed the driver's seat in the investigations and
was driving like an old woman with cataracts.

"Don't worry, Mark," Liddell said. "If it comes down to
it, I'll swear you were never here."

Crowley shook his head. "I'm not saying I won't keep
helping, Liddell. Man, I'm just worried that we could be getting too far over the line."

"I know, Mark," Liddell said. "Sorry I got angry."

Mark Crowley leaned forward and said, "Okay. Let's all
agree that none of us will do anything illegal. We're all
doing this on our own time, so we haven't done anything
really illegal yet. Except maybe violate some departmental
rules, so let's keep it that way. Right?"

And they all agreed. Garcia had been listening to all of
the talk closely and had not said that maybe the men hadn't
broken any laws, but she had stepped *way* over the line when
she hacked into the police department's computer system
and was even accessing confidential federal and state data-
bases. She was a professional and didn't take breaking laws
lightly, but the bastards they were after didn't care about
breaking laws, didn't mind killing kids, and she would be
damned if she let them get away with it.

Jack entered the restaurant kitchen and found Jake Brady
doing something at the stove, his back to him. Besides being
his partner in Two-Jakes, Brady had been in Jack's life so long

that he was like a second father. At sixty-eight years old, he was as strong as Liddell and a little taller, with thick arms covered in coarse red hair.

Brady was mumbling something, or maybe humming, or even singing; it was hard for Jack to tell the difference sometimes because of Brady's gruff voice. He started forward, but a wave of vertigo overtook him, and he held on to the wall behind him.

His hands shook, and his head felt like his skull would split. He closed his eyes to block out the pain and gasped when he saw something shiny flashing toward him. He flinched and felt the bite of the blade cut through his face and neck and deep into his chest. He opened his eyes, and it was gone—the pain in his head, the dizziness, the burning in his neck and chest. He looked up to see Jake Brady staring at him with concern in his eyes.

"What is it, son?" Brady said.

"It's nothing, old man," Jack said and tried to smile. "I just realized how hungry I am."

"Well, you looked like you was going to faint," Brady said, still staring at him. "Old man, my ass," he grumbled, then said, "I'll fix you something up. What do you want?" He turned back to the huge stove and pulled a skillet down from overhead.

Jack's hands started shaking, and he stuck them in his pockets.

"You're creeping me out, Jack," Brady said without turning around.

"Sorry. I guess I'm just not hungry."

"Well, you gotta eat. So bacon and eggs then," Brady said and began cracking eggs into a bowl. "How about the others?" He nodded in the direction of the war room.

Jack braced himself with the wall and opened the door. "I'll go ask, but you can probably just make a heap of everything. Liddell will clean up any leftovers."

Brady laughed. He was well aware of the big man's appetite. He tossed two pounds of bacon on the griddle.

Garcia had two laptops set up in the war room and had "borrowed" a printer from somewhere. She was busy concentrating on the keyboard while Vinnie hovered around her like a gnat.

Vinnie was a small, wiry man, with a tan so deep his skin was leathery. His face was creased with lines that belied his true age, somewhere between twenty-five and sixty. Thick hair, the color of dirty dishwater, was pulled back in a short greasy-looking ponytail. His taste in clothes was tie-dyed T-shirts, faded denim cut-off shorts, and deck shoes, like the flower children of the sixties had worn. But, in his defense, Vinnie was a clean freak. Two-Jakes was spotless, and so was he.

Vinnie had fussed around Garcia since she had arrived early that morning—filling her coffee, bringing her napkins, and anything else that would allow him to be near her. According to Brady, Vinnie was in love. Garcia didn't seem to notice.

Apparently Vinnie wasn't the only one smitten with the petite Garcia. Mark Crowley was leaning over her shoulder when Jack came back in the meeting room, and Jack could tell from the look on Crowley's face that he wasn't admiring the computer screen. But, from Garcia's smirking expression, he was sure she was aware of Crowley's attention and was eating it up.

"What's up?" Jack asked.

Crowley straightened up.

"I was just showing Chief Deputy Crowley what these babies can do," Garcia said, and Crowley's face turned beet red.

"She means the computers," Crowley said, and backed away from the table.

Garcia looked up at Crowley and smiled. "I haven't made a man's face red in a long time."

"That's because most of us are going to hell," Jack told her. "Now quit teasing the deputy and tell me what you've come up with."

"First of all, Liddell had to go to headquarters," Garcia said.

"Whoops. Hold that thought a minute," Jack said and hurried to the kitchen door to tell Jake that he wouldn't be feeding an army now.

"Okay," he said, shutting the kitchen door.

Garcia handed him a printout. Jack looked at the list of forty or so names. "What am I looking at?" he asked.

Garcia turned in her chair and handed him another paper. "The first one is the list of people you've arrested for major felony crimes. Using the files from the parole office, I was able to slim the list by searching only for those with violent crimes or mental problems. The second list is a result of my running those names through BMV and the Indiana Department of Corrections to eliminate anyone who was no longer living in the state or in prison."

Jack noticed the second list had only about thirty names on it. "And, yes, I ran them through the Department of Corrections, too, and all of those people are currently on parole or have been fully released to prey upon the innocent once more," Garcia said.

"Any of them have ties with Dubois County?" Jack said.

Garcia looked slightly embarrassed. "I haven't done that yet."

"That's my fault," Mark said. "Our system hasn't been computerized yet, and I'll have to go through the records manually to check this list out."

Jack sighed. He'd assumed that this was going to be quicker but had forgotten that small departments meant small budgets and significantly more paper to sift through.

He had become spoiled by the technology that was available and wondered if it had helped all that much. The guys coming up through the ranks today didn't have a clue about how to run snitches or build relationships with other departments. In Jack's day, those two things were as important as carrying a badge or gun. He wondered if one day all detectives would only have to Google crimes to get their answers. He hoped not.

"I'll get on this right now," Crowley said.

"I could come and help you," Garcia offered.

Just then Jake Brady came out of the kitchen carrying a large tray laden with platters of toast, bacon, omelets, and fried eggs. The aroma was overpowering.

"Sorry," Jack said. "It looks like it's going to be you and me, old man."

Jake looked at the tray of food and at the others. "You can't leave without a good breakfast," he protested.

Mark Crowley was drooling. "Well. Since you went to all the trouble, it would be rude of me to leave."

"Me, too," Garcia chimed in as they helped set the platters of food out on the table.

The restaurant phone rang, and Brady went to answer. When he returned he had a serious look on his face.

"Jack. That was Franklin. He said the state police ran the DNA, and it doesn't match anyone in the database."

They all traded looks before Crowley said, "Well, shit!"

"Angelina," Jack said, "run your list by Walker to see if any of them are on the list of names from IAFIS." He was referring to the partial fingerprint that was found on the Black Jack chewing gum wrapper.

"I forgot to tell you. I already did that. No match to anyone on that list either," Garcia said.

This time, Jack said, "Well, shit!"

CHAPTER FORTY-ONE

Katie looked out from her classroom window, across the empty playground, and felt a little irritation. She wasn't married to Jack anymore and didn't have an enemy in the world. Why would anyone want to harm her? It angered her a little that Jack had insisted on having policemen watch her house. She felt that, if anything, it would draw attention to her, and she was right. Just that morning, as she walked to her car she had spotted the creepy old van setting at the corner. She immediately made it as the type the police would use for surveillance. Believing it was one of Jack's buddies, she had even given a half nod to the driver. Just to let him know that she had seen him. Jack wasn't the only one that was observant. But the van was so obvious that before she got into her car, her neighbor, Mrs. Rosenbaum, had called out to her.

Mrs. Rosenbaum was a widow in her eighties. She had seen everything, and loved to tell anyone she could corner just how much she knew. This morning she said, "It's that ex-husband of yours, isn't it?" When Katie had asked her what she meant, Mrs. Rosenbaum said, matter-of-factly, "Stalking is against the law, dear."

Katie had tried to explain that Jack wasn't having her followed, but Mrs. Rosenbaum had never liked Jack and had more than once referred to him as a thug. Before Katie could extricate herself from the one-sided conversation, Mrs. Rosenbaum said something funny that Katie wanted to remember to tell Jack.

She smiled now, thinking about how Mrs. Rosenbaum had said in a conspiratorial tone, "I'm afraid to even go to the store alone. You never know when one of them little punks is going to 'cap you with his nine.'"

Katie had laughed at the old woman's remark, but could see that Mrs. Rosenbaum was completely serious.

I really have to tell Jack about that, she thought, as she surveyed the playground for truant children. The little old woman had actually said, "cap you with his nine," and had held her hand out like she was holding a pistol sideways.

"Mrs. Murphy," a little voice said, snapping her out of her thoughts.

Katie looked down to see one of her students dancing from foot to foot and looking anxious. "You may go to the bathroom, Danny. But come right back," Katie said. The boy rushed out of the room.

Two blocks down the street, Eddie sat with binoculars, watching Katie. He was eager to finish this, but Bobby wouldn't have it. Eddie wasn't sure how much longer he could wait. He could just walk right into that classroom and cut her head off with the corn knife. It would only take one swing. But he knew what Bobby would say.

Jack drove down Martin Luther King Junior Boulevard, each bump in the road causing short starbursts behind his eyes. The doctor had assured him that this particular symptom would soon go away, but the headaches were another matter. He felt like he had ridden a rodeo bull.

But there were worse things than headaches. The boredom of sitting around the restaurant, just waiting for something to happen, was unbearable. It was like the killer had vanished. He knew he should be glad there were no new victims, but with the recent bad news, that the DNA didn't match any known criminal, he was starting to feel the cases growing stale.

He pulled his Jeep into the back parking lot of the parole office and wondered what Susan had found. She'd been cryptic on the phone. As he stepped from the Jeep he saw Susan at the back door, motioning him to come inside.

"You're sneaking me in the back door?" Jack said, half jokingly.

"I just didn't want to waste time. Hurry up and come to my office." She headed down the hallway, not waiting for him.

Jack entered Susan's office and looked around. Stacks of files and/or books were everywhere and anywhere there was a flat surface to hold them. The top of her desk was completely immersed in piles of paper. The seats of the two chairs across from her desk were used like bookcases. She ignored the mess and grabbed a couple of folders. "Let's go to the break room," she said, and brushed past him into the hallway.

In the break room Susan grabbed a couple of Styrofoam cups and handed Jack one. When they had hot coffee and sat at a table by the window, she laid the files on the table top.

"First, let me tell you the background so you don't think I'm crazy when I tell you what I suspect," she said.

"It's your story," Jack said.

She took a breath and began. "When you first mentioned the Mother Goose rhymes something bothered me, but I couldn't think of what it was."

Jack nodded, but didn't interrupt.

"It kept bugging me, and I couldn't shake the feeling that

I knew something important." She took a sip of the coffee and made a face, got up, and poured her coffee down the drain. "Anyway, this morning it came to me." She looked at Jack, obviously pleased with herself. "One of my parolees used to quote pieces of Mother Goose rhymes when he would show up for our meetings."

Jack waited. He didn't want to say, "So what?" but the fact that one of her nut-job parolees was spouting nursery rhymes didn't strike him as very unusual. They were all a bunch of smart-asses as far as he could tell.

"Aren't you going to ask me who it was?" she said.

"Who was it?" Jack asked, obediently.

Susan waited a heartbeat before answering. "Bobby Solazzo."

"That's impossible," Jack said, his fingers going to the scar on his face. "Bobby's dead. I killed him, remember?"

CHAPTER FORTY-TWO

Eddie parked the van on the side street. *Just a short walk from here,* he thought. *No one will notice the van parked in this neighborhood.*

He looked over at Bobby, who was leaned back, eyes closed, in the passenger seat. *Always in control. Unstoppable.*

He watched Bobby for another minute before disturbing him. "Wakey, wakey, motherfucker," Eddie said.

Bobby didn't open his eyes. "I got your 'motherfucker' right here," he said, and put a hand over his crotch.

They both laughed. It was good to be working together on this. Good to be brothers. And Eddie felt brotherly pride swell within. He had to admit, Bobby's plan was sharp. Bobby had his shit together, and it was a good thing, because Eddie wasn't feeling too cohesive.

"Bobby Solazzo's dead," Jack reminded Susan. He thought about the last encounter he'd had with Bobby Solazzo. The chase through the alleys behind Turley's Jewelers. Finding the expended shotgun thrown aside by Solazzo. His mistaken belief that Solazzo was unarmed. The surprise of coming up against Solazzo in the rain, the huge blade slicing down toward him.

Pain began to creep up the back of his neck, and he could feel an electric buzz growing inside his skull. "Solazzo's dead," he said flatly. "I put three bullets in him."

"I know. That's why I didn't call you earlier," said Susan.

Jack closed his eyes and rubbed at the base of his skull.

"You should be in bed," Susan said.

Without thinking, he said, "That's all you ever think about, isn't it?"

Susan laughed and said, "Well at least you still have your sense of humor. Or whatever you call that." She got up from the table. "I've got some aspirin in my office. I'll be right back," she said, and started to leave, but Jack called her back.

"No, I'm okay," he said, and he could feel the buzzing diminish from a chain saw down to an electric hum.

"You didn't call me here to tell me a dead man is behind all this."

"Let me finish—then see what you think," Susan said, and Jack nodded.

Susan opened the file she had brought into the break room.

"I thought about Bobby because he was always quoting parts of nursery rhymes to me when I had him under the hammer for some type of parole violation. At the time I thought it was just a defense mechanism. You know. Like trying to distract me, or himself, from the point of our conversation."

Jack nodded understanding, and Susan opened the file to the back page.

"Because Bobby's crimes were so violent he had undergone extensive psychiatric examinations. The court had ordered the first round of examinations to see if he was fit to stand trial, and he was examined again by the Department of Corrections after his conviction to determine where to house such a violent inmate."

Susan got up and poured another cup of coffee, and began pacing. Jack had noticed that when she was thinking something through she tended to walk the floor.

"Guess who his court-ordered psychiatrist was?" Susan said.

Jack raised his eyebrows, seeing where her train of thoughts was leading. "Anne Lewis?" he said.

"Yep," Susan answered, then continued to pace. "But Bobby's dead. So that was a dead end," she said, then looked at Jack and said, "And don't say it. Let me finish."

He nodded for her to go on.

"I was curious," she said, "So I looked up Eddie's file. Bobby's psychiatric report hinted at his being an abused child. So I wondered if Eddie was abused as well. Like I said, I checked Eddie's records and my hunch was right."

"Eddie was examined by Anne Lewis, too," Jack finished her thought.

"Yes," Susan said, "and Eddie hasn't reported to me for a few months now."

Jack hadn't considered Eddie a suspect in these current murders, but now it was all starting to make sense.

"Eddie Solazzo?" Jack said.

"Yep," Susan agreed.

Charlie Toon had been on the playground for only a few minutes when he first noticed the man outside the fence. He was tall, with long dark hair, and dressed like a biker, with one heavy-soled boot stubbed against the front wheel as he leaned against the side of an old panel van. The other kids were huddled in their small groups, talking, laughing, telling stories, and making plans for the coming weekend, oblivious of everything else around them, and impervious to Charlie, but he didn't care if they liked him, or talked to him.

Harwood Middle School was a school where kids were sent when no other school would take them, and, even at Harwood, Charlie was an outsider. He had worn out his welcome at no less than six other schools before landing here. And from "here" there was only one other place to go: the Evansville Children's Psychiatric Center. He'd heard bad stories about that place and was behaving himself. But right now he was watching the man, and the man was watching him.

Charlie's mother was an exotic dancer, and she was real pretty. But "I'm not getting any younger," she'd told Charlie last winter, and when she'd gotten a job offer in a Las Vegas club she had jumped at the chance. She'd told Charlie that he would have to stay behind with Uncle Jon, but it would just be for a while. Just until she got settled.

For nine months now Charlie had lived with his Uncle Jon, who wasn't really his uncle, but that's what his mother had made him call the man who had shared her bed. He knew his mother wasn't coming back.

As he watched the man across the street, he was reminded of the way his Uncle Jon looked at him sometimes, and he'd learned the hard way that it was much tougher on you if you resisted.

When he was nice to Uncle Jon, then Jon was nice to him, and gave him money or took him to a show, but at first he'd resisted Jon's crude, fumbling advances. The very first time he'd screamed until Uncle Jon had choked him unconscious.

"Hi, Charlie."

Charlie was startled at hearing his name. He looked up to see Ellen Sanders. Ellen was the most popular girl at Harwood, and no wonder. She had blond hair and sparkly green eyes, and her smile could melt you down into your socks. He smiled back, but it quickly faded. He knew he could never be friends with a girl like this.

"What do you want?" he said. His tone sounded angrier than he realized, and he regretted it. But like everything else in his life, it just kind of happened. The thought of apologizing never crossed his mind, because apologizing was an action that implied hope—a chance of correcting some wrong. In his short life he had never had much use for that feeling. Life wasn't something to be celebrated; it was something to be endured.

Ellen didn't seem put out with his remark. "Can I sit with you?" she asked, and looked at him with those bright green eyes washing over him like a huge wave. She smiled, and for Charlie it was like the sun had come out. His previous mood eased, and his defenses dropped slightly.

He started to tell her that would be just great, but it came out, "It's a free country."

"You don't have to be rude, Charlie Toon," Ellen said, her smile faltering. Before he could say anything, he was shoved hard from behind and knocked to the ground.

"What do you think you're doing, Charlie Tuna?" Alex Templeton said with a laugh. Alex was the school bully. His father was retired military, and they had lived all over the world. Unfortunately, Alex had adopted his father's demeanor, barking orders and using physical force on anyone smaller than himself.

Charlie wasn't smaller than Alex, but Charlie was on thin ice. One more problem at school and he'd be locked up. He had to bite down his anger as he picked himself up from the ground.

"Why are you hanging around this loser, Ellen?" Templeton said with a smirk aimed at Charlie.

Charlie looked at Ellen, desperately wanting just once for someone to take his side. But she looked embarrassed, and not saying a word, turned and walked away.

Charlie felt his fists tightening into hammers at his sides, but he'd been beaten, and it was no use to resist his fate. He relaxed his hands and just stared away, toward the man across from the playground.

Templeton wasn't satisfied with just beating Charlie down in a word contest. He had to humiliate him further to establish that he was in command. Some of Alex's friends gathered around them, joining Alex in jeering at him, saying, "Why don't you get out of here, Charlie Tuna? You don't belong here. You don't belong anywhere."

"Yeah," one of the other boys said, "Only the best tuna gets to be StarKist."

Another boy chimed in, "He looks more like a mackerel," and they all laughed.

Seeing that Charlie was thoroughly beaten, Alex added, "I'd kick your ass, but you aren't worth it." Alex stalked away, shouting, "Hey, Ellen, wait up," and the other boys hurried away as well.

Charlie stood motionless, eyes trained across the street, but not seeing anything. His thoughts had brought him to an empty place, where there was no Ellen Sanders, no Alex Templeton, and no Uncle Jon. It was a quiet place, where only he, Charlie Toon, could go. A place where he did belong.

Without knowing why, he walked from the playground and toward the man across the street. It didn't matter, really. Anywhere was better than school.

Chapter Forty-three

They were gathered again in the makeshift war room at Two-Jakes. Present were Jack, Liddell, Mark Crowley, and Angela Garcia, and Captain Franklin had decided to risk the wrath of Double Dick to attend the meeting as well after receiving the call from Jack.

"So it's Eddie Solazzo?" Captain Franklin asked.

"Who's this 'Eddie' guy?" Mark Crowley asked. He and Garcia had been halfway to Dubois County when they received the message from Jack and turned around to come back to meet.

"Eddie Solazzo is a psycho who likes to hurt people," Liddell said, scowling, but his face lit up when he saw Vinnie carrying in a tray of donuts and a carafe of coffee.

"Me and Jack arrested Eddie and his brother, Bobby, several times for robberies. They enjoyed inflicting pain more than stealing money. They both have records going back to their preteens. The father was a local preacher who died in a fire when they were teens." Liddell stopped to chomp a pastry.

"In any case," Liddell said, "when their father died, Bobby was old enough to take custody of Eddie, and they just seemed to go wild. Both were pretty much raised by the state through Boys School, and later in the state prison. When Jack killed Bobby, Eddie was doing time in Westville Corrections for armed robbery."

Garcia sneaked a peek at Jack, looking at the thick white scar that ran down his neck. She remembered hearing about the incident with Bobby Solazzo and how Jack had almost died, but she'd never heard the whole story.

Liddell was watching Jack, too. He guessed the thoughts going through his partner's mind, and knew this was Jack's least favorite subject. But the team had to know why Eddie Solazzo was a good fit for the killer. Why Eddie would want to punish Jack. He took in a deep breath and began.

"A couple of months ago, Jack and I got a lead on some guys that had been sticking up jewelry stores all over the state. Turned out to be Bobby Solazzo."

Jack stood up. "I'm going for a walk," he said, and left the room.

Garcia waited until the door shut behind Jack then asked in a hushed tone, "Is that where he got the scar?"

Liddell nodded, and then continued. "Bobby wasn't real careful picking someone to replace Eddie, and the ex-con he used had a problem with spousal abuse. She came to us, spilled the beans about the robbery they were planning, and we set up a stakeout.

"Anyway," Liddell said, "Bobby Solazzo shows up with some ex-cons and they blow the door lock off the back of Turley's Jewelry Store with a pump shotgun and rush inside."

Vinnie brought more coffee and pulled up a chair to hear the rest of the tale. He'd heard it a dozen times, but it never got old. Liddell stopped talking and looked at him dubiously. Vinnie grinned sheepishly and spread his hands. "What? I can't listen to this? It's some big dark police secret or something?"

Liddell refilled his coffee cup and continued. "Okay, so

things went to shit after that. Stuff I won't go into right now, but believe me there was a lot of commotion. Bobby took advantage of the confusion and came out the back door blasting away with a pump shotgun and ran down the alley. One robber was killed by our snipers in the alley, but two of these assholes got stuck inside the store and took hostages. Jack was the only one that wasn't ducking for cover, so he chased Solazzo. Solazzo surprised Jack and nearly cut him in half with a knife. Jack killed him. End of story."

Crowley said, "Yeah, Eddie sounds like a good fit for the killer, but does he use a knife like his brother?"

Liddell had to admit that was puzzling. Eddie generally preferred using a shotgun or a large-caliber pistol. "But if he is getting even for his brother, he might be using a knife to make his point."

Franklin didn't look convinced. "If it's Eddie, we should have his prints on file."

"But Eddie Solazzo is not on the fingerprint list that Walker gave me. And the DNA didn't match anyone," Garcia said, expressing what they were all thinking. "If Eddie Solazzo is our guy, and he just got out of prison recently, then his DNA has to be in the system. Right?"

Tony Walker spoke up. He had been checking the list of possible hits from their DNA request. "She's right. Eddie's not on here," he said.

"How is that possible?" Franklin asked. "I mean, Eddie's been down several times on violent felonies. He has to be in the system."

"Not necessarily," Walker said. "CODIS, the Combined DNA Index System that the FBI maintains, has about seven million offender profiles, but the NDIS, the National DNA Index System, is done state by state. And the fingerprint that the state police got from the gum wrapper was in horrible shape."

He saw everyone looking at him, and he shrugged, "Okay, so I'm a geek. But my point is that Indiana only has about one hundred thirty thousand entries into the database, and depending on the data-sharing between the state and federal computers, it's possible that some of the criminals are not in the system yet." Now he could see they were all interested.

"Check with the state lab and see if they submitted Eddie's DNA," Franklin said to Walker.

"I'll check with the Indiana Department of Corrections," Susan said.

"I'll have another donut," Liddell said, motioning for Crowley to pass the tray back in his direction.

"Susan, can you get a pickup order started on Eddie?" Jack asked.

"I did it this morning. He should be in the warrant computer by now," she answered. "But you know how that works. He can only be held on the warrant long enough to go in front of a judge to determine if he will be sent back to prison for parole violation."

Liddell finished her thought. "And the prisons are full, so the judges really don't bother too much with parolees unless they've committed a new crime, and yada, yada, yada."

"But at least we can get him off the street for a while," Jack said. He'd slipped back in the room quietly. "In the meantime we start working angles for probable cause for an arrest warrant," Jack said, then to Franklin he said, "Captain, can you—?"

"I'll get a BOLO out for Eddie," Franklin said, picking up his cell phone.

"You haven't told us what you found yet," Crowley said to Liddell.

Liddell tried to talk around the powdered-sugar donut he had stuffed into his mouth, gave up, and then held up a finger while he swallowed loudly.

"Real classy partner you got there, Jack," Crowley said with a grin.

"You ought to see him at a buffet," Jack responded, and Garcia made a face at the thought.

"Hey," Liddell protested, powdered sugar stuck to his face and lips. "If you screwups aren't interested, I'll peddle my information elsewheres."

"Go ahead," Garcia said. "But please, stop eating."

Liddell looked around for a napkin, and not finding one handy, wiped at his mouth with the back of his sleeve. "Okay, here's what I got."

Liddell's information had come from one of his informants, named Coin. The ones that knew Coin were skeptical of any information that he would come up with, because he had a reputation of manufacturing what he thought you wanted to hear. An anything-for-a-buck mentality.

Coin told Liddell that he had heard one of the Indian motel owners was "roughed up" a day or so ago. Because his booze-soaked mind worked on quantum time, a "day or so" to Coin might be two hours, or two weeks. It was all relative when Mad Dog 20/20 or Wild Irish Rose had its claws into Coin's mind, causing time to fold in on itself.

But in any case, it was another lead, and it would take at least an hour or so for Walker and Susan to run down the information on Eddie's DNA testing.

Liddell put together a photo lineup containing Eddie's parole photo, and he and Jack decided to run down the Indian motels lead. The thing was, these people were not very cooperative with police, viewing them through their own cultural experience. Police were something to be feared, avoided. But if anyone looked like they had been roughed up, they could at least show the lineup and see if they got a reaction. Besides, they might get lucky and run across Eddie. The strip of cheap motels on Fares Avenue was just the type of place someone could disappear.

CHAPTER FORTY-FOUR

Since he was still suspended from duty, Jack drove separately. If he had to, he could disappear quickly and not get Liddell in hot water with Double Dick. They struck out at the Royal and Schmidt motels, and were beginning to feel like they were on a wild-goose chase.

"Let's try the Arrowhead, and then we'll get back to the others," Jack said. "Maybe Walker will have some information by now."

Jack followed Liddell to the Arrowhead Motel and let Liddell park in the front drive while he took a parking spot around the side. Inside, they were met by a dark-skinned older gentleman who said his name was Haroon. His accent was very thick to the point of being indistinguishable. But when he realized they were there about the "bad man," as Haroon called him, his accent went away entirely, and his English became perfect.

"Sorry about that," Mr. Haroon said, and pulled a hard-bound ledger from under the counter. He flipped through a few pages and then pulled out another ledger and flipped it open. "He checked in on Tuesday, last week, checked out on Wednesday afternoon."

"That would fit Kids' Kingdom," Liddell said to Jack.

"He didn't pay, and he didn't check out," Haroon said, waving his arms theatrically. "He just beat up my aunt. And then he left."

"What room?" Jack asked.

"Room Thirty-seven," Haroon said, sadly shaking his head. "All the way in the back. He's a bad man. A very bad man."

Jack and Liddell took the room key from Haroon, and as they left the office, Haroon followed them. "If you're going to ask why I didn't report the attack, it's because my uncle doesn't want any police involvement, and my aunt wasn't hurt too badly. She understands how things work here."

They stopped outside the door of Room 37. The window next to the doorway was missing, and the curtains were flapping through the opening, held in place by the jagged edges of glass. Haroon stepped back when the two detectives unholstered their weapons and held them low. "Hey!" he said, and Liddell shushed him.

Jack didn't expect anyone to be in the room, but with these ten-dollar-a-night joints, you could easily walk in on a crack deal or a junkie with a gun. Jack eased the door into the room and quickly moved in to the left, his pistol at the ready. Liddell moved inside to the right, and they swept the room in an arc with the muzzles of their weapons until they were sure there was no threat to them. The interior consisted of two rooms, if you could consider a five-foot-by-five-foot bathroom another room. Both men reholstered their weapons and walked back outside, where an anxious Haroon waited.

"Have you had anyone in to clean up this place, yet?" Jack asked, but he was pretty sure nothing had been touched. The couch looked like it had been through a tree shredder. The bed was merely a mattress lying on the floor without any pillow or covers. Next to the mattress a broken lamp sat on a heavily scarred table. The mirror over the bathroom sink had been smashed, and shards of glass hung from the frame like hillbilly teeth. In other words, it was a typical run-down motel that the cops teasingly called a "no-tell motel" because if the cops showed up, you didn't ask, and you didn't tell.

The outside of the stucco building had been painted that shade of pink that you see in third-world countries, and the inside room paint was the color you would associate with Legionnaire's disease and bouts of delirium tremens. The only things interesting about the room were the walls. Each wall had several long gashes that could have been made with a machete or some other heavy-bladed instrument. There were also numerous fist-sized holes in the drywall, but all of this could have been made by tenants previous to Eddie's visit. In most instances the amount of damage in this room would be considered evidence of a struggle and possible murder, but in this type of setting it was called "ambiance."

From the doorway Jack noticed something lying under the edge of the couch. He walked back into the room and leaned down.

"You got some gloves?" he asked Liddell. Liddell handed him a pair of gloves and a plastic evidence envelope. Jack pulled on the gloves and reached under the couch, coming out with a red crayon. He dropped it in the evidence bag and lifted the edge of the couch a few inches. "Shit," Jack said softly and looked up at Liddell.

Liddell leaned down and saw what Jack had found. A Black Jack chewing gum wrapper.

"I'm sure glad I spotted the crayon and the gum wrapper," Liddell said, and that's the way it would go in the report, because Jack wasn't supposed to be there. He took the crayon from Jack. "I'll leave the gum wrapper for crime scene to collect." They went back outside.

"Do you keep crayons in the office?" Jack asked Haroon.

"We keep some in the office," Haroon answered. "For the kids, you know?"

"Where do you get them?" Liddell asked, and Haroon's face colored slightly.

"Look," Liddell said, "I don't care if you steal them from homeless shelters. I just want a straight answer, okay?"

Haroon cleared his throat and looked down. "There is a restaurant near one of our motels where we get them."

"The name?" Liddell demanded.

"It has painted wooden horses," Haroon said. "But I don't remember the name. Honest!"

"I know where it is," Jack said to Liddell, and then to Haroon, he said, "We need to talk to your aunt." Haroon nodded agreement, and led them back through the office to a narrow doorway that was covered by a sheet. On the other side was a room small enough to be a broom closet. The aunt was lying on a camper-type cot with a thin blanket, wearing only a pullover jumper, and bandages covered most of her face. She was of indeterminate age, and was thin, anemic looking. Black rings circled the one eye that wasn't covered with bandages, and her gaze was that of a frightened animal.

"You can talk to them," Haroon assured her in his perfect English.

She let out a small moan as she tried to lift herself up on one elbow. "Is this about the bad man?" she asked in a tiny voice.

"Yes," Liddell said. "Tell us about the bad man."

The woman's name was Akira Patel. She was actually fifty years old, from Bangladesh, and spoke excellent English. They learned during the conversation that Akira meant "graceful strength" and that she was a hard worker. She wanted nothing to do with the police. She had come to America a year ago to work for the family business. Her reticence about the police was a natural tendency of a woman from a country with a caste system. Although she was hesitant at first, she warmed to the detectives and told them quite a lot. At least until they asked if she would look at a photo lineup.

When they were outside alone Jack said to Liddell, "It was like pulling the plug on a toaster, wasn't it?"

"The minute you asked her to look at photos she forgot how to speak English," Liddell agreed. "But can you blame her? I mean, look what he did to her!"

"Yeah, you're right," Jack agreed. "The description she gave us is Eddie, but without a positive identification we can't charge him with anything. Besides, she won't press charges. Hopefully the crime scene guys will find something in that room to verify that it was Eddie. At least then, we can place him in Evansville during the time of the Kids' Kingdom murder."

"So what now?" Liddell asked.

"You go call forensics and tear that room apart," Jack said. "I'm not supposed to be here, and I don't want to put the crime scene guys on the spot by making them lie in their reports."

The search of Room 37 took the rest of the evening. The room was surprisingly clean of any fingerprints or forensic evidence of any type, and the fingerprints they did find were smudged or so light that Liddell was told not to hold his breath. They did find some metal pieces in the large gouges in the walls, and the forensic team seemed pretty excited by that discovery. They wouldn't promise anything, but they told Liddell to check back in the morning. If they ever found the weapon, they might be able to match it to the metal fragments, and to the wounds on the bodies. It was something, at least.

Liddell turned over the red crayon after describing in detail where "he" found it under the bed, and asked for it to be compared with the crayon on the killer's notes. He hoped they would be able to do at least a preliminary comparison without sending it out to the state police lab. After that, Liddell packed it in and headed home. Unless something else came up, there was nothing more to do. Except call Jack and fill him in, of course.

Jack answered on the first ring. "Tell me you found something," he said, and when Liddell didn't respond right away he said, "Damn!"

"Jack, they're taking everything back to headquarters, and Franklin has them working all night on what they have." He then told Jack about the metal fragments that were found in the walls of the room, and the bad news, that the room was almost devoid of any usable fingerprints.

"How can someone be so damn lucky?" Jack complained. "Did you try the Indian woman again?"

"Yeah," Liddell said. "Nothing. She's scared shitless."

Jack was disappointed, but he knew that couldn't force Akira to identify her attacker. Haroon claimed he wasn't able to determine which of their employees had checked the occupant in to Room 37, and the management had closed ranks in silence. Making an arrest for the battery on Akira was not going to happen. Any charge would get thrown out of court, even if they somehow obtained enough probable cause to get a warrant. They would just have to work with the parole violation charge they currently had.

"There's more bad news," Liddell said. "Walker called and said they can't find Eddie's DNA in the system."

"How can that be?" Jack asked. "How do you lose DNA?"

"That's what I asked. He said that there was some kind of problem with the state's computer servers a couple of years ago, and the company they had working on them may have accidentally erased some of the data."

"And they don't back up the servers?" Jack said.

"Walker is still checking. He told them this is a multiple murder case, but the state employee he was talking to didn't seem impressed. Anyway, I called Susan, and she said that she's trying to find out if there's anything that the state parole office may have that can be used for a DNA comparison."

"Well, we still have the DNA from Patoka Lake, so all we have to do is catch Eddie and get some blood from him," Jack said.

Liddell was quiet for a long time.

"What is it?" Jack asked.

"Are you sitting down, pod'na?" Liddell said.

Jack felt a headache coming on. "I was before you called," he said.

"Well, when Walker called he gave me some other news," Liddell said, his voice taking on a chilling note. "He said the DNA in the Patoka case is a match with the urine samples we found on your clothes."

Jack felt his stomach roll. His vision blurred, and pain shot up his spine. His palms became sweaty, and he thought he might throw up. He was startled to realize that Liddell had been talking to him, and was saying, "Jack, did you hear me?"

Jack cleared his throat and said, "Yes. I heard. It has to be Eddie." His voice was stiff, the words forced. He thought, *This must be what victims of rape and assault feel like after . . .*

He had talked to hundreds of victims during his career, but had never really known what they were going through. It was like the most private part of his life was torn from him and cruelly abused. Since the incident behind his cabin, he'd been nervous when he left or arrived home. He had trouble sleeping. His personal safety had been violated, and he'd lost control of his ability to defend himself. For an ordinary citizen that was frightening, but for a policeman, that loss was devastating because it threatened everything he stood for.

How could he protect the public when he couldn't even protect himself?

Jack carried the phone out to the porch, took a Guinness from the cooler he kept stocked by his chair, and sat down. Liddell heard a pop and knew what the sound was immediately. He worried about Jack. He was alone too much, too dedicated to his work sometimes, and too prone to drink when it all became too much.

"It's a good thing you left when you did," Liddell said, to change the subject. "When I called for forensics, they called the chief."

"Really?" Jack said, genuinely surprised.

"Yeah, the crime scene commander has been ordered to call him personally any time I call forensics, or any other assistance," Liddell said. "Guess the chief doesn't trust me."

"Or me," Jack said, and Liddell was glad to hear him chuckle slightly.

"Or maybe he's got wind of our little group, the Holy Jihad team?"

Jack doubted that Dick knew about the team. If he did, he would have Jack up on serious charges and in front of the Merit Commission by now. But he didn't doubt that they would have to be extremely careful. Snitches didn't just work for detectives.

The men agreed to talk again early in the morning. He wondered what the hell he hoped to accomplish by working against the chief's orders. He didn't want to compromise Liddell, and so he couldn't even stay while Crime Scene searched the room. How was he supposed to get anywhere when he had to work blindfolded and hog-tied?

His neck and head throbbed. He went into the bathroom and carried a couple of aspirin back onto the porch and downed them with a Guinness. He didn't know that the morning would hold a surprise for everyone.

CHAPTER FORTY-FIVE

When his phone rang at six o'clock that morning Jack was wide awake and sitting on his porch watching the last boats of fishermen as they sculled along the banks. It was too late in the year to catch anything except maybe a carp or a garfish, neither one edible. He took his empty coffee mug and went inside.

"Are you dressed?" Liddell asked when Jack lifted the receiver.

"Pervert," Jack responded in a dead serious tone.

"What color are your panties?" Liddell said in a raspy voice, accompanied with heavy breathing.

"Does Marcie know this side of you, partner?" Jack said. "What's going on?"

"Maddy got another note. She threatened to burn it if I didn't bring you along. I haven't called the chief yet, in case you're wondering."

Liddell picked him up at his cabin a few minutes later.

The Channel Six television station was housed in a squat brick building with a flat roof that sat on top of a hill surrounded by trees. The structure itself was utilitarian and hideous, with the only advantage being that it couldn't be seen by the public from any of the main roads. The upper parking lots commanded a 360-degree view. Unfortunately the views south and east were of the roofs of an abandoned factory, and the view to the west took in Crescent Hill Cemetery. The view to the north was the top of trees for as far as you could see.

The detectives were met by an excited Maddy Brooks when they pulled in to the Channel Six parking lot. They had not even rolled to a stop when she approached their car.

"Has there been another murder?" she asked, breathlessly.

Liddell and Jack looked at each other.

"Aw, shit," Liddell said, and they got out of the car.

The sun was blocked by black clouds, and to the west Jack could see lightning and could smell the approaching rain. They walked with Maddy to her office. Jack's mood was as dark and angry as the weather as he struggled to control his words.

"So, you got a note from the killer last night and you called the chief of police this morning," Jack said.

Maddy caught the sarcasm in his voice and stopped just outside the doors of the television station. "Let's get something straight, Detective Murphy. These notes are being sent to me. Me personally. I am under no obligation to share them with the police."

Liddell opened the door for them just as the rain started coming straight down in buckets. They hurried in to the foyer.

"You're a paragon of virtue, Maddy. Now can we please see the note?" Jack asked politely.

"You guys better not even think about trying to cut me out of this story," she said, her back to the men as they entered her office.

Jack kept his anger in check. All that mattered was getting the note. He knew if the television station wanted to, they could tie the note up for hours while the police department fought a legal battle over the "right" to see a piece of evidence in a murder case.

He took a little comfort in the fact that they now had a suspect, and that Maddy didn't know about it yet. The forensic boys had come up with a match on a partial fingerprint from a piece of broken mirror. The tech said it was Eddie Solazzo, but to swear to it in court they needed at least six points of comparison and they only had five. It was good enough for Jack, but it still didn't put Eddie at any of the murders because they had no fingerprints in those cases. Crime Scene had also advised that they found a beer can in the room at the Arrowhead and they were rushing a DNA test.

How Maddy had not gotten wind of this development was a surprise to Jack, but he was sure, with all the leaks in the department, she would find all of it out before the day was over.

As they gathered around Maddy's desk, Jack noticed that she had already taken the note from the envelope, no doubt to Xerox, photograph, and get as many fingerprints on it as possible. She saw the disdainful look and said, "Don't worry, I didn't handle anything."

Liddell asked, "Was this one left at the front door again?"

"Lois Thatcher found it lying on the ground beside the front doors when she was leaving the building last night," Maddy said, looking irritated. "I guess she thinks because she's the mayor's mother that she can do as she pleases. Anyway, I had already gone for the day, so she stuck it on my desk and told about it this morning." She looked thoughtful. "Probably would have been about six o'clock last night." She used the eraser end of a pencil to push the note across the desk where Liddell and Jack could read it.

As she said, the envelope was addressed to her. Printed in the familiar red crayon were the words:

> Bring Murphy back
> Or I will kill one
> Every day
> Little Boy Blue is the First.

Liddell gave Jack a concerned look. "He wants you back on the case?"

"You've got to let me interview you," Maddy said, and both men looked at her in disbelief.

"I'm suspended, Maddy. I'm not even supposed to be here," Jack said patiently.

Maddy smiled smarmily. "I bet I can get you back on the job now," she said.

"I don't need your help," Jack said, angrily. "The last time I dealt with you I got suspended."

"You can't blame that on me, Jack Murphy," she said. "You've never respected your superiors, and it's that nasty temper of yours that gets you in trouble."

Jack wanted to come back with something hateful, but she was right. He didn't respect his "superiors" when it came to some limelight-seeking ignoramuses like Double Dick.

Liddell stepped quickly in to defuse the argument. "Maddy, I can't let you interview Jack, but I have something else I can give you if you don't name your source."

Maddy snapped her attention solely on Blanchard now. Her movement was almost snakelike. "What is it?"

Liddell looked around, almost theatrically, then leaned in close to Maddy and said softly, "Forensics think the crayon on all of the notes is from the same batch of crayons."

Jack hadn't learned this information yet, but he was amused watching the look on Maddy's face while she assimilated the new piece of information. It was like she was chewing Liddell's words, tasting them, deciding what to do with his statement. Would she swallow it, or spit it in his face? Then her brow narrowed, and she said angrily, "That's it! That's all I get for this note?"

Liddell plucked the note and envelope from her hands and turned toward the door. "Think of it. Mother Goose's red crayon matched." She was thinking about it. "I'd better get this one analyzed as well," he said over his shoulder.

While Maddy stood with her mouth hanging open, Jack smiled and shrugged and then followed his partner out.

CHAPTER FORTY-SIX

Chief Richard Dick used his master keys to let himself into the Civic Center hallway. The Civic Center wouldn't open for another hour or so, but the mayor was already in and had called for him. Dick stepped off the elevator on the third floor of the Civic Center and walked to one of the mirrored columns to straighten his tie and check his uniform. Everything about him was perfect. He smiled.

It had been over a week since the last killing, and the news media frenzy was winding down. All in all, it had been perfect timing for him. The murders, the publicity, his appointment as chief of police, and the murders had stopped. The media had even played with the angle that it was Dick's reputation as a "no-nonsense copper" that made the killer stop. And best of all, he'd finally humiliated Jack Murphy in a very public fashion. He knew it was Murphy who had started the nasty gossip about him, calling him Double Dick and such.

Dick pulled down the brim of his eight-point police cap and checked his teeth in the mirror. *Things will be different from now on,* he thought, and walked down the corridor to the mayor's office.

"Good morning, Alice" Chief Dick said, giving the mayor's secretary a sincere smile. "You're here early."

She looked up sharply at being addressed so casually. She didn't like it when visitors called her by her first name, and she definitely didn't like the new chief of police. She would have to teach him some manners, she thought.

"Do you have an appointment with the mayor?" she asked, knowing full well that the chief had been summoned by the mayor himself. *Doesn't hurt to put him in his place*, she thought, and was pleased by the grim look that crossed Dick's features.

"I was called," Chief Dick said flatly, and thought, *Controlling bitch.*

She was about to tell him to have a seat while she checked with the mayor, but the door to the mayor's office opened and Thatcher Hensley poked his head out. "Get in here. We've got a little problem," he said to Dick and disappeared, leaving the door open.

Dick entered the mayor's office and took a seat across the desk from Hensley. "You said it was urgent," he said to the mayor.

Hensley pushed a white piece of paper that was stapled to an envelope. "This was left in the Civic Center suggestion box," he said, without further explanation.

Dick reached for the paper, imagining that one of Evansville's citizens had written some hate mail, or some other nonsense. Why the mayor would bother him with these frivolous matters, he couldn't imagine. But he was the chief now. Didn't hurt to brownnose a little.

As Dick read the letter, his face turned pasty white.

While Jack and Liddell were talking to Maddy Brooks, a retired high school teacher, a recent widower, was taking his morning exercise along the riverfront esplanade. The levee system for that stretch of the Ohio River started behind the downtown museum and ran east for eleven miles or so, ending at Angel Mounds State Park in Warrick County. Lenny Clegg had made the walk his morning routine when the weather was nice. In cold weather, or too warm weather, he went to Eastland Mall and walked inside with the other retirees. But he much preferred the scenery and solitude of the walk along the levee.

He climbed the grassy rise behind the museum and looked around. To the east and west the Ohio River wound like a ribbon across the landscape. The old steam engine and boxcar sat in a historically correct train station behind the museum, and a bike path ran westward toward the Blue Star Casino.

In an effort to expand the art culture of the community, the City of Evansville Arts Commission had started displaying various themes of statues along brick-lined Main Street and continuing down the riverfront walkway to the museum. A few months ago, the sculptures—created and painted by local schoolchildren—were race cars. They were actually very good, and after a few months, the statues were auctioned, and the money used to repeat the process. This month, the creations were butterflies. Each one stood about four feet high and was painted in every hue of the rainbow.

Lenny was admiring one of these when he noticed the wings of this particular statue had been draped with what looked like red ropes and someone had splashed blue paint on and around the statue. He pulled out his cell phone to report the vandalism to the police when he noticed a bloody leg bent around the base of the statue.

Chief Dick had recovered sufficiently enough to speak by the time he put the note back on the desktop.

"What are you going to do about this, Chief Dick?" the
mayor demanded.

That the mayor had referred to him by his official title
wasn't lost on him. *What have I gotten myself into?* he worried. But there was only one thing to say, wasn't there?

"I'll look into it, Mayor," Chief Dick said, sounding more
confident than he felt.

Hensley leaned forward in his chair, both hands flat on
top of the desk. "You'll look into it?" He leaned farther forward, and spittle was gathering at the corners of his mouth.
"You'll look into it!" He got up and stood in front of the
bank of glass windows that looked out over Main Street, his
arms straight at his sides, his fists clinching and relaxing.

"I'm doing everything I can, Thatcher," Dick said, and
cringed at the apologetic tone in his own voice.

Hensley spun around, facing the chief. "You'll do better
than that!" Hensley said through clenched teeth. "You'll
catch this bastard, or you'll find another job." With that de-
cree, Hensley turned back to the windows and was quiet.

Dick kept his eyes cast down. He'd seen these tantrums
before and knew that it was best to let the mayor blow off
steam.

In a few moments Hensley turned around and went back
to his seat. "Well," he said, "we'd better decide how we're
going to handle this demand."

"Before we do anything, perhaps I should have my people
verify the note is authentic," Dick suggested.

"What?" Hensley said, "You think it might be from someone besides the killer?"

"Mayor, we suspended Detective Murphy a week ago.
There have been no murders since then. Why would this guy
be demanding Murphy's return now?"

Hensley stood up and paced in front of the desk. "Are you
suggesting that Detective Murphy wrote the note himself,
Chief Dick?"

That's exactly what Dick believed, but he couldn't afford to be wrong. He couldn't afford another murder to prove the point. "I'm merely suggesting that we take a few hours to have this note checked out by my forensic people. Then we can decide."

Hensley stood in front of the chief, looking down into his face keenly. "You'd better do something quick, Richard. He's promised to kill one child for each day we keep Murphy off the job. If the killer strikes again and the public finds out that we sat on this note, it will mean the end of both of us."

Dick understood completely. But he couldn't put Murphy back on the job. Better to be fired than let Murphy gloat over him. "I'll oversee the processing of the note myself, Mayor," Chief Dick promised.

"Get Murphy back, Dick," Hensley said flatly.

CHAPTER FORTY-SEVEN

The responding uniformed sergeant set up an inner perimeter and closed down traffic on Riverside Drive between Walnut and Cherry Streets. Evansville traffic had become familiar with portions of Riverside Drive being blocked by police cars because of the frequent events, such as 5K runs, the Freedom Festival, Frog Follies, and arts and crafts fairs. Because of that, it was strange just how little attention was paid to the police activity by the locals. It looked like just another day in Evansville when Liddell and Jack arrived at the scene, followed closely by a Channel Six news van.

A uniform officer held the yellow caution tape up as Liddell drove under, but stopped the news van from entering.

Outside the tape, Maddy Brooks jumped from the still-moving van, alternately trying to get Jack's attention and giving nine kinds of hell to the uniformed officer who had blocked their entrance.

"Do you think we should let her in?" Liddell asked.

Jack looked back and noticed that the uniformed officer was the rookie, Kuhlenschmidt.

"Fuck her," Jack said, but he felt sorry for the rookie.

"That's why you should be the lead detective on this case, Jack. You're so good with words."

The uniformed sergeant was a wizard at managing things and had already set up a gathering point for the news media at the Four Freedoms Monument several hundred yards distant from the crime scene. A white tent had been erected around the body, properly concealing the victim from the curious and the thrill-seekers that get off on death. All that was missing now were the vendors and kiddy rides.

Jack spotted the mobile command center lumbering up the boat ramp toward the back of the museum. Behind it were two crime scene SUVs, and several officers were busy securing the scene. One of these looked up and said to the other, "Uh oh. We've just been Dick'd."

Liddell and Jack looked in the direction the officer was gazing and saw a black sedan pull up to the crime scene tape across from the Four Freedoms Monument. The news media that had been yelling toward Jack and Liddell now descended on the chief's car like paparazzi on Paris Hilton.

Jack was surprised to see Captain Franklin get out of the driver's side and open the back door for Double Dick. "Where's Dewey?" Jack asked Liddell. He was referring to Captain Dewey Duncan, Double Dick's trusty court jester.

"Hemorrhoid surgery," Liddell commented, and then said, "He's delivering twins."

A uniform officer standing close by said, "I heard he's having Double Dick's love child."

"Children," Liddell corrected him, holding up two fingers. "Twins. Both butt ugly."

"You can quit any time now," Jack said as Captain Franklin spotted them.

Double Dick stood smiling in front of the bank of microphones being thrust in his face, and Liddell said, "You think he'll smoke afterward?"

"Nah, I don't think he knows what postcoital languor is," Jack answered.

The captain walked up to the crime scene tent and stopped to sign in with the officer keeping the crime scene log. Liddell said, "How are your hemorrhoids, Captain?"

Franklin either didn't think it was funny, or had something else on his mind. He said, "Jack. I'm glad you're here. It saves me the trouble of calling."

Franklin turned toward the river, so his face couldn't be seen by the reporters in the news media staging area. Jack and Liddell followed suit and gathered close around. The news media had employed lip readers in the past, and with their long-range cameras they could have any film viewed later to try to discover what the detectives were saying to each other.

Jack had the greatest respect for Captain Franklin, both as a man and as a supervisor. But, Jack thought it was a bad day for the police department when Franklin had been promoted from detective sergeant up through the ranks to captain, because, like most policemen, Jack believed that promotions were bad things, except for the eight percent pay raise. He further believed that for every eight percent in pay that a promotion brought, that eight percent of the promotee's brain was removed. So if his beliefs were accurate, Double Dick was working at about one-quarter mental capacity. Jack wasn't sure how Captain Franklin had managed to avoid the lobotomy and keep his sense of right and wrong.

Franklin kept his voice low. "Chief Dick is considering reinstating you to full duty, Jack," he said.

"No kidding?" Liddell said loudly. Captain Franklin shot him a cautioning look, and Liddell quieted down.

"I saw the note that Maddy got, but I didn't think the chief had seen it yet. Did he?" Jack asked.

Franklin didn't answer. He didn't have to. The killer wanted Jack. He would keep killing until they gave him what he wanted. It was political suicide to not allow Jack back on the case merely because the chief had a gripe with him.

"When?" Jack asked.

Franklin shrugged. Chief Dick had asked Franklin to drive him to the murder scene, and had mentioned that he was "thinking about" putting Murphy back on the case. After that, Dick had said nothing.

"I'm sure the chief is going to want to see inside there," Franklin said, motioning to the tent.

"It's not pretty, Captain," Liddell said.

"Well," Franklin said with a sigh, "we might as well get this over with."

The three men slipped protective booties over their street shoes and then entered the tent one by one, but stayed well back from the two crime scene techs, who were clothed in white protective gear.

"There's nothing on his person to identify him, Captain," one of the techs said. The other tech was on his knees examining the ground around the body, looking for trace evidence.

"Little Boy Blue," Franklin said softly, and looked at the body of what looked to be a ten- to twelve-year-old boy. The body was dressed in well-worn jeans, no shirt, and one dirty sneaker on a sockless right foot, the left foot bare. Blue paint had been poured over the body from head to foot.

Jack looked closely at the boy's wounds. He had been slashed across his face, neck, and chest with something so sharp that the head was almost severed from the neck. The body had then been tied clumsily to the butterfly sculpture with nylon rope and left in a sitting position. There was no sign of struggle or defensive wounds, although an autopsy might give more detail.

"He wasn't killed here," Jack said. There wasn't enough blood.

"He may not have even died from these wounds," one of the techs pointed out.

"If he didn't die from those cuts or whatever, what killed him?" Franklin asked.

The crime scene tech shook his head. "Have to wait for the post, Captain. It's hard to tell what's under all that paint."

The men stepped back outside, leaving the crime scene techs to their work. Franklin sighed, and looked up to see the gangly figure of Chief Dick climbing the grassy hill toward them with a scowl spread across his pinched features.

"This fits the staging of the other victims," Jack said, and Liddell nodded agreement. " 'Tommy Tittlemouse' found face-down in a ditch. 'Little Nanny Etticoat' was dressed in a nightgown, or petticoat."

"You can have as many people as you need," Captain Franklin said to Liddell; then, to Jack, "Don't wander off." He headed for Chief Dick, who had just made it to the top of the hill.

The conversation between the detective captain and the chief of police was so animated that several of the television cameramen had hurriedly turned their cameras on the spectacle. Nothing upped the ratings like a little violence on film. But soon it was evident that the conversation was cooling, and the disappointment on the faces of the cameramen was obvious.

When Captain Franklin walked over to Liddell and Jack his face and neck were still red. Chief Dick stood like a graceful flamingo, his back to the men, nose tilted into the air.

"Jack, come by my office and pick up your gun and badge," Franklin said, causing several of the gathered officers to smile.

"It's about fucking time," Liddell muttered under his breath.

"Liddell and I will be pretty busy, Captain," Jack said. "Can you get some detectives to check paint outlets as soon as we identify the brand of paint? Maybe the state police lab can speed things up with the paint?"

"I'll get it done, Jack."

"You'll get what done, Captain?" Chief Dick said. He had come up behind them soundlessly.

Franklin looked humorlessly at the chief. "We need the cooperation of the state police lab, Chief. Can you help us out there?"

"We need their cooperation for what, exactly?" Dick said.

Franklin pulled a flap back on the tent, giving Dick a view of the splayed and tortured body of the young boy. Dick's expression seemed to freeze on his face, and he made gagging sounds.

"Not a problem, Captain," Chief Dick said, and excused himself on the pretense of going to call the state police superintendant. He almost ran down the hill toward the gathered media and his luxury sedan.

"Good thing he didn't barf on the body," Liddell said, and this time Franklin did chuckle.

"Be respectful, Detective Blanchard," Franklin cautioned. "Chief Dick can be very helpful in clearing the political path for you."

Yeah, if he gets something for himself out of it, Jack thought.

Just then, Liddell's cell phone rang and he answered. A minute later he said, "We've got an ID on the kid."

CHAPTER FORTY-EIGHT

Angelina Garcia had just moved the last of the equipment from the War Room at Two-Jakes to her van. She was about to leave when Chief Deputy Mark Crowley drove into the parking lot.

"Need some help?" he asked.

"All finished," she said, and shut the back hatch. "You have perfect timing, Deputy."

Mark grinned, his face turning red, and said, "I was checking with my boss to see if I could stick around here a while. Maybe help out if I can."

"Is that the reason you came by?"

"Well, not exactly," he stammered, "I just thought—"

Garcia cut him off. "You came by to ask me out."

"Well, I, uh," he said and looked at the ground.

"I'd love to go out with you," she said, and his face showed obvious surprise.

"Would that be okay with your boss?" she asked.

"Hell yeah!" he said.

"You're so cute," she said, and touched his arm.

Mark looked serious and said, "That chief of yours doesn't seem to think so."

"You've talked to the chief?" Garcia said.

"Yeah," Mark explained. "I had to see if he would let me work with y'all."

"Mark," Garcia said, earnestly. "His nickname is Double Dick. What's that tell you?"

"Well, I'm sorry to say this, but the nickname doesn't do him justice," Mark said and rubbed the back of his neck.

Garcia smiled at him. He was country all the way to the bone, and that was what she liked about him. He was a welcome relief from the guys around Evansville, with their toys and attitudes, and their inability to commit to anything more than cable television. Most of them couldn't even stick with a toothpaste brand. But about Mark, her mom would have said, "He's a keeper, Angel." Garcia had to admit, she was interested.

"How about following me downtown?" she said.

Mark smiled and opened the van door for her, and held it until she was seated. "Can't wait," he said, and shut the door carefully.

Garcia rolled the window down and said, "When we get to headquarters, don't hold the door for me, okay? The guys down there take that as a sign of weakness."

"Then someone should teach 'em some manners," Mark said, and grinned.

Just then Angelina's cell phone rang. She looked shocked when she answered, then closed the phone slowly.

"What's the matter?" Mark asked.

"That was Jack," she said, and stared straight ahead. "They found another one."

"Another victim. Who?"

"He didn't say. He told me to go to headquarters and meet Captain Franklin. Now that Jack's not suspended, we're getting a new war room."

"So what do I do?" Crowley asked, hoping he wasn't going to be sent back to Dubois County.

Garcia smiled, and said, "He wants you to wait at police headquarters with me and make some calls to your county. Try to see if someone will check all the motels for someone matching Eddie's description."

"Sounds like a plan," Crowley said, pleased that he would be able to justify his hanging around Angelina.

Jack had arranged with Captain Franklin to have Garcia reassigned to them. He called her and told her about the new murder and asked her to move everything back downtown. Captain Franklin would meet her and show her where to set up shop. After he hung up with Garcia, he and Liddell drove to Harwood Middle School. The victim's name was Charlie Toon, and he was a seventh grader. Jack wondered if Katie had known him, but he didn't want to ask her at the school. He'd call her later.

When they arrived at the school, they saw a young blond girl and a red-haired boy sitting on a bench along the hallway near the principal's office. Whatever the boy was in trouble for, or was required to see the school principal about, he seemed to think it was funny and was smirking. The girl looked both embarrassed and scared. A few feet down the hallway, School Liaison Officer Jeff Townsend pried himself away from a whispered conversation with a cute female teacher who wasn't much older than the students.

"Want me to throw some cold water on him, Jack?" Liddell offered.

Officer Townsend had the physique of a young Arnold Schwarzenegger, along with good looks and an insatiable sex drive. If he had been a woman he would have been labeled a slut, a whore, and a nymphomaniac. But since he was a man, he was well respected by his peers for his ability to get laid.

"Only if he starts humping my leg," Jack answered.

A short and extremely bald man came out of a doorway down the hall and walked in their direction. His brown suit was heavily wrinkled around the waist and tail of the coat, which meant he did a lot of sitting. He was middle aged, but already had heavy worry lines in his brow. When he reached the detectives he stuck his hand out.

"Principal John Spanner," he said.

Jack and Liddell introduced themselves. Spanner's hand-shake was wet and brief before he crammed his hands into his pants pockets. When he spoke there was a noticeable ner-vous tic at the corner of his mouth.

"Let's take this to my office, gentlemen," he said, and Lid-dell and Jack followed after him.

The inside of the principal's office was small and cramped, but clean and carefully decorated. He noticed Liddell look-ing at the floral prints hanging around the room.

"I've only been here since the beginning of the term. I haven't had time to do anything to Mrs. Gleason's office. She was the last principal. She took a faculty position in Col-orado," he said, somewhat enviously. "But you're not here about that."

Liddell said, "Mr. Spanner, what can you tell us about Charlie Toon?"

Spanner opened a thick file on his desk, and Jack guessed that Charlie Toon had quite a history to have generated so much paper for a seventh grader.

"You may not know this, but Harwood School has some-what of a reputation for being a tough school," Spanner started. "We get the castoffs from the other schools. The troubled kids, and I don't mean just special education stu-dents." He said this with raised eyebrows as if making a point.

"My ex-wife teaches for you, Mr. Spanner," Jack said, and nodded for him to continue.

"Katie?" Spanner said, and a lecherous smile lit his face. "I wasn't aware of that," he added, and the nervous tic was back. "Charlie came here—actually was sent here—by his last school because of problems with other students." He leaned forward and lowered his voice, "He has a real problem socializing with anyone, and I mean anyone."

"What kind of trouble are we talking about here?" Liddell asked.

Spanner looked pensive. He obviously was uncomfortable talking about his students in general and maybe about Charlie Toon in particular. He seemed to come to a decision, and continued. "Well, you are the police, so I guess it's all right to speak to you of this."

Liddell assured him that he was doing the right thing.

"Charlie likes to fight. He has a hair-trigger temper. All someone has to do is look at him and he's on the attack. It doesn't matter if it's another student or a teacher.

"He was at Howard Roosa before he came here, and his social studies teacher asked him what was bothering him." Liddell's eyebrows raised in question. Spanner hurried on, "I've spoken to the teacher, and he swears that all he asked was 'What's wrong?' The teacher, Mr. Griffith, had noticed that Charlie was very withdrawn, stayed to himself a lot, and that the other children seemed to be afraid of him. That's usually an indication that something is wrong at home, and Mr. Griffith was trying to help Charlie."

Spanner smiled broadly, and said, "Mr. Griffith is an excellent teacher, I can tell you. He's very interested in his kids, his students, and takes a personal interest in each of them."

Jack was getting tired of waiting for Spanner to say what was on his mind. "So, tell us what happened."

"Well. Mr. Griffith asked Charlie what was wrong, and

Charlie jumped on Mr. Griffith and began beating and kicking him." He looked horrified. Mr. Spanner was a small man, and probably had a lot of fear that what happened to Griffith could happen to him. From what he had seen of school incidents in this day and age, and what he'd been told by Katie, Jack didn't blame Spanner for being concerned.

"It took several male teachers to pull Charlie off."

"Was Mr. Griffith hurt?" Jack asked. He didn't recall seeing anything in any of the newspapers about an incident like that.

"Not any permanent injuries, thank goodness," Spanner answered. "But he was pretty shaken by it and took a leave of absence." Spanner shook his head in dismay. "He didn't return this semester. Mr. Griffith, that is. And Charlie was sent here. Well, it was either here, or the psychiatric institution, and if I may speak frankly, I think they made a mistake sending him here. I think Boys School or the Children's Psychiatric Center might be better for him."

Mr. Spanner looked at the men with concern. "What has Charlie done now?" he asked.

Liddell and Jack exchanged glances. Apparently Officer Townsend hadn't informed Mr. Spanner that Charlie Toon had been found dead an hour earlier. Jack ignored the question for the moment and asked one of his own.

"Who are the two students in the hallway?"

Spanner looked surprised that the men didn't know. "Alex Templeton and Ellen Sanders, of course. They came to the office and said they saw Charlie run off from school yesterday. He didn't show up for class this morning, and Alex was bragging that he'd run Charlie away for good."

Spanner tented his eyebrows again and said, "Alex Templeton is somewhat of a bully."

"I guess Townsend was too busy chatting to tell us," Liddell said.

*   *   *

After they informed Principal Spanner that Charlie Toon would no longer be a problem to his school, or any other, because he was dead, they could not get enough cooperation from the man. Jack wasn't sure, but he thought he'd seen a glow of relief in the principal's eyes.

Principal Spanner looked up the next-of-kin information the school had on file, and told them Charlie Toon lived with an uncle in the Howell Park area. The Howell area of Evansville is the white ghetto. Jack and Liddell passed this information on to Captain Franklin, who sent a team of detectives to find the next of kin. When Franklin called back a few minutes later he told them the "uncle" would have to be sobered up a bit before he could talk to anyone.

Meanwhile, Liddell and Jack had the task of interviewing Alex Templeton and Ellen Sanders. After a few minutes with each they realized they needed more help at the school. It seemed that numerous students may have seen Charlie leave the playground. Jack had the pleasure of speaking briefly with the red-haired smirking boy from the hallway, and came to the conclusion that Alex Templeton might possibly graduate from school, but would definitely become a prison bitch someday, or maybe a serial killer.

Spanner came up with a list of almost thirty students that would have been on the playground at the time Charlie Toon was last seen. Jack decided to stay and interview as many students as they could until help arrived.

CHAPTER FORTY-NINE

"My name is Jonathan Hewett Grant," the man told the uniformed officer sitting with him in one of the police department interview rooms. "Am I under arrest?" he demanded to know. He was dressed in khaki pants and shirt, and had finally been located by juvenile detectives at his newest girlfriend's apartment. He worked at a car dealership as a grease monkey, and the girlfriend as a waitress at one of the county taverns. When he had been told about the death of his charge, Charlie Toon, he had promptly begun to swear that he hadn't done anything wrong and then demanded an attorney.

The remark had bothered Jack and Liddell. Most people didn't swear innocence when they had not been accused of any wrongdoing. So Jack had decided to let him stew while Jack and Liddell watched on a four-way monitor in the detectives' squad room that was hooked into each of the four interview rooms.

It had been fifteen minutes since Jonathan Hewitt Grant had been brought to police headquarters, and he still refused to give them any information about Charlie Toon or tell them why he was being so defensive. Jack was running out of patience.

"Let's try him," Jack said, picked up his coffee, and headed for the interview room.

"There's only one way to do it quick," Liddell said.

"I know," Jack responded, and the two men entered the interview room where Charlie Toon's pro-tem uncle was just finishing another crying spell.

"You can leave him with us," Liddell told the uniformed officer.

"He's all yours," the officer said.

Jack sat in front of Grant, and Liddell scraped a chair across the concrete floor until it was directly behind the man's left shoulder. As Liddell sat down, he slapped a meaty hand on Grant's shoulder and let Grant feel his weight.

Grant's jaws worked, but the mouth was clamped shut. He tried to look around at Liddell, but Jack said, "Hey! Look at me, Mr. Grant."

Grant's attention focused on Jack, but his expression was unchanging.

"You need to talk to us about Charlie," Jack said.

"You got no right doing this," Grant said. "I got rights, you know."

"We don't care about your rights, Grant," Jack said. "We care about Charlie."

Liddell leaned in close to Grant's ear. "Maybe we should look at you for these murders."

Grant's demeanor slipped. "You won't do that, will you, fellas?"

Jack felt bad taking advantage of the man. He knew Grant had nothing to do with the killings, knew it was Eddie Solazzo. But they needed information, and the clock was ticking. Eddie was out there somewhere. Waiting to take another victim.

"You bet we will," Jack said. "If you don't start answering questions, we're going to put you away."

"Well, I'm not even his real uncle, am I? His whore of a mom just dumped him on me." Grant's jaw was still clamped, but his shoulders sagged. He couldn't fight these men.

"Talk to me about Charlie," Jack said.

And he did. Jonathan Hewitt Grant talked for the next fifteen minutes. When he was through they were no closer to having any useful information about Charlie Toon. The last thing they would have to do was take Grant to the morgue to identify the body.

Liddell drove, and Jack and Jonathan Grant sat in the back of the Crown Vic. At the coroner's office, Grant was taken to the small room just adjacent to the autopsy room where bodies could be viewed with more dignity. Little Casket had accompanied him, and now stood beside the shroud-covered remains of Charlie Toon. She folded the cover back to expose only enough of the face for Grant to identify the battered and paint-spattered face of the boy that he had failed to protect.

Grant's tough exterior shattered.

Jack and Liddell dropped Jonathan Grant off at The Lucky Lady strip bar near his girlfriend's apartment, and watched as the man walked inside. He seemed to have made a full recovery from his show of emotion.

"I'm having trouble with the way Double Dick gave in so easy today," Liddell said.

Jack had been thinking the same thing. It wasn't like the pompous ass to miss a chance at punishing Jack. There was something else going on. He was sure of it. But for now he couldn't let himself worry about things that were out of his control.

"Never look a gift horse in the mouth," Jack said.

"What exactly does that mean, pod'na?" Liddell said.

"Hell if I know. I'll call Garcia and let her know what's up. Then we should go back to the morgue. Carmodi should be just about ready to do the autopsy on Charlie Toon."

CHAPTER FIFTY

Lilly Caskins prided herself on a well-run office. In fact, she couldn't imagine doing any other type of work. She had been the chief deputy coroner for almost thirty years, which was no small feat considering that the chief deputy position was determined by the sitting coroner. She had worked for no less than four coroners, both Republican and Democrat. But as she looked at the small body of Charlie Toon on the metal autopsy table, she wondered why she had ever chosen this career.

She thought she had seen everything. Dismemberments, children scalded to death in tubs filled with hot water, infants whose brains had been turned to oatmeal from being shaken by an angry adult, gunshots, knife wounds, fatality accidents, hangings, and worse. But never anything like what had been done to this child.

She looked up as the forensic pathologist, Dr. Carmodi, came in to the autopsy room, wearing a hooded Tyvek suit complete with mask. She had always thought that gearing up like that was a bit of overkill, but she knew it was to avoid cross-contamination with any evidence on the body. Courts today were less forgiving of mistakes made during an autopsy, and were quite a bit more knowledgeable about evidence and procedures for its collection.

Normally she would tease him about suiting up for a space mission. But she couldn't find the humor to speak the words today.

"Hello, John," Lilly said.

"What have we got?" Carmodi asked.

"Maybe another victim of Mother Goose," she answered. They had seen quite a lot of this psycho's work recently, but it wasn't like her to give an opinion prior to the autopsy. For the first time in her career she felt that she needed a change. But what would she do? she wondered.

"Well," Carmodi said, "let's see what we have." And with that, he opened the big catalog case that he carried everywhere with him. As a forensic pathologist, he consulted for no less than seven surrounding counties, and therefore, needed equipment he could count on. Some of the counties were so poor they had virtually no medical equipment. In some cases he had the body transported to the Vanderburgh County coroner's office, where he had X-ray equipment, and all the necessities for examining a body and recording his findings.

He had brought the catalog case in more from habit than from need. All that he required from it was the Pentax DS200 digital camera that he had grown fond of. He turned the camera on, selected the features he required, and began snapping digital photos of the body. He knew that when the EPD Forensic team arrived they would photograph everything in more detail, but he liked to have his own set of pictures to look at while he dictated his findings of the cause of death.

While he was snapping away, a technician from the police forensic team came in to the room and started photographing the body from all angles, beginning with a distance shot and then moving in for close-ups.

When they were finished they all stepped back and waited for police detectives.

When the mayor removed Marlin Pope from his position and appointed Double Dick as the new chief of police, Dick had decided not to raise anyone to his previous rank, that of deputy chief. This left the deputy chief's office vacant, and that office space had been assigned to the murder investigation team. It was probably the only smart thing Richard Dick had done in his life, even if his intentions were not to assist the investigators. By moving Jack and his team out of the noisy and chaotic detective squad room, he had cut off the source of information leaks to the press. Or at least, the leaks that he himself didn't approve.

The little office was cramped and totally inadequate for the number of investigators involved in this serial investigation, but there was no way "Chief" Dick was giving up the chief's offices and conference room as his predecessor had done. Dick was a king, and a king deserved the most spacious and plush surroundings. The worst part, as Jack discovered upon entering the office, was that it still smelled like the strong cologne that Double Dick seemed to bathe in.

When Jack and Liddell walked in, they found Garcia hard at work and Mark Crowley standing behind her, his hands resting on her shoulders as he peered over at her monitor.

"Get a room, you two," Liddell said with a grin.

Crowley asked, "Did you get anything from the autopsy?"

"Not much," Liddell said.

Jack turned on the television. "Maddy Brooks is supposed to make an announcement. The mayor is hoping that if the killer hears that I'm back on the job, he won't make good on his threat to kill more kids."

"You think that will stop the killer?" Garcia asked.

Jack gave a noncommittal shrug and said, "I don't know anymore. I think Eddie is unbalanced and won't quit for long." He looked at the clock. It was almost time for the news.

CHAPTER FIFTY-ONE

Maddy Brooks stormed out of the newsroom in a rage. She knew that Murphy was holding back. He knew something important. And what was worse, that old fuddy-duddy boss of hers, Bill Goldberg, was telling her what to report now. She had been "ordered" to give a breaking news story that wasn't worthy of the title. Just because Murphy had been reinstated, she didn't see why that was news.

She had argued with Bill that the real story was the note—the threat to kill more children, and the subsequent murder of Charlie Toon—and not whether Jack Murphy was employed. But Bill Goldberg was the news director, and he had agreed with the mayor that releasing the note would just panic people, and it was not "responsible journalism." He even threatened to take her off the story altogether if she said anything more about the notes until he gave her the okay.

She was furious. She wanted to blast the mayor for buckling to the demands of the killer. She wanted to put the note itself in her story, along with photos of the crime scene tent at the riverfront. This was a sensational story. Her story! The killer was sending the notes to her! The killer was contacting her!

But, in the end, she had relented and did as she was told for the sake of staying on the story. But why was Goldberg so afraid of the mayor? Hell, Goldberg had even kept Lois Hensley, that impossible old biddy, working well after she should have retired. Was it just to keep in the mayor's good graces?

Maddy promised herself that when this story was through she would use her skills as an investigative reporter to look thoroughly into the news director's relationship with Mayor Thatcher Hensley. Who knew, maybe there was something juicy there. Maybe Goldberg was the mayor's real father, and Lois Hensley had been Goldberg's mistress. But, the thought of Lois having sex—with anyone—made Maddy shudder.

Well, she had done her two-minute spot as ordered, and announced that Detective Jack Murphy was back on the trail of the killer and that his suspension had been a mere misunderstanding.

She slammed the door to her office behind her and picked up the phone. Murphy knew something, and she wanted to know what it was. She dialed a number she had used infrequently, and waited while the phone rang twice and then hung up. She repeated this process and then waited for her informant to return the call. She hoped he would get the information she wanted. The thought of what she might have to do for repayment of the information made her nauseous— hence the reluctance to call in the first place—but if the information was what she thought it was, she would have a story that she could sell to the national news. It could be her ticket out of Evansville.

The thought of anchoring for one of the major national news shows made her smile, but then the phone rang and her smile faded.

* * *

Jack turned off the television in the new war room and looked around the table. The atmosphere was still tense, and no one spoke. True to his word, Captain Franklin had been able to get Channel Six's Maddy Brooks to announce what the killer wanted to hear. Jack felt no pleasure at hearing his name on the news. Instead he felt guilt. All these people had died because Eddie was trying to punish Jack Murphy, because Eddie wanted to kill him. But Eddie'd had the chance and had only knocked him unconscious instead. Jack looked at the maps on the whiteboards and the pinned-up photos of the victims.

Why don't you just get it over with? If you want me, come and get me.

But he knew that Eddie wasn't through with him yet. The pentagram wasn't complete. There was at least one more murder before Eddie would come for him.

Unless I can predict where he is going to go next, Jack thought, and went back to the wall maps. "Angelina," Jack said, "can you pull up that Mother Goose map again?"

Garcia hit a few keys on her laptop and a digital screen overlaid the city map on the whiteboard. Liddell dimmed the room lights, and then stood beside Jack.

"What have you got?" he asked.

"Maybe nothing," Jack said, distractedly. "Give me that Mother Goose book. The one with the map in the back."

Liddell found the book and handed it to Jack. Jack flipped to the inside front pages and found the publishing date and company. This particular book had been copyrighted in 2004, but there might have been an earlier edition.

"Angelina," Jack said, "can you check and see if there are previous editions of this book?"

Garcia took the book. "I get it," she said and smiled. "You're wondering if there was a different map in the earlier editions." Her fingers played over the keyboard like a concert pianist, and in only a few seconds she exclaimed, "I've got it!"

She punched another key, and the office printer whirred into life. Crowley grabbed the paper from the printer tray and said, "Looks like there is an older book with a map. There's a copy at the . . . Central Library" he read off the paper. "Is that close?"

Liddell was already headed for the door. "I'll be right back," he said over his shoulder and then was gone.

While they waited, they looked at the maps. *The pentagram could be a coincidence,* Jack thought. But he didn't believe in coincidence. Besides, that type of thinking didn't take him any further ahead. Just then, Susan Summers came into the office.

"I've got a pickup order for Eddie," she announced.

The library was two blocks from the Civic Center, and Liddell was back in less than ten minutes. He handed the older edition of the book to Garcia. She opened it and folded out the map in the back of the book. "This will just take a second," she said, and placed the map facedown on a scanner.

When the new map appeared she layered it over the top of the old Mother Goose map. It was immediately obvious the locations of the characters in the rhymes in the older edition of the book were different from those in the newer book. Jack took a blue erasable marker and drew a small circle at the location where Anne Lewis and her husband were murdered. He marked this with a number one.

"If the murders were committed in order, this would be the first one, so let's use it as the starting point," Jack said.

"You're assuming that Eddie is smart enough to plan this, Jack," Liddell said. "Eddie was always a nutcase. Bobby was the planner in the group."

"Yeah, but Bobby's dead," Jack reminded him. Jack was frustrated. He wasn't a psychologist, and didn't really believe in them in the first place, but he was a good enough detective to know when he was in over his head.

"Anyone know a good psychologist?" Jack asked the group.

"Dr. Don Shull," Susan Summers said. "I met him at a parole seminar in Las Vegas a couple of years ago. He used to be a forensic psychologist for the Los Angeles Sheriff Department, but got tired of dealing with the violence and moved here last year. He's teaching at Ivy Tech College now."

Jack gave her a sharp look, and said, "You seem to know a lot about this guy."

Susan shrugged and grinned. "He was unhappy with his job, and I helped him find work here. We've gone out a couple of times, but don't worry, he's not my type."

"I'm not worried," Jack said defensively. "Actually, I was going to suggest that you contact him and see if he can help us out here."

"Aren't they cute when they fight?" Garcia said to Crowley.

"We're not fighting," both Susan and Jack said at the same time.

"What is it we're hoping this guy is going to be able to tell us?" Crowley asked.

Jack pointed to the map. "The order of these murders might be significant. If they are, why doesn't the murder at Kids' Kingdom fit the pattern with the rest of them?"

Crowley looked at the map. "This guy's crazy, Jack. You can't figure out how a crazy man thinks."

"You have a better idea?" Jack asked.

"No."

"Susan, would you call this friend of yours?" Jack asked.

CHAPTER FIFTY-TWO

Maddy sat in a dark corner of Duffy's Tavern, averting her eyes from the rough-looking men and women scattered around the room. In total disregard of the local nonsmoking ordinance, cigarette smoke hung like a great cloud in the air. The men were silent, content with their drinks and their own thoughts. The women present seemed to loom garishly over their drinks. Their posture exuded despair or anger, and serious attitude. Maddy didn't want to admit that they were really just a bunch of working folks with nothing more sinister behind their eyes than the fact that not one of them seemed to know who she was.

She was dressed in business attire suitable for the television studio, with a short pinstriped skirt and matching jacket, white blouse, and black high heels. Those around her were dressed in various stages of low-class to homeless clothing. But, as she was in one of Evansville's sleaziest hole-in-the-wall bars, she couldn't expect any better. She was the outsider here.

It took her informant less than a minute to return her call, but she hadn't anticipated that he would insist on a face-to-face meeting. The thought of being alone with him made her skin crawl. But that hadn't always been the case. When she was a newcomer to Evansville, he had given her inside police information that helped her gain status and recognition. She had moved very quickly up the ladder from a research assistant to reporter, to co-anchor. In return she had done some things with him—sexual things—that she would now like to forget. He hadn't asked anything from her for a very long time, but then, he hadn't asked for a face-to-face meeting either.

Two years ago he wasn't the craggy-faced, cigar-smelling man that he was now. He had seemed taller, fitter, and had more hair. It was as if the last two years had magically transformed him into an unpleasant little ogre. That thought was reinforced as she watched him walk into the back door of Duffy's Tavern. *God! I haven't been in a dump like this in forever*, she thought. *But I need that information.*

She put on her sweetest smile, while Detective Larry Jansen pulled a chair up to her small table and looked her over thoroughly. In her mind she could feel his rough hands squeezing, tongue and fingers roughly probing, and she almost changed her mind. She could just get up and walk out.

No, she couldn't. She needed this story. It was her big chance. She took her hands from her lap and placed them over one of Jansen's rough hands.

"What have you got for me?" she asked.

"The killer's name, for one thing," Jansen said and leaned back in his chair, crossing his arms. He openly stared at Maddy's breasts while his tongue darted between the gash that was his almost lipless mouth, like a lizard.

Maddy could smell the nicotine on his breath and choked down a shuddering revulsion at what she had done to get where she was today. "So? What is it?" she said a little too sharply, but Jansen didn't seem to be insulted by her discomfort. He wheezed out more sickening breath and leaned toward her.

"Some piece of trash named Eddie Solazzo," Jansen said, softly. "The kicker is that Murphy killed Eddie's brother a couple months ago."

Maddy was thinking furiously. What did she remember about that case? And then she remembered. Murphy had been on a stakeout and had chased Bobby—yes, that was his name, Bobby Solazzo. Murphy had chased him down and shot him several times. If she remembered correctly, Murphy was cut very badly and nearly died. That's where he got that ugly scar. From Bobby Solazzo. Was Eddie out for revenge? It all made sense now.

"You're sure?" she asked.

"Have I ever lied to you, sweet cheeks?" Jansen said. He reached into a coat pocket and produced a cassette tape.

Maddy found it hard to catch her breath. She was going to scoop everyone. *So this is what Murphy was keeping from me*, she thought. And then she remembered that Jansen had said that he had the killer's name, "for one thing."

"You have something else?" She didn't believe he could have anything better than what he had already delivered.

Jansen handed her the micro-mini audio cassette tape. "This will blow your socks off, toots."

"What's on it?" Maddy asked, suspiciously. This was the first time Jansen had ever given her a tape. He had always been very careful that the information could in no way be traced back to him. Then a distasteful thought hit her.

"What do you want for this?" she asked, no longer smiling.

"I'm already paid," he said, and his face cracked in a hideous grin. Jansen got up and left by the back door without another word, leaving Maddy staring after him.

* * *

Captain Franklin and Jack Murphy sat in armless and uncomfortable chairs that had been carefully placed in front of Dick's large desk. They had been summoned because Chief Dick had somehow discovered that Eddie Solazzo was a person of interest in the murders now. Jack had kept this back with Captain Franklin's permission, hoping to make some progress before Dick leaked it to the press. But someone had beaten Franklin to the chief with the information.

Both men knew that they had really been summoned because Chief Dick wanted to exercise his power, and that any other chief would have left them to their work. But they had been told to sit, and then Dick had quietly stared at the top of his desk for a minute or so. His expression was unreadable.

Finally Chief Richard Dick leaned forward, elbows planted firmly on his desk, fingers steepled in front of his face. His mouth drew into a scowl, his eyes had a haunted, worried look, and he had developed a nervous tic under one eye that made him look pitiable.

From behind his hands he said, "I know that you both had a loyalty to Chief Pope, and I had hoped that you would extend that same loyalty to me as your new chief." When neither man responded, he cleared his throat and went on, anger in his voice now. "I am to be informed of any important developments . . . no, let me rephrase that. I am to be immediately informed of *any* changes in this investigation. Is that abundantly clear to both of you?"

"Yes, sir," Captain Franklin said. Murphy remained silent. This wasn't his fight.

"Then can you explain to me why I had to hear about this Eddie Solazzo character from my secretary?" Chief Dick said with a sneer on his face.

Franklin shook his head. The secretary had told them that the chief was upset because "someone" had told him that they were looking at Solazzo for the murders. She hadn't said that she was the "someone" that had told the chief.

"Chief," Franklin said, "it would really help us if you would issue a department-wide order that this case is not to be discussed with anyone outside of policemen and detectives. If we are leaking information through secretaries and such, we will never catch this suspect."

Dick seemed to mull that over. "Yes, I see what you mean." He seemed to cheer up then. He had something that he could use his chiefly authority on, so he felt better. "I'll issue an order immediately. And believe me, if I catch anyone speaking out of school, so to speak, I'll have their job."

"Thank you, Chief Dick," Franklin said, and then went on to tell him how they had come up with Eddie Solazzo as a suspect, and to explain that they hadn't passed that on to him yet because they didn't want to be premature with a suspect. Dick seemed satisfied with the captain's excuse, but warned them to come to him in the future.

Outside the chief's office, Franklin turned to Jack and said, "There's a lesson in diplomacy for you, Jack."

"Pretty slick," Jack agreed. "That's why you get the big bucks, boss."

A somber look came over the captain's face. "Do me a favor, Jack," he said. "Catch this bastard quickly."

While Susan was locating her psychiatrist friend, Jack and Liddell decided to spend the time running down contacts from Solazzo's past. Garcia had come up with a short list of the ones that were not deceased or in prison. That left them with three names.

"Tony Gaza, Jimmy Sidener, Pat Starkey. The other five are dead," Jack said, reading from the list. "Apparently it's not very healthy to be a friend of the Solazzos."

Liddell chuckled. "I know this sounds cold, but I don't think anyone will be crying over any of those guys."

Jack put the list on his lap and looked through the windshield of the unmarked Crown Vic. They were back in a familiar neighborhood of two-story wood-sided houses with chipping paint and missing gutters. In the early 1920s Rosedale was a thriving community spawned by the industrial boom of steel production and railroad and riverboat traffic. Now it was home to crack addicts, dope pushers, and the worst kinds of criminal element. Only a few older people—either unable to leave or refusing to give up their homes—occupied the homes with blinds pulled, doors and windows locked. They had become prisoners.

"We going to the reverend's?" Jack asked.

"I know he's not on the list," Liddell said, "but we're close to his place. Thought I'd just check up on him." Jack nodded in agreement.

Reverend Payne was one of Liddell's informants, and had a long and colorful history during his life of crime. He had finally become a victim to what sociologists call "aging out"—even hardened killers eventually become too old to continue the life. There is no retirement or benefits at the end of their tunnel, but instead, a homeless shelter or a pauper's grave.

Payne had been an accomplished burglar, thief, and con man during his run. But he claimed that he had found the Lord, and now ran a shelter, of sorts, for the down and out. He provided a bed and meals for anyone and everyone that came to his door. The only rule for admittance was that any criminal activity had to be left at the door. This rule was enforced by mutual agreement by all those that stayed there. Jack knew that wasn't to say that some stolen food or furniture didn't find its way into the place from time to time. Payne thought he was doing good things, but Jack thought he was just fooling himself.

They pulled up in front of a huge two-story home that looked more like a plantation mansion than the single-family residence it used to be. Neither man moved from the car as they watched several window shades, both upstairs and downstairs, twitch upon their arrival. They gave those people inside several minutes to clean up and hide whatever. it was they were doing before stepping from the car.

They stood on the sidewalk near the car until one side of the double French doors opened and a wizened black man with a shock of white hair shuffled onto the porch in house shoes. Reverend Payne was in his late seventies and suffered from severe rheumatism. His skin was the color of dull coal, but his eyes were milky with cataracts. The fingers of his left hand, wrapped around the handle of a wooden cane, looked like twisted tree roots. He kept his malformed right hand in the pocket of the threadbare housecoat he continually wore.

"Come in, gentlemen," Payne said, and shuffled back into the entrance.

The inside of the house reminded Jack of an old-fashioned hotel. Straight ahead was a wide staircase, with heavily worn oak banisters and thick faded carpeting. To the left was an open room with no less than six or seven sofas and several antique chairs. A black lacquered piano sat against one wall, and a frail gentleman of indistinguishable race tickled the keys to a honky-tonk tune. There were ten or more men of various ages and races lounging around the room. All appeared to be immersed in reading newspapers, quietly chatting among themselves, or enjoying the renderings of the piano man. Jack knew that this was all for Jack and Liddell's benefit. An "everything's cool" atmosphere pungent with the smell of incense to cover the odor of marijuana that still lingered in the air.

They followed Payne to a small room just off the main sitting room and toward the back of the house. Payne pointed with the tip of his cane at a table near a big window,

and the detectives pulled up seats. Payne eased his emaci-
ated frame into a padded chair, and his lined face wrinkled
with discomfort.

"Liddell Blanchard and Jack Murphy," Payne said. "Two
of Evansville's finest. It's been a while." His voice was
strong and clear, belying his infirmity. "You're here because
of the murders."

Liddell spoke first. "Actually, we were going to see someone else, and decided to stop by and see how you were."

Payne nodded. "Your visits are always a pleasure. Both of
you." He smiled, his white teeth gleaming in contrast to his
dark skin.

Liddell and Payne chatted for a bit, and then Payne had a
sudden intake of breath and flinched as if he'd had a spasm
of pain in his back.

"Sorry, gentlemen, but I'd best lie down for a while,"
Payne said, and the detectives stood.

Jack decided to ask the question that he'd had in mind
since they had arrived.

"Just one question. What do you know about Bobby or
Eddie Solazzo?"

The Reverend settled back into his chair, his milky eyes
staring at nothing. "Those poor boys." He shook his head
sadly.

Jack and Liddell waited, and after a minute Payne said, "I
knew their daddy." His mouth drew up into a scowl at his
memories. "He called himself a man of God, but he was an
evil man." His voice trailed off as if he was lost in thought,
but then he asked, "Is this about the murders?"

Liddell and Jack looked at each other. No one outside the
war room and Chief Dick knew that Eddie was a suspect.
But they knew it was only a matter of time before word
would get out. Especially since Dick's secretary knew Eddie
was a person of interest. They decided to trust the old man.

"Yeah," Liddell said. "We think Eddie might be tied up in it somewhere."

Payne shook his head again, and said, "That boy's not to blame. Not to blame. He was made mean by his daddy. And crazy, too."

Payne pointed a knotted finger at a small cabinet and said, "Look in the top drawer. You'll find a scrapbook of photos. Bring it to me."

Liddell opened the drawer and took out a leather-bound album that was cracked and faded with age. He brought it to the table and set it in front of Jack and himself. Inside were family photos, some extremely old. Jack saw one of the people in the photo and stared at it, then at Payne.

"This is your family?" Jack asked.

Payne nodded. "The first photo is of my daddy and me. I was only five years old. There aren't many pictures of me when I was growing up because I was in prison most of my life. But I wasn't always a bad man."

Liddell looked through the album and stopped at one photo of a heavyset white man wearing a gray suit complete with white preacher's collar. "Who's the white guy?" he asked.

"That's Giuliani Solazzo. Bobby and Eddie's father," Payne said.

Jack and Liddell left the Reverend Payne in his sitting room. He had told them a story that shed some light on the motivation behind the killings. Not that Eddie needed much reason to kill. Jack flipped open his cell phone intending to call Susan, but the phone rang in his hand. He didn't recognize the number.

"Murphy," he said into the phone.

"Did you miss me?" an unfamiliar man's voice asked.

Jack put the speakerphone on, and the voice said, "Who's with you, the Cajun?"

"Eddie," Jack said. "Why don't we meet somewhere?"

"You don't know how much I'd like to do that, Jack," Eddie hissed. "But you have miles and miles to go before you can rest, Jack."

"Eddie, let's stop dancing around," he said, but Eddie cut him off.

"Shut the fuck up, Murphy, and listen. I'm not gonna repeat this."

Jack looked at Liddell and was glad to see that Liddell had pulled a small tape recorder from his jacket and turned it on. He held it close to the cell phone and said, "Okay, Eddie, go ahead."

"Here's a riddle for you Jack. You're a smart guy. If you figure it out in time, someone won't have to die," Eddie said.

"Wait, Eddie, you don't have to do this. It's me you want," Jack said, his heart pounding in his chest.

"I said shut the fuck up, Murphy! If you interrupt again, I'll take my time killing them. And the blood will be on your head, again."

With great effort, Jack remained silent.

"Okay," Eddie said, "here's the riddle."

CHAPTER FIFTY-THREE

Eddie hadn't blocked the cell phone number. Jack wrote it down, then hit redial. It immediately went into voice mail, and the recorded voice said, "The person you are calling . . ."

Jack hung up.

"He's turned the phone off, and I got the answering service," he said to Liddell.

Liddell stomped down on the accelerator, and drove at breakneck speed toward headquarters. "Call Garcia," he said, and careened around a corner, almost hitting the curb.

"Drive much?" Jack said sarcastically, and then said, "Slow down so I can use my hands to call."

Liddell looked over and saw Jack was hanging on to the door. "Ya' big pussy," he said with a grin. But he slowed, and Jack was able to call Garcia, and then Captain Franklin.

He filled Franklin in, and then called Susan's cell again.

"Where are you?" Susan asked.

"Almost back to the war room," he answered. "Did you find him?"

"We're waiting for you," she answered.

* * *

When Jack entered the war room, Susan and a darkly tanned man with a powerful build were chatting with Garcia. Dr. Don Shull was not exactly what Jack had expected. Shull was shorter than Jack by maybe an inch, and was older by at least fifteen years. But he was compact and looked like he could twist the head off a bull. His hair was pulled into a short gray ponytail, and he sported a close-cropped beard covering only his chin. He was dressed in a multicolored golfing shirt with cargo pants and suede deck shoes, giving him a relaxed and stylish appearance. Except for the hair he could have passed for Harrison Ford's twin.

"Jack, this is my good friend, Don," Susan said enthusiastically.

Don? Not Dr. Shull? Jack thought. He took the doctor's offered hand and was surprised at the gentleness in his grip.

"Jack Murphy," Shull said, "I've heard good things about you."

"So you're the friend of Susan's I've never heard so much about," Jack said with a twisted smile, ignoring the warning look from Susan. "Nice to meet you. At last."

Liddell came in followed by Mark Crowley, and Jack made introductions. While the team chatted with the doctor, Jack whispered in Susan's ear, "Don?"

"Behave," she said with a playful smile.

Jack raised his voice to be heard, "Dr. Shull, how would you like to begin?"

"Please, call me Don," Shull said amiably. He pulled out a chair and straddled it, facing the whiteboards. "Why don't you just walk me through the case from the beginning?"

The meeting with Detective Jansen had left Maddy unnerved. Jansen was a disgusting asshole, and it wasn't like him to not want anything at all from her, not even money. But on the drive to the television station Maddy counted her blessings, and her mood brightened considerably. She hadn't needed to do anything disgusting with Jansen, which was her biggest fear, *and* she had a scoop on every other reporter. This had national news written all over it!

When she reached the station she called her researcher into her office and swore her to secrecy with promises of great rewards. She didn't trust the little twit, but she had no choice. She needed the information fast and couldn't do it all herself. The bouncy blond researcher had gone to the news morgue—that's what they called the temperature-controlled room that held all the video and files on back stories—and was going to pull everything she could find on Eddie and Bobby Solazzo. *Within an hour I'll have everything I need.* Maddy smiled.

She took the tiny audiotape from her purse and scrabbled through her desk drawers until she found a suitable tape player. Maddy put the tape in the player and switched it on.

Oh my God! she thought, and her hands shook as she listened to the voices on the tape.

CHAPTER FIFTY-FOUR

At first the idea of bringing in a psychiatrist had seemed like a good one. But watching the man sit motionless, almost sleepily, as he listened to one after another of the investigators relate their stories, the idea seemed desperate, a waste of time. The only reaction the good doctor had shown was when Garcia had displayed the Mother Goose map. His eyes had widened slightly in some secret knowledge as he watched the computer-generated displays of locations of killings, body dump sites, and homes of the victims. Other than that one telling sign, the man was a statue.

When they were all talked out, Liddell flipped the light switch, and the room was bathed in bright lights. Shull remained seated and quietly chewed a thumbnail.

"So what are your questions?" he asked Jack.

Jack's doubts about bringing in an outsider became even stronger. He'd spoken to psych people before, and they never had any answers, just questions about how you felt. But he'd gone this far. *In for a penny, in for a pound,* he thought.

"What do you think about Eddie?" Jack said.

To his surprise, Shull didn't hesitate or beat around the bush with psycho-jargon.

"Oh, he's your killer all right," Shull said. "He shows strong symptoms of dissociation, schizophrenia, and has a history of violence. Quite frankly, I'm surprised that he hasn't killed more people before now."

Shull stood up and walked to the whiteboard, where photos of Eddie and Bobby Solazzo were taped up alongside the victims.

"My guess is that Bobby was the strong one, although he was psychotic himself, and that he somehow kept Eddie under control. Then when Bobby was, ah, removed from the picture, Eddie didn't have a strong enough personality to function on his own."

"So it's my fault that Eddie lost it?" Jack asked.

Shull looked directly at Jack. "Well, yes, but only because you were the one that actually took his brother from him. Bobby Solazzo was a dead man walking. Someone would have killed him sooner or later."

He pointed to the photo of Bobby Solazzo.

"But the most important thing to remember is that Bobby acted as father, and role model, for Eddie. If what your informant told you is correct, Bobby couldn't protect Eddie from being molested by their father, but he was at least there to comfort him and share the pain and confusion that Eddie felt."

Shull looked around the room as he spoke. "Imagine you are eight or nine years old and your mother has left you in the care of a religious zealot who is also sexually and mentally abusing you. The older brother probably had his turn as well. And for all we can surmise, that may have been what caused the mother to leave. Fear and shame are strong motivators.

"Jack, you said this informant of yours hinted that the

boys may have killed their father in that house fire?" Shull questioned.

Jack nodded. He had checked fire department and police records and the news accounts. "It seems there was a root cellar under the main room of the house their father used for his church gathering. There was a podium in the front, and behind it a trapdoor set in the floor. The fire department report said the fire started near the podium, and when the fire department arrived the blaze was already out of control. The police report said the old man was found in the cellar with a lot of debris on top of him where the floor had caved in during the fire. They believed the father had been trapped by the fire, panicked, and crawled into the cellar. The boys, Eddie and Bobby, were found later. No statements were ever taken from them, but they were turned over to the Welfare Department."

"So there is no evidence that the boys killed their father?" Shull asked.

"Nothing solid," Jack admitted.

"Well, let's take a leap of faith," Shull said. "Let's assume they acted together, or at least conspired in their father's death. These two share some extraordinary bonds. The same abuse at the hands of the father, hatred of the father, and then the elimination of their common enemy."

"I can believe that," Liddell said, "but how does that help us find Eddie?"

"You must understand your prey to track him," Shull said to everyone's surprise. He stood up and went to the whiteboard. "These are all for you, Jack," he said, pointing to the victims' photos. "They are a message to you. One he wants you to understand so that you can finish the game."

"You're saying Eddie is playing a game with me?" Jack looked grim. "What game?"

Shull made an open gesture with his hands. "That's what you're supposed to figure out."

He turned back to the whiteboard and said, "But I don't think he's finished with killing. I think he's going to continue until you get his message. And then he'll try to kill you."

Garcia spoke up. "I don't think Eddie is smart enough to be doing all this. Planning all this. You said that Bobby was the planner and Eddie was just a follower. So how is this just one guy? There must be someone else."

"I agree with Garcia that Eddie's not nearly smart enough to have planned all this. He'd just come at Jack and get it over with," Liddell said, but in the back of his mind he was thinking about the attack on Jack. Eddie was surely responsible for that. They'd have to talk to Shull privately.

Dr. Shull looked unruffled at the cynicism. He was used to it.

"You asked for my opinion, and this is it." He looked around at the faces, and he stopped on Susan's and smiled.

Jack saw the look they shared and knew there was more than friendship there. They had a past of some type. It irritated him that he was bothered by that, because he sure as hell wasn't ready to get serious with anyone. He and Susan got along fine, but he hadn't thought beyond that. His relationship with Katie had ended badly. Maybe he wasn't supposed to be entangled in a serious relationship. He sure as hell didn't care for the drama.

"Dr. Shull, I apologize, and we do appreciate your help. It's just that your theory is confusing in a way. You're saying that Eddie is the killer, but that he is not a planner. Then you are saying these murders were planned," Jack said and sat down on the edge of a desk.

Jack shook his head. "Eddie was always a little nuts, and violent to boot. To him it was not about the money, it was always about inflicting pain."

"That's exactly right," Shull said. "That's the message he has for you, Detective Murphy. The infliction of pain."

Shull looked thoughtful. "He wants you to feel pain. He

wants you to suffer like you've made him suffer. He is punishing you for more than killing his brother. He's punishing you for being you, for being something he could never be, never had the chance to be. He's going to take everything you have away from you and replace it with pain."

"Do you have any idea what Eddie might do next?" Liddell asked. He looked at the map of Mother Goose Land and felt a shudder. There were many locations left on that map. Many people Eddie could kill.

Shull let out a sigh of exasperation. "That's what I'm trying to tell you. You have to quit thinking in terms of Eddie Solazzo." He looked at Garcia and said, "You were right, young lady. There are two killers. But you were also wrong, because only one of them is still alive."

Garcia shook her head. "I'm not following you."

"Eddie is your killer, all right," Shull said, and turned back to the whiteboard and the photos of the victims. "He killed all these people." He turned back to face Jack. But . . ." He stopped talking and took the photo of Bobby Solazzo from the whiteboard and stuck it over Eddie's photo. "There are two killers," he said. "Bobby and Eddie. Inseparable in life. Inseparable in death."

Jack stared at the photos as the meaning of the doctor's words sank in. "Are you suggesting that Eddie has multiple personalities?" Jack said.

Dr. Shull sat down on the middle of a desk and let his legs dangle. He was smiling. "I'm not saying multiple personalities. I'm saying he has a dissociative disorder. Of course he is a good candidate for multiple personalities, but at this point I would be comfortable with the belief that he is mimicking his brother, maybe even hearing his brother in his mind. It is the brother, Bobby, that is keeping him in check."

"You call eight murders being in check!" Mark Crowley said angrily.

"Yes," Shull said. "I know it's horrible, but you have to remember who Eddie Solazzo is and who he 'thinks' he is. It would be hard to say that he would or would not have murdered so many people if his brother were still alive. We will never know that. But it's safe to say that as long as he thinks his brother is calling the shots, he is under some control."

Shull stopped talking and looked at Jack curiously. "I'm surprised that he didn't come after you, Detective Murphy." He saw the look on Jack's face and said, "Then he *has* come after you? Please, tell me about it. It could be important."

Jack looked embarrassed and explained the attack outside his cabin that had put him in the hospital. Shull looked concerned.

"I think you are lucky to be alive, Detective Murphy," Shull said. "Eddie's brother is a much stronger influence on him that I had imagined. The control Eddie showed in not killing you when he had the chance is almost unbelievable. This changes things."

"What do you mean?" Crowley asked.

"I'm not sure yet," Shull said. "I'll have to think about it some more." He saw the disappointed look on Mark's face and explained, "This isn't an exact science. I'm trying to tell you what's in the mind of a man I've never met."

"Sorry, Doc," Crowley said. "I guess I've seen too much BBC television."

Shull laughed. "Yes, like *Cracker* or *Wire in the Blood* where the forensic psychiatrist solves cases for the police in under an hour."

"You mean those aren't real?" Liddell said.

"Of course they are," Garcia chimed in. "Our boy here just ain't as good as those British types." She gave Shull a teasing smile.

Shull took the kidding good-naturedly. He knew this was a way for the stressed-out investigators to let off some steam. That was why on the television news you saw policemen standing around the scene of some horrific shooting or a fatal accident and some of them would be smiling or joking. It's not callousness; it's self-preservation and a way of denying their need to express their shock and pain until they are alone. That was one of the reasons why suicide, divorce, and alcoholism were common among the ranks of law enforcement around the world.

Jack reined them back in, saying, "Okay, quit picking on the doctor, and come up with some ideas. He's given us a lot to think about here."

The snickering stopped, and the seriousness of their situation settled back on them like a storm cloud. Shull saw the bleak looks on their faces and said, "I do have some ideas for you, however."

Everyone looked up with hopeful eyes. Shull picked up an erasable marker and looked at Jack. "Do you mind?" he asked, picking up an eraser.

Jack nodded his consent and Shull erased part of the whiteboard and wrote the name Bobby. Under that he wrote the words: *friends, relatives, employers, news articles, deceased relatives, prison mates.*

"This is just my gut feeling at this point, without knowing more, but I would say that for Eddie, his brother is guiding his actions. Bobby was such a strong personality that Eddie is either acting the way he thinks Bobby would act, or he is somehow being manipulated and controlled by Bobby," Shull said. "In any case you need to find out more about Bobby to get into Eddie's head."

Jack looked at the older man and shook his head.

"What? You disagree?" Shull asked.

Jack smiled and said, "It's just that in half an hour you came up with more than we have in weeks."

"What do you say to that, Angelina?" Shull asked.

She held her hands up in surrender.

"You say that Anne Lewis had worked with both of these men?" Shull asked.

Jack nodded.

"In that case, I'll need to see Anne's files," Shull said. "There may be something in her notes that can help us."

Liddell looked surprised. "Can you do that, Doc? We weren't able to get them."

Shull smiled at Susan, and said, "I'm the director of Mulberry Center, where Anne was employed. I can look at anything I choose to see. Of course, I won't be able to share anything confidential with you, but I'm sure it will shed some light on your investigation."

Jack liked Shull less and less, but said, "Thanks for your help, Don."

Shull took Susan's hand and gently kissed it. "Oh, I'd do anything for this little lady," he said.

CHAPTER FIFTY-FIVE

With her usual efficiency, Susan had already thought of bringing Bobby's files after she had discovered that both he and Eddie had been patients of the first victim, Dr. Anne Lewis.

"This is all the information I have on Bobby," Susan said, handing the file to Garcia. Then to Shull she said, "Would you like to go somewhere to eat?"

Shull's face brightened, and he heartily agreed. "Jungle Mornings on the Walkway?" he suggested, and Susan grabbed her purse.

Jungle Mornings was an upscale restaurant on the Main Street Walkway across from the Civic Center. The service was slow and the menu was a bit pricey, but the food was excellent.

After Susan had walked off, arm in arm with Doctor Shull, Jack said to the closing door, "That's okay. None of us wanted to eat. You two have a good time."

Garcia snickered at him, causing him to blush.

"Well. They could have asked us," Jack protested. He wasn't jealous in the least.

"Would you have gone?" she said to him.

"No. We have work to do," Jack said in an even tone, "but it would have been nice for her to ask."

"Pizza?" Liddell asked, and everyone agreed. He called it in.

With hot pizza and ice-cold soft drinks, they sat around the table discussing what was next.

Crowley shoved a large slice of "extra everything" pizza into his face as if he hadn't eaten for days.

"Be careful, you might get some of it in your mouth," Liddell said and laughed.

"I'm armed," Crowley cautioned him, talking around the huge mouthful of food.

"And he might eat you," Garcia kidded Liddell, and then to Crowley she asked, "Do you like Cajun?"

"Oh, ha ha. You're a real comedian, Garcia," Liddell said in mock sarcasm.

And so it went for the next fifteen minutes. Jack was glad to see them relaxing, having fun. It had been a long couple of weeks, and he knew it was going to get worse before it got better. He didn't know just how right he was about that.

Her researcher was a college student doing an internship, so she wasn't very motivated, or just didn't know shit about research. Maddy tracked the girl down an hour after asking for the material on Eddie and Bobby Solazzo, and found her schmoozing with the news anchor, Clark Jameson.

"Excuse me!" Maddy said, and the young woman gave her a bewildered look and popped her chewing gum.

"You were supposed to be researching some things for me," Maddy reminded her.

"Oh yeah," the girl said, and picked up some papers and a

VHS tape from Jameson's desk and handed these to Maddy. She then went back to her one-sided conversation with the very enigmatic news anchor, *ooh*ing and *aah*ing in all the right places.

"If you showed this to anyone I'll kill you," Maddy muttered under her breath, but the pair had dismissed her from their minds. Maddy stalked back to her office and spent the next hour reviewing all of the video and news stories involving the Solazzos.

She put all the background paperwork and videotape in a large envelope and sealed it. She marked it *Bill Goldberg— confidential* on the outside, thinking that if someone snooped in her office they wouldn't dare open something that was intended for Bill.

Maddy sat back in her chair and mentally sorted through all the information she had. The story about Eddie Solazzo was just icing on the cake. The bigger story was Mayor Hensley. Killers came and went, but crooked politicians had a shelf life that put nuclear waste to shame.

When this story came out there would be an uproar, and not only from the citizenry. Maddy was sure that Mayor Hensley and his political machine would come at her full bore. She decided she could protect herself and her exclusive story with a "poor man's copyright."

She made a copy of the tape and put it aside. She then typed a synopsis of what was on the tape, including a description of how she had obtained the cassette tape and the date and time. She took the paper from the copier, signed it, and then stuck the paper and the original cassette tape in a small manila mailing envelope. By addressing and mailing it to herself, she would have the unopened envelope as proof that she had possession of the contents on the date the post office applied when canceling the stamp. And the original tape would only be out of her hands for a short period while it was at the post office.

The news business was so competitive and cutthroat that she didn't want to risk anyone getting their hands on any of this before she got on camera.

Her hands were shaking when she dropped the envelope in the mailbox outside the station, but she felt safe knowing she had the copy safely tucked away in her pocket.

Back in her office she sat down and looked at the beginning of the news story she had written. It was killer material. Surely Bill Goldberg couldn't refuse to air it? Then she remembered how he had buckled under pressure from the mayor and ordered her to go on air announcing Jack Murphy's reinstatement. She sighed at the idea that her boss was a politician masquerading as a newsman.

She went over in her mind what she would tell Goldberg. He wouldn't expect her to give up her source, but what if he just stalled her again? He could point out that all she had was a confidential source with no verification. And there was no way that weasel Jansen would back her up.

If she could just verify the suspect's name through even one piece of evidence, or another policeman, she could run with the story. Goldberg wouldn't dare get in the way of that. The station owners would fire him if he tried. This was BIG! Murphy was being stalked by a psychotic killer out for revenge. The mayor was on tape saying he doesn't care what happens to the public. What a story!

She picked up her purse and threw a fresh notebook inside. She was an attractive woman. She would find a way to get someone to talk. On her way out she looked at the clock. Almost six o'clock. The second-shift policemen would be on duty. That wasn't good, because she didn't know many of them. She was more familiar with day shift and late shift, because that was when most things happened in this town.

She got in her car and checked her makeup in the rearview mirror. *Oh well,* she thought. *I'm sure someone will talk to me.*

* * *

When Dr. Shull was explaining things, the idea of running down Bobby's contacts sounded pretty good. But after they had eaten four large pizzas and drank a gallon of soft drinks and coffee, the idea sounded like a waste of time.

"Detective Chapman is running down the cell phone number that Eddie used to call me," Jack said to his yawning crew. "He's already sent the subpoena to get the ball rolling, but it may take overnight for them to answer."

"So what do we do next, boss?" Crowley asked.

"First of all, I'm not your boss," Jack said. He hated being in charge, and preferred to work alone. If he hadn't grown so attached to Bigfoot, he would still be working alone.

"If you have to call me something besides Jack, just call me Supreme Commander," he said, and Liddell started bowing toward him.

Crowley chuckled and said, "Okay, boss."

"Anyway, Liddell and I will run down these people," Jack said, and pulled out his notebook that contained the names and addresses of the ten or so contacts for Bobby Solazzo.

"I'll run them through the computer and see what I can find," offered Garcia. She had kept the files at her desk, and though she would have liked to do some fieldwork, she knew that was not her forte. Sure, it sounded exciting, but she was a computer tech and was good at research, not at chases, fights, or gun battles.

"Go home and get some rest. You're no good to us if you're half asleep," Jack said, and then realized that he had sounded curt. "Sorry, Angelina. I guess I'm kind of tired myself," he said by way of apology.

She looked at Mark and was disappointed when he announced that he was going back to Dubois County to update the sheriff on their progress.

He had conveniently forgotten to call his dad and tell him they now knew who the killer was. Conveniently, because if he did, the sheriff would then be compelled to share that information with the state police. His department did all the work, and the state police would take all the credit.

Chief Richard Dick sat staring at the top of his desk. The cassette tape someone had shoved under his door was unmarked, and there was no note left with it. He had almost thrown the tape away, thinking maybe someone had dropped it and it had inadvertently been kicked under his office door. But before he threw it away he noticed it had been used. He could see a small amount of tape wound on the take-up reel. *Does anyone even use cassette tapes anymore?*

Out of curiosity he rummaged through his desk drawers and found a cassette tape recorder. He stuck the tape in and pressed Play. He was shocked to hear his own voice come out of the tiny speaker. He listened in horror, then rewound it and played it through three more times.

Dick: I don't think we should give in to this killer's demands, Thatcher.

Mayor: If we don't he'll kill more people.

Dick: Even if we do he might kill them anyway.

Mayor: You don't get it, do you, Richard? I don't give a damn about the victims. I care about this job. If the public gets this note—and you know that Maddy Brooks probably has a copy—they may get the opinion that I did nothing to stop the killer. It will ruin me. YOU can't let that happen, Richard. I got rid of Pope for you—now do what you're told and get Murphy back on the job, or I'll get rid of you.

Someone had taped his conversation with the mayor. But how? Why? And most importantly, who? And that brought him back to, why? What could they want? There was no note, no message of any kind. He had played the tape all the way to the end, and nothing else was on it.

His hands shook. *If this tape gets into the hands of the media . . . or anyone, for that matter . . .* He couldn't decide what to do. Should he go to the mayor? Did the mayor get the same tape? If so, why hadn't Thatcher called him about it?

Again, he wondered how in the hell someone could tape a private conversation that took place in the mayor's office. Maybe that nasty-mouthed secretary? She hated him with a passion. But wouldn't she be more likely to blackmail the mayor with this?

He put the tape player inside his center desk drawer, locked it, and then took a deep breath, let it out, and rose to his feet. Talking to the mayor could wait. He would see if he was contacted again. Better to find out what was going on before he risked the wrath of that stupid man upstairs. *And besides*, he thought, *there really is nothing on the tape that is negative about me.* He started to feel better as he played the conversation through his mind, analyzing each word. Hensley was the one that would take a beating on this. Dick had said nothing wrong.

He was about to leave his office when another thought crept into his mind, forcing him back to his chair. *If Thatcher is kicked out of office, so am I.* He couldn't go back to being a deputy chief and give up everything he had worked for.

CHAPTER FIFTY-SIX

Maddy Brooks had not found any policeman who would talk to her all evening. One had told her that Chief Dick had put out a department-wide order that she was off limits. Anyone caught talking to her or any other newspeople would be fired. She finally called it a night.

At daylight she made rounds of several coffee shops that were frequented by cops. She spoke to a crime scene tech who confided, "off the record," that he had been asked to compare the fingerprints of Eddie Solazzo with some finger-prints from a motel assault case. He wouldn't admit or deny that Eddie was a person of interest in the string of recent murders.

Admittedly, it would have been better if they were com-paring his fingerprints with ones found at a murder scene, but it would be enough for her to go ahead with her story.

She felt her pocket, assuring herself the tape was still there. *Time to see Bill Goldberg,* she thought. *And if he won't run this story I'll sell it to one of the big stations.* She smiled and was so caught up in her thoughts that she didn't notice Lois Hensley had entered and was standing beside her.

"What are you working on?" Lois asked, and Maddy jumped. She turned the notes over, saying, "What do you want, Lois?" She hoped Lois hadn't seen the mayor's name on anything.

"Pah," Lois said condescendingly. "You newspeople think everything you do is a state secret or something. Always hiding your material, so afraid someone will look or, God forbid, steal your *big story*!"

But then a strange thing happened. Lois's voice turned maternal, and she put a wrinkled hand on Maddy's shoulder. "Take some advice from one who has been in the business longer than you've been alive, hon. Don't take this work so serious. It'll kill you."

Maddy couldn't believe that Lois was giving her motherly advice. But Lois, mistaking Maddy's silence for interest, continued, and said, "You're a young woman now, but someday your boobs will sag, your looks will go, and your career with it. They don't give anchor jobs to wrinkled old dames like me."

If Maddy wasn't so angry that Lois had been snooping, she would have laughed in Lois's face. But she was too close to achieving her goals to ruin things by telling Lois how she really felt about her.

"Thank you, Lois," she said, almost amiably, and patted Lois's hand before gently lifting it from her shoulder.

Lois smiled radiantly, feeling that she had done something quite noble. She was almost out the door when she turned and said, "Oh, by the way, this number is for you." She handed Maddy a piece of scrap paper with a telephone number written in Lois's unmistakable scrawl. "And before you get mad, it was a man's voice and he left the number on the answering machine sometime last night."

Lois turned to leave and turned back once again. The real Lois Hensley resurfaced, and she looked scathingly at Maddy. "I'm not your personal secretary, you know. So tell your gentlemen callers this is a workplace and to call you at home in future."

Lois left and shut the door firmly behind her, while Maddy tried to control her blood pressure. *Just who does that useless old bag think she is?* But Maddy's curiosity overcame her anger, and she looked at the number written on the paper. If she hadn't burnt her bridges with the police department, she would have been able to talk to Murphy. But that would mean sharing what she had with the police, and so far they had done nothing for her that she couldn't have done for herself.

She could feel the cassette tape burning a hole in her pocket. She was torn between the need to go to Bill Goldberg with her breaking story and the urge to call the number first. Of course, the phone number could be some crackpot wanting to complain about something and hoping to get a few minutes on air. But the feeling that her career was about to skyrocket was overwhelming.

She decided to call the number first. If it was some idiot, she would make the call short. But if she didn't call the number, she could miss a piece of information that might clarify what she already had. Maybe it was another police source coming forward with information on the murders and Eddie's connection. She dialed the number.

The phone was answered in mid-ring, but no one spoke. "Hello," Maddy said not trying to hide her irritation. She hated it when people did that. "This is Maddy Brooks," she said, and then added, "with Channel Six News," thinking that would sound important and let whoever this was know they were wasting someone's valuable time.

No one spoke for a full minute, and then a voice came over the line that made her shiver with recognition. It was the man that had grabbed her outside her home.

The soft voice said, "I have a little sister, they call her Peep, Peep. She wades the waters deep, deep, deep. She climbs the mountains high, high, high. Poor little creature, she has but one eye." Then he was silent.

Maddy had scribbled down what the voice was saying, and when he went silent she asked, "Is it you?" Her voice quivered with excitement, not fear.

"Do you know my name?" the voice asked.

Maddy hesitated, unsure how to answer. She didn't want to lose him by lying, but she didn't want to scare him off by telling the truth. Everything in her told her to lie, but she heard her voice say, "Yes."

The line went dead.

"Damn, damn, damn!" she yelled at the phone and hit the redial button. The phone seemed to ring forever. She hung up and redialed. "The number you are calling is unavailable. If you would like to . . ." came an automated voice, and she slammed the phone down on the desk.

"Shit!" she yelled. She knew she should have lied. Then she had a thought. Maybe he would call back. But she remembered that he had called the front desk the first time so he probably didn't have her direct number.

She ran out of her office and down the hallway, and from somewhere ahead of her she heard a phone ringing. *Please don't hang up on him, Lois*, she thought and sprinted for the reception desk. She arrived just as Lois was telling the caller that she was not Maddy's personal secretary. That was when Maddy yanked the phone from Lois's hand and said, "It's me. It's Maddy."

She listened to the instructions the man gave her and then reached over the reception counter and placed the phone in its cradle, her mind churning with what she was about to do.

A smile stretched across her face. The danger involved was great, but then, so would be the rewards. And she wondered what she would wear when she got the award for best story of the year. Oh hell! She would buy something new.

CHAPTER FIFTY-SEVEN

Chief Dick had ordered everyone to meet early. He had just come from another meeting with the mayor, and his ears were still smoking from the dressing-down he'd received. He'd been made to feel like a jackass because he couldn't answer all of the mayor's questions. And it was all Murphy's fault for keeping things back from him. It was time to humble the man, bring him down to his knees. He was tired of Murphy and swore to get compliance or he would give him walking papers, the mayor be damned!

He stepped down the hallway with purpose toward his old office, where he would beard the lion.

Jack had assembled most of the group before daylight. Mark Crowley was telling Garcia about his manly adventures in Dubois County, and she was acting appropriately impressed, when Susan came in with Don Shull in tow. The only two missing were Captain Franklin and Chief Richard Dick.

Susan gave Jack a hug.

"Where's the big dog?" she asked, referring to Chief Dick.

"He'll be here shortly," Jack said, and it was obvious he wasn't very happy about it. "Dr. Shull, he'll want to talk to you, and I apologize in advance, but we have to keep the big boss happy."

"Please call me Don," Shull answered. "It's no problem. I understand how this works. I've worked with police before."

"Attention!" Liddell whispered loudly, as the door opened and Chief Richard Dick entered the office and looked around the room at each face.

He walked to Don Shull and put out his hand.

"I don't believe I know you," he said, severely, "I'm Chief of Police, Richard Dick."

"You have a very impressive police department, Chief Dick. You must be very proud," Shull said, and shook hands.

Dick's entire demeanor did a one-eighty, and he welcomed Shull to the investigation, even though a moment before he had been prepared to deliver a stinging reprimand to Murphy for bringing in an outsider without his approval. "Thank you, Doctor . . . Shull, is it?"

"Yes. That's right. You have a very sharp memory, sir," Shull said, and Jack worried that Don might be pouring it on a little thick. But Dick was eating the flattery up.

"Well, Dr. Shull, are my men treating you well? Is there anything you need?" Dick asked with great sincerity.

"On the contrary, sir. I've been treated like a king, and it is I who am here to help you. I'm sure you have some questions for me," Shull said, and Dick's happy face slipped as he remembered that he had just been dressed down by the mayor for his lack of knowledge.

He didn't want to admit it, but he was intimidated by the doctor. Intimidated by the doctor's inferred intelligence. He rallied quickly, to his credit, and said, "Actually, I just came to listen to what has been done thus far. Detective Murphy, if you would begin, please."

So Jack recounted everything he wanted Dick to know. Chief Dick nodded at appropriate times, as if his intelligence and understanding were omnipresent. Or as Liddell would put it, "he was a legend in his own mind."

Jack also informed everyone that the cell phone Eddie had used to call him yesterday had belonged to Kyle Bannock, the victim from Kids' Kingdom. And that they had, so far, been unsuccessful at any means of tracking the phone. When Jack reached the end of the story he turned the floor over to Don Shull.

Dr. Shull stared at the maps on the whiteboards. "There is no immediacy in anonymity," he said to no one in particular.

"Excuse me?" Dick said. "What did you say?"

"What I mean is, the cat's out of the bag, so to speak. Now that you know that Eddie is the killer, he no longer has the luxury of being invisible, and therefore will have to act soon. I believe that Eddie is going to do one of two things now that we know who he is. He could try to escape. . . ." Shull paused in thought.

"Out with it, man," Dick said sharply. He didn't like being treated like he was ignorant, and the fact that he really didn't know anything wasn't something he wanted to consider.

Susan had had enough.

"Chief Dick, Dr. Shull is here as a favor to your department. He does not work for you and neither do I. If you can't be civil, then we will leave and you can chase this phantom on your own," she said angrily.

Dick's face turned bright red.

"I apologize. Dr. Shull. Miss Summers. I meant no disrespect. I'm sure you understand this has made us all a little off our game."

Jack looked admiringly at Susan. No one had ever dragged an apology out of Double Dick before.

Shull went on as if nothing had happened. "The other thing

that could happen, and I believe this is more likely, is that Eddie will go on a killing spree. I've read Dr. Lewis's files on Eddie and Bobby, and that would be my educated guess."

Jack felt a wave of nausea, and for a moment he was back in that alley with Bobby Solazzo lying dead on top of him, and he could taste the blood in his mouth and feel the rain beating down in his face. He held on to the desk next to him to steady himself, and when the feeling passed he looked around. Luckily, no one had noticed, and he hoped this wouldn't strike him at an inopportune time.

"Can you elaborate, Doctor?" Jack said.

Shull hesitated. If he was wrong he was sure Chief Dick would try to ruin his reputation. But he had agreed to help these detectives, and if he didn't, and then something happened, the man would still ruin his reputation. He regretted his choice to become involved in this madness. Oh, why hadn't he left all that drama behind him when he left his old job?

"There are several things to consider here," he began. "We now know that Eddie and Bobby Solazzo were sexually and mentally abused by their father. The father was an authority figure of sorts, so it is no surprise that both boys took to the life of crime, always at odds with authority. And they have been successful in the past as a team. If what you have told me is correct, I would say that they got away with more crime than they were ever caught and held accountable for."

Jack nodded; that was correct.

Shull continued. "Eddie was the weaker brother, mentally that is. So with Bobby gone, Eddie has poor control over his choices. Except that he has shown a great deal of restraint at times."

Jack interrupted him, not wanting him to say anything about Eddie's personal attack on him. Dick didn't know about it, and Jack had never reported it. "Yes, we've discussed that."

To his relief, Shull seemed to catch on that he was not

supposed to talk about that incident and moved on. "And then that brings us to the matter of the choice of weapon." Shull pointed to the photos of the first two victims, Anne and Don Lewis. "Both of these murders were savagely committed. The killer was out of control, evidenced by the tracking of blood and the torture of the bodies, both before and after death. They were killed in the house, but then the bodies were posed. Supposedly to match this nursery rhyme that was left behind about Punch and Judy.

"And that is another thing. These killings would appear to be very amateurish, except for leaving the note. That shows planning." He looked at Captain Franklin and asked, "I assume your lab guys didn't find any paper or writing instruments in her house that could have been used to write that note?"

"They were very thorough, Doctor," Franklin said. "They didn't find any paper that matched the note, although there were some crayons in the house. We were unable to determine if the crayons were used, but if they were, the killer didn't leave fingerprints. My guys feel strongly that those crayons weren't used."

Shull said, "So the note was brought by the killer."

He then pointed to the next photo. "Tim Ryan. His throat was cut very savagely, and he was disemboweled. His body was then moved to a preselected dump site. The murder shows a rage killing, but the selection of a dump site shows a planned and organized killer. These two types of killing are not necessarily mutually exclusive, but it does stand out."

He pointed at the photo of the three children. "Again, the killing was unnecessarily savage. The killer couldn't control his rage. But then there is a message written on the wall. And the contact with the news media." He shook his head. "It is very puzzling, but the consistency of a pattern is evident."

He summarized the other killings and added, "So that

brings me back to my original statement regarding the choice of weapons." He looked at Jack and said, "Didn't you tell me that Eddie Solazzo normally used a gun to commit his crimes? Even the time you thought he had shot your partner, Liddell, you suspected him because he favored handguns and shotguns?"

"Yes. That's correct. Bobby was the one that liked to use knives," Jack said, and unconsciously touched the scar along his neck.

"That's my point," Shull said. "This is all so inconsistent with the theory of a single killer. You have two different personalities at play here. Maybe we're putting too much emphasis on the relationship with Bobby. Maybe Eddie has found a kindred spirit? Maybe he has recruited some other psychotic individual to help him in these killings?"

"What?" Dick shouted. "Now you're saying that we have two killers and not one?"

Shull looked at Dick and said evenly, "Chief Dick, psychiatry is not an exact science; it is not like mathematics, or chemistry. We deal in personalities and possibilities. I'm not able to tell you anything with certainty."

Dick drew himself up and looked at Franklin, saying, "I'll be in my office. Keep me informed," and he left the room.

"Elvis has left the building," Liddell said, and Shull chuckled.

Jack wanted to get back on track. He said, "So it's possible that it's just Eddie doing the killings?"

"Yes, that's possible," Shull said. "And I want to reiterate that these killings have not had a sexual aspect to them. The victims have been old and young, male and female. Sometimes, by understanding the type of victim that is being killed, you can get a picture of the motive behind the killing. In this case the only motive seems to be you, Jack. He was sending you messages with the bodies, the notes, the type of weapon he chose to use, the amount of violence during the killing. He was also trying to punish you. Rub your nose in it."

"I understand he wants revenge for his brother," Jack said.

"No. It's more than revenge," Shull replied. "He wants to knock you down a peg or two. You are a very confident and capable man, Jack. He wants to show you that he is better than you. That his brother was a better man than you. That's why he wants the media involved. He wants the public to see you fail, and for you to feel helpless and humiliated. No more headlines for the hero, so to speak."

Shull stopped speaking and looked at the whiteboards again, lost in thought. He felt there was something he was missing.

Bobby sat in the passenger seat and stared out the window. Eddie had tried several times to engage him in conversation, only to be snapped at. And when Bobby did speak it was to criticize him, or complain, saying things like, "Don't lose her, Eddie," or, "Slow down, Eddie," and of course Eddie's all-time favorite remark, "Complaining don't get the job done, Eddie." That was the preacher's number-one saying, and Eddie didn't understand why Bobby had adopted it, because he hated the preacher every bit as much as Eddie did.

But it didn't matter what Bobby thought now. Murphy was finally getting the message, and he knew that they would eventually figure out who was sending that message. Bobby was just sore that Eddie was deviating from the plan. But she had called him names on television. And she had acted like he disgusted her when he had grabbed her behind her house. He had only roughed her up a little as a lesson, but she hadn't learned. *This time I'll shut the bitch's mouth for good,* he thought.

He picked up the binoculars and watched the front of the

boarded-up building. It resembled a wooden ranch-style house. The gray paint had faded and peeled, and in some places the roof had caved in. Sitting in the middle of fifty acres on the northwest corner of the county, it had been an FM radio station at one time, but now all that remained active were the twin broadcasting towers. A huge metal star was affixed near the top of each tower, advertising the call letters of the station, STAR. Even though Bobby hadn't said anything about it, Eddie thought he was pretty clever picking this place since the word *star* was the answer to the riddle he had sent Maddy Brooks.

He didn't think Jack would be clever enough to figure the riddle out in the first place, and so, Jack would not think of the abandoned radio station. But Eddie planned to make it easy for Jack to see what he had done there.

He was snapped out of his thoughts when he saw a blue Toyota Camry turn into the dirt drive that led to the station. He trained the binoculars on the car and saw it was Maddy, and she was alone.

CHAPTER FIFTY-EIGHT

It was a worried Bill Goldberg who called Captain Franklin at the police department. Maddy Brooks had missed her afternoon spot, and he'd had to scramble to find someone to fill that time. At first he was angry with her and thought maybe she had done so deliberately, to give him a taste of what it would be like without her around. *Damn all temperamental reporters,* he had thought. But it was getting close to time for the four o'clock news, and she was still missing and wasn't answering her cell phone.

He had hesitated too long, fearing that she would show up at any minute and would be furious that he had called the police. But when four o'clock rolled around and he'd had to scramble around again to fill her time, he knew something had to be seriously wrong. Maddy was too big of a ham to miss any opportunity to get her pretty face on television. If she really meant to punish him, she would just tell his wife about the little fling he'd had with Maddy last year. It was harmless—he'd had too much to drink. But his wife, the old battle-axe, would never see it that way, and he'd be ruined.

He was now waiting for detectives to meet him at the station. *Why didn't I take that sales job out west?* he chastised himself. But it was too late for a job change at this stage of his life. And so he settled into his office and waited for the captain to return his call.

Maddy shut her eyes against the pain. She had tried to scream, but something had been shoved into her mouth. She could feel tape sticking to her lips and face, and the attempts she had made to scream threatened to dislocate her already strained and aching jaws.

Her heart thudded in her chest as she lay naked on the cold concrete floor of the abandoned radio station. She was tied hand and foot. She would be dead before anyone found her, and it was her fault. She had been so careful to keep this interview with the killer an exclusive that she had disregarded the fact that he was completely insane and had already killed at least eight people.

She tried to roll onto her side, but searing pain shot through her entire body. She fell back on her stomach, and tears coursed down her cheeks. She could still feel his mouth at her ear, whispering the things he would do to her, feel his wet tongue on her neck and then in her ear as he entered her forcefully from behind. Mercifully, she had passed out.

She didn't know how long she had lain there before she came to. She couldn't even be sure it was Eddie, because if it was, she wondered why he hadn't already killed her. But the voice was his. It was the same voice she had heard when she was attacked behind her house. The same voice that had called her at the television station.

She wondered if she was alone. Maybe he had just left her like that. But in every other case the victims were killed in a rage. At least that was what she thought had happened. What if the police were wrong? What if Eddie tortured them first? Terrorized them before killing? But if the police were

right about the killings, then maybe he had left her to be
found. Maybe this was just punishment for the things she
had said about him.

Some hope found its way into her thoughts. Maybe he
was going to let her live. Then another, darker thought crept
into her mind. What if Eddie had left her to die? What if no
one ever found her? Eddie had called her as soon as she had
left the station that morning, and had given her directions
that had effectively run her all over the county before he instructed her to go to the old STAR radio station.

She had followed his instructions to the letter and didn't
call anyone so that Eddie wouldn't see someone following
her. The old station was well off the beaten path, but her car
was parked right outside. Surely someone would come by
and see the car? Then gloomily she realized that it could be
days, or even weeks, before anyone got suspicious of a car
parked there.

Maddy was down, but she wasn't out. She forced herself
to think. *How do I get out of here? First I have to get untied.
There are windows. I remember windows. All I have to do is
get loose and then out a door or a window. My car may still
be out there. Maybe I can find my keys.*

She tested the bindings on her hands and wrists. They
were so tight she couldn't feel her fingers. She tried moving
her legs. Her ankles were bound, but she thought she could
feel the restraints loosening, causing her heart to soar.

When I get out of here, I'm going straight to the station,
she thought. *Oh my God! What a story! S*he was just imagining the camera zooming in on her battered face, her audience drawing in a horrified breath as they listened to how
she had been kidnapped by a serial killer, when she heard
gravel crunching outside. She twisted her head around to
look in the direction of the noise when the door slammed
open and a silhouette stood there. The person's hand held
something that looked like a machete.

"Honey, I'm home," Eddie said, and chuckled. He moved forward and loomed over her. "Time to hang your shining star, bitch."

Jack and Liddell had spent the evening and most of the morning running down Bobby and Eddie's comrades with no success. If any of them could be believed, Eddie had dropped off the earth after Bobby was killed.

About noon, they started reinterviewing the victims' families to try to ascertain if any other victims had cell phones missing. By evening, they had determined that the only one that had a cell phone was Kyle Bannock. That was good, but unless they could track the phone it didn't do much for them.

Garcia and Crowley were working on that angle, while Jack and Liddell updated Captain Franklin, who was then to meet with Double Dick and fill him in. There wasn't much to tell the captain, and they were just sitting around looking at each other when Double Dick's secretary stuck her head in the door.

"Message for you, Captain," she said, and handed him a pink phone memo.

Franklin took the note and read it, and then looking at Jack, said, "You'd better read this."

Jack took the note. All it said was *Maddy Brooks missing. Call Bill Goldberg ASAP!*

"Shit!" Jack said and picked up the desk phone and dialed the number for the Channel Six station manager. Bill Goldberg picked up on the first ring.

"This is Murphy," Jack said. "What's going on, sir?"

Goldberg's voice was shaky, and he took a deep breath before speaking. "Well, I hope I'm doing the right thing here," he said.

Jack put the call on speakerphone. "Mr. Goldberg, I've

put you on speakerphone so that my team can listen. Go ahead and tell me what happened."

Goldberg sounded like a man caught between a rock and a hard place. "First, you must assure me that you won't bring an army of police out here," he said.

"Mr. Goldberg, please," Jack said sternly.

"Okay, well, first of all, Maddy didn't show up for her spot at noon. She always does the noon hook. By that I mean, she has about a one-minute spot where she says what police story she will be discussing during the five o'clock news," Goldberg said. "You know, to kind of draw in interest from the audience to watch the five o'clock news?"

Captain Franklin shook his head and said, "Bill, if Maddy is missing we need to get on this right away. Can you cut to the chase, please?"

"Yeah. Right. Sorry," Goldberg said. "Anyway, she never misses that spot, but I thought she was working on a story, so I got a fill-in to do the spot for her. Betsy Johnson did a pretty good job, but she's no Maddy Brooks. She's not bad, mind you, but—"

Jack said loudly, "Please get to the point, Mr. Goldberg!"

"Yeah, sorry," Goldberg said. "Well, she didn't call or come in all day, and then she missed the five o'clock news and no one could get in touch with her. She must have turned her phone off, because it goes right to voice mail."

"Mr. Goldberg, I'm sending some detectives over there right now. Stay by your phone. Someone will be calling you. Okay?" Franklin said.

"She's never missed a spot before," Goldberg said, and his voice sounded strained.

Jack, Liddell, and Crowley were already heading for their cars when Franklin said, "Hang up and wait by the phone, Bill. And don't let anyone leave the station until my guys get there. They'll need to talk to everyone."

Goldberg made a noise, as if he was going to protest, but instead said, "Okay. I'm hanging up now."

Franklin disconnected the phone and addressed Don Shull. "Doctor, will you be available if we need you today?" he asked.

"Do you want me to go to the television station?" Shull asked.

"Well, I don't think that will be necessary just yet, but I'd really appreciate it if we had a way to contact you after they see what they have out there."

Susan took Shull's arm in hers and said, "We'll be available on my cell phone, Captain." Shull smiled brightly, and suggested they go down the Main Street Walkway and get a café latte and pie.

As they left the office Captain Franklin wondered, and not for the first time, where television people came from. One of Goldberg's star reporters was missing under suspicious circumstances during a murder investigation, and Goldberg was worrying about getting more news. It seemed that people in the media were incapable of human emotion. But then, he reflected, cops probably look the same way to the public.

At Channel Six, Jack, Liddell, and Mark were in the station manager's office with the door shut. As they were arriving they had noticed a news van leaving.

"I thought you were asked to keep everyone here, Mr. Goldberg," Jack said, somewhat angrily.

"Look, I have a business to run. This isn't a mom-and-pop grocery. We can't just shut down because . . ." Goldberg said, stumbling for words.

"Because Maddy Brooks might have been taken by the killer?" Crowley completed the sentence for him. "Just because she may be tortured and killed like the rest? Is that the kind of business you're running, sir?"

Goldberg picked up his phone and said, "Margaret, get that crew back in here. Yes, yes, I know, just do it! And tell everyone else they have to stay put to be interviewed by the police. Just do it!" he yelled and slammed down the phone.

"Thank you for your cooperation, Mr. Goldberg," Jack said, and then used his cell phone to call Captain Franklin. "Send everyone available," Jack said, when the captain came on the line.

"Here comes the damn army," Goldberg grumped.

CHAPTER FIFTY-NINE

The conference room, employee break room, and two offices had been taken over by detectives in order to interview all of the news station's dozens of employees. Crime scene techs were busily combing every inch of Maddy's office. Bill Goldberg was sitting impatiently in his own office, waiting for the horde of police to vacate the station, when Jack entered without knocking.

"Good Lord!" Goldberg exclaimed. "Am I to have no privacy? Can you at least knock like a civilized person?"

Liddell looked over Jack's shoulder with a grin on his face and said, "You weren't spanking the old monkey in here, were you?"

A deep shade of red crept up Goldberg's neck and splotched his jowls as his eyes widened and then narrowed to slits. Jack thought he might come out of his chair fighting, but instead, he smoothed his jacket and straightened his tie.

"I have never 'spanked a monkey,' as you put it so vulgarly, Detective Blanchard. Your chief will hear of your behavior. I can promise you that," Goldberg said without looking at either detective.

Jack looked at his partner. "You think old Bill was in here wanking off?"

"Well, like they say"—Liddell put a hand across his chest and raised the other pointing at Goldberg's face like an actor on the stage—"The lady doth protest too much, methinks."

"You're not making any sense. You're both crazy. Get out of my office this minute!" Goldberg ordered, but his voice had lost any attempt at authority.

Liddell said, with a serious note in his voice, "Actually, I was quoting from *Hamlet*, act three, scene two. This is where Hamlet asks the player Queen if she likes the play. Her response is not one of denial, as you would think because of the word 'protest.' But, back in the day, 'protest' meant taking a vow, and because her vows were to such a degree, her objections had lost credibility. Just like old Bill here."

Both Jack and the station manager looked at Liddell with astonishment.

"So what I'm saying is," Liddell continued, "I believe Mr. Goldberg has been trying to hide something from us, pod'na."

Goldberg's face turned pale, and he looked like a kid caught with a hand in the candy jar. "I don't know what you're talking about," he said, "and I've had about enough out of you. Get your men out of here. All of you get out immediately. I shall call the mayor about your callous demeanor." He was leaning forward into Jack's face, glaring at him.

Bill Goldberg was unaware that as soon as Jack and Liddell arrived at the station they had shouted above the noise, asking, "Who is the newest employee here?" A young woman with gelled hair and earrings in her nose and tongue raised a hand shyly. They promptly took the young woman off to the side and badgered her until she told them that under orders from the station manager, Bill Goldberg, several people had left the station before the police arrived, and that Bill Goldberg was in a state, running around yelling orders, and people were carrying boxes of stuff out to their vehicles.

Jack had expected this. But then the young woman told them that she had been doing research that morning for Maddy, and about noon, had seen Bill Goldberg coming out of Maddy's office with a large envelope. When Goldberg saw her watching, he hid the envelope behind him and yelled at her. He had ordered her not to speak with the police on threat of losing her job.

While she had initially been afraid of Jack and Liddell, she didn't seem to be worried about Bill Goldberg or what he had threatened. She shrugged and said, "This place sucks anyway. I'm only doing a summer internship for school, then I'm gone anyway, so screw the old bastard."

Armed with the young woman's information, they soon retrieved the package that Goldberg had taken from Maddy's office and then had lied about. They left a severely humbled Bill Goldberg sitting behind his desk.

"I guess he was going to produce this stuff later on when Maddy turned up. Alive or dead," Jack said. "Which reminds me," he said, and dialed Susan's cell phone. When she answered he said, "You still with Doctor Shull?"

"Are you jealous, Jack Murphy?" she asked.

Jack was irritated that she would think he was jealous. "No," he snapped at her. "I just wanted to see if you and he could track something down for me. Maybe ask Garcia to help. If you're still around the office, that is."

"We're down the Walkway at Jungle Mornings," she said.

Jungle Mornings again, Jack thought. He had only been there once, and that was on police business.

Jack told Susan about the package they had taken from

Bill Goldberg, and about the note that Goldberg had found in Maddy's trash bin and had reluctantly given to them. The note was a riddle that read:

> *I have a little sister, they call her Peep, Peep;*
> *She wades the waters deep, deep, deep;*
> *She climbs the mountains high, high, high;*
> *Poor little creature, she has but one eye.*

"That's the same thing that Eddie said to you on the phone!" Susan said, upon hearing the riddle.

"Garcia is already running that through the computer, but now that we know it was also in Maddy's possession, it's a good bet Maddy got it from Eddie."

"What can we do to help?" Susan said.

Jack noticed the "we" and didn't much care for it. She was awfully chummy with the doctor. "I don't really know. I just thought you could both think about it and see what you come up with," he said, not really wanting to admit that his real reason for calling her was to see what she was doing, and to try to keep her too busy to be charmed off her feet by Shull. Besides, he liked being able to talk things over with her.

"We can do that, Jack," she said. He wasn't fooling her, but she would be nice and not try to make him more jealous.

"Good. Call me if you come up with anything," he said unnecessarily.

"You're an open book, pod'na," Liddell said, wrapping a big arm around Jack's shoulder.

"We better see what everyone's got," Jack said, avoiding a lecture from Liddell about how he should be thinking about settling down, etc.

They made their way to the employee break room and were told that Chief Dick was on scene and was in one of the commandeered offices with Captain Franklin and Lois Hensley, the mayor's mother.

"Uh-oh," Liddell said. "We've just been Dick'd." Both men knew that when Double Dick showed up at a scene it was like a curse. Something always went horribly wrong.

"Why can't he just stay in his throne room like past chiefs?" Jack said.

"It's because he loves you, pod'na. He can't resist your Irish charm or your witty remarks."

"I'm just glad he didn't show up before we confronted Bill Goldberg," Jack said. "He wouldn't have understood the brilliant police tactics we used to beat him down and force his cooperation."

"Kooky" Kuhlenschmidt was standing guard outside the door of one of the offices.

"Officer Kuhlenschmidt," Jack said. "The chief in there?"

Kooky nodded.

"You can call me Kooky if you want, Detective Murphy. It doesn't bother me anymore," the rookie said.

"Where's your partner?" Liddell asked Kooky.

"Off sick today. I'm driving the chief," Kooky said with a sour look on his young face. "You're to go right in."

Jack and Liddell entered the office to find Chief Dick having a row with Lois Hensley.

"That boneheaded son of mine couldn't wipe his own bottom without my help. I tried to warn him about you, but he wouldn't listen to me, and now see what's come of it," Lois was saying.

"Mrs. Hensley," said Dick in a cooing voice, "the mayor is doing a fine job. It's just this situation we find ourselves in. It is very stressful for him, and he doesn't need to be upset further."

Lois sat stiffly, her wrinkled face drawn into a scowl. "I would like to talk to Jack Murphy if you don't mind, Richard," she said scornfully to the chief of police.

"Of course, Mrs. Hensley," Dick said. "I've had him come in to see you," he lied.

As Chief Dick left the room, Lois said to his retreating figure, "That's the only smart thing you've ever done, you hack." Then she turned her piercing gaze on Jack, but the steam seemed to go out of her and she sighed, and said, "When will this be over, Detective?"

CHAPTER SIXTY

After dealing with Maddy Brooks, Eddie drove west on State Route 66 out of Evansville and into neighboring Posey County. He turned right at the Posey County Bank onto State Route 68, heading north toward Poseyville, all the while wondering why Bobby was so quiet. He didn't act mad; he just seemed disinterested. It was like he wasn't really there. But it was almost over now.

Huge farms dotted the landscape as far as the eye could see, and the smell from a pig farm made him roll the window up. *Damn! I gotta find somewhere to get this van off the road. It sticks out like a sore thumb.* Since Bobby wasn't helping, it would be up to Eddie to find a place to hide out until they were ready to finish this.

They couldn't go anywhere near the Whistle Stop restaurant or the nearby motel again because of the scene that Eddie had made. He remembered hearing about a place while he was in prison, an old farmhouse near Poseyville. A new fish had been talking about how he had gotten drunk and driven a stolen truck into a cornfield and got hung up.

He swore he had gotten out to run but then found the old wood-sided house back in the woods.

He'd told Eddie that back in the sticks like that people leave their doors unlocked and windows open. He said he tried the front door, and sure enough, it was unlocked. He decided to go in and sleep the drunk off, but an old woman had caught him, and started screeching at the top of her lungs for him to get out. He said he hadn't intended to hurt her, but she kept swatting at him with a broom and he had accidentally killed her.

Eddie remembered later hearing that the guy had actually been messed up on crystal meth and had driven into the cornfield to hide the truck. The guy had told the truth about the doors being unlocked, but he lied about what happened inside. The guy had come across the old woman while he was burglarizing the house, and because there wasn't anything worth stealing, he had beaten, raped, and then killed her. She was almost ninety years old.

Eddie remembered wondering how some sick bastard could go into an old woman's house and rape her. But the interesting thing was that the guy said that he used to live in Posey County and that the farmhouse and property were going to the state, because the old broad didn't have any family. Eddie hoped the house was still empty. It would be a good hiding place.

A sheriff's brown cruiser going south passed him, and Eddie looked at his speedometer.

"Better slow it down, bro." Bobby said, speaking for the first time since they had left STAR Radio.

Eddie looked in the rearview mirror and watched the cruiser, but it never even tapped its brake lights. He was about to say something when he noticed a narrow track off to the left of the road that ran through a harvested cornfield. He slowed and turned onto the track. In the dome of his bright headlight beams he could see it was more of a path than a road, with tall weeds growing through sparse gravel. At the farthest edge of his vision he could see the peak of a roof in the woods.

He drove through the trees and came to a ramshackle house. Just behind it was the swayback roofline of an old barn that was falling in. He drove to the barn and pulled carefully inside.

"Guess this is where we'll stay tonight," Eddie said, half expecting Bobby to disagree. To his surprise, Bobby smiled.

Eddie found the back door unlocked and walked inside. He felt around the wall at the side of the door but couldn't find a light switch. "Damn!" he muttered, and walked back to the van and came back with a flashlight. He shone the light around the room and saw he was in the kitchen. The room didn't have a lamp or an overhead light fixture. In fact, he didn't see any electrical outlets. He'd never seen a home without electrical wiring before, but then, he was out in the sticks. Probably wasn't even a septic system here, but the whole house was a toilet by the looks of it.

His light shone over a hurricane lamp lying on its side near the doorway that he guessed led into the rest of the house. He picked it up and found it still had a small amount of oil and a wick, but the glass chimney was cracked. He removed the chimney, lit the wick with his cigarette lighter, then carefully replaced the damaged chimney.

In the surprisingly bright illumination of the lamp he surveyed the room. Near a window that looked out over the back of the house stood a kitchen table with two legs missing, and someone had used paperback books to prop it up. Cans, trash, and empty fast-food packaging littered the floor. Eddie figured the house was probably used by migrating homeless people because railroad tracks were located less than a mile away, and because there wasn't enough damage to the house. If kids had found the house, all the windows would be broken and the walls spray painted or destroyed.

He looked at his brother, wondering what he thought about staying there, but Bobby just stood there and smiled without speaking. "I know what you're thinking, Bobby, but we're only gonna be here tonight and then we're moving on." Again he was surprised when Bobby didn't challenge him.

"Aren't you gonna say something?" Eddie demanded. At first he had felt exhilarated to be the one making the decisions, but now the adrenaline rush he'd felt with the demise of that bitch reporter had bottomed out, and he was feeling uneasy. Bobby had kept him out of trouble for so many years, and it wasn't like Eddie to show such disrespect.

Bobby stopped smiling. "What do you want me to say, Eddie?" Bobby said, a vacant look on his face. "End game, bro. You know what to do from here."

Eddie took the flashlight and went out to the van, then came back in with an army duffel bag and a black plastic tarp. He busied himself by tacking the plastic over the window so that no light would show from outside. He then pulled a sleeping bag from the duffel and laid it on the floor.

Bobby was pissing him off, and he didn't know why. All he wanted was for Bobby to tell him what the next step was, and instead, all of a sudden, Bobby was making Eddie decide. He didn't want to decide. He just wanted Murphy dead. All the rest of this crazy shit had been Bobby's idea.

It's a test, he thought. *Bobby's hoping I make a wrong move so he can criticize me and tell me I fucked up again.* He plopped down on the sleeping bag and pulled the lamp close. *Screw it. I'm going to sleep. Tomorrow I'll know what to do,* he thought. And with that, he turned the lamp wick back to a bare flicker and went to sleep.

CHAPTER SIXTY-ONE

"Jack, you'd better hear this," Liddell said, tugging on Jack's sleeve.

Jack said good-bye to the coroner and closed his cell phone. "What's up?"

"Earl got a call from one of the station people that was off work. She called Earl to tell him that she saw Maddy going into Duffy's Tavern this morning," Liddell said.

"Duffy's?" Jack knew that other than locals, the only people that went there started out with bad directions. "He bringing her in?"

"She volunteered to come to the station. Be here in about ten minutes. Name is Letty Breeden."

True to her word, Letty Breeden came through the back doors of the station in exactly ten minutes. She was young, blond, pretty, all legs and boobs. Kooky, who was now on guard duty at the back door, looked embarrassed when Letty caught him checking her out.

"Ahh, to be young again," Liddell murmured.

"You're married. Get your mind back in your pants, Bigfoot," Jack replied.

"I was talking about Kooky. He's about her age."

"Ms. Breeden," Jack said, getting her attention. She excused herself from the chatty rookie and walked toward the two detectives. Jack was disappointed to see that her initial allure was ruined by her way of walking. She stomped forward, like a superthin model on a fashion runway, with a lurching, leg-pumping motion that looked neither attractive nor graceful.

She came to rest in front of them like a locomotive that has had the emergency brakes applied and smiled at them in what she obviously thought was a seductive manner. "You're Jack Murphy," she said, her eyes growing wide.

Liddell stifled a laugh and said, "Yep, that's him. In the flesh. But don't you think he looks bigger on television?"

Letty ignored Liddell and moved close to Jack. "I've heard a lot about you around here. You've killed a bunch of people," she added, to Jack's irritation. He took a disliking to this leggy transport system for a pair of plastic boobs.

"He's a legend in his own mind," Liddell said, seeing Jack's discomfort in talking about things he would rather put behind him. "Why don't we sit over here and you can tell us everything you know?" Liddell showed her to an empty desk, and Jack reluctantly followed. He wanted to hear what she knew, but he hoped she would keep to the point.

During the interview with Letty, whom Liddell later renamed "Leggy," she said she had been visiting a friend on the south side when she drove past Duffy's Tavern and saw Maddy Brooks turn into the back lot. She was curious, knowing that Maddy was so stuck up she wouldn't be caught dead in a place like that. And so she had turned down the alley and watched Maddy to see if she was really going into the tavern. She saw Maddy take a small tape recorder from her handbag, do something with it, and then put it in her pocket and enter the back door of the tavern.

Letty said, "I sat there a couple of minutes, you know,

wondering if I should go in and let her know that I'd seen her." She had a lopsided grin on her face like a mean kid. "I wanted to bring her down a peg or two, the snooty bitch. But just as I was getting outta my car, another car pulled into the lot next to Maddy's and parked. I recognized it right away as a cop car. I've seen that guy before, but I can't remember his name." She described the man she saw get out of the police car and go into the back door of Duffy's. "Of course, all of this happened yesterday morning, so I didn't think it was important."

Jack and Liddell got her contact information and advised her they might want her to look at some pictures. She left the station, lurching in that strange Frankenstein walk, smug in the belief that she was now a key witness in something, or at least important in some way.

"You know who she was describing?" Liddell said. It wasn't a question.

"We need to talk to the captain," Jack said, and took out his cell phone.

Franklin spent several minutes calming an angry Bill Goldberg and had just left the television station when he received the cell phone call from Jack.

"Go ahead, Jack," Franklin said, and turned onto Tree Top Lane heading south from the station.

"Are you close?" Jack asked. The seriousness of his voice made Franklin pull into a nearby drive and begin turning around to go back.

"I can be there in less than a minute. What's up?" Franklin said.

"Meet us at the back door," Jack said.

Liddell and Jack walked toward the back of the station when they were stopped by Earl Chapman, the detective who had found Letty Breeden.

"Hey, guys. Let me give you some other tidbits." He looked at his notes and said, "One of them"—he hooked a thumb over his shoulder at the mass of employees hustling about—"saw Maddy in her office yesterday morning about ten o'clock." He flipped the page, "Another one saw Maddy come flying out of her office like her ass was on fire and head out to the parking lot. That was shortly after ten yesterday."

Liddell looked at Jack. "It was about ten minutes after that when Letty saw Maddy," he said.

Earl was smiling tightly. "You know who she's describing, don't you?" he asked them.

Jack put a finger to his lips, and said, "We don't want that getting out, Earl."

"Kind of figured that," Earl said. He closed his notebook, then, as if remembering something, opened it again and said, "Also, I chatted Lois Hensley up a little. I knew her husband, Thatcher Hensley, Sr., before he was the mayor here. Knew her son, too, before he got into the mayor's position." Earl was in his late fifties, but well preserved, with a mind like a steel trap. He had become a police officer back in the days when "who you knew" was more important than "what you knew." But he was no dummy.

"Anyway," Earl continued, keeping his voice low, "she said she saw Maddy kind of sneaking into her office about eleven o'clock this morning and something about the way she was acting made Lois curious. She went back to Maddy's office and listened at the door for a minute. She thought she heard someone in there with her and so she opened the door and peeked in. Maddy was bent over a tape recorder listening to a tape, and Lois said she recognized one of the voices on the tape." Earl stopped talking and looked at Jack and Liddell, as if to say, *Guess who it was?*

"Okay," Liddell said. "I can't stand the suspense."

Earl leaned in close and told them.

CHAPTER SIXTY-TWO

Lois sat in a chair by Bill Goldberg. Goldberg sat at his desk. Her hands were folded in her lap, and her wrinkled features carried a look of importance. Across the large office, Jack, Liddell, and Franklin sat in visitors' chairs. There was a feel of electricity in the room, the kind of feeling Jack always associated with major breakthroughs in cases. It was like the thunder you could hear in the distance and the smell of dampness that preceded a storm.

"This time we're going to get all the information," Franklin was saying. The station manager, Bill Goldberg, had protested the intrusion on his time and was threatening legal action when the men had entered his office and told him to call Lois Hensley to meet with them. His protestations were quickly overcome when Franklin reminded Goldberg that he, Goldberg, had tried to hide evidence in a missing-person case, and that the evidence may possibly relate to the series of murders. Goldberg had relented, but now sat rigid, staring at the floor in front of the detectives as if there were an answer stenciled into the carpeting that would relieve him of the presence of these damned policemen.

"Mr. Goldberg, I apologize for talking so roughly to you earlier," Jack said, and was glad that for once, Liddell didn't make some silly remark, like "not me," or "me too." Then he turned his attention to Lois Hensley, and she smiled.

"Mrs. Hensley, you've been a great help so far, and we just have a few more questions."

"I'll be more than glad to help, Detective Murphy," she said, obviously delighted at the attention she was receiving.

"Now, Mrs. Hensley," Jack began, "you told Detective Chapman that you heard voices in Maddy's office and you thought you recognized one of them. Is that correct?"

She drew herself up and said, "Well, I believe I would know my own son's voice."

Bill Goldberg shot her a startled look. He didn't know what they were talking about, and he didn't like not knowing everything that went on in his station. He was about to say something when Captain Franklin held a hand up to silence him.

Jack smiled at Lois and moved a chair close to her and sat. "Was it just one voice that you heard?"

Lois stared at Jack. "No, there were two voices. One was familiar, but I didn't hear much of the conversation, you see. I opened the door to check on Maddy, and saw she was writing something down on a notepad. The tape recorder was on her desk, but it was turned off."

"What did Ms. Brooks do, or say, when you came into her office?" Jack asked.

"She was concentrating so hard on what she was writing that she didn't see me. When she saw me she jumped a little and then hid her notes. You know how these newspeople are. Everything is a big secret." Lois looked chagrined, and said, "I know you think I was snooping, but I wasn't." She said this while looking directly at Bill Goldberg. He had as much as accused her of being a gossip before, and she wasn't a gossip. She couldn't stand gossips.

"So what did you hear?" Jack asked soothingly.

Lois looked at her lap and crossed and recrossed her feet before answering.

"Lois?" Jack said, and when she looked up he gave her his most charming smile.

"Oh, all right," she said, and looked worriedly at Bill Goldberg. "But I'll only talk to Detective Murphy."

Goldberg's face grew red. "I'll be damned if I'm leaving my own office. This has gone on long enough."

"We can step out back," Lois said to Jack, and got up. She stopped at the door and turned to Goldberg. "This wasn't always your office, Bill," she said.

Jack hid a smile as he followed the feisty old woman from the office, but he was also quite curious about what she had to say that she couldn't say in front of the others.

Once outside, Lois seemed to come alive. Jack watched her take a deep breath as she looked to the west, where the sun was just beginning to settle on the horizon in a riot of crimsons and wispy whites. Jack guessed she was probably in her late sixties, but she looked much older. Her mouth was drawn and wrinkled from years of tanning or smoking or both. She would have been pretty once, but the years had not been kind to her, and her manner of speaking belied the bully just beneath the exterior of civility.

"I'm going to tell you something that I probably shouldn't," she began. "But I know quite a few policemen, and all of them seem to respect you."

Jack felt his face getting red. Somehow he had never thought about what anyone else thought of him, or even cared much for that matter. He didn't know how to respond.

She looked concerned, and then said, "I don't want my son hurt, but I think someone may be blackmailing him."

"Go on." Jack said.

Before he could ask a question, she said, "The tape I

heard couldn't have been anything else except an attempt at blackmail. I mostly told you the truth, but I did hear a little more than I let on. I mean, Maddy was so intent on listening to that tape that I could have marched around her office naked and clashing cymbals and she wouldn't have noticed."

"Tell me why you think it was blackmail, and what this has to do with your son," Jack said. The first thought he had was that maybe Maddy had some dirt on the mayor, but she just didn't strike Jack as a blackmailer.

"You're not going to like it," Lois said. "But the conversation was between my son, Thatcher, and that despicable chief of police."

Jack was confused for a moment and wondered if she meant Marlin Pope, but then he didn't think she had ill feelings toward Pope. She did, however, hate Richard Dick. He remained quiet and let her tell the story in her own way.

She took a breath and let it out before continuing. "I saw Maddy come in the back door, looking around like she didn't want to be seen, and then she went into her office, alone, so I knew she didn't have anyone in there with her. That morning I'd found a message on the station's answering service. It was a man's voice, and he just left a telephone number for Maddy to call. Something about his voice made me think this was a personal phone call. You know, like a boyfriend or something. And before you ask, I don't remember what the number was. Anyway, I was about to knock at the door of Maddy's office to tell her that I wasn't her personal messenger girl, when I heard men's voices." She looked at Jack, worried that he would think her a terrible snoop, but she decided to finish.

"You must promise me something first, Detective Murphy," she said. "If I tell you what I know, you must promise not to use it against Thatcher."

Jack thought of telling her that her son was in his early forties and didn't need his mommy to protect him, but he knew that granting her promise would not cost him any-thing.

"I promise," Jack said, then added, "as long as it doesn't bear directly on one of the murders."

Lois looked in his eyes for several seconds, and then said, "Someone must have bugged the mayor's office. The conversation I heard was between my son and Richard Dick, but they would never have said those horrible things if they thought they were being listened to."

Although the idea of the mayor's office being bugged sounded rather paranoid, Jack waited for her to continue.

"What I heard was Dick saying to Thatcher that he didn't think they should give in to the killer's demands. But Thatcher was horrified and said that if they didn't, that the killer would kill more people in retaliation. Then that dreadful chief of yours suggested coldly that 'he might kill more people either way.' " She hesitated, unwilling to say any more.

"Lois, what else did they say? This doesn't explain why your son would be getting blackmailed. In fact, from what you've told me it sounds harmless," Jack said.

"In a nutshell," Lois said, "my son made some remarks very unlike him. And they were afraid that Maddy had a copy of some note that could hurt Thatcher's career if it became public." She had decided not to tell him about her son admitting that he had "gotten rid of Pope" and threatening to do the same thing to Dick.

Jack had listened carefully to what she said, and her eyes belied her words. She was still holding something back, but he thought he had a good idea what note she was referring to. Maddy had shown them a note that threatened to kill more people if Jack wasn't put back on the case. But Chief Dick had pretended to not know about the note until Captain Franklin mentioned it after Jack and Liddell had met with Maddy at the television station. Why would Dick keep the note from them? Was it out of some political loyalty?

Lois broke the silence and said, "The last part of the conversation I heard was about you."

Jack looked surprised, but then it all made sense. Eddie had threatened the mayor with the same note he had sent to Maddy Brooks. Dick and the mayor had gotten into it about putting Jack back on the case.

"Your son made Chief Dick put me back on duty, didn't he?"

Lois smiled. "You're as smart as they say, Detective."

Jack returned her smile. "Then you should also believe that I know that you are holding something back from me, and that I will eventually find out what that is. Wouldn't it be much easier to just tell me now? I promised not to do anything to hurt your son's reputation. You have to trust someone."

That bullying look crossed her face again. It was amazing to Jack how this tiny woman could look so threatening, but then, she was power hungry, not for herself, but for her son.

"I haven't lied," she insisted. She turned to the door, and Jack thought the conversation was over, but she stopped and said, "Wait here," and then she went into the building.

This is getting stranger by the minute, Jack thought. But he stayed where he was, hoping she would tell him the rest of what she knew. So far what she had to say wasn't particularly pertinent to Maddy's disappearance, or to the other murders, unless you considered Double Dick or the mayor as suspects.

Lois returned carrying a small brown mailing envelope. She held it out to Jack. "Maddy must have mailed this to herself yesterday," Lois said.

Jack took the envelope and saw that the return address was for the television station, and the addressee was Maddy Brooks, c/o Channel Six News.

"How do you know Maddy mailed it to herself?" Jack asked.

"Because that's Maddy's handwriting," Lois said.

CHAPTER SIXTY-THREE

It was almost midnight as Chief Dick sat in front of Mayor Hensley's desk, his hand trembling as he pressed the play button on the small tape recorder. Maddy Brooks's disappearance had forced his hand. He hadn't wanted to go to the mayor with the tape, but what choice did he have?

Hensley sat silently and listened to the tape twice before reaching over and shutting it off.

"Who else knows about this?" Hensley asked.

Dick's face went red. He didn't want to admit that he didn't know. He said, "Like I said, that tape was shoved under my office door, so it had to be a policeman or cleaning person."

"Or it could be someone from maintenance, or one of your record room clerks, or even some damned homeless person, or an alien for all you would know," Hensley said. All the blood seemed to drain from his face in his rage and fear. What Dick didn't know, and what he debated not telling him, was that his mother had called him last night to warn him that Jack Murphy was in possession of the contents of the tape, and possibly the original tape itself. She had told him about the package that Maddy Brooks had mailed to herself, and that Jack had found it contained a cassette tape and a note. The fact that Murphy had not informed the chief of police about the tape made him wonder what Murphy was playing at, and how he could manipulate things to control any damage to his career.

His mother had assured him that if he just kept away from Murphy and let him do his job, Murphy would eventually clean this mess up. The killer would be caught; the news would eventually die down. But she had warned that if he continued to keep Richard Dick as chief of police he could kiss his career good-bye.

She had also told him that one of the Channel Six employees, a brainless little blond thing named Letty Breeden, was bragging about having information about the disappearance of Maddy Brooks. Thatcher allowed himself a small smile, thinking about how his mother had slyly gotten the name of Detective Larry Jansen out of the girl. He was sure that Jansen was the one responsible for the tape, but he wouldn't share that bit of information with Dick yet. However, he couldn't allow anyone to get to Jansen yet.

"What you will do, Richard," Hensley said, "is suspend Detective Jansen immediately. With pay."

Dick looked surprised, saying, "Why would I do that? What justification do I have?"

"You're the damned chief of police, Richard. You can do anything you want." Hensley gave a sigh of disgust. It was like talking to a moron. He wondered why he had ever thought this egotistical asshole would be beneficial to him.

"Listen. I want you to go to him. Quietly. I want him to disappear for a while," Hensley said, patiently, as if he were speaking to a young child.

"But where?" Dick questioned.

Hensley glared at him as if he was at his wit's end, and Dick recoiled as if a snake had bit him. "I'll take care of it,"

Dick said, and partially rose, then stopped to see if he was dismissed.

"Get out of here," Hensley snapped at him. "And don't let anyone talk to Jansen. If you screw this up, Dick, I swear that will be the final straw."

Chief Richard Dick hurried from the mayor's office, his feelings smarting with the chastising he had received, but not so much he couldn't snap at the mayor's secretary on his way out.

"Don't you have something to do besides sit there all day doing your nails?"

She just glared at him and then dismissed him from her mind. They both knew his days as chief were numbered.

"I hope you have a good reason for asking us to sneak out to a marina restaurant at midnight," Captain Franklin said to Jack and Liddell as they entered the back room at Two-Jakes that they had come to know as the war room.

Captain Franklin and Marlin Pope were occupying seats around a small conference table. After Pope's removal as chief of police, he had been relegated to the nether regions of the Police Personnel Unit. Pope actually had no authority to be involved in the murder investigation, but Jack needed to get his take on what was going on.

Jack had a lot of respect for Pope's ability as an administrator and as a policeman. He hoped that Pope might have some insight that could get the case back on track again.

But first he wanted to let both Franklin and Pope hear what was on the tape that Maddy had mailed to herself. He cued up the tape player he'd brought with him and switched it to play. The sound quality was not great, but then, Jack thought, the method of recording the conversation may not have been exactly legal to begin with.

Lois Hensley had suggested that the mayor's office had been bugged. While that wasn't very plausible, Jack remembered hearing tapes recorded by undercover narcotics officers using a directional mike, and this tape sounded similar to them.

When the tape began to play, Chief Richard Dick's voice could be heard saying: *"I don't think we should give in to this killer's demands, Thatcher."*

The next voice was not familiar to Jack, but Pope stiffened when he heard it say, *"If we don't he'll kill more people."*

"That's Hensley," Pope confirmed.

The men listened to the rest of the short tape—the mayor's *"I don't give a damn about the public"* remark, and then the admission that *"I got rid of Pope for you."*

"Does Dick know about this tape yet?" Pope asked.

Jack shook his head. "I haven't told him. But that doesn't mean he doesn't know. It may be why he's keeping Jansen out of reach."

Pope knew that the conversation alone would not be as damaging to the men politically as Jack thought. But combined with the disappearance of Maddy Brooks, and the interference of the chief and the refusal of the mayor to assist Murphy in his inquiries, it might be enough to get him ousted in the next election.

"What I don't understand, Chief," Jack said, "is how they can deny me access to Jansen. He's one of the last people to see Maddy Brooks before her disappearance."

Pope sat with his hands folded on top of the conference table and considered his possible answers to that question. On one hand, he didn't want to be involved in this matter any more than he had to be. He had been angry and depressed about being removed from his position as top cop in Evansville, but then he noticed that he was sleeping more soundly, feeling better during the day, and his wife was even paying more attention to him in the bedroom. He'd lost almost ten pounds over the last several weeks, and he credited this miracle with the lack of stress in his new job. He no longer ate constantly to be doing something.

On the other hand, he was still a cop, and he had a lot of empathy, not to mention sympathy, for the impossible position that Captain Franklin and Detective Murphy found themselves in. As chief of police, he'd played the political game long enough to know that you can't fight city hall.

Pope had an idea, but it would mean putting his job on the line. If Dick or the mayor found out—and it was almost a sure thing that they would—he would find himself being forced into retirement. But then, he was going to be sixty-five next year, and would have to retire anyway. *Better to get kicked out for doing the right thing,* he thought, *than leave with my tail tucked between my legs.*

"Quit calling me Chief," Pope said, and then told Jack and Franklin his idea.

Al Leathers turned his work van into the gravel drive that jaunted north from the county road and stopped to admire the sunrise just peeking over the pine trees in the east. *No one should have to be up this early. Sun's barely getting up.* But he knew that his job with the power company was on shaky legs right now.

He checked his clipboard. The radio towers were on his list. Yeah, he was two days behind schedule, but a little creative writing would fix that problem. On the top of the work order, he backdated his inspection, then marked the order as completed. *That oughtta do it.*

Brushing some donut crumbs from the top of the work order, he inspected his work. No one would be able to prove that he hadn't been there two days ago. It would be their word against his.

Doing the inspection was unnecessary in the first place. This type of equipment never needed repair. But he would get out and check it anyway, just in case those rats back at the office were still checking up on him. He was still furious that someone had told the boss about the place he'd found to hide his van and take a nap.

· He remembered old man Casselman, sneaking up on him, knocking on the van window, waking Al from a pleasant dream. It still rankled with him. There was no way Casselman found his hiding place without someone ratting him out.

Just go through the motions, he told himself, and putting the van in gear, he drove back to the deserted STAR broadcasting station, where he was to inspect the twin radio towers.

Chapter Sixty-four

Jack and Liddell rode to the scene together. Liddell turned east onto Mohr Road from St. Joseph Avenue and the uniform car that was blocking that street backed up enough to let them pass.

"Stop here," Jack said, and Liddell saw that Jack was squinting into the sun. Liddell stopped the car, and both men got out, shielding their eyes against the early morning glare.

The twin radio towers of the old FM radio station pointed at least one hundred feet into the sky like metal fingers. About halfway up the side of the nearest tower, a naked body was secured somehow to the structure in an inverted cross position.

"I think we found Maddy," Liddell said.

Jack said nothing. Both men got back into the car and continued down Mohr Road until they reached the next roadblock.

The area was crawling with police activity. Marked uniform cars were set up at hundred-yard intervals to discourage or detain any curious sightseers or aggressive news media. Techs in white Tyvek protective suits were combing every inch of ground around the abandoned station building, while uniformed officers moved in a line down both sides of the road, searching the high weeds, looking for anything that didn't belong.

Liddell pulled off the side of the road, and they continued on foot to where a heavyset man wearing a blue work suit was sitting in the back of an ambulance being looked over by paramedics.

Al Leathers wore a strained look. One of the medics whispered to the detectives that the poor guy had a weak heart and they were discussing transporting him to a hospital as a precautionary measure.

Jack was surprised to see the rookie cop, Kuhlenschmidt, looking composed and confident as he comforted Leathers.

"Kooky," Liddell said to the young officer. "I see you have things under control here."

Kooky smiled shyly, guessing that Liddell was referring to the fact that he wasn't pale or shaking like a leaf at what he had just seen. In fact, he had felt a little light-headed when he first got a look at the killer's handiwork. But he fought it back in time and now it didn't seem so horrible. Still, he was glad they hadn't posted him to guard the body.

"I'll talk to"—Liddell looked at the name tag sewn on the blue work shirt—"Al."

Jack nodded and walked down the gravel road that led to the twin radio towers. He had spotted the body when Liddell turned east onto Mohr Road from St. Joseph Avenue. The station was several hundred yards in the distance, but Jack was sure it was going to be the body of Maddy Brooks. He crossed under the yellow caution tape and signed the crime scene entry log handed him by the uniform officer on duty.

"Walker's waiting for you," the officer informed Jack.

Jack walked the gravel path that led to the radio towers. Sergeant Walker was near the base of the closest one, looking skyward, when he spotted Jack and motioned that it was okay for Jack to come closer.

"We've only been here a short time, Jack," Walker said. "An employee, Mr. Leathers, was here to inspect the tower and discovered the door to the old station was standing open. Mr. Leathers said he figured kids had broken in. He just pulled the door shut and walked back here to the towers to do an inspection. He looked up and saw the body, and, well, you can guess the rest."

Jack stepped forward, but Walker put a hand out.

"You might be careful right there," Walker said, and pointed to stains on the bottom metal strut. Jack saw what appeared to be dark stains splattered down the side of the tower, and a pile of something dark and sticky-looking lying at the base.

"The glorious life of a policeman," Jack said sarcastically, and Walker smiled.

"Well, at least this time the mess wasn't from one of our guys," Walker said.

Jack looked up and shielded his eyes from the glare of the sun. It had rained overnight, and the bright morning sun was causing a mist to rise from the vegetation and the metal tower. The heat was also adding to the already-pungent smell of decaying human matter.

"Maddy?" Jack said.

Walker nodded, and then said, "Here comes Li'l Casket now."

Jack turned and saw the diminutive figure of Chief Deputy Coroner Lilly Caskins, dressed in white protective clothing, descending on them with her perpetual scowl firmly fixed.

"Morning, Lilly," Walker said. Jack nodded at her. She ignored both men and looked at the stains on the side of the tower and the pile of dark matter on the ground near its base.

She looked up at the body, and if she hadn't been told it was probably Maddy Brooks, she would have had a hard time determining even the sex, much less the identity, of the bloody mess that had been roughly tied to the metal struts in an inverted cross.

Lilly stepped back a few paces and examined the ground, making special note of the mass of internal organs splashed over and around the bottom brace of the radio tower.

"I'm assuming she's been gutted?" Lilly asked Walker.

He nodded. "That's my guess. We haven't really started yet," he said, meaning they had not documented or collected anything yet.

"How the hell did he get her up there?" Lilly said to no one in particular.

"We'll examine the tower when we take her down," Walker said. "I have a bucket truck coming."

"When it gets here I'd like a look before anyone touches her," Lilly said, and the men agreed.

There was nothing else Jack could do here until the body was lowered to the ground. He already knew this was Maddy. Knew that she had been killed by Eddie. Knew that the autopsy would only confirm the level of violence she had been forced to endure before she was killed. And none of that knowledge would help him find Eddie faster.

Jack told Walker to call when he got something and then walked off to find Liddell.

Jack was making his way to the area of the ambulance when an older officer named King yelled, "The Cajun's over at the abandoned station, and he told me to bring you."

They hurried along a path to the abandoned STAR Radio Station building. Jack had heard that Al Leathers had found the door open and thought it was kids that had gotten in. Officer King was saying something about another crime scene now, and Jack cursed himself for not thinking of it sooner.

Liddell was just inside the doorway. "Jack, we found some

clothing in here." He looked pale when he added, "There's not much blood, but it looks like drag marks leading to the door. It's gonna be hard to tell where she was killed. In here, or after she was dragged outside." Liddell shook his head and added, "We haven't found a definite kill spot out here, either."

Jack shuddered, thinking about the condition of Maddy's body up in the tower, and the pile of what might be her intestines spread on the ground below her. *Could Eddie have killed her up there?* Jack wondered, imagining what kind of strength it would have taken to carry a person up the outside of that gigantic metal structure, be able to hold on and still tie the body to the struts. He hoped that Maddy was already dead when this happened, but since he was a cop, he always imagined the worst.

"Who's been in here?" Jack asked.

"Already taken care of," Liddell said. "Officer King came to me after finding the clothes, and I've been standing by until we can lock this place down."

Jack filled him in on what he'd learned at the tower, and he could see Liddell's features darken.

"Eddie," Liddell said.

"Yeah," Jack agreed. "Maddy must have agreed to meet him, and he either brought her here, or she came on her own to meet him here. Has her car been found?"

Just then, Officer King's radio crackled and someone asked for Detective Murphy. Jack took King's radio. "Go ahead for Murphy."

"Detective Murphy, this is Kooky—I mean Officer Kuhlenschmidt," the voice on the radio said.

Jack thought again about how not everyone was cut out for police work. Kuhlenschmidt had a rough road ahead of him.

"Officer Kuhlenschmidt, go ahead for Murphy," Jack said patiently.

* * *

What Kooky had was Maddy Brooks's car. He had been relieved of duty at the crime scene, and had been put out with the teams scouring the countryside for any further evidence. He had literally stumbled upon the car when he fell into a large drainage ditch.

The area around the old radio station was farming country, and had been spared the normal urban spread. Because of the heavy rains in the Midwest, large drainage ditches were a necessity to keep the crops from washing away.

Kooky was born and raised inside Evansville's city limits, and even though he'd seen the behemoth ditches from the road, he had never been this far out in a farm field. He had just come out of copse of scrub trees that bordered another field when the ground disappeared beneath him. He toppled right over the edge and onto the hood of a small blue Toyota.

Liddell looked at the shiner Kooky was sporting around his right eye. "You really get into your work, don't you son?" he said with a grin.

"Think you can find the car again?" Jack asked, glaring at Liddell.

"Yes, sir," Kooky said. His right eye was beginning to swell shut, and his uniform was covered in mud from his climb out of the ditch.

CHAPTER SIXTY-FIVE

Chief Dick arrived at the crime scene like a visiting dignitary. All that was missing from his black limo with its dark smoked windows was a couple of flags displayed on the front hood. Captain Dewey Duncan, newly recovered from his hemorrhoid surgery, jumped from the vehicle and smartly moved to the passenger compartment to hold the door open.

Dick unfolded his lanky frame from the backseat and barked orders to the uniformed officers around him, thinking that this is what he was meant for, command at a major crime scene. He felt alive for a change, and even the ass-chewing he had received from the mayor wouldn't bring his mood down.

"Where is Detective Murphy?" he demanded of one of the uniformed officers.

The officer looked at the chief with a confused expression and shrugged.

"Dammit, Officer! What's your name?" Dick sputtered. Had to be a rookie to not recognize the chief of police. And he didn't even address him as sir. *What kind of dummy is the police academy turning out these days*? he thought.

"Officer Parker, sir," the officer said, coming to attention.

Well, that's better, Dick thought. He didn't know that Officer Parker had been on the police force for nine years and had been awarded for bravery twice. He didn't know these things because the lives of the police officers under him were of no concern, except when they crossed his path. He was also unaware that Officer Parker was actually mocking him by coming to an exaggerated stance of attention, or that several of the other officers present were sniggering behind his back.

"Find Murphy for me, son," Dick ordered, and while Parker saluted smartly and hurried away, he looked around for the command center. He had expected the crime scene commander, or Captain Franklin at the very least to meet him when he arrived at the crime scene. He was visibly upset that no one of any rank was present. *But, at least I'm here now,* he thought, and with that he began barking orders again.

He pulled three officers off perimeter security duty and told them to set up a tent near the entrance to the gravel drive, to create a place for the news media to gather. He brushed off their questions of how they were supposed to get a tent and bullied his way to the open door of the radio station. He was glad that the news media hadn't arrived yet because he hadn't been briefed. He just hoped Murphy would arrive soon, so that he could find out what was going on here.

Jack watched as a crime scene tech photographed the blue Toyota from every angle, and then he descended into the ditch. There was no hurry to get inside the car because the license plates had come back to Maddy Brooks. Unlike crime shows on television, things didn't happen in thirty minutes, and it could possibly be late night or even tomorrow before the vehicle would get a thorough going-over, inside and out. Time was important, but destroying evidence for the sake of satisfying curiosity was plain stupid.

"No blood visible," one of the crime scene techs said to Jack. "There's a purse inside. Do you want me to look?"

Jack thought about it. "Leave it until you get the car out," he said. "We can move the car if you're ready."

Jack motioned for Kooky to call the waiting wrecker. He just hoped the wrecker wouldn't get hung up in the muddy farm fields before it reached the ditch. The ground had taken a good soaking from the overnight rain, and he could feel his feet sinking slightly from his own weight.

"Star," Liddell said from beside him, gesturing to the call letters on top of the towers.

"What?" asked Jack.

"The riddle or rhyme that Eddie told you on the phone," Liddell said. "The answer is a star. He hung her on that tower deliberately so that we would find her, and to complete his riddle. STAR radio station."

"That's too smart for Eddie," Jack said, but maybe Eddie was smarter than he was giving him credit for.

CHAPTER SIXTY-SIX

Chief Richard Dick hurried to his car, almost bowling Captain Duncan over in his haste to get into the driver's seat.

"Sir?" Captain Duncan said, reaching for the door handle on the passenger side and finding it locked. The window came down, and Dick snarled at him, "Get a ride back to headquarters with someone," and then drove away.

Dick glanced in his rearview mirror at a dumbfounded Captain Duncan, who was standing in the gravel lot looking every bit a lost child. He liked Duncan. Duncan was useful. But what he had in his coat pocket was more important at the moment than anyone's feelings.

He took the cassette tape from his pocket and, with sweating palms, looked at it in horror. It was identical to the one that someone had shoved under his office door. *It had to be Jansen*, he thought. Jansen was the one that bugged the mayor's office. Jansen was the one that gave the tape to Maddy and left a copy under his office door. *That's why Jansen had looked so relieved when I ordered him to take a long vacation out of town,* he thought. "But I'm on to you now, you bastard," Dick said angrily.

Suddenly, the sheer lunacy of what he had just done struck him like a hammer blow, and he could hardly take a breath. He pulled the car onto a turnaround and stopped. *Dear God, what have I done?* he thought. Then, *Maybe I can take it back.* But he knew that would not be possible now.

He had gone into the abandoned STAR radio station building, and had bullied his way past the young patrolman standing guard. Crime scene officers seemed to be everywhere but inside the building. He saw the pile of clothes lying a few feet away and approached curiously. Somewhere deep inside him a warning voice was telling him not to touch anything, to leave it for the crime scene techs to collect. But then he had spotted the corner of something hard and plastic sticking out of the jacket.

He had stooped and, to his credit, used the end of his pen to extricate the object without touching it. But when he saw what it was, his heart almost stopped. Without even thinking, he had picked up the cassette tape and was looking at it when that moron patrolman stuck his head in the door and asked if he needed anything. He had yelled, "Yes, I need you to stand your goddamn post!" The officer had hurried back outside, and Dick had pocketed the cassette tape.

There would be no way to explain having the tape. *No excuse to have handled evidence. And at a murder scene, of all the stupid things to do.*

He had luckily brought his briefcase with him and now took out the cassette player that he had put inside. He pushed the cassette he'd found back at the crime scene into the slot of the player, clicked the Play button, and turned the sound up. He heard himself saying on the tape: *I don't think we should give in to this killer's demands, Thatcher.*

He ejected the tape and stuck it in his pocket. *Now what do I do? Destroy it?* He was out in the county. Nothing around except long stretches of nothing. He could just throw it in the road and drive over it a few times. Leave it there.

But that might be risky if someone saw him doing that. And what if one of the officers at the scene had seen the tape with the pile of clothes before he took it? He had to get to his office and erase it. Then if someone came looking for it, at least it wouldn't have anything incriminating on it. Better yet, he might burn it. He knew that with the new technology out there, someone would probably be able to recover the sound on an erased tape. And once again he wondered, *Who uses cassette tapes these days?*

Eddie had spent a fitful night in the abandoned house. The dream was worse this time, and he had awakened with bloody knuckles and found fist-sized holes punched in the thick plaster walls of the room where he had slept. He couldn't remember getting up or punching the walls. He could barely remember what the dream was about. But he remembered the preacher, and he could still feel the pain in his backside.

He also remembered what he and Bobby had done to the preacher. The revenge they had got for what they had endured during their childhood. Burning was too good for the bastard. But burning the preacher alive was a good way of acquainting him with the place he surely was now.

He looked around for Bobby, but he wasn't there. Lately, Bobby seemed to be gone a lot. Eddie dug around in his duffel bag and took out an emery stone and the book of rhymes. He sat Indian-style on the floor and propped the emery stone between his feet and sharpened the corn knife with one hand while clumsily flipping through the book with the other.

"What'cha doing, bro?" Bobby said from behind him, causing him to jump and drop the knife.

"Dammit, Bobby!" Eddie said sharply. "Don't do that!" He picked up the knife and noticed the book had flipped open to a page.

"That's the one," Bobby said, nodding at the open book.

"Yeah," Eddie agreed, with a grin on his face. "You're right, Bobby. Time to get it done, man."

Bobby smiled at him, and for a second Bobby looked like death itself—a skull with red eyes staring straight into Eddie's soul. Then the specter was gone.

"We're gonna do him at the last place anyone would suspect, Bobby," Eddie said, and then stuck the point of the sharpened knife deep into the floor at his feet. On the open book, the caricature of a man in a white dressing gown and cap was jumping over a lit candle.

"That's perfect Eddie," Bobby said, proudly. "Perfect. But how about we go out in a blaze of glory, bro?"

Eddie listened closely to Bobby's idea, but he didn't tell Bobby that he had already planned on doing just what Bobby had suggested. Bobby liked to be the one that came up with the plans. No harm in letting him think this was all his idea.

CHAPTER SIXTY-SEVEN

Liddell was waiting for Jack outside the war room. "Crowley and Garcia have been working full bore on the telephone angle," Liddell said.

Garcia looked up as they entered the room and smiled. "Mark has been working with someone with the military to try and locate the Kids' Kingdom phone by its signature."

"Any luck?" Jack asked.

Mark rubbed the back of his neck, looking very much like the stereotype of a country boy. "Well, I met this fella at a training session in Washington, D.C., who works for Army CID. He owes me a little favor."

Jack knew that CID was the Counter Intelligence Department, the military equivalent of the CIA, or the FBI, but with more limited authority. Actually, they had no authority outside federal property, specifically military bases.

Garcia gave Mark a reproachful look and said, "Some little favor, big guy." Then she explained, "He saved the guy's life, Jack."

"Anyway," Mark said, quickly, "he's going to see what he

can do to locate the phone for us. He's got some connections that might be able to trace the phone even if it's turned off."

"Can they do that?" Jack questioned.

Mark grinned. "He said he'd do what he could, so I guess he can get it done."

Jack wondered what other technology was out there that regular street cops, like him, would never know about, never have access to on a regular basis. "That's great, Mark. I knew there was some reason we kept you on this."

"What do you mean we?" Garcia said, a smirk playing at the corners of her mouth. "I only wanted him around because he's eye candy."

Crowley turned red and excused himself from the room.

"Angelina, you've got to cut him some slack. He's not ruined like most of us around here. I think you embarrassed him," Jack said.

"You think?" Garcia said, with a big smile.

"You'll never get to her," Bobby said. Eddie was sitting behind the wheel of the van and watching the front of Harwood School. He'd spotted Katie Murphy's car in the parking lot and had decided to watch for a while. He spotted the plainclothes cops immediately. He'd have to get her during school, and that would be risky. He smiled.

"I'm gonna take her right out of class," Eddie said.

"Well, you'd better have a place to stash her right away," Bobby said. "Cops are gonna be on us like flies on shit."

"I got the perfect place," Eddie said with a sneer. "We'll be right under their noses where they won't be sniffing around."

"So, how you gonna get her out of the classroom, Eddie?" Bobby said. The sound of his voice made Eddie look closely at him.

"You feeling okay, Bobby?" Eddie asked. But it was obvious that Bobby didn't feel okay. He looked terrible. His complexion was ghostly pale, and he kept rubbing at a spot on his forehead like a dog with a rash.

Bobby didn't answer. He just laid his head back and looked out the side window.

"Go ahead and take a nap," Eddie said. "I got this covered, bro." He looked at the back of Bobby's head for a long minute, and was concerned for him. He hadn't been the same since Eddie got out of the joint. But it was almost over now. Just one more to go, and then they would end Murphy's worthless existence. *And about fuckin' time, too,* he thought.

The brown Crown Vic rolled down the street in front of Harwood School. The two men in front had been assigned by Captain Franklin himself, to keep an eye on Jack Murphy's ex-wife. They'd never seen the woman, but Franklin had given them a good description and they soon found her car. They weren't clear on why they were not to approach her and introduce themselves so they could be sure what she looked like. All they had been told was to watch and report and not let anyone go near Katie.

"How much of this shit have you done before, Charlie?" the younger of the men said to his plainclothes partner.

Charlie had been a uniformed copper for fifteen years before he managed to get into the detectives division. The fifteen years had seemed to fly by compared to his last two years in plainclothes. Most of the last two years he'd had to take every shit job that came down the pike.

It was always, "Charlie, go get us some lunch," or, "Charlie, you got the midnight shift." They, his superiors, didn't seem to think he could do anything but sit on his ass or fetch things for them. It was like being a rookie patrolman all over again, and he was wondering if he should have just stayed in uniform where his seniority counted for something. But then, he remembered, the little puke he'd gotten stuck with on this detail was even newer than him. So . . .

"There ain't nothing going on here," Charlie said with more anger in his voice than was necessary. *The better to keep the new guy in line.* "Murphy's ex can take care of herself for an hour or so. Take me to get some coffee, Mike," he ordered his junior partner. "And shut the fuck up for a while, will ya?"

Mike chuckled at his partner's insults. He was just happy as hell to get a chance to work plainclothes.

Mike put the car in gear. He had pulled out from the curb, when he heard his call sign come over their radio, saying, "Two-David-three."

Charlie picked up the microphone and said, "Two-David-three, go ahead."

"Signal nine your last detail," the dispatcher said.

"Ten-four," Charlie said and put the microphone back in its hook. "Well, I don't know what's going on, but let's go get coffee."

Mike didn't understand. "Won't that be dangerous for Mrs. Murphy, Charlie? I mean, what if something happens to her because we ain't here?"

Charlie gave him a disgusted look. "You heard the dispatcher, junior. Signal nine. That means we aren't assigned to this detail anymore."

When Mike still looked unsure, Charlie said, "Look, maybe they have another team set up. Maybe someone in the neighborhood spotted us and called in, so now we gotta move out of here. Hell, I don't know. All I know is that a signal nine means we're done. So move it!" he ordered his junior partner.

Mike pulled away, looking back at the school until it was out of sight. He had a bad feeling about this.

*   *   *

Chief Dick found himself once again riding the elevator to the third floor of the Civic Center. He was on his way to get another ass-chewing for things that were not within his control. And once again, he stopped at one of the mirrored columns in the third-floor hallway, checking that his brass was polished, his shoes shined, and seams straight. The face that looked back at him from the column was gaunt and pale. Rings had formed under his eyes overnight, and his mouth was dry, lips chapped.

He took several deep breaths and then pushed open the heavy door to the mayor's office, where the cynical look of the secretary made his blood boil. As she announced him on the intercom, he swore under his breath that one day he would get even with that bitch. Then he stood erect and pushed through the inner door.

He'd found out about Captain Franklin's little stakeout detail on Murphy's ex-wife, and since Franklin hadn't consulted him about it, he called them off. They needed all the detectives they had for other duties. Besides, Franklin was being paranoid. No one was going to bother Murphy's ex-wife. Now if it was his current wife, maybe he would have thought twice about pulling the detail. Or, if Franklin had come to him and requested it, he might have let them stay a little longer. But in the end, the decision was up to the chief of police. And that was him. Not Captain Franklin. And definitely not Jack Murphy.

He decided not to tell the mayor about any of this. *No need in worrying him with every tiny detail*, Dick thought, and straightening his tie, entered the mayor's inner sanctum.

Captain Franklin hung up the phone on his desk and dialed Murphy's cell number.

"Murphy," Jack answered, and Franklin could hear the tiredness in his voice.

"Jack, you need to talk Katie into leaving town for a while," Franklin said, hoping he didn't sound as angry as he felt right now. He'd just spoken with the detective sergeant who had been keeping a team of plainclothes at Katie's house and at Harwood. The sergeant had told him that Chief Dick ordered him to recall his men and put them back on the street.

"What's up, Captain?" Jack asked, although he had an idea.

"I had a team of plainclothes watching Katie for the last couple of days. Just to be safe," Franklin said. "The chief just canceled them."

"I appreciate the heads-up, Captain," Jack said. "I'll call her."

"Listen, Jack, the chief just called them off, so they may still be in the area. If you want them to go back over there, I'll see what I can do."

"Thanks, Captain. I'll run over there to see if I can get her to go to her mother's house for a while. She lives in Maine. Thanks for looking out for her, Captain," Jack said and hung up. He hadn't really considered Katie to be in any danger. But now that he thought about it, why wouldn't she be? Or Liddell or his wife, Marcie, for that matter. He would have to come up with something himself. Maybe some of his buddies could look after the women. He would pay them to do it off duty, but no one would take money for that. That's what cops do. Look after each other.

He closed the phone and told Liddell what had just happened.

"Call Katie," Liddell said, "and I'll call some guys to set up some protection."

"Better have some of them watch Marcie, too," Jack said.

"Hadn't thought of that," Liddell remarked and called his wife.

Jack called Katie's school. He hoped the detail was still there, but knew they were probably long gone since they had been ordered off by the chief.

CHAPTER SIXTY-EIGHT

Jack and Liddell had been standing outside Liddell's car when Franklin had called. Jack walked a little distance away and called Katie's cell. It went immediately into her voice mail, indicating that the phone was turned off. Could mean she was still in class, or a meeting, but Katie never turned her phone off. Maybe on vibrate, but never completely off. He dialed the number for Principal John Spanner.

"Just a moment, Detective," Spanner's secretary said. There was a click, and Spanner came on the line.

"Detective Murphy," Spanner said. "So good to hear from you. Wonderful news, isn't it?"

"What are you talking about?" Jack said, confused.

"I thought you would be celebrating, Detective Murphy," Spanner said.

Jack started to grow concerned, and said, "Celebrating what, exactly?"

Spanner's tone changed, not quite so jovial. "Why, the fact that the killer has been caught. It is great news, isn't it?"

Jack felt his blood turn cold. "Where's Katie, Mr. Spanner?"

"Well, she's on her way to police headquarters, I imagine. You sent for her, didn't you?"

Jack punched off and dialed Captain Franklin.

"Captain, did you send someone to bring Katie to headquarters?" he asked as soon as Franklin answered.

"No," Franklin answered, and then catching the serious tone in Jack's voice asked, "What's going on?"

Jack told him and hung up.

Seeing the look on his partner's face, Liddell said into his phone, "I've got to call you back. Yeah, get them started. Okay." Then he hung up.

"What is it, Jack?" he asked.

Jack ignored him and jumped into the driver's seat, peeling out and leaving his partner standing in the middle of the road. Jack wasn't planning on obeying any traffic laws, or any other law for that matter, until he was sure Katie was safe. Better that Liddell was not in the car during this trip so that he wouldn't have to testify against him later.

His mind raced ahead to the school, planning what he would do when he got there, finally coming to the conclusion that he'd better get the troops in on this. He pulled his phone from his pocket, and it rang in his hand.

"What the hell are you doing, Jack?" Liddell asked.

"Katie's not at school. She may be in trouble."

"What do you need?"

"Get me some troops. I'm on my way to her classroom," Jack said.

"I'm on it," Liddell said, and hung up.

Several red lights and blaring horns later, Jack thanked God that he hadn't run over anyone or crashed during the mind-numbing ride to Harwood School. Out of habit, he had scanned traffic all the way there, looking for anyone driving unusually recklessly, or too carefully, or for anyone that looked like Katie or an unmarked car, or anything that seemed out of place. His mind was in overdrive, his senses taking everything in at a time when most people would have tunnel vision, because cops trained themselves to function differently. An adrenaline dump would send a normal person into a form of shock, triggering the fight-or-flight syndrome. But he wasn't most people.

He spotted Katie's car in the school parking lot, but then reminded himself that if someone had picked her up she would have left it behind. He also made a mental note of every car in the lot, and nothing jumped out at him as not belonging or being out of place. He squealed to a stop at the front doors of the school and jumped from the car. His cell phone ringing startled him, and he swore.

He looked at the cell phone display and recognized the number. He forced himself to stop and take a couple of deep breaths before answering.

He punched the on button, "What is it, Eddie?" he said, trying to keep his breathing normal.

"Jack?" It was Katie's voice.

Jack's throat constricted, but he forced himself to speak calmly. "Katie, are you all right?"

The voice that answered was not Katie's. "Katie's not able to talk right now, Jack," Eddie said.

"Eddie, you son of a bitch," Jack began, but Eddie yelled into the line.

"That's right, hero!" Eddie said, and chuckled mirthlessly. "I'm the son of a bitch that's going to screw your old lady."

Jack bit back his anger and said, "Eddie, let me talk to Katie."

"No, I don't think so, Jack," Eddie said.

"It's me you want, Eddie, not anyone else. Let's get this

over with. I'll meet you anywhere you say. Let her go and you can have me."

"Well, let me think about that," he said, and then immediately responded, "NO! How's that, motherfucker?"

Just keep him talking, Jack thought to himself. He knew that time was running out, but if he could just keep him talking, he could maybe figure out where Eddie was. Find him. Kill him.

Katie's voice cut through the silence. "Don't do what he asks, Jack!" she yelled, and then came sounds of struggling and a scream. The phone went dead in his hand.

He held the phone to his ear feeling helpless as he said, "Hello? Hello?" into the dead line. Maybe Spanner was wrong. Maybe Katie was still inside somewhere. It didn't sound like the call was coming from inside a car, or outside. *So maybe, just maybe,* he thought and jumped from his car and rushed across the front playground. He ignored the screams of children as he rushed in the front doors, and from somewhere in the back of his mind he realized that his gun was in his hand. Maybe the sight of a man running into a school with a gun in his hand was what was frightening them.

Halfway down the hall to Katie's room he bowled over Principal Spanner, who had just come out of an office.

"Detective Murphy?" Spanner said while getting up from the floor. "What are you doing?"

He was looking at the gun in Jack's hand. Jack ignored him and rushed down the hallway. Katie's room was the fifth, or was it the sixth, on the right? *Damn!* he thought. *Which room?*

He decided on the fifth, and positioned himself near the door, gun held at combat ready, barrel pointed out at a downward angle, only needing a few inches to acquire a target. He took some deep breaths to steady his shaking hands, and then used his foot to ease the door inward.

He bladed his body against the door frame, sweeping the room with the gun barrel, finger outside the trigger guard. It wouldn't do to shoot some kid, and with the Glock .45 it only took about two pounds of pressure to pull the trigger. He'd practiced this so often he was on autopilot, except that he wasn't concerned with the police department policy of yelling "Stop" or "Freeze, police," and would go right to the part of shooting the bastard until he ran out of ammo.

The lights were on, but her room was empty. He knew it was her room because her purse was still on the floor beside the desk. Then something touched him on the back. He spun, bringing the gun barrel into the wide-eyed face of Principal Spanner.

"No one goes into this room except police," Jack said, and holstered his weapon.

Spanner swallowed loudly and croaked understanding. He took a key and locked the door behind them, then seemed to stagger. Jack helped him to a bench in the hallway.

"Put your head down, sir," Jack said, gently helping him put his head between his legs. After a few moments Spanner sat back upright, his complexion as blotchy as if he'd run a marathon.

"What the fuck is going on?" Spanner hissed between clenched teeth.

Jack told him, and Spanner shakily resumed the position with his head down.

CHAPTER SIXTY-NINE

Charlie and Mike were having coffee at the local Donut Bank when they heard the run come out at Harwood School. "Get in the car! Get in the car!" yelled Charlie, and they ran to the unmarked unit. Charlie had the car in gear before Mike had shut his door, and rocketed forward with such force his door slammed shut, nearly taking his fingers with it.

"Listen up, Mike," Charlie said, breathing hard. "When we get there, just let me do the talking. You back up whatever I say, understand?"

Mike didn't understand, but he knew that their jobs were probably on the line, so he agreed.

They were only a short distance away. As Charlie slowed and pulled down a side street paralleling the school, he hoped with all his heart that they would be the first to get there. *Why did I have to get stuck with a rookie?* Charlie thought, ignoring the possibility that he was the one to blame for their predicament.

"Maybe it's just some missing kid, or something," Mike suggested.

"Dispatch said 'kidnapping,' idiot," Charlie yelled, and Mike looked thoroughly chastised, making him feel even surer that it was the rookie's fault.

John Spanner's color was coming back, and he was anxious to answer a few questions for Jack.

"The man came to my office," Spanner was saying. *The killer was in my office.* Spanner turned pale. "He said he needed me to call Katie Murphy to my office. He said the killer had been caught and we could all relax now."

"Describe him," Jack said.

"About your height, slim, muscular, dark long hair. He looked like he might be working undercover or something. I don't know, maybe thirty years old. Could be younger. I'm not good with ages," he said.

Jack nodded understanding. It was a perfect description of Eddie.

"He acted like a cop. He was wearing a sport coat and jeans." Spanner looked at Jack, and his eyes were misting up. "I'm so sorry, Detective Murphy. We all love Katie. I would never have called her if . . ." His voice trailed off, and he looked down at the floor.

"Did he show you credentials?"

"A badge?" Spanner turned red in the face. "Well, no, actually. He just seemed like a policeman. You know? He was very confident, smiling even."

I'll bet he was, thought Jack. *The bastard walked right into her school and took her. He had her called to the office so he could catch her away from everyone.*

"Which direction did they leave? Did you see a car?" Jack asked.

"He met her at the doorway of my office and led her down the hall toward her classroom. Her kids had just gone to lunch," answered Spanner.

"Did he touch her?"

"Well, he did take her arm, like maybe he was helping her for some reason." Spanner looked ashamed. "He was forcing her out, wasn't he? He must have threatened her when he leaned over and whispered to her."

Jack wasn't surprised. Eddie must have threatened to kill Spanner or some of the kids if she didn't leave with him. Katie would have gone willingly to save her children. She knew about the killings, and she was probably smart enough to figure out who he was.

Jack's phone rang.

"Jack," Captain Franklin said, into the line. "I've got several detectives on their way out there. Liddell told me what happened. What have you got?"

Jack told him.

"What do you need?" Franklin asked.

Just then two men came running down the hallway, faces flushed with excitement. They showed their badges and said they were just outside when they heard the run come in. The older one explained that they were the surveillance team. Jack had seen him around the office recently, and it shamed him to think that Katie's life had been left to men such as these. He ignored them and turned his attention back to the captain.

"I need Katie back, Captain," he said, and closed the phone. It suddenly felt like the whole world had collapsed. Why hadn't he made her leave town? Or, at least, hired some guys that he trusted to stay with her? Better yet, stayed with her himself? If anything happened to her, he would never be able to live with himself. And at that moment he realized that he still loved her. More than anything in his life. More than his life.

The two plainclothes had wandered down the hall. They weren't in any real trouble from the brass because they had been officially relieved of the detail. But they were in deep shit from the rank-and-file cops who would never forget that they had let another officer's wife be abducted by a killer. But for Mike, who had little experience with such things, and had dreamed of getting into some action as a detective, the look of deep hurt and loss on Detective Murphy's face was not something he wanted to remember. He blamed himself for not standing up to Charlie and insisting they hang around a little longer. Instead he had driven to a donut shop and stuffed his face. It was their fault.

Jack walked down to them and noticed chocolate icing smudged on the younger man's shirtsleeve. "There's nothing you could have done. He pretended to be a detective and then walked her right out of here," Jack said, although he knew that it was their fault. They might have seen Katie leaving with Eddie if they had been doing their job. But his dad had always told him, "Fix the problem, not the blame." Blame wouldn't bring Katie back. He needed every policeman available, and such as they were, he needed them to work on this. He looked at the two shame-faced men and knew they'd never make the same mistake again. But even though he instinctively knew all that and also, that Double Dick was to blame, he would still have taken great pleasure in smashing both men's faces bloody.

"Can you start talking to the teachers and kids? See if someone saw Katie leaving? What kind of vehicle she got into?" Jack asked the men.

"We're on it," Charlie said, glad to have something to do, and they went with Principal Spanner to gather up the teachers.

Jack's phone rang again. His arm felt like lead when he answered.

Eddie said, "There's a neat little clock, in the schoolroom it stands, and it points to the time, with its two little hands."

Jack jogged down the hall and caught up with Spanner, silently motioning for him to unlock the door to Katie's classroom. "What do you mean, Eddie?" he asked. Spanner unlocked the door and stood back while Jack donned a pair of latex gloves and entered the room.

"Don't fuck me around, Jack," Eddie said. "You know the rules. If you solve the riddle you get the prize."

"What's the prize, Eddie?"

"You'll get to know exactly when she dies," Eddie said. "But I'm gonna have me some fun first," he added with a chuckle, and the line went dead.

Jack closed his phone and looked around the empty classroom, Eddie's taunting words bouncing around in his mind. The rational side of him said the best way to help Katie was to remain calm and think this through. There was probably no reason to worry about prints.

He looked behind him, over the doorway, and saw the large white-faced clock. The glass had been smashed, and the hands were stuck at twelve o'clock. He glanced at his watch. It was one forty-eight now. *The answer to Eddie's riddle,* he thought. *Katie has until midnight.*

CHAPTER SEVENTY

Liddell arrived at Harwood in the back of a uniform car and impatiently waited for the officer to let him out. He'd never ridden in the back of one before and was surprised at just how uncomfortable the seat was. His underwear was up somewhere inside, near his throat, and he remembered that when he was a kid they called this an atomic wedgie. He fought the urge to adjust his clothing, but then gave up and did what was necessary to keep from walking like a duck.

He spotted Jack at the front doors and rushed up.

"Sorry about dumping you, partner," Jack said.

"It's all right. What do we know?" Liddell looked more angry than concerned. Jack was glad now that he'd left him behind. If Liddell had known the two rookies were slacking off when Katie was snatched, he'd have rearranged their faces.

"Right now, not much," Jack said. He told Liddell about the telephone call from Eddie and the clock in the class-room.

"So we have until midnight?" Liddell asked.

"Who knows with Eddie?" Jack said, feeling sick. He

didn't have to say that she might already be dead. But somehow he felt that she was still alive. Eddie would probably
want to play this out longer to make him suffer. If Eddie was
trying to punish him, he'd done a fine job. If he was trying to
commit suicide by cop, that could be arranged.

"What's the next move, Jack?"

Jack had no "next move" in mind. He was running purely
on instinct now. His gut told him to get back to the war room
and gather his team. The storm was coming, and he'd need
them.

"Let's let Franklin's guys do the questioning here. We
need to get back to the war room," he said to Liddell, and
pitched him the car keys.

"Don't ever leave me behind like that again," Liddell said
seriously.

Susan was sitting at a table near the window of the Main
Street Café on the Walkway, cell phone pasted to her ear.
Katie was supposed to meet her for lunch almost an hour
ago, and it wasn't like Katie not to keep an appointment,
much less not to call and say she wasn't coming. And now it
seemed that Katie's phone was turned off.

She pushed the last of her wilted salad around her plate
and listened to Katie's phone go into her answering service
for the third time. She closed the phone and put it in her
purse. *Where is she?* Susan wondered.

She thought about how quickly she and Katie had become friends. Here she was dating Katie's ex-husband, and
neither of them had a jealous thought about the other. In
fact, she sometimes felt that she got along better with Katie
than she did with Jack. He could be distant and focused
only on his work, where Katie was attentive and didn't look
through her when she was talking. She knew Jack meant
well, but his job occupied most of his waking thoughts.

When he's not thinking about sex, that is, she thought and smiled.

"Oh well," she said out loud, and gathered her things. Katie would call her when she had time, and then would explain what had kept her. Maybe there had been trouble in her class. She had told Katie once that the students Katie taught were the same ones that would grow up to be Susan's clients, and on parole. Katie had laughed. But Susan firmly believed that kids that grew up in a violent environment, without love or affection, would always end up in a bad way. And that described most of the kids at Harwood School.

Susan took one more look outside and watched the businesspeople scurrying up and down the street on their way to lunch or back to work. Main Street had been refurbished when the Blue Star Casino had opted to build a floating riverboat casino in Evansville. But the casino hadn't brought the prosperity to the downtown area that the politicians had promised, and now it was starting to look shabby again. She sighed, put a generous tip on the table, and left the Café.

She looked up at the clear blue sky and wished now that she had walked to the Café instead of driving. But she had planned on a short lunch and then to do some much-needed clothes shopping before returning to work. Waiting for Katie had used up all of her time, and now she would have to hope she could find a parking spot back at work. Parking, anywhere in the downtown area, was always at a premium.

Susan turned left and headed down a wide alleyway between the buildings. She was digging in her purse for her keys and almost didn't notice the van parked in the narrow alleyway. It was faced away from her, and she could tell the hood was up. *Bad place to break down,* she thought, and began to squeeze between the van and the wall, when she became aware of a presence. She barely had time to turn her head before she was propelled sideways into the open side door of the van. Then rough hands were on her throat, and a knee stomped down into her ribs, forcing all the air from her lungs. She thought she heard a buzzing sound before she lost consciousness.

The fifty thousand volts Eddie had administered with the tiny stun gun hadn't been necessary, but it tickled him to see the parole officer jumping and jiving like a fish out of water as he held the device to her neck.

"Yippy-ki-yaaay," Eddie said, shocking the unconscious woman's body again and again.

"Where're Susan and Dr. Shull?" Jack asked when he entered the war room. Garcia looked at Crowley, and they both shrugged.

"Jack, I'm so sorry about Katie," Garcia said. "But listen to this." She looked at Crowley.

Crowley's face was hard as stone. "Jack, my friend with CID was able to pinpoint the cell phone. It was last used in the downtown area. He's sending me a piece of equipment that we can use to manually track it. But I was wrong about the phone not needing to be turned on. Apparently we don't have that capability yet."

Jack was pleased. It was the first break they'd gotten in a long time. "Let's get everyone together, and then we'll tackle this monster," he said.

Garcia, who had been on the phone, said, "Susan's phone didn't pick up."

Jack pulled out his phone and called Susan's cell. The call went to her answering service. "Her phone's turned off," he said.

"Maybe she's with Shull? Maybe the battery's dead?" Liddell suggested.

Jack shook his head. "She'd never turn her cell off." *Not even when we're in bed,* he thought to himself. "Besides, she's too efficient to let the battery go dead."

Garcia had picked up the desk phone, and held a finger up, motioning everyone to silence. "Hello, Dr. Shull," she said into the phone. "Yes. Angelina. Yes. Yes. Thank you, Dr. Shull, I like my name, too. Listen, Doctor Shull, is Susan with you? No? She's not? Okay, thanks. If you hear from her please call us. No, nothing is wrong." She thanked him and hung up.

"Jack, he thought she was meeting Katie somewhere downtown for lunch," Garcia said.

"Downtown!" Jack said, and an uneasy feeling settled in his gut. He tried Susan's phone again, and was surprised when it was answered. "Susan, where are you?" Jack asked, feeling relief.

"Don't worry, Jack. She's with Katie," came the reply. It was Eddie's voice. Jack's legs turned to rubber, and he sat on the edge of a desk as a feeling of despair washed over him. *Eddie has both of them,* he thought, and the line went dead.

CHAPTER SEVENTY-ONE

After the mayor had removed Marlin Pope from his position as chief of police and replaced him with Richard Dick, the first move Dick made was to relocate Pope to the nether regions of the Civic Center. Pope had been relegated to a sparse office on the third floor of the Civic Center with no windows and the closest restrooms at the far end of a long hallway.

His new duties were to oversee two sergeants who monitored the accreditation system for the Police Department. The sergeants' offices were moved from an office near the chief of police, and had been relocated in the basement area near the maintenance facilities. Apparently Chief Dick didn't value the work of the Accreditation Unit as much as Pope had when he was chief of police. But he knew the real reason for putting him in this broom closet was to keep him out of sight and out of mind.

As it turned out, Dick had done him a favor. His office was so removed from the police department that he could come and go as he pleased without attracting much attention. He was now sitting in Penny Lane Coffee Shop, and across the table was a nervous-looking Detective Larry Jansen. Pope was rather pleased with his investigative abilities, having been removed from the action for so many years. Of course, if Chief Dick found out that Pope was talking to Jansen, there would be serious repercussions.

"So. What's this about, Chief?" Jansen was saying.

"First of all, I'm not the chief anymore, Larry," Pope said, wanting to be clear that he was not acting as the chief. "This is a social call."

Jansen looked suspicious, and then a smile played across his face. "Dick don't know dick, does he?"

"No. He doesn't know I'm here, Larry," Pope said.

Jansen smiled at some secret knowledge, but the smile soon faded, and was replaced again with a suspicious look. "You're playing a dangerous game, Chief," Jansen said.

Pope was more than aware of Richard Dick's reputation for retribution, and how long he could hold a grudge. Many a policeman's career had been ruined by Dick over the years, and sometimes for as little as a perceived personal slight.

"I'm not playing a game, Larry," Pope said, locking eyes with Jansen. "More than careers are at stake here. Maddy's dead, and now Katie Murphy is missing." Pope saw the startled look glimmer in Jansen's eyes for a microsecond. *So. He hasn't heard about that yet,* Pope thought. He decided to drop the bombshell while he had the man off balance.

"I know you were leaking things to Maddy," Pope said.

Jansen had committed a mortal sin against law enforcement policies. He just hoped that Jansen still had a little fear or respect for an ex-chief of police.

Jansen started to get up, and Pope said, "Sit down, Officer. I still outrank you, and I can make your last years of work a living hell." He delivered this stone-faced, no menace in his voice, only a promise. Jansen sat down, and his hands covered his face.

"What do *you* want?" Jansen said, with the practiced tone of a habitual victim.

Pope smiled and leaned across the table. "I want it all, Larry," he said.

An hour later he was on his way to Two-Jakes with a reluctant Larry Jansen sitting in the passenger seat. Pope had arranged a meeting with Captain Franklin, Jack Murphy, Liddell Blanchard, and the city attorney, Dan Grossman. He hoped that Grossman didn't go running to the mayor before he heard Jansen's story. It would ruin all the fun of telling the asshole himself.

Dan Grossman, Larry Jansen, Captain Franklin, Marlin Pope, Murphy, and Blanchard sat around the large table in the meeting room at Two-Jakes. Jack looked impatient, and understandably so, thought Marlin Pope.

"First," Marlin Pope said, "let me assure you, Dan, that I in no way am representing the chief of police. I'm acting alone as my duty as a lieutenant in rank demands. These other men, with the exception of Detective Jansen, know little to nothing of what we are about to discuss here."

Grossman smiled and said, "That's a load of bullshit, Marlin, and you know it. But . . ." He shrugged as if to say, *It's your funeral.*

Pope looked at Jansen, who was looking at the door as if he was wondering what his chances of escape were. "Tell them," Pope said sternly.

Jansen looked pleadingly at Grossman, but saw no help from that corner. He knew he could tell now, or he would be forced to tell in a full internal affairs inquiry. Even the chief of police wouldn't be able to stop that if the public got wind of what had been happening within the ranks of the police department.

"I've been doing—" He stopped and cleared his throat.

"I've been doing certain things for the chief over the years," Jansen began.

"What chief?" Grossman demanded.

"Richard Dick, sir." Jansen took a deep breath, let it out, and then continued like many criminals that need to get things off their chest. And like most criminals, he started with an excuse for his actions. "My wife, Annabelle, has been sick for many years. Many, many years! She's got lupus. The doctors have done everything they can, but there's no cure. Over the last ten years, it's been hell for her. And for me. I used up all my savings and cut into my pension money to get nurses at my house round the clock."

Everyone just looked at him. He took another breath and continued, and for the next half-hour he told how he had been approached by *then* Deputy Chief Richard Dick, with an offer. All he had to do were certain "tasks" for Dick, without question, and Dick would make sure that Jansen would be in jobs that would allow him to spend as much time at home as was necessary to curb the costs of medical care for his wife. For the last five years he had done things that he knew were wrong, but it wasn't his fault.

Jack was stunned, but now it was clear to him how Jansen had earned the reputation of being a "missing person detective." Jansen was missing almost all of the time, and instead of being fired for absence, as any other detective would have been, his absenteeism had been kept quiet by Double Dick all these years. He wanted to have some compassion for the pitiable figure of Detective Jansen, but it was because of people like Jansen and Double Dick that Katie had been so easily kidnapped in broad daylight.

When Jansen was talked out, and staring at the tops of his shoes like a dead man, the first one to speak was Dan Grossman.

"The city owes you a huge debt, Detective Murphy," he said sincerely. Or at least as sincerely as an attorney was capable of being. "And we owe you an apology, Marlin," he said.

Pope noticed he had used his first name, meaning of course that Grossman was trying to suck up to him and limit the damage to the mayor and the city.

"Of course we'll take immediate action. I believe the first thing is for me to contact the mayor and hopefully have you reinstated as chief of police immediately," he said to Pope.

Liddell Blanchard spoke for the first time since entering the room. "It's about goddamn time!"

The soon-to-be-reinstated chief couldn't agree more.

Within an hour, Richard Dick had been removed from the office of chief of police and was on temporary leave with pay until his fate could be decided. Marlin Pope had been placed back in his old position, and his first act as chief was to declare all-out war on Eddie Solazzo. He had started amassing enough forces to search the tri-state area if necessary, calling in county police, FBI, and anyone else that was able-bodied.

But even with all this, Jack left the meeting with a sense of gloom. Pope coming back as chief was a dollar late and a day short. Eddie had already done his damage, and there seemed to be no way of stopping him now. The only chance they had now was to use the tracking equipment that Chief Deputy Mark Crowley had borrowed from his friend.

CHAPTER SEVENTY-TWO

Back in the war room, Jack and Liddell met with the team, including an anxious Dr. Don Shull, but minus Susan Summers.

"Let's see where we're at," Jack said, and pointed to the map of Mother Goose Land on the wall. "We finally figured out there was a pattern, but now Eddie has seemingly abandoned that. Doctor?"

Shull was standing in front of the map, arms crossed, looking at each scene marker. "I've never seen someone so confused. And that's saying a lot."

He pointed to the first murder scene. "Anne and Don Lewis. It seemingly started there, with the murder of his court-ordered psychiatrist." He looked at the photos and descriptions of the victims.

"Anne was very good at what she did, Jack. If she had a chance to talk to Eddie, she probably would have been able to talk him down. That fits with what you told me of the scene. The unprovoked attack on the husband and then the savage killing and staging of the scene. I would say he probably displayed her husband's dead body to her. The rage was controlled until the actual killing occurred. The killing was animalistic. However, the initial attacks were ritual. Planned. Well thought out. And that's what is most confusing still."

Shull looked at each person in the room, and then continued. "There are two minds at work. One planning and one killing. Until the killing of Maddy Brooks, it appeared that the planning mind was in control. That would be Bobby. Now Eddie is in control. He has become strong enough to resist what he thinks Bobby would do."

"This is taking us backwards, Doc," Liddell complained.

"No. It is deciphering the mind of your killer," Shull replied. "Maybe I can explain it this way. Eddie was so lost without his brother's guidance that he invented his brother. Like a kid with a secret friend that no one else can see. It was Bobby's influence that kept him from killing Jack. He's probably still holding on to his brother's memories, discussing his moves with the imaginary brother. But make no mistake, Eddie is in charge now."

"How do we know that for sure?" Crowley asked.

"We don't know anything for sure," Shull replied. "But from what you've all told me, Bobby wasn't suicidal. Some of the things that Eddie has done recently indicate a death wish."

"Are you saying he wants to be killed?" said Liddell.

"Well, yes and no," Shull answered.

"Typical psychiatrist answer," Crowley said.

Shull grinned and said, "Typical police interpretation."

Liddell cringed. "Ouch! I think he got you there, Mark."

Crowley apologized and said, "Okay, so what does your answer mean, Doctor?"

Shull looked at the map again, and said without facing the others, "He wants to die, but he just won't admit it to himself. And in particular, he wants Jack to do it. If he can."

"Oh, I can," Jack said, matter-of-factly. "So. How do we find him?"

"That's the point I'm making, Jack. I think he will be the one finding you."

They looked at each other, and were all wondering the same thing that Shull now voiced. "He's likely to come here if he doesn't lure you somewhere alone."

Liddell leaned in toward Jack's ear and said, "We've gotta talk. Now!"

CHAPTER SEVENTY-THREE

"I'll handcuff myself to you if that's what it takes to make you do this the right way," Liddell was saying heatedly. A couple of uniformed officers, who had been standing in the hallway chatting, moved off quickly. Liddell was the size of a gorilla and just as strong. You didn't want to be in this man's face when he was mad.

"It's not about me, Cajun," Jack said as forcefully as his angry partner. "He's got Katie and Susan, and every minute we play patty-cake here he's spending with them!" Jack had tried not to think about what might be happening to the women, but he had not realized the full extent of Eddie's sickness until Shull brought it to his attention. Now he couldn't get it out of his mind. They must be frightened beyond fear by now. *If they're not dead,* he finished the thought. And with that thought he rushed back into the war room.

Shull was talking to Mark and Angelina when Jack interrupted. "Hey, Doc," Jack said, and then told Shull his idea.

* * *

Bill Goldberg was angry. Not because of the death of his reporter, but because he was being ordered by the station's owners to participate in what he viewed as a highly illegal, not to mention legally liable, act by the police department. Who the hell did this detective Murphy think he was, anyway?

"I'll do it," he said to the station's attorney, David Wires. "But you'd better remember, that when this goes to hell, and it will, that I was against the idea." Wires was tired of listening to the manager vent and decided the conversation was over. The line went dead in Goldberg's ear.

"Damn! Damn! Shit!" Goldberg said into the empty line and slammed the phone into its cradle. "Get the Bobbsey Twins in here!" he yelled at his secretary, referring to anchors Clark Jameson and Tonya Simpson.

Everything had been put together in a rush, but Jack was confident that this would get the results he wanted. Shull had given him the idea when he said that Eddie was still talking to his brother, Bobby. If that was so, he hoped Eddie was still watching the news reports on the case. He had a surprise for Eddie.

It was already five o'clock, and Jack was sitting in the same chair he had occupied when Maddy Brooks had interviewed him a week ago. But now, Tonya Simpson sat across from him, patting and prodding stray hairs into place as she practiced her smile. *They actually practice smiling,* Jack thought.

Somehow it hadn't sunk in that the chopped-up mess they had found tied to the STAR radio tower was all that was left of Maddy Brooks. She had been a beautiful woman once, but her pride and curiosity had gotten her killed. He hoped

that same pride and curiosity would be Eddie Solazzo's un-
doing, as well.

The newsroom lights brightened, and Clark Jameson
looked into camera one, as the cameraman gave him the
countdown. Jameson came in on his cue, did the agreed
spiel. Jack was sickened by the idea of using the deaths of
these innocents to draw Eddie into a trap. But he reminded
himself why he was here, and thought about how Double
Dick had denied taking evidence from a crime scene. Jack
would never understand how someone supposedly of leader-
ship caliber could just up and piss a career away like that.
But before he could complete the thought, the light over
camera two came on. *Nearly showtime,* he thought.

Tonya Simpson looked into her camera, showing more
teeth than a great white shark, and said, "We have with us
Detective Jack Murphy, the lead investigator on the recent
series of murders committed by the man that has been
dubbed 'Mother Goose.' "

As planned, Jack interrupted her before she could ask a
question. Only Bill Goldberg and Dave Wires had been informed about the content of what Jack was going to say. Jack
needed Tonya Simpson and Clark Jameson to look startled.
He just hoped that they wouldn't blurt something out before
he was finished.

"Tonya, I'm not here to answer questions," Jack said,
leaning forward into the camera. "I'm here to give a message to Eddie and Bobby Solazzo."

Tonya Simpson looked confused. Bobby Solazzo was
dead. What was Murphy up to this time? "But Detective,
isn't Bobby Solazzo—" she got out before Jack interrupted
her again.

"Bobby Solazzo has always been the brains of that crew.
Eddie couldn't take a dump without consulting Bobby. So

it's clear to me that Bobby is behind all of these recent killings. Eddie's not smart enough to come up with something like this." Jack stood and walked toward the camera with a threatening look on his face. "I just want Eddie to know that he's in the clear if he'll turn himself in. I'll personally meet him anywhere, anytime. Alone! Bobby Solazzo is the killer. He's the one we want."

"But, Detective Murphy," Tonya tried to speak but saw her camera light go out. Looking over, she saw Bill Goldberg motioning for the camera crew to cut to a commercial. "Bill, what the hell is going on?" she yelled across the stage, and when she turned back to Murphy she found an empty seat.

As soon as the camera light went out, Jack had yanked the tiny mike off his jacket and thrown it down in the chair. He hoped that Shull was right and that Eddie was a crazy as he thought. His plan had been to get Eddie so worked up that he would come after him. The problem being, that even if it worked, there was no guarantee that he wouldn't kill the women first.

"I hope I never lay eyes on you again," Bill Goldberg said to Jack as he walked across the newsroom stage to where Liddell and Crowley were waiting.

"You'd better hope that's true," Jack said menacingly, and Goldberg cringed back like a typical bully.

Liddell slapped Jack on the shoulder, saying, "Great job, pod'na. Now what kind of jobs are we going to be looking for when this all goes to shit?"

Jack said, "You wanted to know what the next move was. Well, the next move is Eddie's now. If Shull is right, I've just caused some dissension in the ranks of the Solazzo boys. Eddie will have to show his brother that he is a man by killing me."

"Great plan, Jack," Crowley said.

They followed Crowley outside to a white panel van with

smoked windows. Crowley opened the back, and Liddell said, "Holy shit, Batman! Where did you get all this stuff?"

Jack looked inside the van's cargo area. Every square inch of wall space was taken up with electronic equipment, and then he noticed the tall antennae on top of the vehicle. Crowley reached inside the front driver's door and pulled out two large magnetic signs and stuck one on the side of the driver's door, the other to the rear door. The van now looked like a *Channel Six News* van, complete with tower antennae.

"Your friend from CID loaned you all this?" Jack said.

"Cool stuff, huh?" Crowley answered.

"Hell, yeah!" Liddell shouted. "Know how to use any of it?"

Crowley climbed in the back of the van, dropped into one of two roll-around chairs, and reached out to Jack, saying, "Give me your cell phone."

Jack handed him the phone, and Crowley wedged it into a holder on one of the control panels. He punched a couple of buttons, and everything powered up. Lights subdued, and a screen that looked like a sonar screen from television came to life. "I can handle everything from here, Jack," he said, and reached in his pocket, coming out with a tiny ear plug. "Put this in your ear," he said.

Jack put the flesh-colored earbud into his ear. "What's this for?" Suddenly he could hear Liddell chuckling as if he were right in his face.

Crowley said, "I can control the volume from here, and it's two-way so we can hear you talk even if you whisper. It also has a sound enhancer that will enable you to hear things more clearly at a distance. My friend said this is an outdated system, so he didn't have a problem loaning it to me for a few days."

"For the taxes I pay, I would expect something newer," Liddell joked, but no one laughed. "Hey, that was a pretty good joke," he complained.

"Won't I need my phone?" Jack asked.

Crowley smiled, saying, "That's another cool thing about this getup. I plugged your phone into the computer system. All you have to do is say a series of numbers and your phone will dial it for you." Liddell reached in to touch something, and Mark smacked his hand. "Don't touch anything. I don't know what half of it does."

"And you're just now telling us this?" Liddell said.

"Look, I know how to operate the parts we need. I can trace any phone call that's made to Jack's phone back to the originating phone. I even had my friend program in Maddy's, Susan's, and Katie's phones as well. Believe me, when he calls, we'll be able to track him," Mark said.

"If he calls," Liddell grumped, and the men settled down to wait for the call, Jack in the back with Crowley and Liddell driving. Liddell pulled out of the station parking lot and headed for the downtown area since that was the last place that Eddie had used the cell phone.

CHAPTER SEVENTY-FOUR

The flickering of the television was the only light in the cabin. Eddie sat in a comfortable recliner, the corn knife with its razor-sharp edge lying across his legs. His eyes were closed as if he was asleep, but he wasn't. He had been asleep most of his life, but now his eyes had been opened. He knew exactly what he had to do. How things would end. With or without Bobby's help.

He opened his eyes and looked at the women bound to wooden chairs in front of the kitchen entrance. "Murphy shouldn't have fucked with me, Bobby!" he shouted, leaping from the chair and swinging the knife through the air. Both women cringed as the blade smashed into the wood of the door frame, mere inches from Katie's head. Then he stood rigidly, looking across the darkened room at nothing, and yelled, "I'm in charge here, Bobby," and spittle flew from his mouth. "I'm in charge!"

Susan managed to twist her head enough to see Katie's bruised and battered face. One of Katie's eyes was swollen shut and the other was wide with fear. Duct tape wound tightly around both of their faces, completely covering their mouths, but Eddie had been careful not to cover their eyes.

Susan knew this wasn't a good sign. If he planned on keeping them alive, he wouldn't want them to be able to recognize him, and she sure as hell knew who he was. The look on Katie's face said that she had guessed their fate as well.

She had felt something wrong in the alleyway before Eddie grabbed her. But she had let her guard down. She wondered what had happened to the intuition that had served her so well in the past. But it didn't matter now. She and Katie were going to be killed by this raving lunatic, and there wasn't anything they could do about it.

Susan tried again to loosen her bonds, but Eddie had not only tied them up with rope but also used rolls of duct tape. Suddenly her head was roughly yanked up by the hair, and a fist came down into her face. She was dazed and felt her mouth filling with blood.

"I told you not to move, bitch!" Eddie struck her again, this time so hard that she lost consciousness. He continued to beat her.

Katie sat still, facing forward, and felt shame that she was too afraid to even watch as her friend was beaten senseless. *Where is Jack?* she wondered. *Jack, please come for us!* And even though she hadn't moved, it was her turn next.

"Eddie, you son of a bitch, where the hell are you?" Jack muttered.

Mark checked all of the equipment settings for the hundredth time. Jack had done his thing at Channel Six around five o'clock, and it was now going on seven o'clock. It felt like they had been driving for hours, and he could feel a gloom settling over them. He had never met Katie, but he knew Susan to be a good and brave soul. The cop side of him

vowed that Eddie would never make it to jail, and he knew
Jack felt the same. He wasn't so sure about the Cajun. Liddell didn't have the killer in him that he felt in Jack. Mark
had spent some time in Desert Storm and knew the look of
someone who has killed. Jack had that look.

"He'll call, Jack," Mark said.

But Jack wasn't listening. He was staring out the darkened rear window at the receding businesses along Main
Street. Just down the street was the little jewelry store where
he and Katie had picked out wedding rings. He remembered
how her eyes had widened and then sparkled when she
found "the one." And he wondered why he hadn't tried
harder. But he knew the answer. His work had always been
more important to him than anything else. He always had
some case, or some bad guy, or a murder to solve, and he
would get around to his friends and his life later. That included his wife.

For some reason, he had always expected her to just be
there. His mother had always been there for his dad, and his
father had been a cop for almost forty years. So, how had
they put up with each other for all that time? He remembered his father missing most of his birthdays and ball
games when he was growing up, but he had always loved his
father. Maybe if he and Katie had had children it would be
different.

Something beeped on the control panel in front of Jack,
and a green light came on. He looked excitedly at Crowley,
who was busy flipping switches.

"We got a signal," Crowley said, looking at one of the
screens. "He's turned on Katie's phone."

"Where?" Jack asked through clenched teeth.

"I'm not sure I can tell you," Crowley responded.

"Goddamn it, why not?"

Crowley looked offended. "Because it seems to be coming from the Ohio River."

Jack looked at the screen. "Where on the Ohio?" he asked, and Crowley told him. Jack pounded on the back of the partition separating them from Liddell and yelled, "Stop!" Liddell hit the brakes, and the van lurched to a halt. Before Crowley could stop him, Jack grabbed his cell phone from the control panel and bailed out, disappearing in the darkness.

Liddell slid a panel aside and looked through it into the back of the van. "What's going on?" he asked, and then saw the back doors hanging open. "Jack, you dumb shit!" he yelled and jumped from the van. He came around to meet Crowley, who was standing behind the van and looking down the street for a sign of Jack.

"We got a signal," he explained to Liddell, "from Katie's phone. It came from somewhere along the river, east of here. Jack just dived out!"

"See if you can pin it down any better," Liddell said, and Crowley climbed back in the van. Liddell pulled out his cell phone and dialed Captain Franklin.

"Aw shit!" Crowley said.

"What is it?"

"Jack took his phone."

"Well, can you track his phone?" Liddell asked.

"I can try," Crowley said uncertainly.

"Shit!" Liddell said out loud, and then into the cell phone, "No, not you, Captain. It's about Jack," he said, and then told the captain their situation.

The van was less than a mile from Two-Jakes, and Jack was headed there at a dead run. If he could get there quickly, he had a plan that might work. He stopped to catch his breath and looked at the luminous hands on his watch. It was just after seven o'clock. If Eddie had told the truth, he still had five hours. But his little stunt on television might have pushed Eddie over the edge. Pissing Eddie off was a risk, but he'd had to flush the bastard out somehow.

He sprinted again. It would have been much faster to have gone there in the van, but then he would have had to tell Crowley and Liddell what he was doing. Then they would know that he planned on meeting Eddie alone, and he didn't want half the police department and the SWAT team breathing down his neck. He didn't like leaving Liddell and Mark with their dicks hanging out, but if he didn't, he would be putting them in the position of having to lie for him.

It took almost five minutes at a full run to reach the inlet area at Two-Jakes where people stored their boats. He was puffing like a steam engine when he let himself into the locked gate that separated the inland marina from the parking area.

Since he was part-owner of the business, he kept his own boat docked here when he needed it serviced. He prayed that the service crew was finished and had put it back in the water. He ran down the dock to the last slip on the left and was relieved to see that his boat, a twenty-five-foot Day-cruiser called the *Miss Fit*, was tied up there.

He untied the lines and jumped aboard, fired up the two large inboard engines, and pulled out of the dock. He was going too fast and narrowly missed the end of a barge tied up outside the inlet, but then he was on the river, running the big engines to their capacity. The cloud cover was thick, and the river was as black as the sky. He thought about running without lights, but he couldn't risk running into half-submerged debris in the pitch blackness that spread before him. The current in the Ohio was famous for carrying whole trees downriver, and even in daylight he had to keep his eyes peeled for any obstacles.

He made his way upriver a couple of miles, thinking his cabin was just around the next bend in the river. He cut his lights and navigated by memory, staying close to the bank.

The shore began to look familiar, and he knew he would have to depend on his instinct now. He would have to time this just right, or he would run aground and alert Eddie that he had arrived.

He throttled back and then let the boat glide forward. The boat slipped quietly in beside the floating dock at the bottom of his property.

If he was right, Katie and Susan were inside. And so was Eddie. But if he was wrong, he may have doomed any chance they had of finding the women before time ran out.

He had spent most of his summers as a boy here, fishing with his granddad and his dad, so he knew every inch of the surrounding terrain. He jumped to the dock, and without taking time to tie the boat off, moved silently across the deck and up the riprap to the bottom steps of his cabin, where he paused.

There was no light coming from inside his cabin, and even though he had been careful in his approach, he knew someone had turned off the outside lights that were on motion sensors. He listened, and at first the only sound was that of water lapping against the shore. But then he heard a voice, or a moan, or both, and it seemed very nearby. He looked around in the dark and saw nothing. Then he remembered the earbud that Crowley had him wear. Crowley had said it would enhance his hearing. Were the sounds coming from inside his cabin?

He had to get closer. He eased up the side of the bank, ignoring the steps that led up to his porch, and scrabbled up the gritty bank to the base of his cabin.

Huge pilings had been driven into the clay for the foundation, and to keep the cabin higher than the flood stages of the river. As he lay against a piling and tried to steady his breathing, he thought that Eddie had to be totally mad to bring Katie and Susan to this particular cabin. But, in a crazy sort of way, it made sense. Eddie wanted to "beard the lion in his own den." He was doing just what Don Shull had predicted. Bringing Jack to him.

Jack's eyes adjusted to the darkness, and he surveyed the surrounding area looking for any sign of light escaping from the cabin. There was none. He had a feeling of dread that maybe he was too late. Katie and Susan could be dead. But then he heard the soft moan again and again a loud thud.

Jack crawled farther under the cabin and lay motionless, listening, waiting, and was rewarded by the sound of someone walking across the floor toward the door that led onto the porch. If Eddie was looking outside, he was probably seeing only darkness. Jack knew there was no way to make out the boat from that distance. He still had the element of surprise. Then he remembered that he had the cell phone with him.

Oh, shit! he silently mouthed. If the phone rang, he was directly beneath Eddie. He reached for the phone, hoping he had left it on vibrate, but it rang in his hand.

He knew that if he didn't answer, Eddie might kill the women. If he did answer, Eddie might hear him and kill the women. "Fuck it," he said under his breath and slid out from under the cabin and walked up the steps and onto his porch. He sensed, more than saw, the movement inside the cabin as he reached out and tried the door. It was unlocked. He pushed the door open and said, "Eddie, I'm coming in. I'm alone."

He wasn't sure he'd been heard and was about to repeat himself when he heard a whimper from inside. He stepped into his front room just as a bright light shined into his eyes.

CHAPTER SEVENTY-FIVE

Captain Franklin pulled into Two-Jakes and parked by the surveillance van loaded with electronics equipment. There were five uniform patrol cars, several unmarked police cars, two from the narcotics unit, and two K-9 cars. He was amazed that dispatchers had managed to coordinate this meeting without alerting the news media to the event. He walked to the back of the van and noticed the newly reinstated chief of police, Marlin Pope, leaning inside and talking to Dubois County Chief Deputy Sheriff Mark Crowley.

"I guess I should say something like 'Great Caesar's Ghost' or something appropriate about this equipment," Pope was saying, obviously impressed with the technology. Franklin knew that this type of equipment would never be in the future budget of the Evansville Police Department.

Crowley smiled and looked a little embarrassed. "I was just telling your chief here that I've pinpointed Jack's cell phone, and it's in the same place as Katie's cell phone. Liddell thinks they're inside Jack's cabin."

"That crazy son of a bitch," Franklin said, shaking his head.

Liddell asked, "Mark, did Jack ever answer his phone?"

Crowley shook his head.

"What's the plan, Captain?" Chief Pope asked.

Liddell spoke up, and said angrily, "The plan is, we surround Jack's cabin, and then we go in and kick Eddie's skinny ass to the moon."

Pope rolled his eyes. He'd forgotten how plainspoken the big Cajun was. But, on the other hand, he would never want to be the target of Liddell's rage. He'd seen a few of those unfortunate persons, and they were almost always in the back of an ambulance, or in a hospital.

Franklin looked at Liddell, but spoke to the chief, saying, "We are going to set up a perimeter around Jack's cabin. I called the Coast Guard, the sheriff's department, and the fire department, and asked for the use of their boats to take some of our SWAT team out to set up a river perimeter. For all we know, Eddie may have a boat out there. Other SWAT members are going with one of our crisis negotiators to set up a command post near the cabin. I've also called for a couple of ambulance units to stand by."

"You sure Jack's in there?" Pope asked, and Franklin nodded that he was.

"I already called Little Casket," Liddell said, and when the chief looked at him, he shrugged his big shoulders and said, "Hey, if Jack's in there, Eddie's coming out in a bag."

Before Jack entered his cabin, he had slipped his gun from behind his back and held it to his side, keeping his body slightly angled to hide the weapon. The light that was in Jack's face remained steady.

Eddie said, in a singsong voice, "To market, to market, to buy a fat pig. Home again, home again, jiggety-jig. We've been waiting for you, Jack."

The light in Jack's eyes shifted to the right, and Eddie

said, "Now drop the gun before I cut this one's head off." To emphasize his point Eddie caused one of the women to give a muffled scream.

Jack heard a cry, but couldn't tell who it came from. The light had obliterated any night vision he might have.

"Is that another of your riddles, Eddie?" *Keep him talking. Get a location on him, then bye-bye asshole.* Jack's finger tightened on the trigger.

"I always thought you were the brave one," Jack said, and Eddie laughed. "But I see that you're a bigger coward than your brother. Hiding behind women in the dark. What does Bobby say about that, Eddie?"

Eddie stopped laughing. A lamp clicked on, and Jack could see both women now. What he saw made his stomach lurch. Katie and Susan were tied to kitchen chairs, and duct tape was wrapped around their faces. Eddie was crouched low behind them, the blade of a long knife, like a giant machete, held so close to Katie's throat that blood had trickled down her neck and onto her clothes. Katie had been beaten. One eye was swollen shut, the other electric with fear.

Susan was in worse shape. Her jaw looked misshapen, maybe broken. And though her face was covered in blood, Jack saw anger flashing in her eyes. Susan was a fighter. A survivor. But poor Katie was a sixth-grade schoolteacher. Her only association with violence was through the rare stories that Jack had shared with her when they were married, or perhaps what she read in the newspapers. She looked as if she was going into shock, and Jack felt he had to do something now or she wouldn't make it. There was no time for negotiations. He hadn't come there to talk.

"Drop the gun, hero," Eddie said with a crazy grin on his face. "I won't ask again." He used the blade to slice Katie's face, causing her to give a painful scream, and then dropped the blade to her throat.

Jack was a good shot, but Eddie was not making himself

a target. Eddie was crouched so low Jack feared he would hit Katie if he tried. Then he had an idea. He used his thumb to push the release on the backup and felt the loaded magazine slip loose.

He slowly moved his left arm out where Eddie could see the gun, and as he did so he said, "I didn't come here to bargain with you, asshole." Jack laid the gun on the floor and carefully kicked it toward Eddie. The gun came to rest under Susan's chair and a surprised Eddie glanced down.

"Pick it up," Jack said.

"What?" Eddie looked at Jack as if Jack were the one that was crazy.

"Haven't you ever heard the old saying? You should never bring a knife to a gunfight, dick-for-brains."

Eddie's mouth quivered; his eyes widened with rage. He dropped the knife and grabbed the gun, but Jack didn't move. Eddie reached around Katie, pulling the tape loose from her mouth. She drew in a huge breath, but he grabbed her roughly by the jaw, pulling her head upright. "I want you to see this, motherfucker. This is for me 'n' Bobby."

Eddie put the gun to Katie's temple. "Who's the dick-for-brains now, Murphy? Who's got the gun now?" he said, and pulled the trigger. Katie screamed, and her head lurched to the side in an attempt to avoid the blast that she knew was coming. But there was only the sound of an empty click.

Jack knew the gun would never fire with the ammo clip disengaged. It was one of the safety features of that particular model. He reached inside his coat and pulled his .45 Glock from its holster. "You're the dick-for-brains, Eddie," he said, and squeezed the trigger.

The bullet caught Eddie in the forehead, blowing bits of tissue and skull onto Katie and Susan, and sending a large portion of Eddie's brains flying into the kitchen.

Jack watched Eddie crumple to the floor like a blow-up doll that had a massive air leak. In the movies the bad guy was always blown backward twenty feet, or his entire head explodes when you put a hundred and forty-five grains of lead into his skull. But in real life, the bullet only made a little hole where it went in, and it took out a chunk about the size of a plum where it came out.

It took Jack a moment to realize that Katie was still screaming hysterically and was trying to spit something out. Later he would realize she was spitting out bits of Eddie's skull.

And then all hell broke loose. The living room and kitchen windows broke simultaneously, and objects clattered around the rooms, soon filling them with tear gas. Jack moved to the women and covered them with his body to shield them from the concussion of the stun grenades that he knew would come in right behind the tear gas. The blast was meant to stun, and the grenade did its job. With the blinding flash and concussion, Jack became too disoriented to move, and it appeared that men in gas masks were moving toward him in slow motion.

EPILOGUE

Liddell and his wife, Marcie, stood at the elevator bank in the lobby of St. Mary's Hospital. Jack came into the lobby carrying a beautiful bouquet of daffodils in one hand, and another bouquet of some kind of yellow flower that looked like small sunflowers in the other hand. Jack was never good with flower names, but knew that daffodils were Katie's favorite, and he had seen the sunflower-looking ones around Susan's place.

"Oh, what beautiful flowers, Jack!" Marcie said, and rose onto her tiptoes to kiss his cheek.

With a big grin, Liddell tried to kiss him, too, and Jack pushed him away. "Not in front of your wife, Cajun. She might not let us be partners anymore."

Marcie slapped Liddell on the arm and, in a low voice—the one his mother called an "inside voice"—she warned him to behave himself in the hospital.

Jack wondered why people kept their voices low in a hospital. Was it like a church, or was it because of the mystery of medicine or the sense of death lingering in the halls? He wasn't sure, but the last couple of times he'd been in the hospital, all he wanted to do was scream.

The elevator came, and they all rode to the fifth floor, where Katie and Susan were sharing a room. When the elevator doors opened they were all surprised to see Susan standing there, waiting for the elevator.

"You've already been released?" Jack asked happily.

Susan pulled him back on the elevator. "We have to talk," she said seriously, then to Marcie and Liddell, "Hi. Sorry, but I'm in a hurry. See you later." And then the door shut and the elevator headed back down.

"What is it?" Jack said.

"I have to get out of here," Susan said, and Jack just then noticed that she had dressed hastily and hadn't even tied her shoes.

"Are you escaping? Oh, you're a bad girl?" Jack said with a grin.

"Damn right," Susan answered, and as the doors opened at the lobby, she said, "Just walk to the lot with me. I've called a cab already."

"There's no need to do that, Susan. I'll take you home."

"No," she said a little too quickly, making Jack look at her. Something was wrong, and he wondered if it was just the aftereffects of her harrowing ordeal with Eddie.

"Look," Susan said, "you and I both know that you executed Eddie."

Jack was shocked into silence. He hadn't thought of it that way. He did what he had to do to save their lives. If he had given Eddie any chance at all, one or all of them might be dead. "I had to make a decision," Jack said. "I chose for Eddie to die, instead of you or Katie."

Susan's eyes grew moist, and she looked away from him. "I just . . . I just never thought that I . . . or that you would . . ." Tears slid down her cheeks, and she looked at Jack. "I just can't deal with this right now. You should go and be with Katie. She needs you more than I do right now," she lied.

The cab pulled up, and Susan slipped inside. She didn't look at Jack as the cab pulled away. He stood there for several minutes looking after her.

She's been through a lot. She doesn't know what she's saying, he thought. But it felt as though she hated him. The sad thing was, he could easily understand why.

He trudged back into the hospital and rode the elevator to the fifth floor. As he entered Katie's room, he found her propped up in bed looking at a huge basket of flowers. He was chagrined to see Don Shull sitting beside the bed, holding one of her hands in his and patting it gently.

"Look who's here," Liddell said, smirking.

"Yeah." Jack said, wearing a grin. "Look who's here. Dr. Shull."

"Hi, Jack," Shull said happily. "I heard about that rescue of yours last night. Man, they ought to make a movie about you. I'm just so grateful that you got our little Katie out of there in one piece."

Jack looked at Shull, wondering if he was being facetious or serious. He decided that Shull wasn't being a smart-ass, but he was sure that Shull was attracted to Katie. He hated to admit it, but he sort of liked Shull. And besides, maybe Katie could use a friend like him. She would have some hard days ahead of her. But Jack was so preoccupied by Shull's presence in Katie's room, in her life, that he hadn't noticed the look that crossed Katie's face when he walked in.

"Are those flowers all for me?" Katie asked, and Jack realized he was still carrying both bouquets of flowers. He had forgotten to give Susan the one he brought for her. But she had been so rude with him that he decided instead to give them both to Katie.

"Yes," he said, setting the flowers on the table beside her bed, "they're both for you."

"Daffodils," she said, and tried to smile, but winced instead.

Shull said, "Katie's being released this afternoon. Her doctor said there were no major injuries. Her jaw is bruised badly, but it isn't broken. I've offered to take her home later."

Jack looked at Katie, but she seemed to deliberately not look at him. He decided not to offer to take her instead of Shull, and he wondered why he was the recipient of all this anger from her and Susan for saving their lives. He decided that he'd never understand women as long as he lived.

The next few days were spent with Internal Affairs and in front of the Public Safety Board's Shooting Inquiry. Franklin had again taken Jack's duty weapon and ordered him to take the required three days of paid leave. Per standard operating procedure, his duty weapon would be examined to be sure that it was the weapon that killed Eddie, and that he was using police department-approved ammunition. Normally it would be test fired and the bullet would be compared to the one that blew Eddie's head apart, but the crime scene techs had been unable to locate that bullet.

Liddell kept him up to date on the departmental goings-on, and Jack was glad to hear that the Safety Board and the mayor had agreed to leave Marlin Pope in the position of chief of police until the next election, three years down the road.

He also learned that the missing persons detective, Larry Jansen, had somehow dodged federal charges of illegal wiretapping by recording a private governmental conversation between Mayor Thatcher and Double Dick. Instead of going to the federal pen, Jansen had been moved from Missing Persons to the Vice Unit. To Jack, that was tantamount to inviting the fox into the henhouse. But then, that was politics.

Double Dick had also survived the fracas, even after it had been discovered that he had taken the cassette tape from the pile of clothes that was evidence in a murder investigation, and then had attempted to destroy the tape by running it through a magnetic eraser, and then lied to internal affairs investigators. He had been cocky, thinking he was in the clear, until the sneaky internal affairs guys told him that the tape had been miraculously resurrected by the FBI. Of course that was a lie, but Dick fell for it because they said FBI, and Dick didn't know dick about whether a tape could be "brought back to life." He confessed tearfully and had to be shut up by Dan Grossman, the city attorney, before he let any super secrets slip out.

End result, Dick maintained the rank of deputy chief, along with all the pay and privileges, and was riding a desk in Personnel and Training in perpetuity, or at least until another mayor came along with toe jam for brains. Who says crime doesn't pay?

Jack made several attempts to contact Katie, but each time she declared she was busy, or ill, or any other thing she could say to get shed of him. He had been too embarrassed to call Susan after her remarks that day at the hospital. Liddell assured him that both women were recovering from their injuries, both mental and physical, and advised his partner to just give them some time to come to grips with what happened.

"They'll see that you had no choice, buddy," Liddell had said. Jack wanted to believe that, but he felt that their injuries were so deep that things would never be the same between them.

By the end of the week Jack had been cleared by the Safety Board and reinstated to duty once again. But the reactions shown by Katie and Susan made him feel guilty. It was his fault they were involved in the first place. His fault that they had been terrorized by Eddie and nearly died. Definitely his fault they had watched Eddie die.

He also worried that he felt no remorse for killing Eddie, or actually, he should say that he felt glad that Eddie was dead and that he was the one that killed him. *How normal is that?*

Anytime a policeman is involved in a shooting, he is encouraged to take advantage of the police department's mental health program. Jack had always wondered how a shrink that had never done anything more violent than tear open his Gummi bears could counsel someone that had just committed the ultimate act of violence by taking a life. But he decided to take Chief Pope's advice and see the counselor, if for no other reason than to make some sense of Katie and Susan's anger with him.

And that was how he found himself sitting on a bench in Garvin Park on a beautiful sunny day in late October, awaiting the arrival of the shrink that had been assigned his case. The doc's secretary had insisted that his caseworker liked to work outdoors when the weather was nice. Jack attempted a joke with the secretary, suggesting that *caseworker* was a nice name for a squirrel doctor, so maybe they should meet in a park. She giggled politely, and Garvin Park was agreed on.

Jack looked around and thought that in a couple of months the park would be covered in snow, the ponds would be iced over, the green grass and foliage would be gone, the squirrels would be hunting for food, and he suddenly realized just how negative he had become. "I *really* do need a shrink," he said out loud, not caring if the other squirrels heard him.

"And here I am," came a friendly voice from behind him. Apparently the shrink had arrived.

Jack looked up and was shocked to see the stunning woman who stood there. He'd expected a female Sigmund

Freud, beard and all, but this young lady was gorgeous. As tall as Jack, with strawberry-blond hair worn down to her shoulders, she had the figure and muscle tone of an Olympic skater. *Thank you, God!* he said mentally, and then offered her a seat on the bench beside him. And for the next hour he began to enjoy the green of the grass, the buzz of bumblebees on the purple clover, and even the playful squirrels that skittered around in search of goodies. Maybe it wasn't so bad being a squirrel.

ACKNOWLEDGMENTS

I would like to give special thanks to my editor, Michaela Hamilton, of Kensington Books, for her guidance, confidence, and unending patience with me. If I could give advice to new writers it would be to "listen to your editor."

I would also like to thank all the staff at Kensington Books who have worked so hard. Without them my book would still be on my hard drive.

For my special friends at The Church Street Coffee House in New Harmony, Indiana; Laura Hudgins and her son Elliot; Molly and Mickey Grimm and their son Grafton; and all the rest of you New Harmony town characters, a big thank-you for your unending support and for allowing me to spend many pleasurable hours in your company.

I would also like to thank Linda Cutteridge, Deborah Wozniak, Buffy Baker, and Gillian Robertson for reading and proofing this story when it was still in its infancy.

Don't miss Rick Reed's next page-turning thriller
featuring Detective Jack Murphy . . .

coming from Pinnacle in 2011.